TRISTAN STRONG

PUNCHES A HOLE IN THE SKY

TRISTAN STRONG
PUNCHES A HOLE IN THE SKY

KWAME MBALIA

RICK RIORDAN PRESENTS

DISNEY · HYPERION

Los Angeles   New York

Text copyright © 2019 by Cake Literary
Introduction copyright © 2019 by Rick Riordan

All rights reserved. Published by Disney • Hyperion, an imprint of Buena
Vista Books, Inc. No part of this book may be reproduced or transmitted
in any form or by any means, electronic or mechanical, including
photocopying, recording, or by any information storage and retrieval system,
without written permission from the publisher. For information address
Disney • Hyperion, 77 West 66th Street, New York, New York 10023.

First Hardcover Edition, October 2019
First Paperback Edition, September 2020
5 7 9 10 8 6
FAC-025438-21162

Printed in the United States of America

This book is set in Minion Pro, Hoefler Text, Courier Std/Monotype;
Astoria, Bouledoug/Fontspring
Designed by Tyler Nevins
Map illustration by Sveta Dorosheva

Library of Congress Cataloging-in-Publication Control
Number for Hardcover Edition: 2018057192
ISBN 978-1-368-04241-3

Visit www.DisneyBooks.com

SUSTAINABLE
FORESTRY
INITIATIVE

Certified Sourcing

www.sfiprogram.org
SFI-01054
The SFI label applies to the text stock

For the stories untold
and the children who will tell them

CONTENTS

THE WORLD BEYOND THE SKY

Don't get me wrong, Greek myths are great! But you can't swing a gorgon's head in any bookstore without hitting at least a dozen Greek-myth-inspired books.

Try finding great adventures based on Western African gods like Nyame or Anansi. Try finding stories about modern kids who encounter African American folk legends like High John, John Henry, and Brer Rabbit. Those books are a lot harder to locate, despite the fact that millions of kids would relate to *those* gods and heroes even more than they would to Hercules and Perseus (sorry, my Greek dudes).

Can you imagine what it would be like if you could find a book that wove the whole brilliant, beautiful tapestry of West African and African American legend into one magical world? A world that made young African American readers think, *Yes! This is MY awesome mythology. This is MY magic world to explore, and these heroic kids are just like me!* A book that left *all* readers thinking, *Wow. Why didn't I know about these amazing stories sooner?*

Kwame Mbalia has written that book. You are about to discover *Tristan Strong Punches a Hole in the Sky*, and your world will never be the same.

I won't even try to describe all the incredible adventures facing Tristan Strong in this debut novel. That would spoil the fun! But when Tristan accidentally punches a hole into the sky of the MidPass, the world of African American legends, he starts on the most *epic* of quests. Awaiting him are a malicious haint, relentless iron monsters, creepy bone ships, flying rafts, burning seas, talking animals, ancient gods, and more.

But for all its great fantasy elements, what I love most about this book is its human side. Tristan is struggling with grief after the death of his best friend. He has just lost his first boxing match, thereby disappointing his father's and grandfather's hopes for him carrying on the family legacy. Sentenced to a summer at his grandparents' farm in rural Alabama, this Chicago city kid is struggling to figure out who he wants to be, and whether his parents (and society) will let him be that person. Tristan is tough but tender, smart but cautious, courageous but insecure. He is someone every kid will relate to, and you will immediately want to be his friend.

I'll tell you a secret: I cried while reading *Tristan Strong*. Several times, I just got overwhelmed with happiness, thinking about what this book would have meant to many of my students back when I taught middle school. I was delighted to see old friends like Brer Fox, John Henry, and Gum Baby in such a fresh, modern, page-turning adventure. I felt grateful to Kwame Mbalia for writing it so that new generations of young readers could grow up with Tristan and get to know the rich stories of West Africa and the African Diaspora. In a lifetime full of highlights, I have to say that helping to publish this book is right up there at the top!

I know you will enjoy *Tristan Strong Punches a Hole in the Sky*. I envy you reading it for the first time. As for Tristan's further adventures, the sky's the limit. Wait, no. Tristan punched a hole in the sky. There *are* no limits.

THE MAP

THE THICKET

MIDPASS

THE DROWNED FOREST

THE BURNING SEA

1
THE CAR RIDE

THERE WAS A RHYTHM IN MY FISTS.

Pop pop

It told a story.

Pop pop

Everybody thought they knew the story. They'd seen it before. *He'll get over it. It's a phase. Give him space.* But they only knew fragments. They didn't want to hear the rest....

Oh, you do?

Hmm.

Well, what if I told you that I went to war over my dead best friend's glowing journal? Or that I battled monsters big and small, with powers I didn't know I had, with gods I didn't know existed. Would you believe me?

Nah, you wouldn't. You got your own problems. You don't wanna hear about my struggles. Right?

Oh, you do? Well, I gotta warn you, it's a wild ride, so buckle up, champ.

Let me give you some truth, and I hope it returns back to me.

"Tristan! They're here."

Pop

Mom's shout interrupted my groove. I stopped pummeling the small punching bag Dad had installed in my room and loosened the straps on my boxing gloves with my teeth. The gloves fell on the bed, and I dropped down next to them. Eddie's journal sat on my tiny desk in the opposite corner. Still glowing. Still unopened since his mother had given it to me after the funeral two weeks ago.

My room was so small I could've reached out and grabbed the leather book, but that would mean dealing with it, and who deals with their problems by choice?

Pffft. Not me.

"Tristan Strong!" my dad yelled from down the hall.

I hated that name.

It made me appear to be something I'm not. My name should've been Tristan Coward, or Tristan Failure, or Tristan Fake. Maybe Tristan How-Could-You-Lose-Your-First-Boxing-Match.

Anything but Tristan Strong.

Mom's footsteps echoed through our tiny apartment, and then soft knocking sounded on my door. "Tristan, baby, did you hear me?"

I cleared my throat. "Yeah, I'm coming."

The door opened and Mom peeked in. She was still wearing the TEAM STRONG T-shirt from last night. I don't think any of us had gotten much sleep after we came back from my first bout. I stayed up nursing my pride, the only thing I really injured. My little fan club—Dad, Mom, and my grandparents on Dad's side—had tried to cheer me up, but I could see the disappointment written on everyone's faces, so I pretended to go to bed while they held whispered discussions into the wee hours of the morning. And now it was dawn, time to get this show on the road.

Mom's eyes took in the organized chaos of my room and crinkled when they landed on me. She crossed the floor in two steps—avoiding yesterday's untouched dinner in the process—and sat down on the mattress. "It's only for a month," she said, not even playacting that she didn't know what was wrong.

"I know."

"It'll be good for you to get away."

"I know."

She rubbed my head, then pulled me into a hug. "The grief counselor said it would be good to get a change of scenery.

Some fresh air, work around the farm. Who knows, maybe you'll find out you were meant to work the land."

I shrugged. The only thing I was sure of was that I wasn't meant to be a boxer, despite what Dad and Granddad thought.

I pulled free of Mom's hug, stood, grabbed my duffel bag, and headed out to start my month of exile.

"Aren't you forgetting something?" Mom asked.

I turned and she held Eddie's journal out to me. Her hand and wrist were bathed in the emerald-green glow that was coming from the cover. But, like everyone else I'd shown the journal to, she didn't notice any strange light.

Mom mistook my confused frown for apprehension as she slipped the book into my bag. "He wanted you to have it, Tristan. I know it's tough, but . . . try to read it when you can, okay?"

I didn't trust myself to speak, so I nodded and headed to the front door.

The decision to ship me to Granddad and Nana Strong's farm down in Alabama had been made without my input. Typical. My parents had talked about it a few times before, but after Eddie's death, and my third school fight in the final two weeks before summer break, well, I guess the time was right.

At least I'd held my own in those school fights. Unlike in the ring last night.

It was just my luck that my grandfather had been there to witness my humiliation.

"You outweighed that other kid by seven pounds!" Granddad had said after the match, in his growling rasp of a voice. "Set the family name back by a decade."

That's me—Tristan Disappointment.

Son of Alvin "Wreckin' Ball" Strong, the best middle-weight boxer to come out of Chicago in nearly twenty years. I had Dad's height and Granddad's chin, and boxing was supposed to run in my veins. I'd worn Granddad's old trunks, and Dad had worked my corner. The Strong legacy was expected to take another leap forward during my first match.

Instead, it got knocked flat on its butt. Twice.

"You'll get him next time" was all Dad said, but I could tell he was let down.

And that hurt almost as much as getting punched.

An early summer heat wave greeted me with a blast of humidity as I left the apartment building with my backpack over my shoulder and my duffel bag in hand. Thick gray clouds huddled in the distance, and I added that to the list of totally not ominous things. Glowing journal? Yep. Storm on the horizon? You betcha.

Dad and Granddad stood at the curb while Nana (no one ever called her Grandma, not if you wanted to eat) knitted in the car. Dad towered over his father, but you could see the family resemblance. Deep brown skin like mine, a wide jaw, and a proud stance. I got my hair from Mom's side of the family, thankfully, because both Strong men had identical bald spots peeking through their short afros.

"Get him in the fields, put him to work," Granddad was saying. "That'll put some fire in his belly."

Dad shrugged and said nothing. To be fair, no one did much talking when Granddad was around. That old man could yak a mile a minute.

Nana saw me coming down the stairs, dropped her knitting, and rushed out of the car. "There he is! How you doin' today, baby? Are you sore from last night?"

She gave me a hug that muffled any answer, then shooed Granddad to the side. "Get the boy's bag, Walter. Alvin," she said, addressing my father, "we've got to hit the road before that thunderstorm hits."

Granddad looked me up and down. "Is that all you kids ever wear?"

I glanced down. Black Chuck Taylors with gray untied laces. Loose khaki cargo shorts, and an even looser gray hoodie. That hoodie went with me everywhere—it had a picture of a flexed bicep on the back in faded black ink. Call me sentimental, but it's what I always wore when Eddie and I were hanging out. He called it the Tristan Strong uniform of choice, perfect for all occasions.

So yeah, I wear it a lot.

Nana shushed him and pulled me into another hug. "Don't listen to him, Tristan. I can't wait to have you back with us on the farm. You were so little last time, but them chickens you used to chase still haven't forgotten you! I packed a lunch and even rustled up a new story or two for the ride...."

And so, just like that, with a clap on the shoulder from Dad and a hug from Mom, I was someone else's problem for a month. Good-bye, Chicago, and all your glorious cable TV, internet, and cell phone service. I hardly knew ye.

One thing became very clear during the twelve-hour car ride to Alabama—I was never going to do this again.

Never ever.

Sitting in an enclosed space with Granddad was like wiping your tears with sandpaper. Painful—excruciating, even—and you wondered why you ever thought it was a good idea.

Oh, think I'm playing?

Ten minutes into the trip: "When I was your age, I had a full-time job and I'd already fought in two title fights."

Three hours in: "Oh, you're hungry again? Did you bring some stopping-for-snacks money?"

Six hours in: "Man, I shouldn't have ate those leftover beans for breakfast."

Eight hours in: "Can't believe I drove all this way to see a Strong boy fight so soft. That's your grandmother's side of the family. Ain't no Strong ever look like that in the ring. Why, I remember..."

Anyway, you get it.

By the time we crossed the Alabama state line, I was ready to claw my way into the trunk. I don't know how Nana could just sit there and hum and knit for most of a day, but that's what she did. The Cadillac rumbled down a two-lane highway, kicking up trails of dust and exhaust, a dented rocket ship blasting through time in reverse from the future to a land that Wi-Fi forgot.

I'd put my earbuds in somewhere back in Kentucky, but the battery on my phone had long since run out. I just kept them in so no one would bother me. Nana kept knitting in the passenger seat, and Granddad tapped a finger on the steering wheel, humming along to a song only he could hear. Things seemed more or less calm, except for one thing:

Eddie's journal sat on the seat next to me.

Now, I could've sworn I'd stuffed the book under the clothes in my duffel bag. Which Grandad had put in the trunk. And yet here it was, waiting on me to do something I'd put off since the funeral. The late afternoon sun, occasionally peeking out from behind the storm clouds, made the journal look normal, ordinary. But every so often I'd shade the cover with my hands and peek at it while holding my breath. Yep, still glowing.

Why not open it, you might ask, *and see what's inside?*

Well, believe me, it wasn't that simple. Before Eddie's death, the cover of his brown leather journal had always been blank. Now a weird symbol appeared to be stitched into it, like a sun with rays that stretched out to infinity, or a flower with long petals. The same symbol was embossed on a carved wooden charm that dangled from a cord attached to the journal's spine. I'd seen the tassel before—Eddie had used it to mark his spot, or to flick me in the back of the head—but the charm was new.

And, even more weirdly, the trinket pulsed with green light, too. I'd been staring at that book every day for minutes on end, but the glow always stopped me from opening it.

I mean, I knew what was in there anyway. The stories Eddie had jotted down in his goofy, blocky handwriting, from his own silly creations to the fables Nana used to tell us when we were younger, when she'd come up to visit. John Henry, Anansi the Spider, Brer Rabbit's adventures—I'd read them all. Our end-of-semester English project was supposed to be a giant collection of stories from our childhood. Eddie was doing the writing, and I was going to give the oral presentation. Then the accident happened. The counselor Mom took me to every Wednesday had said I should try to finish the writing part, even though school was now over for the year, as a part of healing and other stuff.

(Before you say something slick you might regret, Mr. Richardson is pretty cool for a counselor, you get me? We play *Madden* while we talk, which means I can focus on running up the score on his raggedy Eagles squad and not on being embarrassed about answering questions. It helps . . . some. If it gets too tough, he knows when to back off, too. So you can keep your *Sensitive* and *Man up* comments to yourself. Chumps.)

To avoid thinking about the haunted journal, I watched the weather outside the car window. The clouds had never let up, even once we were in the Deep South. They just switched from hurling lightning bolts at us to hurling fat drops of rain that splattered across the windshield like bugs. Everything everywhere was miserable, and that pretty much summed up my life at the moment.

I took off the earbuds and sighed. Nana heard and turned around in her seat to look at me.

"You hungry, sweetie?" she asked.

"No, not really."

"No, *ma'am*." Granddad's deep voice rolled back from the driver's seat. "You answer 'No, ma'am' to your grandmother, understand?"

"Yeah."

Granddad looked at me in the rearview mirror.

"I mean, yes, sir."

He held my eyes a moment longer, then went back to looking at the road.

"Well," Nana continued, turning around and picking up

her knitting, "despite what your granddad said earlier"—she gave him a glare—"let me know when you are. Your mama told me you ain't been eating much, and we're gonna fix that. And don't you have some writing to do? That's what your counselor wants you to focus on."

"Boy don't need no counselor," Granddad rumbled. "He needs to work. Ain't no time for moping when horses need feeding and fences need mending."

"Walter!" Nana scolded. "He needs to—"

"I know what he needs—"

I shook my head and stopped paying attention. After spending a day in the car with them, I'd realized that this was what they did. They argued, they laughed, they sang, they argued again, and they knitted. Well, Nana knitted. But they were two sides of the same old coin.

With Granddad, everything was about work. Work, work, work.

Bored? Here's some work.

Finished working? Here's more work.

Need someone to talk to? Obviously, that meant you didn't work hard enough, so you know what? Have a little bit more work.

Nana, on the other hand, sang and hummed when she wasn't talking, which almost never happened, because she always had a new story to share. "Do you know why the owl can't sleep?" she'd say, and off the story would go, and you'd sit there and listen, just being polite at first, but by the end, you'd be on the edge of your seat.

I smiled. Eddie had loved listening to my grandmother. When she'd come to visit earlier this year, he'd practically followed her around, his journal in hand.

Speaking of which...

My left hand rested on top of it in the seat next to me, and I traced the symbol stitched into the front cover.

"What's that, sweetie?"

I looked up to see Nana peeking back over the seat.

"Hm? I mean, uh, yes...ma'am?"

Granddad nodded, and I let out a sigh of relief.

Nana smiled. "Is that for your writing?"

I hesitated. "Yes, ma'am." I held up the book so she could see it, and her eyes widened at the symbol on the cover.

"Where'd you get that?" she asked. Granddad turned to see what she was looking at, but Nana flapped a hand at him. "Watch the road, Walter."

"From Eddie..." I began, then paused. "I mean, his mom gave it to me. It is...was for us. For our school project. Why? What's wrong?"

Could she see it? Could she tell that the book was glowing, even in the daylight?

Nana pursed her lips. "That symbol. I just haven't seen it in a long time."

"You know what it is?"

"Well..." She glanced at Granddad, who'd tuned us out as soon as we started talking about writing. "It's the spider's web, an old African symbol for creativity and wisdom. It shows how tangled and complicated life can be. But with a little imaginative thinking, we can solve most of our problems and those of others."

"Do you notice anything else about the journal?" I asked her.

Nana laughed, a bright, joyous sound that infected anyone listening. "Is this a test?"

"No, ma'am."

"I don't see nothing but procrastination. Go 'head and give it a try."

"Yes, ma'am." I frowned. So Nana could see the symbol, this spiderweb, but not that it was glowing. Well, that didn't make me feel any better.

Granddad smacked the steering wheel. "Y'all need to stop filling his head with that mess about symbols. He needs to stay in the real world, think about what he did wrong last night. The boy need to focus! Boxing ain't gonna just happen—you got to train your body and your mind."

"Granddad, I don't want—"

"I don't want to hear it. You're not a kid anymore. You're a Strong, and—"

"Walter," Nana interrupted, "don't be so hard on the boy."

"He needs some toughening up—y'all being too soft on him!"

"Now look—" Nana started whisper-lecturing Granddad, who shook his head and grumbled beneath his breath.

I slid down in my seat and tried to block out the argument. I let my thumb trace the cover of the journal, and before my brain could tell me not to, I yanked it into my lap and flipped to a random page. So what if it glowed? It was still a book, and reading it would be better than listening to any more of Granddad's insults disguised as life lessons. Or reliving that bus accident.

I mean, really, what could go wrong?

2

THE BOTTLE TREES

TWO FIGURES CROUCHED NEAR THE BASE OF A GIANT OAK TREE. Huge knotted roots sprawled in the center of twisting, creeping shadows. The first figure—a large Black man with arms of mahogany, fists like rocks, and shoulders broader than mountains—went down on one knee in the soft, damp earth. He rested his hand on a smooth log beside him.

"You sure this is necessary, BR?" His voice rumbled like a thousand trains all heading to the same place.

The second figure—a rabbit as big as a kindergartener—twitched nervously and snapped, "Of course I'm sure, John! Hurry up! We need to get this over with." Something clanked in the distance and the rabbit jumped. "Now!"

"Okay, BR, okay," John said. He straightened up ... and up ... and up, until his silhouette seemed larger than the old tree. "But you need to lend this ole tool some power. I can't do it alone."

"Whatever, just get on with it!"

John picked up the log, except it . . . wasn't a log. It was a handle—the smooth shaft of a massive hammer. Carvings were etched up and down the wood, and it hummed as giant hands found familiar grooves.

John. With a hammer. No way. . . . I knew that name. Those *characters*. John Henry, and BR . . . BR . . . *Brer Rabbit*? But—

Brer Rabbit put his paws on the huge iron head of the hammer and began to speak in a low tone. His whispers swirled and grew until they sounded like shouts and drumming and stomping feet. The hammer's head—a thick metal block marred with pits and scrapes—began to glow with blazing, red-hot light, and John pressed it against a tangle of roots.

A yawning black hole opened in the ground at the base of the tree.

John bent over and picked a small object off the ground. I couldn't make out what it was. "Go," he said to it, setting it gently into the hole. "Go now and find it. Find it. FIND IT!"

Click click click

I yanked my hands off the journal with a gasp. Sweat poured down my face, and I was pressed against the back seat of the Cadillac as we motored along. The storm clouds had finally dissolved, and the sun was almost at the horizon, its orange and red rays pouring through the window.

What was that? A dream? Had I fallen asleep while reading?

Then why had it felt so real? And why was the journal closed on the seat next to me?

"You okay, baby?" Nana asked without turning around.

Click click click

Her knitting needles moved furiously. Was it my imagination or was she sweating, too?

"Tristan?"

Click click click

But the pressure of that ... whatever it was still sat on my chest and locked my mouth. It felt hot and cramped and smothering in the car, like I'd been tucked in with a giant itchy wool blanket, and suddenly I couldn't breathe. I somehow managed to lurch over to the door and open the window to try to get some fresh air.

"Tristan!"

"Boy, put that window up!" Granddad barked from the front. "Lettin' all the dust get in here. Is you out your mind?"

One breath. Two breaths.

"TRISTAN!"

Granddad twisted around, but it was Nana who placed a hand on my knee, and suddenly the pressure was gone. I reluctantly shut the window, then took a deep breath. The feelings of something pressing down on me had faded to a lurking presence. I could handle that, though it made my neck itch. Nana removed her hand but kept peering at me, a worried look on her face.

"You okay, baby?"

I nodded.

"Answer your grandmother when she—"

"Hush, Walter," Nana scolded. "Mind the road."

I shook my head. "Just...got a little carsick, I think."

Nana watched me as if she suspected that wasn't true, but she didn't pry any further. "Why don't you try to take a nap, dear. Only another hour or so and then we'll be at the farm, and you and Granddad have some work to do before supper." She turned back around, but, just for a second, I could've sworn her eyes glanced at the journal.

Click click click

Nana continued knitting, and I looked at the journal on the other end of the seat. After a moment's hesitation, I reached over and shaded it with my hands, already knowing what would happen but checking anyway.

The journal pulsed quicker and stronger, with a bright green glow.

Sometime later, Granddad slowed down and turned onto a bumpy gravel road that climbed up a long hill. "We're here," he said.

I jerked out of a daze. I slipped Eddie's journal into my

backpack, then stretched and looked warily out the window. Everything looked . . . well, it looked like the country.

Yay.

"We are? Where?" I asked.

"Home, sweetie," Nana said, packing up her knitting and turning to smile at me again. "Just in time for me to get dinner started."

"Still about an hour left of sun," Granddad said. "Can at least get part of that old fence fixed."

The car chugged to the top of the hill, and I sat up as the Strong family farm sprawled out to the horizon. A patchwork quilt of green and brown fields surrounded a huge barn and a slightly smaller house. Rows of corn stood at attention as the Cadillac ambled past, like a chariot returning with the land's king and queen. And Nana and Granddad did seem to sit up straighter as we got closer to the house. Even I could feel it, a tug from something that had been in my family for generations. This was our duchy, our territory. The Strong domain.

My nose pressed against the window, breath fogging the glass, I spotted a stand of trees at the far corner of the farm. They were old, like a section of forest that time had forgotten. Their twisted, giant trunks were bunched together like some sort of crowd . . . or guards. As I stared at them, the pressure on my chest came back—the feeling from before. Someone . . . or some*thing* was out there searching.

Searching for *me*.

A flash between the branches caught my eye as we drove past.

"What's that?" I asked.

"What's what, sweetie?"

"In those trees over there. Something's shining."

Granddad shook his head. "More foolishness, that's what it is."

"Hush, Walter," Nana said. "That's just the Bottle Tree forest, baby."

"The what?" What sort of trees were those—and there was another one! Something flashed again, like light on a mirror or glass.

"Bottle Trees. Oh now, would you look at that? I skipped a stitch. What was I saying? Oh, the Bottle Trees. I could've sworn I've talked up one wall and down the other about this before." She turned around in her seat. "Slaves carried the practice over with them from Africa as a way to capture and dispose of any haints wandering around."

"Haints?" I pressed my nose against the glass and squinted.

"Evil spirits, baby. Lord knows, plenty of those ramblin' about, what with . . . Well, anyway, don't you worry about it none," Nana continued. "I don't want you messing around over there. Them old trees aren't for playing on. You liable to hurt yourself."

"Need to cut 'em down," Granddad grumbled, but Nana just shooed the words away with her hand.

"Hush, Walter. Now look, Tristan, over there...." She started playing tour guide as we drove up to the house, and I settled back, unable to shake the tingling feeling that something weird was going on.

"Grab that end, boy, and lift. Lift! Stop half-steppin' and put your back into it."

I heaved at the end of a log as Granddad and I slid it into the empty top slot of a pole. We dropped it into place, and I sagged against the repaired fence with a sigh. We'd been working for the last hour, racing the sun to get this section of fence fixed, and I was exhausted. I hadn't even had a chance to drop off my bags. I picked up my backpack, and Eddie's journal nearly fell out of the open compartment. I could've sworn I'd closed the zipper....

Granddad watched me put it away and shook his head. He mopped his forehead with an old rag he kept tucked in the back pocket of his overalls, then put it away and rolled his sleeves down.

"You need to leave that writing nonsense alone, boy. Ain't gonna get you nowhere but confused."

I didn't say anything.

"What you got to write about, anyway? Video games? TV?

All that city life got you boys soft. I would've had your dad out here at the break of dawn. How you think he got them heavyweight shoulders? Strongs work, boy."

I squeezed the straps of the backpack until they cut into my palms, but I still didn't say anything.

He spat out the twig he was chewing. "Hmph. Go on, then, and run that extra wire back to the barn. Then clean up for dinner. Hurry up, now—your grandmother's waiting."

I grabbed the spool of wire and stalked down the trail toward the barn. I heard Granddad grumbling to himself, and I tried to ignore it. No matter what I did or where I went, someone always wanted to tell me what I was doing wrong and what I should do different.

You're pretty big, Tristan. Go play football.

Stop reading comic books, Tristan, and go read a real book.

Stop . . .

I looked up, suddenly aware that the world had gone quiet. I mean, nothing made a sound. No birds, no squirrels, no rustling leaves—even the wind held its breath.

The old stand of trees loomed in front of me.

How long had I been walking? How had I found myself here?

The shadows on the ground deepened and stretched toward me. Thick vines around the trunks seemed to curl like fingers beckoning me closer. They felt desperate, needy. The trees grew larger and larger, and it took me a second to realize that it was because I was walking toward them.

FIND IT.

The words boomed and crashed in my head, a thunderstorm of a command, and I froze. They were the same words, the same voice, from my dream in the car. That *had* been a dream, right?

I had reached the edge of the trees. A breeze gusted softly from the dark center of the forest, almost like a breath. It smelled... old. Earthy. Like whatever was in there hadn't been disturbed in years. I didn't want to be the first new intruder.

And yet...

I took a step forward.

"Tristan? Tristaaaan?" Nana's voice broke whatever spell had fallen over me, and I shook my head to clear the cobwebs. My right foot hovered in the air, inches away from entering the shadows. I slowly placed it on the ground, then retreated a few steps. I squinted into the trees. Something was in there, and it wanted me. I could feel it.

"Tristan, dinnertime!" Nana's voice floated out of the sky, riding the breeze in the way only an elder's voice could.

I backed up farther, then turned and ran through the cornfield to the farmhouse.

No way are you going in those woods, I told myself. *No way.*

I was wrong.

3
GUM BABY

WHEN THE ATTACK CAME, I WAS HALF-ASLEEP.

The car trip, the weird dream-that-wasn't-a-dream, working on the farm... By the time I went to bed, my eyelids felt like they weighed a ton. Still, I couldn't quite get to sleep.

It wasn't the darkness, though I wasn't used to nighttime in Alabama. I was used to the almost-night of Chicago—with the glow of streetlights and the flicker of neon signs outside my window.

Here, the complete lack of light made everything seem... different. A flashlight lay on top of the blankets next to me. Not that I'm scared of the dark, you get me, but in case I had to use the bathroom or get a drink of water.

Man, what I wouldn't have given for a couple of streetlights.

It wasn't the silence, though it was also way too quiet. Instead of the comforting sounds of cars and trucks and sirens and people talking on the street, I heard cornstalks rustling in the wind. The window wouldn't close all the way because of the warped wooden frame, and that was good and bad. Good because I didn't feel so pressed in, so enclosed, but bad because of the crickets.

Maaaan, those crickets. Talk about annoying. How could anything so small make that much noise? It was like a million of them surrounded my window and were screaming the lyrics to the most annoying song you could think of.

Yep, that one you're thinking of right now.

Sucks, doesn't it?

And yet it wasn't the darkness, or the strange sounds, or the unfamiliar house that was keeping me up. The pressure I'd felt on my chest in the car was back, waiting for me to relax. I knew that as soon as I did, it would seize me like an opponent in the ring, clinching my head between its gloves and waiting for the right moment to let go and hit me with that perfect punch. I could feel it. As soon as—

Thump

The noise had come from across the room, by the window, like something falling to the floor.

Instantly, I sat up, straining to see in the dark.

Now, if I were back in Chicago, I'd just stuff a pillow over my head to block out the noise, figuring it was a neighbor. Our walls were so thin in that apartment, you could sneeze and people two floors down would say *Bless you!*

But this definitely wasn't Chicago. So, when something

went bump, I paid attention. Especially because I was already on edge. Double especially because the sound was followed by sticky, mucky, stepped-on-a-piece-of-tape footsteps.

I stared around the room. There wasn't much furniture—a dresser with my backpack (Eddie's journal still zipped up tight inside), a coatrack, and a chair with my clothes from the day on it. Still, nighttime eeriness turned the shadows of ordinary objects into something twice as creepy. Fingers stretched out of empty space. Shapes combined into creatures that crept toward the bed.

"Who's there?" I whispered.

Nobody answered. The crickets yelled their chorus outside and the wind cackled in the dry cornstalks. But those were normal farm sounds, right?

I don't know what I expected. I took a deep breath and rubbed my eyes. This was silly.

"Stop being a baby, Tristan," I said, embarrassed. "There's nothing here."

Something scraped along the floor, and I swear I heard a voice whisper, "Where is it, where is it, where is it?"

My heart skipped a beat, and I scrambled to the foot of the bed with the flashlight clutched in both of my shaking hands. I clicked it on, but nothing happened.

"C'mon, c'mon, c'mon," I muttered, slapping it against the palm of my hand. The switch was stuck. "Why doesn't anything work around here?"

Click

The beam flickered on after the fifth or sixth try. "Finally!"

I swept the cone of light around, looking for anything remotely creepy, relaxing a bit each time something strange became familiar. The fingers turned back into a coatrack. The creeping monsters turned back into the chair covered in clothes. The doll baby in the middle of the floor—

—rotated its head when the flashlight beam hit it.

I froze.

The doll looked homemade, like someone had carved it out of wood, painted it a dark molasses brown that hadn't quite dried yet, drawn two black dots for eyes, and glued curly black wool on its head in two afro puffs. It stood still in the light, almost a foot high, and the two of us stared at each other.

"Okay," I said, then licked my lips. The flashlight turned off again. "Okay. This...is not weird. Right? There's nothing weird about—"

"Who you calling weird?"

I looked around, confused, as I tried to locate the owner of that voice. It sounded strange and high-pitched, like when you breathe in helium from a balloon and your voice gets squeaky.

"Oh, so you don't see Gum Baby now? She invisible now?"

It came from down low. The flashlight came on just in time to catch the doll starting to walk across the floor toward me. Each of her footsteps made a sound like Velcro strips separating.

It—she?—stomped closer, glaring and pointing. "Where is it? You'd better tell Gum Baby, and fast."

Gum Baby? No way.

I'd heard that name before. Not the little doll from the stories...? It couldn't be!

In the Anansi tales, Gum Baby was a doll Anansi used to trap an African fairy while he was on a quest. But in the story, the doll remained silent and wore leaves for clothes. This one, on the other hand, had on a black turtleneck and black pants, but her tiny feet were bare. And what were those stains she was tracking across the floor?

"Hey, Gum Baby's talking to you, big boy." The doll marched across the floor, the serious expression on her face ruined by the plopping sound each of her footsteps made.

"Don't make Gum Baby climb up there."

Plop plop plop

"Is Gum Baby talking to a brick wall?"

Plop plop plop

"Oh, you're asking for it now."

Plop plop plop

She was up the side of the bed and leaving dark stains on the blankets by the time I finally shook myself out of the daze and extended the flashlight like a weapon. "Who—who are you?" I whispered.

The ten-inch-tall doll glared at me, climbed atop my foot, and struck a pose. Both chubby arms spread wide, one foot planted on my big toe, she laughed in her tiny voice.

"Ha-ha-haaaa! You want to know who Gum Baby is? Gum Baby is the reason you sleep with the door locked. Gum Baby is the reason the sun runs away across the sky. Gum Baby is your nightmare, and people whisper her name and tremble around the world. Aha-ha-ha-haaaa!"

"*Shh!*" I said, waving both arms in warning. "You're gonna wake up my grandparents."

Gum Baby cocked her head and looked at me like I'd just slapped her.

"Did you..." she began. "Did you just shush Gum Baby? Didn't you hear the introduction? Being a nightmare and all that, and you locking your door? Did...did that not make sense?"

"No, it made sense, it's just—"

"Should Gum Baby clarify?"

"No, it's fine, I just don't want—"

"Oh good. In that case, GUM BABY WILL GO UPSIDE YOUR HEAD IF YOU EVER THINK ABOUT SHUSHING HER AGAIN!"

Gum Baby scrambled across my lap and flailed at my chest with both sticky hands.

"Let another shush come out of that mouth. Let it! It'll be the last shush your shush-maker will shushify!"

"Okay, okay!" I batted away the irritating blows, ducking and dodging more of that sticky stuff. "Stop it, that tickles, and you're getting . . . stuff all over the bed."

Gum Baby wrestled with my shirt one more time, then stood on my lap, both hands on her hips. I wiped a glob of goop off my cheek and made a face. What were Granddad and Nana gonna say about the mess in the morning?

"That's better. Now, where is it?" Gum Baby folded her tiny arms across her chest.

"Where's what?"

"Don't play dumber. You know what."

"No, I— Look, I don't know who you are. . . . Well, I think you're . . . but that wouldn't make sense, those were just stories, and . . . Can you just tell me why you're here?"

I meant why was she alive and not just a fable, but Gum Baby misunderstood. She glared at me for a second. "Gum Baby's on a mission, Bumbletongue. Where is the sign? Gum Baby knows it's glowing around here somewhere."

I tried to form words, to come up with some sort of answer to her questions, but the whole situation was too unreal. It was like I was being interrogated by a twelve-dollar toy from the bargain bin. Eddie would never have believed this. In fact, this was just the sort of story Eddie would—

Wait a minute.

Glowing around here . . .

Could it be?

My eyes flicked to the backpack on the dresser—only for a second, but Gum Baby saw, and an evil smirk crossed her face. Quick as a flash, she flung more goop in my face.

"Think fast!"

"Gah!" I yelped.

While I pawed the stuff out of my eyes, the blankets shifted and I felt her run to the end of the bed and leap off. By the time I could pry my eyes open, the stupid little thing was nowhere to be seen. A line of dark globs led to the dresser. I kicked off the blankets and ran over, looking around wildly.

The backpack—with Eddie's journal—was gone.

I spun around and aimed the flashlight at the floor. Gum Baby had disappeared. I looked under the bed—nothing.

Then I heard sticky footsteps sneaking to the wall behind me.

I twisted around just in time to see Gum Baby leap out the window, fleeing into the night with my pack, green light escaping from the slightly open zipper.

"Get back here!" I whisper-shouted as I ran to the window.

Gum Baby sprinted on her stubby little legs along the dirt path outside, around the Cadillac, and up the hill leading to the cornfield. Seconds later, I couldn't spot her anymore.

I slowly sank to the floor, hugged my knees to my chest, and closed my eyes.

What had just happened? This was a nightmare. That was it—my dream in the car must've never ended. This couldn't be real. I couldn't have lost the only thing I had to remind me of Eddie. And to a sticky toy at that!

Stupid, stupid, stupid.

My hands shook, and I pressed my palms against the floor to keep them still—right into a puddle of something soft and sticky.

What *was* that stuff? Honey?

Strands of whatever it was stretched and folded like taffy as I rubbed it between my fingers. It smelled sweet, but not exactly like honey. Something familiar, though. More of it dotted the floor, and I looked at the wall behind me. Sure enough, little dark splotches went all the way to the windowsill.

A trail!

I clenched my fists, then looked at the corner of the dresser where the backpack had been. That journal held Eddie's humor, his silly jokes, his stories, his dreams. It was everything.

Maybe there was a chance I could get it back.

I grabbed the flashlight, tugged on my hoodie and cargo shorts, and stepped into my sneakers. The window creaked as I eased it up, and the smell of horses and other farm odors hit me, right before the wind issued a warning.

Stay in bed.

I ignored it.

I squeezed through the window and dropped to the porch.

For a moment I hesitated. The darkness, the whispering wind, the rustling cornstalks—they all tried to change my mind.

Go back inside.

This ain't for you.

No telling what might happen to a city boy around here this time of night.

I was about to cave in to the fear and go hide in my bed, when the flashlight beam landed on a small patch of sticky residue on the edge of the wraparound porch. And then one on the grass a few feet away. And another. And another.

I gripped the flashlight so hard it hurt. The wind whistled louder, rattling the corn, but I gritted my teeth and shook my head. "You don't scare me. I'm getting that journal back. Strongs keep punching, you get me?"

I felt silly saying it, but Dad's mantra gave me courage. Before I could think twice, I plunged off the porch and into the night.

4
FIGHT IN THE FOREST

MY SNEAKERS PADDED ON THE DIRT PATH AS I RAN UP THE TRAIL.
Stars twinkled above, but with no moon, I could barely see
where I was going. And the sounds... It seemed like the
night was alive... and angry. Animals and birds and more
dang crickets all wanted a piece of this Chicago boy who was
invading their turf. The only thing keeping me going was the
sound of something scurrying through the cornfield on my
right. If I moved fast enough, I could cut off the tiny thief.
From the sound of Gum Baby's complaining, she was facing
more obstacles than I was.

"Who plants corn in the middle of a field? Ooh, child, if
Gum Baby had the time, she would show this world a thing or
two. Who's that? Move along, bird! This ain't a party. Gum
Baby said move! Hey, let go of that.... Let go! So you want
some of this? Sap attack!"

A flurry of feathers erupted out of the cornfield, and a crow squawked and flapped awkwardly away.

Sap...So *that's* what the sticky stuff was. In the stories, Anansi covered the doll in the sap of gum trees. This little thief seemed to produce it like Granddad did sweat. And, yes, neither image is pretty. Sticky, sweaty sap missiles. Lovely.

I put on a burst of speed and rounded the bend just in time to see Gum Baby scurry across the road, leaves and feathers stuck to her back, and plunge into the trees on the opposite side.

"Hey!" I called.

Gum Baby gave me a glance, then took off sprinting. "You again? Well, you're too late—Gum Baby's like the wind!"

I lunged forward, but she and my backpack disappeared into the darkness. I skidded to a stop at the edge of the road and swallowed. The creepy old Bottle Tree forest stood in front of me, its canopy creating the illusion of a tunnel. In the beam of my flashlight, the gnarled trunks looked like faces. Sentinels on watch, they eyed me suspiciously.

I gulped.

The wind blew, cackling through the leaves.

Told ya, boy. You don't want this.

I backed up a step, then stopped. A soft green light bobbed deep in the woods.

Eddie's journal. I clenched my fists. I had to get it back.

The wind gusted stronger, but I made a rude hand gesture at it. "You don't scare me," I whispered. One deep breath, then another, and I ran headlong into the forest.

The wind howled, and branches scratched and clawed my face, but I pressed on. Trees creaked and groaned, and roots tangled my feet, but still I moved forward. It grew harder and harder to run, with the branches and knots of the trees forcing me to scoot and sidestep, but eventually I forced my way through and stumbled into a clearing.

I thought I was ready for anything.

Wrong. WRONG.

Gum Baby stood in front of the weirdest tree I'd ever seen. It was only a few feet tall, maybe coming up to my chin, but its arms sprawled out straight as a ruler in all directions. Bottles of every shape and size—but all a glimmering shade of blue—were stuck on the ends of the branches.

When the wind gusted, the bottles moaned. Sweat beaded on my forehead as that pressure from earlier in the day smothered me like a wet blanket. My arms and legs felt like the heavy bags from Dad's gym, and moving them took more effort than I ever imagined possible. I was so distracted by the dread curling around me I didn't notice that the Bottle Tree was now leaning in my direction. A flash of blue alerted me.

Deep inside the largest bottle on the tree, up near the tippy-top, something moved. It shifted like dirty oil moving through water, and the only thing I wanted to do at that moment was run screaming back to the house.

"You don't know when you're beat, do you?"

Gum Baby's squeaky voice grabbed my attention. She leaned against the Bottle Tree, one hand clutching the backpack, the other pushed *inside* the trunk.

"Hey!" I shouted.

"Who you shouting at, boy? If Gum Baby had more time, she'd wear out that hide of yours, up one end and down the other. But you ain't worth the crusty sap on the bottom of Gum Baby's foot, so you get off with a warning."

"Give me back my stuff!" I said, forcing myself to move closer to her and the tree. The branch holding the creepy large bottle at the top of the tree seemed to lean over more and more.

She laughed. "Just go home, fool! Enjoy life's little pleasures, like breathing and eating solid food." She turned and stepped farther into the trunk. One strap of the backpack was now gone, heading to wherever that freaky little tree led. Cold anger made me clench my teeth, ignore the sense of evil growing in the forest, and focus on getting back Eddie's journal.

"Look, you . . . you . . . doll baby! Gimme back that bag, or I'll—"

Gum Baby froze. She turned slowly toward me and tilted her head. "What'd you say?"

"Give me back—"

"No, hush, before that. What'd you call me?"

I licked my lips. "Uh...nothing. I just wanted my friend's—"

"Oh no, it wasn't nothing. It can't be nothing now. You said it. You let the words come out of your mouth, and you need to stand by them. For as long as you have legs to stand on, anyway. So come on, big boy—what'd you say? Huh? WHAT'D YOU SAY?"

The wind died down and the Bottle Tree stood up straight again, as if the forest wanted to hear my answer. I looked around, suddenly wishing for a witness, or a shield. "Um, I just, I mean, I may have said, or called you, a doll—"

Gum Baby leaped toward me with a murderous scream.

"CALL GUM BABY A DOLL, WILL YOU? SAP ATTACK! TWO SAP ATTACKS! GUM BABY HOPES YOUR HANDS STICK TO YOUR FACE FOREVER AND YOU HAVE TO EAT WITH YOUR ELBOWS. TRIPLE SAP ATTACK, YOU...YOU...GIANT TURTLE-FACED THISTLE-HEAD!"

"Ow, stop it!" I fell backward as she scrambled up my legs and onto my chest. She unleashed a miniature onslaught, and it took everything I had to shield myself as her tiny fists and feet pummeled me. Finally, I batted Gum Baby away with my hand, but she got up and ran at me again. I grabbed one strap of the pack, ignoring the sticky residue squelching under my hands, and pulled it out of the tree, stumbling backward. Gum Baby hung on to the other strap, and the weirdest game of tug-of-war ensued in the middle of the clearing. "Let go!"

"*You* let go! Gum Baby's on a mission."

"A mission? What mission?"

"None of your business, fool!"

I swung the backpack around, trying to dislodge the thief, but Gum Baby held on with grim determination. I slammed it into the ground, whirled it over my head, but no matter what I did, I couldn't dislodge her. I let a growl of frustration escape and ran toward the Bottle Tree.

Gum Baby flapped behind me. "Oh, you're running away now? You better! Gum Baby was just about to— Hey, what're you doing?"

I swung the backpack in a circle and slammed it—and Gum Baby—against the trunk. She yelped, then wrapped herself even more tightly around the strap.

"Wait, stop it, fool! You'll damage the tree!"

"I don't care," I growled. "Give me my backpack!" I whipped it into the tree again.

The bottles shook and clinked together, echoing like haunted wind chimes. I began to whip around again for an even heavier slam.

"No, you idiot, you're fixing to get us both—"

"Shut up, shut up, shut up!" I shouted. I grabbed a handful of the backpack, balled my fist around the strap, and punched the Bottle Tree with all my might.

Crack

The punch smashed into the large blue bottle near the top, shattering the glass. The backpack ripped, Eddie's journal tumbled out, and bright green light flared in a blinding flash.

Heat.

Wind.

Everything blasted me at once.

But beneath it all, I heard a sinister laugh. The pressure on my shoulders suddenly disappeared. Out the corner of my eye, I saw a shadowy shape ooze from what was left of the broken bottle on the ground and creep along the grass. The wind howled in agony, the forest roared in pain, and a chasm ripped open at the foot of the tree. A giant sucking sound filled the clearing, like air rushing toward a hole.

The fissure split and grew, like those scenes in disaster movies when an earthquake cracks the streets apart and chases the hero.

I tried to get away, but the tear in the earth widened to reveal a swirling coal-red tunnel of fire. It burned like a thousand suns, and at its edge, something glowed a soft green.

I sucked in a breath.

Eddie's journal teetered there precariously.

"No!" I shouted, just as Gum Baby yelled, "The stories!" Gum Baby leaped from the backpack to the book.

Without thinking, I dove for it, too, desperate to rescue Eddie's journal from the flames and from Gum Baby.

My fingertips grazed the cover just as Gum Baby plopped a sticky hand on it. I started to yell at her, but then I realized, too late, that we were falling.

We'd tumbled into the glowing slash in the ground. We plummeted without slowing one bit, spinning and twisting at dizzying speeds. It was like a sink of burning anger, and we were swirling down the drain.

I tried to scream, but the forest's pained roar drowned me out. Gum Baby clutched my wrist tight as we fell for what seemed like forever, dropping like stones through the whirlpool of fire.

5

HAINTS AND BONE SHIPS

PAIN.

Confusion.

Fear.

Darkness.

And then, echoing all around me, a voice: "Hey now, hey now...I gotcha, big man, I gotcha."

A match was struck, and a lantern flared to life overhead. The soft yellow glow didn't eliminate the shadows so much as it outlined them. I was lying in the middle of a rustic room, like the inside of a cabin or a wooden shed. Who was speaking? I couldn't make out much except for the shadows and that lantern.

Water dripped from the ceiling, and the smell of old swamp and rotting vegetation filled the air. My eyes started to tear up, and I coughed as the vapors got into my nose and lungs.

"Easy now, Tristan. That is your name, right?"

"W-who's that?" I asked in mid-cough.

"Aw shoot, big man, I'm nobody. Just didn't want you to fall to your death, is all. I saved you, just like you saved me."

My chest burned, but I stood up and wiped the tears from my eyes. "Where are you?"

One shadow detached from the rest, but it had no shape. It oozed up, and I shuddered as a familiar pressure gathered around my shoulder blades. This was the thing from the Bottle Tree forest, from the broken bottle. I'd recognize that feeling of despair anywhere.

"I saved you?" I asked.

"You did, Tristan, so I had to repay the favor. I've been waiting for you. You got something I need, and if we work together—shoot, this whole world can be ours. They won't know what hit 'em. But I'm getting ahead of myself. Why don't you hand me that book of yours and we can get started."

"Book?" I shook my head, then froze. Eddie's journal. The fight. Gum Baby. I whirled around, looking for the little terror and my backpack, but all I saw was darkness.

"Yes. The book." The voice went from smooth to impatient. "Where is it?"

"I—I don't know." I dropped my head into my hands. "I lost it. I need to find it."

A growl echoed around the room before it faded to a soft purr. "Yeeeeah. You do that. I need that book, Tristan, so when you find it, you bring it to me, and we can get this party started, you hear? Don't you tell a soul, boy, and don't dally.... Naw, don't you try and play me one bit. 'Cause I'll know."

Wind whistled in my ear, and my clothes fluttered as if a huge gust was blowing through.

"Wait, where am I? Who are you?"

Why was everyone after Eddie's journal? Why did this...
thing need it so badly?

"We saved each other, so we're practically kinfolk." The voice began to disappear in the howling wind, and I could barely hear the final words. "Just call me Uncle C."

"Tristan! Tristaaaan!"

I was falling again. Whatever that place was, whoever that voice was, it all got driven to the back of my mind when I opened my eyes to a nightmare.

Gum Baby's back was stuck to my wrist as if it were glued there as we continued to tumble down the fiery tunnel. Luckily she was holding on to Eddie's glowing green journal for dear life. Swirling below us was a dark, boiling sea, so horrifying that even my screams started screaming. Wind whipped my cheeks and pulled tears from my eyes. I squeezed them shut. Whatever was going to happen next would happen—I didn't need to see it.

Splash!

The impact drove the breath from my lungs. My skin

prickled. The water temperature bubbled a few degrees above comfortable—not scalding as I'd feared, but hot enough to scare me. Panicking, I opened my mouth to cry out in surprise, and water surged inside. I swallowed by accident and it burned on the way down. *Swim!* I told myself. *Swim, Tristan, or you're done for.*

I forced my eyes open and tried to figure out which direction was up. Blurry light flickered in the distance. My legs kicked me toward it on their own, my lungs screaming for air, and I clawed my way to what I hoped was the surface. Shadowy shapes streaked past, and—oh, man—something slimy brushed my ankle.

I'd had it by that point. *This* was how Tristan Strong was going to meet his end? In a giant dirty hot tub?

Just when I thought I couldn't go any farther and my chest felt like it was going to explode, my head broke the surface. I coughed and spluttered.

"Blech!"

My mouth tasted like old pennies and warm spoiled milk. Yeah . . . think about that flavor.

"Gum Baby?" I called out hoarsely. I kicked and paddled, doing my best to tread water as I sucked down air, and looked around in confusion. "Gum Baby, where . . . ?"

The question died on my tongue as I took in my surroundings.

Fires burned on the sea. Not little fires, either, but massive walls of flame that licked high into the air. The current carried infernos everywhere, and their bright blazes turned the water into swirling oranges and reds. Steam hissed up from the surface and collected into clouds a few feet above my head. Through an occasional break in the mist I could see that it was still nighttime. And there, high above, the fiery tunnel we'd fallen through scarred the sky.

I looked down. Lights twinkled on and off in the depths, and at first I thought it was the reflection of the stars. Then I saw a long shadow pass underneath me—a leviathan somehow lit from beneath—and I gulped.

Where the heck had we landed?

"Bumbletongue!" The cry came from behind me. "Help! Gum Baby can't sw—*glublublub*. Gum Baby can't swim!"

I tore my eyes away from the shape below and whipped my head around. Sure enough, there was the little thief, flailing in the water a short distance away. I paddled over, a million questions fighting to be first out my mouth.

Gum Baby floated on her back, hugging the journal tightly like a life preserver. Her little legs kicked helplessly in the air, and a tiny fire burned on one foot. I splashed her to douse the flame, then grabbed the journal and lifted it—with Gum Baby still attached—out of the water with one hand. I hoped it wasn't ruined. (The book, not the doll. She could float there forever for all I cared.)

"About time!" Gum Baby, now hanging on from below,

coughed and glared at me. "What took you so long? Gum Baby ain't a fish. Come on, we have to—"

"Where are we?" I asked, cutting her off.

"What?"

"Where are we? What happened? Did you see a shadow thing, with the voice and the smells, before we splashed down? Why am I floating in an ocean of fire, and why are there stars under us, and what happened to my backpack?"

Gum Baby waved one arm and a wet glob of sap plopped into the sea. "*Shh*. Gum Baby don't know what you talking about half the time, and the other half she ain't got the patience. No time to answer all those questions. Well, maybe there is, but you drain me. Like a straw. Here you come, and—*fwoop!*—all my energy is gone."

I growled and shook the journal. She nearly lost her grip.

"Okay, okay! Stop messing around. Gum Baby don't feel so good."

More sap plopped down as if to prove her point. As I continued to tread water with only one arm, I gave thanks for Dad's swim training. He used to make me do laps in the local community center pool when it was too cold outside to go running.

I tilted my head, trying to get water out of my ears, and for a second I thought I heard a drumbeat and clapping. But that was silly. I turned back to my sticky little companion.

"Where. Are. We?" I asked again through gritted teeth.

"*Shh*. Gum Baby's trying to tell you, now ain't the time for talking. If they hear us, we're in trouble."

"*They?* Who's they?"

Just then, a splash sounded in the distance, and Gum Baby shushed me again. She stared into the fire and fog, her wet black curls plastered to her carved wooden head. After a second, she relaxed.

"Can't be so loud," she muttered.

I didn't know if she was talking to me or to herself, but either way, it wasn't reassuring. I blinked salt out of my eyes and spat out another mouthful of sour seawater. *I'm going to need eight bottles of mouthwash after this*, I thought.

"What is this place?" I asked. "Some sort of underground salt lake? I didn't think Alabama had these."

"What? No." Gum Baby looked surprised, as if I should know. "This ain't no Alabama, wherever that is."

"Maybe Mississippi, then?"

"I don't know no Mrs. Ippy, and you can tell her Gum Baby said that."

"No, that's not—"

"Look, enough with the flappy-lip jibjab. We need to hurry before—"

There was another splash, then another that sounded even closer, and Gum Baby froze up.

"They're coming," she whispered.

"Who is *they*?!"

A rippling sound echoed across the water. We both turned to see a column of floating fire curving through the water toward us, and with every second it picked up speed. The ripples it made turned into flame-capped waves as a long, gnarled shape sliced up through the surface and into the air.

My eyes nearly fell out.

"Holy—"

"Ship!" Gum Baby screamed.

A vessel unlike any I'd seen before rose from the deep. Its hull was two giant white hands cupped together, the fingertips touching at the prow. Knobby knuckles poked out along the side. It had no sail, just a single bare mast that jutted up mid-ship, a daggerlike tower that cut through the curtains of steam. No one could be seen on deck. It was just a weird hand-ship the size of a yacht, sailing without a captain, roaring across a burning sea toward us.

Oh, and it wasn't made of painted wood, like I'd thought.

"Those are bones!" I yelled at Gum Baby.

"Stop shouting and swim, fool!"

The spooky ship creaked as it listed to one side, turning to sweep down on us. Horrible sounds floated to us across the waves: a thousand sufferers moaning and crying out. Desperate. Infuriated. Scared. Hungry. I didn't know who—or what—was making the noise, but I wasn't planning on sticking around to find out.

I shivered despite the hot water, floundering with one

arm, the other supporting Eddie's journal and Gum Baby. "I can't swim *and* hold you," I said.

"Hand over the stories and put Gum Baby on your back. Now!"

"On my back? I'm not—"

"Put Gum Baby on your back, Bumbletongue! Stop chit-chattin' and move it!"

I swallowed several choice angry words and slipped Gum Baby onto my shoulders. I didn't trust her with Eddie's journal, but the ship was barreling toward us and I needed both hands free.

"You lose that book," I said, "or run away with it again, and I'll turn you into an incense holder."

Gum Baby patted the top of my head. "*Shh,* fishy. Just swim toward the cloud of steam when Gum Baby says go. These things don't turn around easy, so even your dusty tail should be able to escape."

I hated that doll. I hated it with a burning passion.

"Ready . . ."

The ship moaned at us. It was a white and sharp predator trailing fountains of fire behind it.

"Steady . . ."

I licked my lips. "Gum Baby, it's nearly—"

She smacked the back of my head. "Hush, fool! We've got one shot at this. Bone ships look scary, but you can avoid them easy enough if you know how."

Oh great, they were even called *bone ships*. That didn't make things better.

Just when it seemed like we were moments away from being crushed, just when the front of the bone ship—no way!—groaned open, the fingertips lowering to SCOOP US UP . . . Gum Baby shouted in my ear, "Go, go, go!"

My body responded to the command before I could protest. Dad used to shout the same thing at me from the side of the pool when I did my laps. I gave a mighty kick, my legs scissoring through the water, and I darted forward. I didn't look behind me, but I knew the ship was close. The surge it was creating nearly pulled me under. I fought it, my arms flashing in and out of the water like Dad had taught me, and then the ship passed us by. We were safe.

"Go there!" Gum Baby screamed, pointing.

A thick gray-white cloud of steam hovered ahead. It drifted over a calm spot just beyond the waves, and, thankfully, no fires were burning nearby. I dug deep for a bit more energy and kicked forward. Another moan echoed over the water, taking my mind off how heavy my arms felt. Exhausted and free beats resting in the bowels of a skeleton ship, you get me?

Gum Baby patted my head as we approached.

"Good fishy. Scoot on in there and wait until—"

A bellowing moan—even louder, deeper, and scarier than the first—sounded right in front of us. I could feel it through the water, in my chest, and I threw my arms out and floated to a stop.

Gum Baby squeaked, and something rolled down my back.

"Please tell me that was sap," I whispered, treading water.

"Um . . . okay."

I couldn't even get angry. I was too tired. Too drained. Too afraid that . . .

Another bone ship lunged out of the thick cloud of steam in front of us. Cloudy wisps clung to it like spiderwebs. Even though it was about the same size as the first, its horrific shape made it seem larger.

It was the jawbone of some enormous reptile. Long and thin and pale, it cut through the sea like a powerboat. Strands of something I didn't want to look at too closely trailed from between its enormous teeth. Burning seawater streamed down its sides, and it let loose a soul-crushing bellow as it began to pick up speed.

Out of the corner of my eye, I saw yet another streak of white in the water. A third ship surfaced from beneath, like a submarine from a horror show. This bone ship looked like a rib cage, curved bones curling up as it erupted out of the sea.

The first ship, Bone Hands, circled around behind us.

We were trapped.

"Gum Baby, where do I go? What do I do?"

Silence.

I could feel Gum Baby lying between my shoulder blades, shivering.

"Gum Baby, get up! What do I do? Where am I going?"

The three ships closed in. Rib Cage rattled as it drew near. Jawbone continued to blast us with that deep groaning bellow. I turned to see the Hands open again, the hungry maw between the fingertips dark and foul. A chorus of moans tortured my ears while a gust of hot, rotten air clawed up my nostrils.

"Gum Baby, what do—?"

A high-pitched whistle split the night.

Gum Baby leaped to her feet and scrambled to the top of my head. "Gum Baby don't believe it!" she said, her voice excited.

"What?"

"We're saved!"

"Saved? How?"

But she didn't answer. Instead, she jumped up and down on my head and started shouting at the top of her tiny little lungs. I didn't know doll babies *had* lungs.

"HERE!" Her shrill voice—and her tiny feet beating on my skull—made me wince. "WE'RE DOWN HERE!"

Nothing happened.

The bone ships surged closer, hemming us in, and I looked around wildly for some way to escape. I could dive beneath them, but Eddie's journal (and yes, I guess, the annoying, sticky little creature holding it) would be hard to hold on to while I swam. Besides, my legs felt like anchors by then, and those ships had come from beneath the sea—there was no telling how many more of them lurked below. I couldn't avoid them for much longer.

The Hands swept forward, seconds away from funneling me inside....

Something splashed down into the water next to me.

"Grab the rope!"

The voice—a girl's—came out of the air above us. A giant wooden raft the size of a boxing ring floated in the night sky, a rope dangling over its edge. A hysterical chuckle bubbled in my chest. Of course. A flying raft. Why didn't I think of that?

"Grab it, grab it!" Gum Baby shouted, and I lunged for the thick line. I felt the doll crawl into my soaking-wet hood, and not a moment too soon. The rope grew taut, and whoever was on the raft pulled us up. The razor-sharp mast of the Hands barely missed slicing the sole of my foot open, and then we were clear, soaring into the night.

6

THE RAFT

THE FIRST THING I SAW WHEN I ROLLED ONTO THE RAFT WAS A carved staff. Its golden tip, a face twisted into a snarl, stared down at me.

"Who are you?" the staff's owner demanded.

I stared at the tip, which moved from side to side hypnotically, like a cobra getting ready to strike. "Uhh..."

"I won't ask again. Who are you?"

"My name is Tristan," I said. "Tristan Strong."

"Tristan Strong. Hmph. Well, Tristan Strong, what are you doing flopping about in the Burning Sea? You could've dragged us all down into a right nasty time trying to rescue you."

"Sorry."

"Sorry don't feed the hungry." The staff lowered, though, and I finally snapped out of my trance and glimpsed who was wielding it.

A short round girl with honey-brown skin and gold snake bangles curling up her arm glared at me. She looked my age, maybe a year older. Her hair was pulled back in two thick braids that disappeared behind her head, and she wore a sleeveless gold tank top, black pants with gold trim that stopped mid-calf, and brown sandals with beaded straps that tied around her ankles.

Someone—no, several someones—huddled behind her at the other end of the raft. A group of about a dozen clustered together, all wearing long, dingy gray cloaks with hoods that hid their faces. They stood among rumpled leather sacks, and they clung desperately to rope handrails on the sides of the raft. My eyes shifted between them and the girl.

"Well, get up," she ordered.

I stood slowly. My legs jiggled like wet spaghetti, and I could barely lift my arms. *Tired* didn't even begin to describe it. It felt like everything, from Gum Baby to the Bottle Tree to the weird shadow man to the Burning Sea to the bone ships, was piled up in a wobbly tower in my mind. Any second now, it would all come tumbling down and bury me in confusion.

Sometimes you just have to fight off your brain.

"Who are you?" I asked the girl as I began to pull up the rope that had saved me, coiling it around one arm. "Where did you all come from?"

"Why are you so nosy?" she asked.

"Sorry, I—"

"Never mind, we don't have time for this. Just be quiet before I throw you back."

I obeyed.

One of the cloaked figures in the rear shifted. "Ayanna, we must go."

The girl huffed and turned. As she walked by, I felt Gum Baby jerk up in my hood. "Ayanna? Is . . . is that you? How . . . ? Why . . . ? You're so big!"

"Gum Baby!" Ayanna dropped to her knees and swept the doll out of my hoodie and into a huge hug. "How did you . . . ? Where have you been? We looked everywhere for you. We were worried sick. You were supposed to come right back!"

"Gum Baby only meant to stay for a few hours, but Bumbletongue here was selfish and insisted on tagging along. And then there was the whole fight over this book"—she held up the waterlogged journal—"and—"

"A few hours?" Ayanna held Gum Baby at arm's length and looked at her. "Gum Baby, you've been gone for a year. What—?"

"Ayanna! Bone ships!" The tallest passenger leaned over the side of the raft and pointed to the Burning Sea beneath us. "There!" he called in a pained yip. Others craned to see, but I stared at the one who had called the warning.

I must have been tired. Half-asleep, even. His arm looked like it was . . . covered in fur.

But there was no time to linger on that. Ayanna put Gum Baby down, and, with a promise to talk later, dashed to the rear and jammed her staff into a knothole.

"Hold tight!" she called.

Everyone grabbed the ropes, and my eyes grew wide.

"Wait—"

But it was too late. With a thrust of Ayanna's stick, the raft jerked forward and I toppled head over heels, landing in a pile of cloth. *What is propelling this thing?*

"Oomph!" Someone pushed me off them. "Watch it!"

"Sorry," I muttered, but when I turned to meet the eyes beneath the hood, I froze. They glinted yellow. And was that a . . . snout? "What the—?"

But the person—it *had* to be a person—turned away as a bright orange flash seared the night sky.

Ayanna blanched. "Why are there so many ships?" she whispered.

I looked at her face, swallowed, then scooted back and peeked over the edge of the raft.

"Sweet peaches," I said under my breath.

Bone ships swarmed beneath us like sharks smelling blood. The Hands, the Ribs, the Jawbone—they were all there, but there were more, too. They fought and jostled to get right underneath the raft, as if at any moment we'd tumble out of the air. The sea flared with light every time one ship crashed into another, and the impact sounded like a crack of thunder. Flames shot up like lava from an erupting volcano, and more than one scream echoed around me. Ayanna tried to swerve and keep going forward, but another blast nearly singed the front of the raft.

"Toss some of those supply bundles overboard," Ayanna instructed someone. "We have to get higher. I'm cutting off the search and heading home." It looked like the words pained her as she turned the raft around.

The search? What were they searching for? Not the journal...

Gum Baby was still holding it under her arm as she clung to the handrail, looking around in confusion. "Gum Baby was gone a whole year?" she muttered to herself. "That ain't right."

I leaned over to look down at the violent sea, then sat back in a hurry and prayed we would go even faster. "Gum Baby, how long did it take you to get from... this place to my grandparents' farm? Did it take months?"

"No! Seconds—minutes, maybe. Gum Baby told you she move like the wind." She rubbed her face in confusion. "It don't make sense."

"Well, where are we going now?"

"Back," she said, her squeaky voice low and sad. "Back to the Thicket."

"Where's that?"

Gum Baby pointed to a smoky white line in the distance, barely visible beyond the flames on the water. From here it looked like a mere smear on the horizon.

I bit my lip. "It's too far away," I said. "The ships will get us before—"

Gum Baby shook her head. "Ayanna can make it."

"I hope you're right," a low voice behind us muttered.

All the passengers held each other as Ayanna coaxed and pleaded with the raft for more speed. The bone ships moved slowly, but others kept popping out of the deep on either side below us. Just when it looked like we'd left some pursuers behind, another three or four would lurch out of the water like the unearthed remains of prehistoric monsters. Or sea zombies. Yeah, sea zombies. They moaned with hunger and joined the chase.

Finally, after the last supply bag went over the side, and just when I was wondering how far a drop it was to the ocean, we began to pick up speed. The bone ships drifted farther and farther behind us, until eventually they disappeared into the flames. Several passengers exhaled in relief, but my muscles wouldn't relax, and I started to shiver.

"You cold?" Ayanna asked. "We have blankets—"

"No, I'm good." I didn't want to tell her the real reason I was shaking. I don't do heights. Especially not on a flying raft with no seat belts and flimsy ropes for railings. But it felt silly complaining about that after nearly being swallowed by an oversize science-class skeleton.

We kept gliding until the line of smoky white became a cloudy smudge, then a curtain of fog. Finally, the vague outline of a coast appeared. It stretched far and curved slightly in the distance, disappearing into mist.

Once everybody had settled down, and a few passengers even began to chat among themselves, I scooted closer to Gum Baby and leaned over. "Those ships back there... What...? How—?" I broke off, trying to get my words together and my shivering under control. "What were those things?"

Gum Baby picked at a smear of sap on her pants. "Everybody just calls them bone ships."

"But what *are* they?"

"Scavengers," Ayanna broke in. "Vultures. Miss—uh, someone I know calls them echoes of a nightmare from another realm. But still, they're more of a nuisance than a real danger. At least they used to be. I've seen them group up before, but never like that."

"But the sounds. The people I heard moaning—"

"Those are just echoes. Nothing is alive on those things, trust me. You just heard memories from a different time, a bad time."

"Memories of what?"

But she waved me off. "Not now. We're almost there."

The raft slowed and started to drift lower and lower. As we sank through wispy white clouds, leafless dead trees appeared, leaning out of the water like spears. Ayanna beckoned us all close. "Gather whatever you have left. We've made it to the shallows—we can wade to shore from here. I'd rather land now than try to navigate through that mist and those trees. Leave what you can't carry, or anything that would bog you down. Head for the trees, follow the signs, and we'll be back in the Thicket before you know it."

I started moving to the back of the raft to get out of everyone else's way, trying not to rock it. Ayanna looked at me, then at Gum Baby, who'd climbed up on my shoulder, and shook her head. "I don't know what y'all did, or where you came from, boy, but you might as well come with us, too. If Gum Baby brought you, that makes you one of us."

I coughed, and Gum Baby shifted on my shoulder, but neither of us tried to argue with her. I met the little doll's eyes, and an unspoken agreement passed between us. *Get to safety, and then we'll explain everything.* I got the impression from Ayanna's reaction that Gum Baby had done a bit more than she was supposed to.

Ayanna stared at the sea. "I've never seen the Maafa's minions act like this."

"The Mafia?" I looked from her to Gum Baby. "Why would—?"

The raft touched down on the sea with a bump and a splash, making me stumble. Ayanna clapped her hand over her mouth, like she'd said something she shouldn't have, and moved to the center of the raft, calling out instructions.

"Gum Baby?" I asked. "Why would the Mafia—?"

"Not the Mafia, the *Maafa*!"

"Oh. What's the Maafa?"

"*Shh.*" Gum Baby patted my head absentmindedly and scanned the area. The curtain of fog hung about a hundred yards away. So close, yet so far.

"Boy! Hey!" Ayanna motioned to me. "We need your help."

"The name's Tristan. Not *boy*."

"Tristan, then. We made the shallows, but the water's still too deep for some of the Midfolk."

"Midfolk?"

She gestured at the cloaked people gathering their things. I shrugged. Whatever the weird cult members wanted to call each other made no difference to me. But a few of them *were* on the small side, and I didn't want a current to drag them back to where the bone ships waited.

Sometimes you just have to join the party, no matter how strange it is.

"What do you need me to do?" I asked, rolling up the sleeves of my hoodie.

"You and BF hop over the side. You two are the biggest.

I'll keep the raft clear of the flames—y'all take the rope and haul us to shore."

The person with the yellow eyes came forward, carrying a bundle in his arms. Ayanna stepped close to talk to him.

"Be careful," she said in a low voice. "If you get tired—"

"I will do my part," the person said. It sounded like a snarl, but Ayanna didn't look offended. She just nodded.

The person held the bundle out to her. "Watch Chestnutt, will you? She hasn't recovered yet."

"Of course." Ayanna accepted it and cradled it like a mother would a baby. "Is she—?"

"She's fine. She just . . . scares easily."

Gum Baby stood on the edge of the raft and cupped both hands around her mouth. "Bumbletongue! Head into the trees!"

"My name. Is. Tristan."

"Tristan, Bumbletongue. It all sounds the same. Gum Baby can't keep track."

"Just try and keep the journal out of the water this time," I said. It had already gotten wet once, and while I couldn't believe I was actually trusting her with it, I needed both hands free.

"BF," Ayanna said, "give me your cloak. It'll drag you down."

The person named BF nodded, then shrugged off his garment. My jaw dropped and I choked on my words.

"Sweet. Peaches."

The yellow eyes.

The snout.

The person Ayanna spoke to . . . wasn't a person.

My mind turned to goop.

7
IRON MONSTERS 101

"GAAAAAH," I SAID.

A reddish-brown-furred fox, easily as big as Ayanna herself—the largest I'd ever seen—dropped his cloak on the raft. It—he—stood on his hind legs, and his muzzle twitched in wry amusement.

"I think I broke him," BF said to Ayanna.

BF. *Brer Fox.*

"Gaaaaah," I said.

Gum Baby shook her head. "See? That's why you're Bumbletongue."

Ayanna tossed the rope toward me. The end smacked me in the forehead and fell across my outstretched arm, which was pointing at the walking, talking animal in front of me. In fact—I took a quick glance back at the other cloaked figures and inhaled sharply—he wasn't the only one. A tail poked out here. A wing there.

"Gaaaaah."

"Did he do this with you, too?" Brer Fox asked Gum Baby.

The little doll nodded sadly. "Gum Baby worries about him. He's so fragile."

Talking dolls.

Bone ships.

Burning seas.

Flying rafts.

Human-size foxes.

"Gaaaaah."

Brer Fox slipped over the side of the raft with a wince, then grabbed the other rope that Ayanna tossed to him.

"Well," he said, his whiskers glistening in the night, "shall we save ourselves?"

The long, mournful moan of a bone ship floated across the waves. The sound jostled me to my senses—sort of.

"Gaaaaah." I nodded, and we both began to wade through the waist-high shallows, fleeing the desperate haunted ships behind us.

We slogged through the foggy shallows. The height of the water slowly dropped until Brer Fox and I splashed instead of waded. We grunted and snarled (guess who did which) as we dragged the raft forward. White mist hung in the air like frozen spiderwebs, and the roaring flames of the Burning Sea faded as a blanket of eerie silence covered us.

"Where are we?" I asked Brer Fox.

"The Drowned Forest," he said, his breath coming fast and heavy. "For obvious reasons, wouldn't you say?"

The marshy water, thick and clouded with dirt, leaves, and branches, smelled and looked awful. My socks squelched, my shorts were turning slimy green, and I didn't even want to think about what my Chucks looked like. Mom was gonna kill me when I got home.

If I got home.

Something snagged my ankle and I nearly fell.

Mom was gonna have to get in line.

"Just a bit farther," Ayanna said from the raft. She spoke in a whisper as she steered around a jagged tree stump, but the sound carried over the still water like a shout. "Keep close, everyone. Cloaks off. We need speed now. No time for stealth."

Gum Baby hopped up next to her. "We're safe here, right, Ayanna? They've never come this far into the trees."

"Who's *they*?" I asked. "The bone ships?"

Ayanna winced, someone gasped, and Gum Baby shook her head. "Not unless they grow some legs. Naw, it's the—"

"Hush now, Gum Baby," Ayanna whispered.

She glanced back over her shoulder, and I did the same, trying not to gawk. Some of the Midfolk were watching us, while the rest pretended to be busy. They had discarded their cloaks to reveal other furry faces, along with three feathery ones, and even a turtle. There were a couple of human chil-dren as well. I took a deep breath, but surprisingly, that was my only reaction. At this point they all could've started doing the electric slide and I would've shrugged and joined in. The mind can only take so much weirdness before it accepts it as a new normal.

Ayanna turned back to me. "Enough questions. You'll scare the others. Just get ready to run—we can talk all we want back in the Thicket, I promise. But right now? We need to move."

I tried to nod calmly, even though my face was burning. I turned back around and resolved to keep my eyes forward. A chuckle sounded to my left. Brer Fox licked his graying muzzle, and his left ear twitched forward. The right one was mangled, as if something had once chewed on it.

"You're not from 'round here, I suppose," he said. It wasn't a question, but I shook my head anyway. "Where, then, if I may ask? You've the look of the Ridge people—or maybe the Crescent folk, now that I think about it."

I bit my lip and kept my eyes straight ahead. See how you'd feel, talking to a fox. Gives you all sorts of willies.

"I don't know any of those places," I said.

"You don't know the Alke territories?"

"Who's Alke?"

This made Brer Fox stumble. He huffed and chuffed, emitting a yipping cough, and it took me a second to realize he was laughing.

"Who—who's Alke. Oh, that's...that's a delight." His laugh turned into a raspy wheeze, and he stopped hauling on his rope to hunch over and cough. When it didn't stop, I quit pulling as well.

"Brer Fox?" Ayanna called, worried. "You all right?"

He waved a paw at her, but it was another minute or two before he could stand upright and breathe without coughing. He took a deep, whistling breath, then wiped his muzzle. He picked up the rope floating near his hind legs and began to pull again.

After a few moments, I cleared my throat. "I'm serious. I'm not...I don't know this place."

"Where are you from, then, if I may be so bold?"

My eyes flicked up to the sky, to the hole that burned like a second sun, and he followed my gaze. He stiffened and his ears flattened to his skull. The look he turned on me, as if he was struggling to hold back a snarl, made me flinch.

"You don't believe me?" I asked.

"No." The word came out almost as a bark. "No, quite the opposite. I *do* believe you."

"Really?" I pulled the raft in silence for another few seconds, then sighed. "I don't quite believe it myself right now. I just...I just want to get back?"

He didn't answer, though from time to time he'd glance up at the sky, then look around. I took that to mean he didn't have a clue as to how I would do that, and I trudged along in a sour mood.

The water was only ankle-deep now, and the mist cleared a bit to reveal glimpses of a sprawling forest of moss-covered trees. Vines dangled from low-hanging branches, and roots dipped in and out of the water, while the treetops disappeared into blurry white, as if some supreme cartoonist had forgotten to finish drawing them. The air felt thick and humid, and my neck tingled like someone was watching me.

Brer Fox stared at me as I tried to shake off the feeling. "Good. You sense it as well. Be wary, my boy. We've not escaped just yet. That hole in the sky is causing creatures far worse than bone ships to go into a right frenzy. You want to know how to get back to wherever you tumbled from? Stay alive."

I swallowed hard, and we entered the forest.

I watched him out of the corner of my eye. In his prime, Brer Fox would have been glorious and fearsome. Even now I could see traces of his red-and-silver fur through the gray. His tongue lolled out as he panted with exhaustion, and his teeth still looked wicked and sharp.

"My friend," I said suddenly, "used to tell me a story."

"Good friends will do that," he commented. "But I'd be wary of telling the full tale here. Stories are powerful magic. You'll find that out soon enough. Best only summarize."

I nodded, though I didn't entirely understand what he meant. "It was an old story. A folktale, really. About a rabbit, a bear... and a fox. The bear and fox would try their best to catch and eat that rabbit, but he was too smart. He always got away."

Brer Fox made a weird noise in his throat. A chattering, whining sort of sound. He shook his head. "Too smart indeed."

"So...?"

"Am I that fox? Hm. I suppose I am."

I nodded. "And the rabbit and bear?"

"I suspect you'll see Brer Rabbit soon enough."

As soon as he said that, I remembered the vision in my grandparents' car. The large, weary, and bruised rabbit, anxious and jumpy. So had that been real, and not a dream like I'd assumed? My mind reeled. First Gum Baby, now Brer Fox and Brer Rabbit. All of them from stories Eddie had collected, that Nana had told, that I'd read in some form while growing up. And now I stood with the very same characters, plucked straight out of a book.

Or had I been plunked *into* one?

"And the bear?"

Fox's tail swished angrily, and he bared his teeth. "Bear isn't here," was all he said, and that was that.

The raft ran aground—now the Midfolk would have to continue on foot to this Thicket place. Wherever it was, everyone seemed eager to get there. I could read the hope in their eyes as they helped each other get ready. Ayanna whispered soothing reassurances, and Brer Fox and I assisted as they disembarked. I kept my face neutral as I took wrinkled paws as well as brown hands like mine and lifted the Midfolk off the raft. An old crow cawed her thanks and flapped ahead with two smaller crows following after her, joining the rest as we started to walk.

Some of the puddles on the forest floor were too deep for Gum Baby, so she rode on my shoulder, still holding the journal, and shouted encouragement.

"Pick up them feet!"

"This ain't a field trip!"

"Don't make Gum Baby put some pep back in your step— Oh, sorry, Ayanna. Didn't know it was you."

With Gum Baby blaring in my ear, I fell back to check on an old turtle the size of a dinner plate ("Call me Tarrypin, sonny. Mr. Turtle is my pappy."), who was struggling to climb over a partially submerged root. I lifted him over it, then we scrambled after the rest of the group.

Ayanna shook her head. "How you and Gum Baby paired up should make a fine tale."

Gum Baby bounced on my shoulder and nearly fell off as I hurdled a stump. "What, him?" she said. "Gum Baby barely knows the guy."

I shrugged without warning her, and the little doll toppled

backward. She just managed to grab on to my hood and screamed at me in her shrill voice.

"BUMBLETONGUE, GUM BABY GONNA WHOOP YOU LIKE YOUR BUTT'S ON FIRE! THIS AIN'T FUNNY! YOU GONNA PAY, YOU HEAR GUM BABY?"

"*Shh*, y'all!" Ayanna whispered, but a small smile slipped across her face.

Gum Baby managed to scramble back up to her perch on my shoulder, where she whispered other gruesome threats in my ear. Then she dropped Eddie's journal in my hood, jumped down onto Tarrypin's back, and made rude gestures at me with her little carved hands as the two trundled off after the others. I rolled my eyes and slipped the journal into my cargo shorts' pocket. Ayanna's smile transformed into a grin.

"She's a trip," she said.

"She's something, all right," I agreed. We separated for a moment to help the others navigate the trees and branches but were soon running side by side again. I hesitated, then asked the question that had been bugging me.

"Who are you?"

She wrinkled her eyebrows in confusion. "You don't know my name?"

"No. I mean, yes, but like, all of you. Brer Fox, Gum Baby—you all are from stories, but now..."

"Oh."

I waited, and she dodged a low-hanging branch (I didn't, in case you cared) and thought about her answer.

"I'm not sure how to explain it. Brer Rabbit, or John Henry—they normally do all the introductions."

I stumbled over a tree root and nearly face-planted in a smelly, squelchy mud puddle. "John Henry?" The giant man from my vision popped into my mind. Of course. If Brer Rabbit and Gum Baby were there, he would be as well.

"Mm-hmm. Watch out for those roots, by the way."

Her sarcasm made my ears burn. "Oh, thanks. I'll try."

She took a deep breath. "I heard you and Fox talking earlier. This world, as messed up as it is right now, is called Alke. We're in MidPass, an island in the Burning Sea."

I stopped in my tracks. "Does that mean we're trapped here? Surrounded by fire and those bone ships?" Panic started to bubble in my chest until Ayanna grabbed my wrist.

"We're not trapped. Just . . . waiting for the right time."

I nodded, though I didn't really understand, and she let go. We hurried to catch up with the group.

"The Burning Sea back there cuts us off from the mainland," Ayanna went on, "but we're still a part of Alke. A territory, if you want to call it that."

"Like Chicago is in Illinois," I said.

She shrugged. "Sure, I guess. But, for better or worse, this is our home."

"Okay, I get that now. But . . ." I hesitated, unsure of how to ask my next question. "People and"—I started to say *animals*, but stopped short—"creatures. From stories. How come?"

Ayanna grinned. "Okay, I'm starting to see where the nickname Bumbletongue came from." She ducked a twig I threw at her, then got serious. "The way John Henry tells it, your world and ours are like twins. No, wait, that's a bad example." She wrinkled her forehead, then sighed. "How does he put it? Alke . . . Alke is the dream to your world's reality. The tales, the fables, the things you think are made up, they exist here. We aren't just stories—we're real, with hopes and dreams and fears just like you, and right now we're all just trying to make it back home before—" She broke off, but I knew where she was going.

"Before the Maafa, whatever that is, captures us with the bone ships," I finished.

"It's not just bone ships."

I stopped. She started to say something more, when a hissed warning sliced through the trees. Everyone skidded to a stop. Brer Fox stood tall, his good ear flicking and his head whipping left and right as he sniffed the air. Ayanna and I crept up to his side, comforting Midfolk as we went. When we reached him, his teeth were bared and his hackles raised.

"We're being hunted," he said, and a chill went down my spine.

8
FETTERLINGS

HUNTED.

By what? I wondered. I couldn't hear anything. The forest was dead silent. We were the only things breathing or moving. I hoped it stayed that way.

"There's a bridge, just up a ways, that marks the edge of the Thicket," Ayanna whispered. "We'll cross it, run north as fast as we can, and then other Midfolk should be able to help us."

"And if whoever is hunting us follows?" I asked. "What then?"

Ayanna didn't look at me. "Don't. Let them. Follow. Got it?"

Brer Fox's mangled ear twitched. He pawed at it, then noticed me watching. "Lets me know when trouble's afoot, it does."

"And?"

It twitched again, then quivered and went flat. I guess that was answer enough.

"What are we running from?" I asked. "In the stories—"

"This ain't nothing like the stories you've heard," Brer Fox said. "And we try to keep their names out our mouths if at all possible. Seems like discussing them brings them around faster."

With that cryptic comment, we started off.

"The river's just ahead!"

The call got passed back like a relay baton, and everyone who heard it found a new burst of energy. A dot of light pierced the gray-green stillness. The break in the forest grew as we sprinted to it like moths to a flame. If we could make it there, it felt like our troubles would—

A rattling sound filled the forest, like a bunch of chains swinging in the wind.

I slowed to look around and Brer Fox snarled at me.

"Keep moving!"

The rattling came again and again from everywhere all at once. Behind us, from our left, from our right—like something was herding us onward. The sounds rolled in on top of each other.

We all huffed along, wheezing and choking.

"Quickly now! To the bridge!"

We burst out of the Drowned Forest into a clearing. There the thick mud had dried to a dark, flaky crust like an old scab, and a layer of leaves covered the ground like a raggedy Band-Aid. We skidded to a stop. A rickety bridge made of split logs and woven vines dangled across a steep, rocky ravine. The largest river I'd ever seen surged along beneath it, roaring and carrying branches over sharp rocks and around twisty turns.

A high-pitched scraping sound, like nails on a chalkboard, ripped through the air. I clapped my hands over my ears and winced, and Tarrypin moaned. Brer Fox dropped to the ground and yipped in pain. The others reacted similarly. Even Ayanna scrunched down like the noise hurt her. Only Gum Baby seemed unaffected. She ran over to each of us in turn, pushing with her tiny arms, trying to get us to move. She said something, but I couldn't hear her over the screeching. Finally she gave up and ran to the bridge.

Near the edge of the ravine, just before it dropped off to the hungry river below, she paused. Something in the leaves grabbed her attention, and she seemed transfixed by it.

Frozen stiff, almost.

With my ears still covered, I stumbled over and stopped short of Gum Baby and the steep drop-off behind her.

"What's wrong?" I yelled.

She didn't answer. Her body jerked—first left, then right—and I squinted.

"Gum Baby? What are you doing? We need to— Oh my sweet peaches."

At first I thought it was a snake. An easy mistake, really.

It wrapped itself around Gum Baby, and a trick of the dim light gave it a link pattern, like a rattlesnake.

But then I realized quite a few things at once.

First: The "snake" was actually a chain-like creature with a metal shackle for a head.

Second: It held Gum Baby fast, its cuff-head snapping around her neck like a collar, the long chain attached to it coiling around her tiny wooden body.

Third: More of those things were filling the tiny clearing.

Fourth: My shorts were glowing.

Green light grew brighter and brighter, filling the clearing and dashing away the shadows, and it took me a few seconds to understand that the light was coming from my pocket— from Eddie's journal.

Soft moans floated up from the Midfolk huddled behind me, but my attention stayed glued on Gum Baby's helpless struggles. She jerked left and right, but the chain-thing only squeezed tighter.

Brer Fox staggered forward out of the cluster into the middle of the clearing, his ears flat to his skull. He was still yards away from me and Gum Baby, too far to help, and he froze when he saw the chain creatures rising out of the grass, dangling from trees, and creeping along the ground. His hackles rose like needles on a porcupine, and he snarled.

"Fetterlings."

"Fetter what?" I shouted back.

"A type of iron monster."

Two of the creatures—fetterlings—swayed from branches just off to my right, near the edge of the ravine, and I got a good look at them. They ranged in size. The littlest, like the one that had trapped Gum Baby, only had the collar head. Their chain links were no longer than my thumb. The bigger ones had the collar, much thicker chains, and chain-like arms that ended in open manacles.

"See those pincer hands?" Brer Fox said as the fetterlings' appendages clacked together. "They use those to drag off their victims."

I paled and my mouth went dry. "Drag off?"

"To their leader."

I gulped. "You mean the Maa—"

"Don't. Don't say it." Brer Fox dropped to all fours and called out instructions. "Slowly, and carefully—"

"One of them has Gum Baby!" I blurted out. I hated the way my voice cracked with fear, and the way everyone seemed to look at me when they heard it. Even the monsters. But it was just the two of us, a boy and a doll, and you know what? It was scary. There. I said it.

More fetterlings rose off the ground. We were trapped.

Some blocked our path to the bridge on the north side of the clearing, right where Gum Baby and I stood. Others crept through the grass on the east and west. And back by the forest edge behind us, across the clearing and near where Ayanna had been bringing up the rear, more fetterlings swarmed out of the trees.

"Ayanna?" Brer Fox called.

"I'm thinking, I'm thinking," she said, her voice filled with desperation.

The fetterlings swayed back and forth as they slipped closer and closer. The group blocking the bridge rattled threateningly, tightening the trap. I prayed Ayanna would come up with a plan soon, but as I looked back and our eyes met, I saw the despair in her face, the same expression she had worn back on the raft when we were above the bone ships. There were just too many adversaries.

Brer Fox recognized her expression as well.

His posture relaxed. Suddenly he seemed so old, just a graying forest fox living out his final days, a fact he had made peace with.

"Make sure Chestnutt gets home safe," he said to her.

He lifted his muzzle to the sky and a whining scream ripped from his throat. Then, before anyone could stop him, he threw himself at the group of fetterlings near the forest edge.

"Noooooo!" Ayanna and I screamed at once, and the night exploded into a frenzy.

I don't think the fetterlings expected their prey to hunt them. Fox's attack took them by surprise, so he was able to dispatch several bigger monsters before they knew what had hit them. His jaws clamped down on one, his claws swiped at another, and it looked like a silver tornado whirled in the clearing as the metal monsters disintegrated into broken links and rust.

But the fetterlings soon recovered and began to overwhelm him.

"Go!" Brer Fox roared before he disappeared beneath a wriggling pile of iron monsters.

The group of fetterlings blocking the bridge swarmed past us to attack the threat, and Ayanna jumped into action.

"Quickly now," she said to the Midfolk, her voice alternating between a yell and a sob. "To the bridge. Come on, Tristan!" She ran ahead.

I stomped my foot on the small fetterling holding Gum Baby, and it screeched in pain. I did it again, then a third time, driving my heel into the thin chain link just below the base of the collar head, until it opened with a small click.

"Tristan!" Gum Baby cried. I snatched her up along with Tarrypin, who'd disappeared into his shell, and put both of them in my hood. I sprinted to the bridge, covering the distance in a few steps, and skidded to a stop next to Ayanna. The bridge wobbled and swayed under the Midfolk's rushing feet and paws.

When everyone else had made it safely to the other side, I set Gum Baby and Tarrypin down and gave them a nudge forward. "Your turn," I said.

Yips and howls echoed behind us, and I turned to see fetterlings peeling themselves off the pile to creep toward the bridge. Big ones. They shook and rattled, their lower bodies slithering like snakes while their cuffs snapped and their collar heads clacked.

A feeble gray paw emerged from the pile behind them, struggling to evade their grasp.

The green light from Eddie's journal still pulsed in my pocket.

A memory unlocked itself in my mind.

A hand extending from beneath a mangled school bus seat.

The image hit me square in the chest. My hands trembled, and I started breathing faster and faster. Just for a second I could see Eddie reaching for me on the day of the accident. The day I failed to save him.

"Tristan? We have to go. Now, Tristan!"

Two voices echoed in my ear. One in the present, one in the past. Ayanna's . . . and a teacher's aide. Both wanted the same thing—for me to leave someone behind.

"Tristan?" Ayanna called. "What are you doing? Move!"

But it was too late.

Two fetterlings dashed forward. One tried to encircle my ankles, while the other went for my wrists. I started to skip backward, but my foot hit something. A third fetterling had slithered through the leaves behind me and tripped me up.

"Tristan!"

I landed hard on my back, but immediately I rolled to my right, away from the fetterlings. A collar head snapped shut on the dust where my own head had been moments before. Eddie's journal kept glowing. I struggled to my feet and was just about to give Brer Fox the signal that I was coming to help, when something slammed into my left side.

"Ooomph!" The air abandoned my lungs.

Click

The fetterling who'd crashed into me snapped a cuff on my left hand, and cold iron bit into my wrist.

9

THE PAPER GIANT

I PANICKED.

"Get off me!" I battered the fetterling with my right hand. Just when its grip seemed to loosen, another monster curled around my right bicep. More fetterlings slithered forward and tangled up my legs. No matter how much I struggled, I couldn't free myself.

A loud scraping screech came from the trees.

All the iron monsters in the clearing grew still for a moment. Then the group holding me and those locked around Fox hauled us both toward the forest. The treetops rustled and branches snapped as more of the fiendish creatures raced to join the fight.

"Tristan..." Brer Fox said in a low voice.

"Don't say it."

"You have to get them to safety."

"Don't say that," I whispered. "You're coming, too."

"Ayanna!" BF shouted. "I know you're still there. You never follow your own orders. Tell the others what I did! You hear? Give my story a good ending for once. Tell them I—"

A fetterling collar snapped over Brer Fox's mouth. The chain grew taut, and he was yanked off his feet and hurtled into the forest gloom.

All the fetterlings turned to me.

My eyes stayed on the spot where the fox had disappeared. He'd been taken to the Maafa, and I hadn't been able to stop it. Once again, I'd failed to save someone who had needed my help.

I thought fairy tales were supposed to have happy endings. What was the moral of this story?

Rustling noises pulled me from my daze as the other fetterlings approached me.

Eddie's journal began to flash in my pocket.

Green light pulsed quicker and quicker until it surged in a hot white flare that blinded everyone in the clearing. When the light faded and my eyes adjusted, my heart leaped into my throat. A rusty fetterling collar hovered inches away from my neck, looking rough and sharp. But that didn't matter.

Hundreds of pages were floating in the clearing.

The leather binding of Eddie's journal lay open and empty on the ground. How had it gotten there? I tried to feel my pocket, but the fetterlings still had my arms and legs pinned. They rattled as I struggled but otherwise didn't pay me any mind. The wondrous display had them riveted, like cats watching a laser pointer.

The journal pages spun and coiled in the air until they formed a humanoid figure. It stood between me and the mass of fetterlings. One arm reached up and touched its featureless face, as if it was adjusting something. It was a gesture so familiar, so routine for anyone who'd ever worn glasses, that my whole body locked up like cement, then went limp.

"Eddie?" I whispered.

The paper giant raised its arm.

If you'd been in my place, you might say you saw a casual wave. I saw my best friend's fist raised, his standard greeting when he couldn't be bothered because his nose was buried in a book. A tear rolled down my face, followed by another.

The fetterlings screeched their challenge, and the forest swelled with the harsh sound.

The ones holding my arms and legs let go. They rattled and clacked their manacles, and then charged the paper figure. But the iron monsters couldn't get a grip on any of the pages. I worried as more and more fetterlings rushed to enter the battle, but the giant just kept swinging blow after blow, scattering monsters to the trees. Still the chain creatures swarmed.

I stumbled backward.

Several fetterlings had managed to coil around Eddie's

page giant like a python, but huge paper fists were hammering them left and right. The minions surged in a frenzy around the figure's legs, snapping and clamping, snatching pages with each attack. The battle edged closer to the trees, and I realized the fetterlings were dragging the giant away, back to wherever they had taken Brer Fox.

"No!" I shouted, sprinting after them. Fetterlings broke off to attack me, and I punched them like I'd never punched before. My knuckles had no protection, but the pain didn't matter. Nothing mattered except reaching my best friend. He'd returned when I needed him. He'd come back for me, to save me from a nightmare, just like he'd said he always would.

Losing him again would destroy me.

"Eddie!"

The battle moved into the forest and I followed.

"Tristan!" Ayanna called to me from across the bridge. I'd forgotten about the Midfolk before. I ignored them now.

A fetterling reared up in my face. I ducked its attack and slammed home an uppercut. Another slithered up and I snapped two quick jabs and a hook. Dad would've been proud.

"Eddie!"

I couldn't see the giant or any fetterlings now, but I could still hear the rustling, rattling skirmish. I scrambled after it, but soon the sounds faded away, too. I tried to follow

the signs they'd left behind. Broken branches. Crushed logs.
Then even those disappeared. I spun in circles, tears flowing,
searching for a trail, for any clue that would give me hope.

Nothing.

I staggered up to a tree and collapsed under it in the deafening silence.

They found me there some time later. Crying. Knuckles
bleeding. Sitting in mud. Knees drawn to my chest, my back
against some dead tree.

Alone.

10
THE THICKET

I WOKE UP IN A PANIC, DRENCHED IN SWEAT.

A voice echoed in my ears. *Thanks for the book, boy.*

Uncle C.

As the shadows and whispers faded, everything seemed fuzzy and distant, like a dream dissipating in the morning, but a throbbing pain in my knuckles quickly brought me back to reality.

I was tucked in a small wooden bed beneath soft covers that didn't reach my feet. My current sanctuary was a room with thorny branches covering the walls and the ceiling. Not little thorns, either, you get me, but knife-size prickles that looked like they were daring you to test them.

I didn't, of course. Even if I'd wanted to, every inch of my body hurt.

Not to mention my heart.

That hurt worst of all. I'd lost Eddie's journal to monsters,

monsters serving something called a Maafa. And now it was in the hands of a haint—one of those evil spirits Nana had mentioned. Was Uncle C the Maafa? There were too many questions and not enough answers. None I liked, anyway.

I squeezed my eyes shut, sending the tangled nightmares back to the corners of my mind, then opened them to continue to examine my surroundings. Sunlight trickled in through gaps in the ceiling. The room was warm—and cozy, despite the thorns. My bed and a rough wooden chair beside it were the only pieces of furniture. The walls were made of branches as thick as my arm, woven together like wicker baskets. Vines with tiny wildflowers crept up to the ceiling, filling the air with the scent of summertime fields. And the floor . . . I leaned over the side of the bed to get a better look.

Yup.

Dirt. Dark as night, soft and crumbly, with tender green shoots poking through. With a start I realized that the bedposts and the legs of the chair were growing out of the floor, thick at the base like roots, and coiling together.

Something rustled as I tried to make sense of everything, and a small circular door I hadn't noticed opened across the room.

"Hello?" I called when no one appeared. I sat up a little. "Gum Baby?"

"Oh, you're awake! Good. They were getting worried."

The voice came from the end of the bed, light and energetic, like a child's. But it wasn't the doll.

"Who's there?"

"You can't see—? Oh, right, sorry." There was a struggle, like someone wrestling with something heavy, then a sharp intake of breath, and the smallest rabbit I'd ever seen hopped onto my bed. "Hi!"

She had deep brown fur with a splash of white on her front paws, and one of her hind legs was bandaged tight. She sat back gently, twitched her nose, and waved. I found myself waving back.

"I'm Chestnutt," she said.

"Tristan," I said slowly.

"I know. I'm supposed to come fetch you. Are you ready?"

"Ready for what?"

"Everyone's at the meeting. We have to decide—well, not me, but *they* have to decide who's going to go. No, wait, first we have to see if we *are* going to go, and then, if yes, *who's* going to go. I hope it's me. It sounds really exciting and—"

"Wait, wait," I said, hopelessly lost. I wriggled up into a fully seated position and rubbed my temples. "How long have I been asleep?"

"A day."

"A whole day?"

Chestnutt nodded. "Yup, yup! They carried you in night

before last. You slept all yesterday and most of this morning. Do you always scream in your sleep?"

"What? I don't know. No," I said. "Why does it matter?"

Her nose twitched and her ears went back at my defensive tone. "It doesn't. Sorry. Brer Fox says I should try and hold back all my questions. Says they make everyone angry."

At the sound of Brer Fox's name, the memory of him fighting beside me—and losing—crashed my senses and I had to take a deep breath. I balled the blanket in my fists, and my arms trembled.

Chestnutt watched me. "Do you know him?"

"Sort of. Not really. We escaped through the forest together. He fought and distracted the . . . He fought so the rest of us could escape."

"Really?" She leaned forward on her front paws. "He hates violence. BF says it never solves anything, and only spreads more violence and hatred."

I pictured the fox leaping, snarling, into the midst of the iron monsters, and I frowned, but Chestnutt didn't notice and kept talking.

"He says wounding or hurting someone else leaves just as big a mark on the attacker," she went on. "You can't see it, but it's there."

I remembered the bundle Brer Fox had carried on the boat, before gently handing it over to Ayanna. *Make sure Chestnutt gets home safely,* he'd told her.

"How did you and Brer Fox...How did he become—?"

"My guardian?"

"Yeah. How did that happen?"

Chestnutt sat up and twitched her ears proudly. "Well—"

But she never finished. Something rustled in the walls, and her ears stood tall on her head and flicked to the door.

"Oh, I was supposed to fetch you! The meeting's started. Come on, we have to hurry." She hopped down from the bed and bounded through the small round door, her voice fading as she disappeared into the shadows. "Hurry!"

The childlike insistence in her tone had the blanket thrown aside and my feet hitting the cool soil-covered floor before I could think. What was it with me chasing weird little talking creatures into dark spaces? First Gum Baby, and now this.

As I stood, I thought about refusing, maybe playing up my injuries until I could figure things out, but I quickly dismissed that option. If I wanted to get back home and leave this nightmare behind, I'd need help, and it sounded like this meeting was a step in the right direction, even if I had no idea who was going to be there.

My shoes were dry and waiting for me by the door, along with my socks. Both had a slightly mildewy odor, and I sighed as I slipped them on. It had taken me seven Sundays' worth of chores to save up for those Chucks. The sacrifices we make for the greater good. Boy, I tell you. . . .

I squeezed nervously through the thorny door, ducking and holding in my stomach, and entered a long, twisty hallway made of woven branches still carrying leaves and flowers. It smelled refreshing. There was more than enough room for me to move easily, but a thorn jabbed me when I got too close. I hunched over, sucked my injured thumb, and limped on.

Chestnutt waited for me around a curve. The corridor split, and she twitched her ears at the path on the right. "This way," she said, hopping ahead.

"What is this place?" I asked, staring at the grass growing underfoot, a living carpet that felt as soft as anything you could buy in a store.

"This tunnel?"

"All of it. This whole inside forest-like thing? Where are we?"

"Oh, that's easy. You're in the Thicket."

"The Thicket . . . Ayanna mentioned that name. Is this like some sort of hideout?" And speaking of my savior, where was she? Would she be at the meeting?

"Yup, yup." Chestnutt wiggled an ear at me. "It's a good thing Ayanna found you. And Gum Baby, too, I guess. She's good at that sort of thing—finding, rescuing. I want to be like her when I get bigger. Or Brer Fox. Or both. Yep, both. That way I'll be superstrong and I can protect all of Alke."

"Alke? Not MidPass?" I ducked a particularly nasty

collection of thorns dangling from the ceiling. All the place names were starting to run together, and I'd never been good at keeping details like that straight.

"MidPass is *in* Alke, silly! I want to protect everyone." She stopped and thought for a second. "Though things aren't that great between MidPass and the rest of Alke right now. But you didn't hear that from me!"

"Um..."

"BF says not to mention it to strangers, on account of we shouldn't be worrying everybody, even though the Thicket is under siege, and it's our last hideout, and if anything happened to it we'd all be lost, and the M—"

She stopped and I nearly stumbled over her. Chestnutt flicked her ears in worry.

"What's wrong?" I asked.

"I'm doing it again. Talking too much."

"About the Maafa? That's what you were going to say, right?"

The little rabbit shivered violently, as if she was seconds from falling apart—literally. I gingerly sank down to one knee, keeping a close eye on a thorn at butt level, and said, "Hey, hey, it's okay. Forget I said that, all right? I'm new here, and everything's kind of freaking me out right now."

Chestnutt's chest fluttered in and out, and she shook her head, continuing as if she hadn't heard me. "Brer Fox says not to say that name. Talking about it gives the iron monsters strength, and then nobody will be safe. And I've been blabbing, and now we're going to get attacked, and it'll be all my fault, and why do I do that? Stupid, stupid, stupid, stupid—"

"Hey." I reached a hand out but paused just before I touched her. Some people didn't like to be touched, and I figured animals might feel the same way. "Hey, that's not true."

"It's not? How do you know?"

"Because someone once told me it isn't."

"They did?" She sniffed.

I remembered one of my first sessions with my counselor, Mr. Richardson, after the bus accident. "He said we can't hide from our fears. We have to be able to talk about them, or else they'll fester like poison, eating us from the inside."

Chestnutt began to calm down. "BF says I have to work on not panicking so much."

"Brer Fox has told you a lot, hasn't he?"

"Yeah. Yeah, he has."

"You two were—*are* very close?" Did Chestnutt know that Brer Fox was gone? I had to choose my words carefully.

Chestnutt began to hop forward, and I stood up and followed. "Yup, yup. He rescued me when I was a baby, you know? A couple of those stupid monsters attacked my family's burrow. Brer Fox says I was the only one left, and he carried me back here. He taught me everything." She hopped on. "A lot of lectures, though," she added.

I grinned. "Yeah. Grown-ups will do that."

We continued on in silence. The tunnel started to widen and lighten, and the buzzing noise of a large crowd floated down. Just before we reached the exit, Chestnutt slowed to a stop and looked back at me.

"It's not your fault, you know, what happened to Brer Fox," she said.

That took me by surprise. So she *did* know.

"I . . . I'm sorry," I stuttered. "If I had been quicker, or stronger, I might've been able to reach him. He might still—"

Chestnutt shook her head. "Brer Fox told me we can't harp on past mistakes. He said a lot of stuff like that. I don't remember it all, but what I do remember, I keep telling myself so I won't forget it. Keeping someone's words alive is like keeping them alive, right? I know you tried, and I know what Brer Fox did, and I know he's gone, but as long as I have his words, I'll have him. So it's okay. Right?"

"Right," I said softly. Eddie filled my mind, and the loss of his journal stabbed my heart anew. I'd lost his words. Did that mean he was completely lost to me now?

Chestnutt hopped on out into the noise. "Come on! It's starting."

I followed, still sorting through a heap of feelings, and not sure if I'd ever untangle them.

We entered an amphitheater-like space and I stumbled to a halt.

"Sweet peaches."

Above the humongous oval-shaped room, thorny branches arched like the roof of a dome, with creeper vines and yellow seed pods hanging down like streamers from rafters. To my left, thick roots were layered on top of one another, going up and back like stadium seating, which, I realized while looking around, was exactly what it was.

Brown-skinned people of all sizes and ages sat among woodland creatures. All of them huddled in groups.

All of them bore scars on their necks, wrists, and ankles.

"Survivors," Chestnutt said quietly. When I looked at her, she twitched her nose sadly.

I almost asked *Survivors of what?* but I already knew. I could still feel the bite of the fetterlings on my wrists. "Where did they all come from?" I asked.

"All around MidPass. Once the iron monsters started terrorizing us, John Henry convinced Brer Rabbit to open up the Thicket. But if someone was too sick or too old—"

"You all would go find them," I finished, and the pieces came together in my head. "That's what Ayanna and you all were doing. Rescuing those who couldn't save themselves."

Chestnutt beamed. "Yup, yup! People like Ayanna, we call them pilots! BF used to be one, but he started getting aches, so Ayanna became his student. I was going to be next. . . ."

She trailed off, and I swallowed a sudden lump. Her ears sank and I heard her sniffle, so I looked away to let her mourn privately.

The larger-than-usual animals, birds, reptiles, and amphibians scattered among the people in the stands were also grieving. A turtle with a gash along his shell comforted a weeping older woman who was clutching a child's doll. Two rabbits sat on either side of a boy of about five or six. He stroked their fur gently with each hand.

"Come on," Chestnutt whispered, and she hopped away to the right.

"This isn't the meeting?" I looked back over my shoulder at the sea of faces, so different and yet all sharing something familiar: fear.

The other side of the amphitheater was set against what looked like a giant, wrinkled brown wall. Thick knobby whorls of the same brown extended from the wall's base. A giant stone was nestled between them, and they curled around it to form an elevated stage of sorts. I jerked in surprise. Roots. I was looking at roots. Which meant . . .

"That's the bottom of a tree?"

"That's *the* tree," Chestnutt corrected. "The Tree of Power."

She hopped forward, but I stood there and craned my neck as far back as possible, trying to take in the incredible aura. The giant oak tree felt ancient, like the Bottle Trees on my grandparents' farm. But while the Bottle Trees were guards, making sure evil spirits like Uncle C didn't escape, the Tree of Power seemed like it wanted to protect *you*.

It was like being in the presence of a relic, or even living history. As I stood beneath the shelter of its limbs and the shadow of its trunk, it felt like I was in one of Nana's stories. I heard something—a whisper, or faint music, maybe even a drumbeat—and it sounded so familiar. The bark on the trunk began to shimmer, like something was hidden in plain sight, and any second it would reveal itself—

"Tristan!" Chestnutt's call broke the spell. "Hurry, the meeting's starting!"

I shook my head and looked back at the Tree of Power, but it was no longer flickering. The moment had passed. Still . . . something lingered in the air, like electricity after a lightning strike. An energy. I could almost—

"Tristan!"

I frowned and, with one last glance at the enormous tree, trotted after Chestnutt to find some answers.

It took me five minutes to decide that maaaaybe going to the meeting was a bad idea.

Don't get me wrong—I still wanted to find someone who could help me rescue Eddie's journal and get out of this place. Adventures are cool, just not when three-foot-tall handcuffs are chasing you. But as Chestnutt led me down the gently sloping Thicket tunnel, this one with cherry-red flowers budding along the walls, I heard the echo of Gum Baby's voice ahead of us.

"And then Gum Baby had to run for her life! That boy chased Gum Baby, screaming and hollering like his feet were on fire."

"Mmmm," somebody said. A woman, by the sound of it, and I hesitated. I knew that tone of voice.

"And he started calling Gum Baby names. Horrible names. Too bad to even repeat."

"Mm-hmm," somebody else said. Another woman. What was this, an after-church luncheon? "A year, Gum Baby. You were gone for a year. You had one job, simple, and you failed. And then you bring this boy with you—what were you thinking?"

I grinned. *Serves the little loudmouth right*, I thought, *fibbing on me like that*.

Chestnutt hopped down the tunnel and came to a stop beside a large entrance cut into the Thicket wall. The conversation continued ahead of us, but I stopped paying attention, because I heard that music again. Drums and rhythmic clapping, louder than before. I shook my head to clear it and tried to focus on what was in front of us. Light spilled into the tunnel, bright and inviting, but I'm no fool. I could see from Chestnutt's expression that she wasn't eager to hop through. She twitched her ears in hesitation.

"Well," she whispered, "I should probably leave you here."

I looked at her, then at the giant doorway, then back at her. "Nuh-uh."

"What?"

"I'm not going in there alone. I don't even know who, or what, is in there."

"It's just where they plan strategies and hold meetings and stuff like that."

"Who's *they?*"

We were holding a whispered argument, neither of us in a hurry to attract attention.

"Brer Rabbit and the others."

"Folktale characters?"

"They're gods, Tristan! Maybe they were something else in your world, but here, they're the only ones who can keep us safe. You have to remember that. Like, the Thicket? Brer built it all by himself. You never wondered how all the tunnels are just the right height for whoever's walking through them? And the thorns aren't just for decoration, either. Yup, yup, they're gods."

My jaw dropped open. In the stories, the Thicket is where Brer Rabbit tricked Brer Fox into releasing him. But it was just a prickly bush thing....This...this was a whole city of vines and thorns. A citadel. A fortress. It was all so incredible....

And I wanted no part of it.

"Look, I'm done with this," I said. "I appreciate all the help, and please thank whoever it was that tucked me in, but how about you just show me the exit to this place and we'll call it a day. I'm tired, I'm hungry, and I just want to go home now, so if you—"

A shadow fell across the doorway, and Chestnutt and I shrank back against the tunnel wall. That might not have been the best idea. For little Chestnutt it was fine—she just ducked in between a couple of branches and hid. But me? The tall kid with the too-wide shoulders? Big mistake.

"Gaaaaah!" I shouted as a thorn jabbed me right in the bottom.

So if you ever think you've made a bad first impression—maybe you tripped and fell over your own feet, or you had ketchup on your face—just picture me, Tristan Strong, hopping into a room full of gods while trying to pull a thorn out of my butt.

11
THE GODS OF MIDPASS

BY THE TIME THE OFFENDING PIECE OF THICKET HAD BEEN REMOVED from my posterior and Gum Baby had stopped laughing, a trio of adults stood over me with their arms crossed and serious expressions on their faces.

"Tristan," a massive voice rumbled, "I'm glad you decided to join us."

Oh my goodness.

And I thought *I* was tall.

The deep voice belonged to a chest. At least, that's what I thought, until I looked up . . . and up . . . and up . . . and finally saw the face looking down at me. It seemed familiar. Deep brown, with wrinkles at the corners of his eyes and also on his forehead, like he could only smile or frown.

Right now he was frowning.

"My name is—"

"John Henry," I blurted out. "I . . . Sorry, I didn't mean to cut you off, it's just . . . John Henry. Whoa."

Out of all the folktales, "The Ballad of John Henry" was my favorite. Eddie and I had done research on him once. According to some tales, he hammered steel drilling spikes into granite for a railroad company. At the turn of the nineteenth century, men and women like him carried progress on their backs, laying tracks across America, around valleys and lakes and through mountains. John was the biggest and the strongest, the first to land a hammer blow in the morning and the last to trudge home in the evenings. In the early years after slavery, when Black people were struggling to find their way, John Henry was a rock to his small community. When he accepted a sadistic railroad magnate's challenge and raced a steam-powered drill through a mountain and emerged victorious on the other side, he became a source of pride, even after the effort stopped his heart and he collapsed dead.

That's what Eddie and I had found.

When Nana saw what we were doing, she'd made us sit and listen to her tales. Her stories were a little darker.

According to her, John Henry was a farmer, a former slave turned sharecropper, who got arrested for something ridiculous.

"You have to remember," Nana had said while sitting in her easy chair, a pile of knitting in her lap, "people were in an ugly mood at that time. When they banned slavery, it stripped thousands of plantations of free labor. Now they had to pay us. You think that went over well? Child, please."

She'd snorted, clicked her needles together, and looked over her glasses at us.

"No, they weren't going to pay for something they used to get for free. So they invented laws. Then they said we broke them. Tossed us into prison, and guess where they made those prisoners serve time? That's right. On those farms, or, like John Henry, on railroad chain gangs, hammering spikes from morning till night."

She'd leaned forward and pointed a knitting needle at us.

"So remember that. A lot of times those little facts get smudged out of the history books. If you gon' tell a story, you better be sure you're telling the right one."

What I'd thought was just a room at first was actually a forest glade, sheltered by a loose weaving of Thicket branches high above that let light in. Butterflies fluttered around flowers that filled the air with light scents of vanilla and cinnamon. A stream bubbled through the middle, surrounding a medium-size hill with a flat top. Two elderly women stood nearby, with Gum Baby between them, and they all stared at me.

And from somewhere, just like when I was beneath the Tree of Power, I heard the faintest drumming. A rhythm that, if I tried to capture it, would disappear. It was infuriating!

But my eyes were quickly drawn back to John Henry, and I forgot everything else. I mean, he was huge! He wore blue overalls, one strap undone, and a white collared shirt soaked with sweat, the sleeves rolled up above his elbows. Both arms were folded across his chest, and I couldn't help but look around for his massive hammer.

He cleared his throat (I thought someone had fired a cannon) and nodded at the hill, the frown fading and his eyes twinkling. "Care to meet with us up top?"

I meant to say something profound. Something along the lines of how much his story meant to me, and how it had inspired me. Something deep and intelligent.

"Gaaaaah." I nodded and rubbed my sore butt.

Hi, my name is Tristan Please-Let-Me-Hide-in-a-Corner.

John Henry's frown disappeared completely, and he tried and failed to hide a smile before turning to follow the two women, who were already climbing the hill. They carried Gum Baby by the arms while she swung her legs in the air. I trailed after John Henry, thinking I hadn't had to jog like this to keep up with someone since kindergarten. Chestnutt struggled to keep pace, too, so I kneeled and she hopped gratefully into my arms.

When we got to the bottom of the hill, John Henry stopped, still towering over the women now on top. He motioned for me to climb up.

No getting around it, I thought, and that made me scowl. As I hiked the slope, I prepared a defense against whatever accusations they were going to make. That's what this was about, right? I was in some kind of trouble. That's the reason you get called to a place where you're the only kid in a gathering of adults.

As soon as I reached the top, where a wide tree stump rested in a clump of tiny white flowers, I said, "Look," trying to get ahead of the inevitable lecture headed my way, "I didn't do it. Whatever it is, I'm not sure how it happened. I just want to go home."

The women parted, and the rest of my words mushed together into a lump on my tongue and refused to come out.

A sandy-brown rabbit reclined on his back beneath the shade of a giant mushroom cap. He used his long ears to shade his eyes from the rays of sunlight leaking in through the Thicket ceiling. Plump berries lay in a pile on a leaf beside him, and he popped one into his mouth. His fur was patchy, and long scars crisscrossed his body. Every so often his legs would twitch uncontrollably, like he was trying to shake something off.

I recognized him. I just didn't expect him to be so . . . real.

"You're . . . you're Brer Rabbit," I stammered out.

"Brer."

"I'm sorry?"

"Brer. Not Brer Rabbit. Just Brer now—I really don't see a need to specify anymore, do you? I mean, Bear is gone, and now Fox is gone. It's just me, old Brer, last of the trio."

"Nice to meet you. I'm—"

Brer flapped a paw. "I know who you are. You're the one responsible for the end of the world. So, you know, thanks."

"Now, hold up. I—"

But two more voices cut me off, and each other. They spoke quickly, in light tones that sounded like birds chattering, and they finished each other's sentences like twin sisters would.

"What Brer means to say—" the first began.

"—is that you have some explaining to do, and quickly," the other finished.

A tingling, hot feeling started at the base of my neck. I tried to remain calm as I turned to the two women and really looked at them for the first time.

One was tall, with hair cut lower than mine. She wore glasses perched just at the tip of her nose, and she glared over them at me like I'd tracked mud on her new carpet. The other woman was short with thick dreadlocks that were wrapped in multicolored cloth and piled high atop her head. Their deep brown skin glimmered beneath what at first I thought were black shawls draped over their shoulders.

Then a feather, black as midnight dipped in shadows, fell to the ground.

Those weren't shawls.

They were wings.

And I knew.

"They say the People could fly," I whispered.

The women caught each other's eyes, then leaned forward and stared at me even more closely.

The first said, "It seems we have—"

"—a storyteller," the second finished.

I looked between them, breathless. Nana used to tell me stories about how, over in Africa, before the horrors of slavery, people used to fly all the time. They'd whisper the powerful words, the phrases dripping in old magic, and shoot off into the sky. Brothers raced sisters. Mothers and fathers carried babies over shining lakes and snow-covered mountains.

Then came the chains and ships, and pain and whips, and the people's wings fell or were torn off. But the words of power were never forgotten. Sometimes, in the middle of the night, after a brutal day of working in blistering-hot fields, the elders would whisper them into the ears of those who needed it most, and *whoosh,* off people would soar toward freedom.

I'm not gonna lie—I gawked at the two women. John Henry chuckled.

"Tristan, this is Miss Sarah and Miss Rose." He didn't point out who was who, or I missed it, so I stood there confused until the tall, skinny woman with glasses gave a small *harrumph* and waved at her partner.

"Really helpful, John. That's Rose. I'm Sarah. Now that the introductions are finished—"

"—perhaps we can get back to who *you* are," said Rose, "and just what the two of you were thinking."

"The two of us?" I looked around, confused, until my eyes landed on the tree stump. There sat Gum Baby. She raised a sticky hand and waved.

"Hey, Bumbletongue."

"You! What lies have you been telling now? Huh?"

To my surprise, Gum Baby didn't jump up and start shouting nonsense. She didn't get angry, she didn't sap attack anything. . . . She didn't even look up at me. She just stared down into her lap, weaving tiny little crowns out of grass and flower petals.

"If you're quite done with your questions—" Miss Sarah said.

"—maybe you can answer a few of ours," said Miss Rose.

I flushed and turned back to the women. They glanced at each other—I'd seen that type of look before. Nothing good came after a look like that.

"Questions?" I asked.

John Henry cleared his throat. "Gum Baby here was sent to find . . . something—"

"I know. The book."

He frowned, and Brer sat up. "How do you know that? No one outside this room knew anything about that."

I took a deep breath, paused, then shook my head. "Doesn't matter." How could I explain the vision I'd had in the car and the other weird magic Eddie's journal had?

John Henry leaned forward, and the giant folk hero let a rumbling growl escape his chest. "I reckon we'll be the judges of whether it matters or not, understand?"

I looked around at all of them, glaring at me with either suspicion or outright anger. There's a time to be stubborn, and this wasn't it. "Yeah, fine."

"Good. Now . . . what do you know of Gum Baby's plan?"

I sighed and scratched my chin. "Uh, you and Brer sent her. Y'all were scared of something . . ." I remembered the sound of clanking in my vision. "The fetterlings, I guess."

Brer flinched at the mention of the iron monsters.

It was all starting to make more sense now. "You and Brer made a hole—a tunnel—by the Tree of Power and sent Gum Baby through, telling her to find it. Find the book."

Everyone stared at me. Brer scrambled to his feet and hopped in front of me with one giant leap. "Spy!" he snarled. "How did he follow us? Is the Warren compromised? Who told you where to find us?"

"I didn't spy on anyone," I said angrily.

"Liar!"

"I saw it when I touched..." There was no use trying to the hide the truth now. "When I opened my friend's journal."

Brer jerked back as if I'd struck him, and he swallowed whatever accusation he'd had on the tip of his tongue.

Ms. Rose looked at me skeptically. "A journal?"

I nodded.

"This journal..." Brer said slowly. "Did it have a symbol on it?"

"Yeah. Though it didn't always...."

"Describe it."

"Um..." I squinted in concentration. "Golden. My grandmother said it was an old African symbol for a spiderweb. Something about being creative."

Brer hopped back a few paces, wonder all over his furry face. He stroked his ears and nodded at me to go on.

"I mean, that's it," I said. "Well, except that it's been glowing...."

"A green light? Pulsing every three seconds or so?" Brer asked eagerly.

I nodded, and he clapped his front paws and laughed.

"I knew it. I knew it!" He jumped up and punched John Henry in the shoulder. "Didn't I tell you? I said we'd find it, and we did! Took a bit longer than expected, but we found it!"

John Henry grunted. "Why *did* it take so long?"

Brer stopped in mid-cheer. "Eh?"

"Why did it take so long? Gum Baby thought she was there for an hour or two, but it was a year. And the flaming tear in the sky—did that have anything to do with it?" He turned to me. "Was that because of you?"

I took a deep breath and described Gum Baby's break-in, the chase through the Bottle Tree forest, and finally our fight.

Brer tapped his foot impatiently, until finally he flapped his paws and cut me off. "Oh really, John, it's simple time distortion. Various realms experience time differently—that's been known for a while. Without proper precautions someone could theoretically live a lifetime in their world and a moment in ours. It's quite complicated, you know, something I don't expect you all to pick up on right away. But you add that rip in the sky into the equation . . . why, all bets are off. Gum Baby pops out in the boy's realm, spends an hour upworld, but comes back through the tear between realms instead of the spell we cast?" He tutted. "Nasty stuff. She could've been smooshed."

Gum Baby gasped. "Gum Baby could've been Gum Gravy?"

Brer waved a paw. "But you're all missing the bigger picture! We can fix the tear and everything else once we build . . . you know." Brer turned to me, his ears practically quivering with excitement. "So, where is it?"

"Where's what?"

"The book! Where are Anansi's stories? We should get started right away. Preparations need to begin, no time to waste, chop-chop."

"Anansi's stories? No, it was my friend's journal." But the words died on my lips. *An old African symbol for a spider's web,* Nana had said. Anansi the Spider, whose hunger for story-telling and spinning a thrilling yarn was legendary. Anansi, who bugged the sky god Nyame into giving him the first stories, and whose legend grew as his tales spread.

I unclenched my fists and rubbed my temples. This was all giving me a headache. Could it be true that the journal was actually a magical collection of the Spider's stories?

I squeezed my eyes shut. Fine. Believe it, if only just for a second. Let's say the greatest storyteller to ever entertain *had* infused it with magic somehow. I mean, I *was* talking to a giant rabbit at this moment....

But why would Anansi give such a powerful item to a nerdy black boy from Chicago?

I opened my eyes to see everyone waiting.

"The book is more than you think," John Henry said gently but insistently. "It is the key to everything. Now hand it over."

12
THE BUTTERFLY WHISPERER

I OPENED MY MOUTH TO ANSWER, BUT NOTHING CAME OUT. GUM Baby peered up at me, then cast her eyes down quickly. Brer looked between us, his excitement fading and his suspicion returning.

"Where is it?"

I explained, slowly and with great difficulty, about what had happened in the Drowned Forest, nearly losing it when I admitted I hadn't been able to save Brer Fox, and clenching my fists when I got to the part with the paper giant.

Brer groaned and collapsed on the ground, his ears flopping over his eyes. "No, no, no, noooo! You lost it? We're doomed. Doomed!"

"Enough, Brer," John Henry said. "That won't get us anywhere."

Miss Rose sighed. "Fighting with Gum Baby, honestly. Damaging a Bottle Tree. Ripping the fabric between worlds . . . You could've destroyed everything we've built here. It's bad enough the other Alkeans won't talk to—" She broke off, and I wrinkled my forehead.

"The trouble between us and the rest of Alke only started after that blasted rip appeared," Brer muttered. "Those arrogant—"

"Brer!" Miss Sarah folded her wings firmly and narrowed her eyes. "Enough. For now, we have to deal with these two." She frowned at me, then turned to Gum Baby. "To think we gave you another chance, and this is how you chose to behave."

"Shameful," Miss Rose added.

"Disrespectful, even."

Gum Baby shrank even farther, her head nearly touching her stubby little legs. I actually —and I can't believe I'm saying this—I actually felt bad for the little villain.

"Maybe she's just not ready."

"Maybe she never will be."

They went on like this for several minutes. Back and forth with their criticism, sometimes of me, sometimes of Gum Baby. Brer would occasionally drop a disappointed sigh or a snide comment here or there, and John Henry lectured everyone. I tried to interject, but I couldn't get a word in. When grown-ups get on their high horses, those things gallop for days.

Finally I just threw up my hands. "What exactly is it you

want me to say?" I asked loudly. "And if I answer the questions, will y'all tell me how I can get back home?"

Everyone fell quiet.

Brer snorted. "Get back home. Right."

I glared at him. For an inspirational god, he was becoming super annoying. "Yes, back home. Through that flaming hole."

Brer hopped toward me, his long hind paws thumping the ground. He came up to my chest, had muscles that would put a Westlake Academy football player to shame, and now that he was standing up, one of his ears drooped. He stopped just inches from me and folded his paws across his front.

"Go back. Just like that. Leave the mess you created behind for someone else to clean up."

"The mess *I* created?"

"Yes, you. You think you can just disappear after all the trouble you've caused? Think you can go around disrespecting the hard work of others, upsetting the balance between worlds like a little punk? Just for some fun? I don't think so. No, you're down here in the muck and mud with the rest of us, hiding and running for our lives."

I shook my head, more to clear the tingling heat creeping down my spine than anything. "I don't understand what you—"

"That's right, you don't understand. I've seen your type before." Brer hopped around the hilltop, pointing at the

Thicket and then at the other gods. "No respect for anything you didn't make. No respect for others. Wild and uncaring."

"I have respect—"

"Impulsive. Dangerous. No pride in appearance."

I straightened my hoodie and clenched a fist. "I am not—"

"And..." Brer said, as if I'd never spoken. He leaned forward, his paw and left ear both pointing at me accusingly. "This is possibly the worst trait of all—consistently lets others down. He said it himself! He nearly killed everyone chasing after the iron monsters just to look like a hero. What sort of friend—?"

"YOU DON'T KNOW ANYTHING ABOUT ME!" I shouted.

Silence settled over the glade like fine ash after a scorching fire.

"You have no idea who I am," I said, my anger throttling my words into a hiss.

Everyone was staring at me, and I bit my lip. *Calm, Tristan. Gotta stay calm. Adults don't like it when they're not the only ones yelling.*

Miss Sarah looked at Miss Rose and they shook their heads. Brer hopped back a step with a smug expression on his face. John Henry sighed.

The tingling anger rippled out from my core again. My fists clenched as I tried to suppress the feeling, but those looks they gave each other...

Adults passed those looks back and forth when they didn't want you to know what they really thought about you. Those looks could travel around a room as quick as the wind, replacing all conversation as soon as you entered. They were exchanged by adults you knew and by adults who thought they knew you. Mr. How-You-Doing-Sport and Mrs. Are-You-Okay-Sweetie would flash the looks between them before trying to dissect your last twenty-four hours.

I hated those looks.

"Tristan."

Gum Baby's voice snapped me out of the fog, and I realized my hands were shaking. The tingling had built to a furious itch that needed to be scratched, and I was too upset to hold back any longer. The drumming that had been lingering in the back of my head all day began to grow louder.

"You don't know anything," I repeated in a low growl. "You only see what you wanna see. You sent somebody to steal from a boy, because *you* wanted something. But did you see that boy? Did you know he had lost a friend? And not just a friend, but his best friend, his brother, his partner, his road dog, his *Say no more, no words necessary* homie until the end? Did you know that all this boy had left of his friend was a book, a single book that they had worked on together, collecting the stories they had loved hearing as kids? Their big project, their shared thoughts, right? Did you know that?"

I was moving around the hilltop now. Everyone stayed

silent. All of a sudden, no one had any comments. No looks. No adult-code phrases. I stared at Brer, who was examining his paw with great interest.

The tingling had moved to my fingertips. It felt as if at any moment all that pent-up energy would burst from within and sweep everyone aside.

I stopped and clenched my fists, then bent over, knuckling my temples and gritting my teeth.

"Did you know that? Huh, gods?" I asked again, straightening up. "Can you picture that boy, in a strange place, and that book is the only thing reminding him of home and good times, and someone *steals* it? That's right. Somebody breaks in and steals the only good thing this boy has left! Can you believe that?"

The anger piled behind my eyes in a pounding headache, thumping in a rhythm that felt strangely familiar. I needed to punch something, but there were no gloves, no punching bags nearby. My skull was going to split open if I didn't lash out, if I didn't channel that energy somehow.

"Tristan."

I ignored Gum Baby's call again. Everything was too much. Sadness. Confusion. Frustration. Emotions on top of emotions, all fighting to be expressed, and all anyone ever saw on the outside was an angry boy.

Unfair.

Un. Fair.

"Bumbletongue!"

"Can you picture it?" I asked again. The tingling and the throbbing headache raged out of control in one powerful surge, like a giant wave crashing on a beach and wiping out the sand castle you worked on all day. It ripped out of me and I screamed.

"CAN YOU PICTURE IT?"

Little hands grabbed me, and I could feel Gum Baby scramble up to sit on my shoulder. She patted my cheek with sticky hands.

"Tristan...look. Look."

"Let go of—"

I opened my eyes and froze.

Brer and John Henry, Miss Sarah and Miss Rose—they were all staring in amazement, their jaws hanging open.

The forest glade was filled with soft, pulsing green light, and just down the hill, all the butterflies—millions of them, it seemed—fluttered in tight formation, moving together in shapes and patterns that looked just like—

"My story?" I whispered.

And it was.

The butterflies were reenacting my tale. There was Gum Baby, slipping through my window. Over there, large black-and-yellow butterflies formed the shape of a boy, who chased her. And there was the forest, and the Bottle Tree, and the fight, and the burning rip.

I looked around. Nobody said a word as they watched, awestruck. Everyone except Gum Baby. She seemed relieved, as if she'd been proven right.

"See?" she said to the others. "You told me bring you Anansi's sign, and I did." She patted my cheek again. "I brought you an Anansesem."

13
ANANSESEM

"ANANSESEM?" I ASKED, TRIPPING OVER THE SYLLABLES. "WHAT does that mean?"

"A storyteller," John Henry answered. He stroked his chin in thought. "But more than just words, more than just *once upon a time* and *the end*. It's about the entire experience, from the audience to the stage to the spectacle. There's music, too, I reckon, but—"

"Enough!" Brer shouted. He leaped high in the air, off the hilltop, and down to the field below, scattering the butterflies. The spell was broken. They fluttered off to the flowers and trees, and Brer turned around with a glare. "Do you want to bring those iron monsters down on our heads? Of all the—"

"Brer," John Henry rumbled in warning.

"—stupid, idiotic, brainless—"

"That's quite enough, Brer," Miss Sarah said.

"—dumb, selfish—"

"BRER!" all three gods shouted, and Brer finally ended his rant. He turned and, with three powerful leaps, hopped out of the forest glade and into the network of Thicket tunnels.

John Henry, Miss Sarah, and Miss Rose huddled together, murmuring under their breath, and I rolled my eyes. More "adult" conversations. But I had to admit I was spooked. The paper giant I maybe could have ignored as a one-off freaky occurrence in a freaky place with freaky creatures. But now the butterflies... All of a sudden, *I* felt like the freaky one.

That was *not* a good feeling.

"Tristan," John Henry called, startling me. The giant man motioned for me to join them. Gum Baby broke off from harassing a cluster of butterflies and ran over as well.

"So?" she said. "Did Gum Baby do good or not?"

John Henry patted her on the head, nearly smooshing her, then looked confused when he lifted his hand to find Gum Baby stuck to it.

"Yes, you did fine. But what's important is what happens next."

I frowned. "What do you mean?"

Miss Sarah smoothed one of her wings and cleared her throat. "The Thicket is in danger. We were discussing that before you, ah..."

"Before he hopped in with a thorny bottom?" Gum Baby asked.

My face grew hot with embarrassment and Miss Rose rolled her eyes.

"Yes, thank you, Gum Baby," she said. "The point is—"

"—in his butt," Gum Baby whispered and snickered.

"—we have a dilemma," Miss Sarah said loudly.

I looked around at all the grim faces and blew out a puff of air. "The iron monsters you all were talking about. The fetterlings."

"And hullbeasts and brand flies," Miss Rose murmured.

I didn't know what those were, but I shuddered at the names. Why did everything around here have to sound so painful? Why couldn't we be up against creatures called fluffbirds and taffypaws?

"Yeah, I guess," I continued. "Brer Fox said the iron monsters are all worked up because"—*of me*, I wanted to say—"of that giant rip in the sky. And—"

"And they're picking us off one by one," John Henry finished. "They're hunting us for some reason. Everyone who's caught gets dragged to . . . well, to a bad place, never to be seen again."

"To the Maa—?" I started to ask, but three voices shushed me, and someone threw sap at my head.

"We try not to call attention to that *thing*—" Miss Sarah began.

"—and *you* need to be especially careful," Miss Rose finished.

"Me? Why?"

"Because you're an Anansesem," John Henry said. His voice rumbled and he got down on one giant knee. "When you tell stories, something special happens, like you just saw with the butterflies. That's why we call them things iron monsters, and I reckon you especially ought to do the same."

"You have to be careful," Miss Rose warned.

Miss Sarah nodded. "You have to focus. Concentrate on what you're speaking about, and learn control."

I threw up my hands. "I don't even know what Anna... Anon...what that means!"

"It means you have Anansi's gift," said John Henry. "I'm still not sure how the Weaver created this magic, but what I do know is the world listens to you. And you listen to it."

A thought jumped into my mind and I inhaled sharply. "The music..." The others looked confused, and I explained. "I've been hearing music ever since I arrived. Drums. Clapping. Even some singing, but it's real faint and..."

I paused as a giant yawn escaped my mouth. The events of the past night were catching up to me, and I still didn't know how I was going to get home, or *if* I could get home. With the tear in the sky making everyone's lives down here a living nightmare, I wasn't even sure I *should* go home, not without trying to help. But being some kind of magic story-teller wasn't going to be of much use in an iron-monster attack.

Tristan Strong the butterfly whisperer. Whoop-de-poop-de-do.

Another yawn threatened to break out—all this stress was exhausting. If this was how adults felt all the time, you could miss me with that mess.

John Henry frowned. "All right, that's enough for now. We need to do some figuring about this. Gum Baby, take Tristan to get some food with the others. And send Ayanna in here if you see her."

Gum Baby saluted and started trotting down the grassy hill to the doorway in the thorns. I began to follow, but a deep voice stopped me.

"Tristan," John Henry said. He pointed a massive finger at me. "This ain't over. Somethin' ain't adding up completely, but there ain't no time to toss over it now. We will speak again."

I swallowed and nodded, then hurried after Gum Baby.

What had I gotten myself into?

14
GROWING DESPERATE

GUM BABY LED ME BACK UP THE WINDING TUNNEL. SHE STOPPED every so often to examine a branch ("Gum Baby never saw this one before") or a corner ("This is new!") or a footprint ("Who's been walking in Gum Baby's halls?").

I was only half paying attention and almost stepped on her when she stopped and scratched her head. "Gum Baby don't remember this fork being here," she said.

"Wait, what?" I looked around. We were at an intersection. "Are you lost?"

"Gum Baby don't get lost, boy. She just decides to go somewhere different sometimes."

"Uh-huh."

"Got it. It's this way." Gum Baby started marching off down the leftmost path, and I sighed and followed. We walked in silence for a few seconds before she spoke again. "Everything's so different."

"What?"

"Everything." Her voice was softer and less brash. "Everyone. People used to dance and sing and play—now they all quiet. Scared."

I pursed my lips. "They said you were gone a year. A lot's happened in that time."

She stopped at another intersection, listened, and looked both ways before moving forward. I could hear faint voices now, and Gum Baby seemed more confident in where she was going. She glanced up at me and shook her head.

"Gum Baby wasn't gone no whole year. She left yesterday! It don't make no sense."

Something savory wafted up the hallway and my stomach rumbled. We rounded a curve and entered a large room crowded with Midfolk. Long picnic-style benches stretched in rows from end to end, with a small aisle in the middle so people could walk up to the circular cooking station in the front.

Gum Baby stopped. "See what I mean? They look so..."

"Sad," I finished.

A line curled around the room, and people and animals shuffled forward. Nobody spoke, and all eyes were fixed squarely on the floor. A baby cried and was quickly shushed. Children sat in groups, some wolfing down their food and others listlessly picking at it. We got in line and Gum Baby scrambled up onto my shoulder.

"Gum Baby don't know anybody in here," she said in frustration. "All these new faces."

"Refugees?" I guessed. "From around MidPass."

"But those ain't MidPass clothes."

She pointed to a little boy who was draping his beaded cloak around his even littler sister as she clung to his shoulder. The boy offered her a drink of water from a tall jug, but she batted it away and buried her face in his chest.

"Gum Baby," I said slowly. "Did you . . . see anything weird when you fell into the Burning Sea?"

"Flaming death?"

"Well, yes, but anything else? Did you . . . see a shadow in a room?"

Gum Baby shook her head. "Nope. Why?"

The haint's cackling laughter echoed in my ears again, along with his warning.

Don't you tell a soul, boy. . . .

"Just wondering."

She patted my cheek and went back to looking for anyone she might know, while I grimaced and wiped off her sticky residue and wrestled with secrets.

The haint had fallen through the tear, too. I knew that now. The presence in the Bottle Tree forest, the shadow that had seeped out of the bottle, the weird conversation with Uncle C . . . each encounter had involved the same evil aura that lingered like a bad aftertaste or that weird smell in my gym bag. And now he was lurking somewhere out there, doing gods-knew-what with Eddie's journal. He had seemed eager to possess it, and now he did, as much as it pained me to admit that. I had to get it back.

But how? I stared at my hands, then flexed my fingers. Apparently butterflies were at my beck and call, so maybe—

"Stew?"

The question startled me, and I blinked. "I'm sorry?"

The girl manning the cook pot sneered. "Do you want stew or not?"

"Oh, uh, yes. Please."

"Bread?"

"Yes, please."

She handed me a rough clay bowl full of steaming vegetables, seasoned rice, and a crusty chunk of bread, and I thanked her and moved on. I found a seat near the back of the room, at the edge of a table, and sat down next to a family of Midfolk with four children, each of them staring at me. They really stared when Gum Baby hopped off my shoulder and stuck her face into my food. The little terror even had the nerve to hum to herself while she scarfed my meal.

I ate from the other side of the bowl. The vegetables—onions and celery and something that resembled a purple carrot—were spicy and made my eyes water. It was also delicious. I devoured it, dipping the steaming bread in the remains to sop up every trace.

"Daaaaang, Bumbletongue, you were hungry, weren't you? Gum Baby wanted your bread, too. Now she's gotta get up and go ask for some more. You just selfish." Gum Baby walked down the table, scrounging for leftovers.

I looked around. Everyone was watching me, and my face got so hot with embarrassment my cheeks could've started a fire. One of the younger kids snickered before being shushed by his older sister, who looked to be around my age.

She smiled apologetically. "Sorry. I know how it is—you don't realize how hungry you are until you sit down in front of food."

"Yeah." I studied the bowl, eyed the piece of onion in the bottom, and decided against slurping it up.

"My name's Netta."

"Tristan."

"You just get here?" she asked. One of her siblings climbed into her lap, and she began to rock him automatically.

"Yeah. Well, yesterday. Apparently I slept for a while." At the mention of sleep, a yawn forced its way out, and I blinked in surprise.

Netta grinned. "Beds are too comfortable after nights spent on the soggy Drowned Forest floor."

"Yeah, I guess."

"Sorry for all the questions. It's just . . . not a lot of kids our age make it to the Thicket."

I looked up, confused. Netta shrugged and nodded at the crowd. "You didn't notice? Look around. Those iron monsters seem to prefer us older kids for some reason. Nobody knows why."

I scanned the room. She was right—all the kids, apart from a few like Netta and myself, were younger. Children who, back in Chicago, would be in kindergarten. Why? I felt sick to my stomach.

I've been waiting for you, Uncle C had said.

Netta frowned. "You okay? You don't look so good."

I got up, jostling the table in my rush. "Sorry, I . . . I gotta go." I hurried through the jam-packed chamber, mumbling apologies as I squeezed through, until I reached a clear space against the wall and bent over, my hands on my knees.

All those people. All those families, ripped apart and hounded through the forest, just because of me. That haint had been hunting Midfolk, somehow working with the Maafa, whatever that was, and sending iron monsters searching for me, but taking everyone they captured and . . . I felt like I was going to vomit everything I'd just eaten. How soon before everyone made the connection? How soon before they figured out it was all my fault?

I sank to the floor and laid my head on top of my crossed arms. A wave of exhaustion swept over me. I just wanted to sleep and wake up and the nightmare would be over. I'd be back in Chicago, Eddie would be knocking on the apartment door, and everything would be back to normal.

I just wanted to sleep.

Sleep...

Darkness.

Two torches burned on either side of me, barely illuminating a long, damp corridor. The kind of space you walk away from, not into.

But I couldn't walk away.

Something wouldn't let me.

One foot moved, then the other, and I stepped into the gloom. As I walked, the torches floated alongside me, and faces appeared in their dim light. People and animals looked out at me from inside the semitransparent walls, their horrified expressions lining each side of the hallway like twisted portraits. Manacles held them in place, and their mouths moved but nothing came out. I passed two or three before I came to one I recognized.

"Brer Fox?" I tried to stop, but my feet wouldn't obey my commands, and I kept walking. When I looked back, his silver muzzle moved as he tried to respond. "Brer Fox!" I yelled.

He was alive! There was still a chance to save him.

This thought dominated my mind so thoroughly that I didn't notice when the darkness began to lighten. Water dripped and things scurried past my feet as I trudged down the hall. Whispers echoed, and I heard a nasty laugh. Just when I thought I'd be marching forever, a door emerged out of the darkness.

I wanted to turn around, but my hand moved on its own and I couldn't stop it from pushing the door open. My feet took me through.

"Hey now, hey now. Look who it is! Where you been, Tristan?"

The shadow from before, the one I had seen when I was falling through the hole, stood in front of me. It had a form now—a body. I could see it outlined, though only in parts, as if someone had just started drawing a monster with ink and anger.

A single eye blinked open, and the haint smiled, showing a row of perfect white teeth. "You ain't avoiding old Uncle C, are you?" Something dropped out of the shadow—something I couldn't make out completely, but it looked like a flower with fuzzy white petals. It immediately withered in the darkness.

"What do you want?" I whispered.

"You ain't been square with me, Tristan." The shadow sounded sad. Betrayed. Like I'd stolen a dollar from it. "Naw, you ain't been square at all. After I saved you, this is how you treat me?" A lantern flared to life, and I saw more shriveled flowers on the ground. Next to it was a book full of warped pages with a water-stained leather cover. Eddie's journal! Somehow, someone had put it back together. I squeezed my fists so hard my fingernails bit into my palms.

"That's mine!"

The shadow's edges hardened, and just for a second I thought I saw a full face glaring at me—one-eyed and scowling.

"This ain't what I thought it was, but you knew that. Where's the magic? I can't do nothing with this mess. I should burn this piece of trash!"

"No!" I shouted.

"Well, then you should've been square with me!"

I shook my head. "I don't know what you're talking about." But as I said that, the story scene from the Thicket glade popped into my mind.

The lantern flared again, and the smell of old rot nearly choked me. "You know exactly what I'm talking about! You made a fool out of me. But I'm a kind uncle, yes, I am. You know what I need, and you gonna get it for me. I want that spider's power, and you gonna bring it to me, or I'll light this wad of toilet paper on fire and come find you. And when I do find you, I'm gonna put an end to everything and everybody who ever helped you or looked at you or even thought nice things about you. I'll bury them all!" The lantern flickered as the haint spat out, "You hear me? I WILL COME FIND YOU!"

The words punched me in my chest, and suddenly I was

flying backward, yanked by an invisible string through the door and down the hallway, until I was abruptly dumped at the entrance.

Get me Anansi's power, boy, or this journal of yours and everything else is kindling.

The threat followed me, or maybe it was burned into my head. I had control of my body again, but as I turned, another voice stopped me in the darkness.

"Hey, nimrod, you're talking to the wrong one."

The breath left my lungs, and I whirled around. I recognized that voice. I just never expected to hear it again. "Eddie?"

"You're talking to the wrong one."

"Eddie! Where are you?"

He didn't answer, though. My best friend's voice just kept repeating that phrase, and I gripped my skull as panic and confusion and helplessness pulled me in seventeen different directions.

"EDDIE!"

Nothing.

15

FUEL FOR THE GODS

"TRISTAN?"

My eyes snapped open. Ayanna stood over me in the crowded common area, her eyes narrowed. I stood up and swallowed a few times.

"Hey. Where've you been?" I asked her.

She watched me, then glanced at the people trying not to listen in. She turned and beckoned me to follow. "Not here. Somebody wants to speak to you. Come with me and I'll explain."

Curious, I followed Ayanna through the Thicket's shadow-filled tunnels. Slivers of sunlight squeezed through the cracks in the branches, and I caught a glance of cloudless blue skies more than once. MidPass should've been a peaceful place, somewhere you could play, grow up, sing, dance, and let the magic of the world carry you along.

Instead, it was horror.

Nightmares.

Because of me.

What did the haint want with storytelling magic?

I needed to find a way to fix this. Maybe if I explained everything to John Henry and Miss Rose and Miss Sarah, they could somehow take the Anansesem power away and I'd be free to go.

"I had to go talk to some of the Midfolk," Ayanna said suddenly. I looked at her, confused, and she sighed. "You asked me where I'd been. I had to tell some families that we weren't able to find their loved ones."

I winced. "That sounds hard."

"It is. And it never gets easier. I don't know how Brer Fox did it. . . ."

Brer Fox. I wondered if I should tell her he was still alive . . . somewhere. But then I decided against it, remembering Uncle C's threat against anyone who even looked at me.

"And after that I had to try to convince Miss Sarah to let me go out on patrol one more time. There are still Midfolk out there we can save, I know it!" She pounded her fist into her hand. "There have to be."

I didn't know what to say to that. We walked in silence for a long time until Ayanna slowed, and I realized we were back at the indoor Thicket glade where John Henry and the others had quizzed me earlier. She turned around before we stepped inside and studied me again.

"What?" I asked.

"Did you really do it?" she asked.

My heart skipped a beat. Did she mean the tear in the sky? "Do what?"

"You know. Bring that story to life. With magic." She said it with a bit of anger, as if I'd betrayed someone.

I let out a breath of relief. "I don't know. That's what the gods told me."

"I'm not asking them, I'm asking you. Apparently you can hear things, too?"

"I don't know, okay? I sense . . . something. Drums, clapping, faint music . . . I can't explain it, other than to say it's like having a memory just out of reach." I balled my hands into fists and sighed in frustration. "I don't know if it's that Anansesem thing, but . . ."

Ayanna continued to watch me. "I hope so," she muttered. "We need all the help we can get, and maybe . . . just maybe, with your help, we can tip the balance in our favor for once." She offered me a small smile, then walked inside.

I waited for a moment. She wanted my help. . . . Even after everything I'd done, and all the problems I'd caused, I could still make this right.

So why did that thought paralyze me with fear?

"Tristan?"

I exhaled and followed her inside.

We walked past the hill, crossed the stream, and headed toward the trees in the back, where a large boulder sat between several trunks. At first I thought there was a breeze, because of all the motion in the treetops, but then one of the many leaves separated and fluttered down to us.

"The butterflies!" I said in hushed awe.

The trees were covered with the butterflies from before. They'd made their homes in the branches, folding and unfolding their wings, until it looked like the entire grove was a living painting. I held out a finger and the largest butterfly I'd ever seen landed on it. Sky-blue wings splashed with yellow and white dots flapped slowly before the insect took off to flutter elsewhere.

"Peaceful, ain't it?"

John Henry's voice rumbled out of the shade. What I'd assumed was a boulder was really the giant folk hero sitting against a tree trunk. Now he turned slowly and looked at me, and my eyes widened at the hundreds of butterflies covering his arms and shoulders.

"Come here to think sometimes," he said. He glanced at Ayanna and smiled. "Thanks for bringing him. Sarah and Rose went to do a flyover of the Drowned Forest, see if they can find any stragglers. You get something to eat?"

She shook her head. "Later. I'm going back on patrol. I'll take the east side."

John Henry's eyes grew sad. "Ayanna, Rose said—"

"I'm going on patrol," she repeated stubbornly, and after a brief standoff, he sighed and nodded.

She looked at me with that almost-pleading expression again, like I was the answer to an unspoken question, before gripping her staff and stalking to the exit.

"Sit down, Tristan," said John Henry. "We need to talk."

I eased down opposite him and leaned my head against the tree trunk. John Henry watched Ayanna leave, then turned and studied my eyes. I avoided his, choosing instead to gaze at the butterflies flying above us.

"These iron monsters are killing us slowly," the big man said grimly. "It's getting to the point where folks can't step outside the Thicket without one of us gods escorting them. Even then it can get iffy."

"But," I said, "you're John Henry. You're all heroes, gods! Right? How can they—?"

"Easily. All it takes is a bunch of those sneaky metal creatures to suck up our attention, and then other ones start snatching folks left and right. They're smart—smarter than they should be. Smarter than they used to be. The Ma—their leader is devious in ways we never could've imagined. They're learning, and they're taking our people. They're even taking our children. Our CHILDREN!" John Henry pounded his fist on the ground, sending tremors through the whole forest, and I flinched as hundreds of butterflies took flight in a flurry of silent wings.

"Who's their leader?" I asked.

He rubbed his forehead with his eyes closed for several seconds. "It ain't really a *who*. It's more of a feeling. Of devastation and destruction, hunger and greed. It's pain, and that's what it survives on. It came here with the first of us, with me and Brer Rabbit and Brer Fox and the Flying Ladies. The sadness to our joy. We managed to defeat it once. We thought if we let it sink to the bottom of the Burning Sea, and stayed vigilant, and forbade anyone from mentioning or even thinking of it, we could live peaceful lives." He looked up at the sky. "But something's brought it to the surface again, worked it up into a right fury, and it's sending everything it has after us. All the iron monsters it can dredge up from the depths are headed our way."

When he stopped speaking, I struggled with the enormity of his words.

Something had disturbed a monster it had taken all the gods to defeat.

That something was me...and the haint I'd brought along.

John Henry cleared his throat. "Brer says he has a plan. And you're part of it."

I frowned. "But..."

He winced. "I wish we could keep you out of it, but I don't see how we have a choice. We need your help."

There it was again. That word.

Help.

I started to shake my head. "I don't think I can..."

"Tristan, an Anansesem...that's something special. You may not realize it, but this world and yours are connected. The legends, the fables...all the tales you heard growing up, they give us strength. They're like fuel for us folk heroes here, the reason everyone calls us gods. And when an Anansesem tells them, they're even more powerful. You are linked with Alke more than any of us, because you carry the stories that brought us here—stories from your world and mine."

I opened my mouth, then closed it. How was I supposed to respond to that? Suddenly all of my excuses sounded trivial. I closed my eyes and squeezed my fists tight. Everyone was after this power that I didn't understand. I just longed to get rid of it, not save the world. But if I wanted to get home, what choice did I have?

"What's the plan?" I asked.

16
THE WARREN

IF YOU TOLD ME A DUDE JOHN HENRY'S SIZE COULD SQUEEZE through a tunnel of thorns I had to duck through, I'd laugh in your face. But somehow the Thicket seemed to shift and grow and stretch around him. Chestnutt had said the Thicket had magic woven into its vines, but it was still amazing to watch as we made our way through the maze of hallways unimpeded.

We found Brer sitting in the middle of the floor in a dome-like room. Small holes dotted the space from floor to ceiling, and behind the walls I could hear the sounds of scratching and scampering.

"Mm-hmm." Brer grunted as crumbled leaves tumbled out of an opening near his head.

"Got it," he said as a flash of gray fur disappeared into a burrow by his feet.

"I'll pass it along," he muttered as a fluffy white tail dashed away.

"This is the Warren," John Henry whispered as we watched Brer work. "Them little holes are tunnels that lead all over MidPass, and even beyond. Somebody once said a few of 'em go clear over to the mainland. Brer's friends gather information and bring it back here, where he organizes and files it away for future reference."

"He's got spies?" I blurted out. "And you accused me of being—"

"Collecting information is hardly spying," Brer snapped back, his ears flattening in annoyance.

"Enough, you two," John Henry said. "We've got a problem that has to be dealt with, and I reckon it's time we talked about how to fix it."

"Fine, fine. Of course," said Brer. "But I'm waiting until the others get here—no sense in wasting my breath twice."

The rabbit collected his scribbled notes and began sorting them without another word. John Henry shrugged an apology to me and I rolled my eyes. God or no god, Brer was working my last nerve.

Miss Sarah and Miss Rose arrived a short time later, and I was surprised to see Ayanna trail them inside. While the winged goddesses both murmured greetings to me, the raft pilot gave me a brief smile that I hesitantly returned.

"Ah, good. About time." Brer shuffled a stack of his notes and cleared his throat. "I, for one, will not dally, as I'm incredibly busy."

"Doing what, sitting?" I said before I could stop myself.

Brer hopped to his feet in a huff. "*Some* of us, boy, actually contribute around here. *Some* of us believe that helping everyone survive is important. I solve problems—problems that you created—so spare me the insolent sarcasm and start pulling your weight."

"I didn't ask to come here!" I snapped.

"We didn't ask for you either, and yet here you are."

"Well, help me go home and I'll get out of your hair!"

"THERE IS NO GOING HOME!" Brer exploded. He hopped inches from my face and glared. "That's the problem! Nobody here has the ability to fly you up to a burning spiral of death that's been hanging over our heads for a year, growing bigger and bigger. Not with hordes of iron monsters lurking in the mists! Not with brand flies swarming in the skies, chasing you this way and that! Until the tear is closed, and those iron monsters dealt with, you're not going anywhere. So lose that idea until I tell you otherwise."

I bit back a retort and remained silent, struggling with what he said. I was trapped there. For how long? The time difference between my world and Alke continued to throw me off. When I escaped—*if* I ever escaped, that is—how many days would have gone by at home?

"So then, what's the plan, Brer?" John Henry threw up his arms, and his fingertips grazed the walls on opposite sides of the room. "If we can't get up there, that hole will keep growing, and those iron monsters from the bone ships will keep boiling out of the Burning Sea!"

Brer rubbed his furry face and sighed. "From what we've been able to gather, there's some connection between the abnormality in the sky and those creatures. I just haven't been able to figure out what it is. What we do know is that when young Fisticuffs here"—he pointed his ears at me—"battered the poor Bottle Tree, that upset something, and the iron monsters, a minor nuisance since you-know-what was defeated, have been a menace again. If we can push this boy back through and close the hole behind him, it stands to reason whatever is aggravating them will be cut off...."

Miss Sarah said, "That's all well and good—"

"—but someone still needs to get up there," her partner continued.

"And we're not trying again," they finished at the same time.

Miss Rose sniffed. "My wings still twinge in the mornings, you know."

Miss Sarah nodded, and I imagined the two goddesses beating their wings in time as they shot toward the tear in the sky.

A crash of thunder, and black feathers falling, a shriek of pain, and—

"Tristan, honey, you all right?" Miss Sarah peered at me, and I shook the vivid image from my mind. I could even smell the singed feathers.

"Fine," I croaked out.

John Henry was still arguing with Brer. "And like you just said, them monsters ain't letting no one get close enough to try," he rumbled.

Brer hesitated. "Provided we figure out a way past them, which I'm working on, there are two people I know who can make it through that fire unscathed, but only one of them can fix the rip in the sky *and* perhaps rid us of our unwelcome guest."

We all leaned forward to hear the name.

"Anansi."

17
THE WORST PLAN EVER

A BREATH OF WIND BRUSHED ACROSS MY FACE, AND I THOUGHT I heard someone whisper my name, but when I looked around, nobody was talking to me.

John Henry and Ayanna were arguing with Brer, who had both paws crossed over his chest and a determined look on his face.

"That tear in the sky needs to be sealed shut, and who better to do it than the Weaver himself?"

"Kwaku Anansi hasn't been seen in months," Miss Sarah said.

"If we could find him, though . . ." said Miss Rose.

"Ain't happenin'." John Henry shook his head. "It just ain't. Even if he wasn't long gone by now, hiding somewhere, what makes you think an Alkean god is gonna help us MidPass gods?"

"Because he has to!" said Brer.

"And how do you expect to find him?"

The bickering continued, growing into shouts and hand-waving, and I shook my head. Adults are so quick to jump on us kids for acting like that, when they do the same thing. Hypocrites.

"Excuse me," I said loudly. "Hey! Excuse me!"

Everyone broke off their debate and turned toward me.

"How could Anansi help us?"

Silence greeted my question for so long I started to think I had food in my teeth, until Miss Sarah slowly asked, "You don't know about Kwaku Anansi?"

"Oh, I know about him. Spider god. Stole stories from the gods and brought them to the people. The original trickster. Makes Brer, here, look like a teacher's pet. I mean the teacher's favorite kid, not the teacher's animal, though I guess you've got that going for you, too."

Brer snarled, and Miss Rose hurried to cut him off. "Yes, all of that is true. But Father Anansi is also known as the Weaver. The threads he spins are powerful magic—"

"—and right now, that's what we need," said Miss Sarah. "Powerful magic to close the tear in the sky."

John Henry frowned. "But even if we can find him, and even if he bends that stiff neck of his, his help don't come cheap."

"No," Brer said. He sighed and dropped back to his

reclining position. "It doesn't. We'd have to offer something mighty valuable to lure him out and over to our side."

I looked around. "And we don't have anything? What about your hammer?"

My suggestion brought a grunt of disapproval from John Henry. "That hammer might come in handy next time those iron monsters come 'round. And besides, what's the spider god gonna do with a hammer?"

We all fell quiet for a moment, and then Brer cleared his throat.

"There is ... one thing."

"No," John Henry said promptly.

"Johnny Boy, I'm just saying—"

"It's too dangerous, Brer."

"So is lying around here waiting to be snatched away by some overgrown bracelet!"

I waited for an explanation, and from their looks, so were Miss Sarah and Miss Rose, but John Henry and Brer just glowered at each other. I swear, adults act worse than sixth graders sometimes.

"Sooo ... anyone going to tell us what's too dangerous?" I finally asked.

John Henry glared a warning at Brer but didn't say anything. Brer sat up, his ears flat to his skull.

"The Story Box," he said.

Miss Sarah and Miss Rose drew back in a flutter of black

feathers and sharp inhales. John Henry clenched his fists. Ayanna gripped the carved end of her staff and narrowed her eyes.

And me?

I stood there like an idiot, confused.

"A story what?"

"Story Box. A treasure vault for tales and ballads. A repository for lullabies and fables older than the sun, some familiar, some no one has ever heard before." Brer hopped to his feet and stretched his arms wide. "This wide, and this high—though it changes in appearance depending on who carries it—and every city in Alke has their own version. The original, however . . . the true Story Box, Anansi's Story Box, the one he outsmarted Nyame to get . . . is unique."

"And you think this treasure that is already his will lure him because . . ."

Brer fidgeted suddenly. "Because we were working on a project for it together. Then the iron monsters attacked, and we fled our separate ways. I came back here, and Anansi disappeared, but the Story Box was left behind."

I thought about every Anansi tale Nana had told me over the years. He always had to prove himself the smartest, the trickiest, and above all, the most renowned. Losing the Story Box had to be a blow to his pride. "Anansi is a glutton for stories," I muttered.

"Watch it. It's bad business to insult a god," Brer warned.

"Not that I expect someone with your manners to know that."

"It *is* a well-known fact, Brer," John Henry said. "Get that Story Box and the Weaver is liable to spin his way to us quick, fast, and in a hurry."

I looked at the giant man. "Wait. You said it was too dangerous, but Brer says every city has its own. Why don't we just use the MidPass Story Box? Isn't it good enough to lure out Anansi?" Maybe this could work.... And once Anansi was reunited with a Story Box, there'd be no need for me to stick around as the new Anansesem on the block.

John Henry looked away and sighed. "We actually don't have one. A Story Box is an important icon of our history, and we haven't yet hit on just the right combination of materials and spirit to build one with yet."

Miss Sarah said, "We've tried many times before—"

"—but each disintegrated after only a day," said Miss Rose.

"There's some wood over on the Alkean continent," John Henry mused. "Heard that it's right powerful, but with things the way they are, the iron monsters and them being stubborn, it's liable to be months before we can try again."

That comment floated between us for a moment. Ayanna shook her head sadly like this was a constant source of disappointment.

"Okaaaaay," I said. "We need a Story Box, and we don't have one."

Brer cleared his throat and John Henry's face went grim, and again he clammed up. It was obvious that he didn't approve of what Brer was going to say next, and after hearing it, I understood why.

Brer moved closer, both ears shading his eyes as he looked at me. "No, you're not understanding. There's a perfectly good Story Box waiting on its next owner. I just told you we left it behind. It's there, right now, in the Golden Crescent. That's where Anansi and I were studying it."

"The Golden Crescent?" I asked. "What's that? A city or something?"

"It was the jewel of Alke," Ayanna explained. "But soon after the tear appeared, Brer said the iron monsters came and destroyed it. Any hope of Midfolk taking refuge there or in any other Alke territory disappeared after that. The cities are all afraid they'll be the next to be overrun. And I don't blame them."

"But we're not talking about taking refuge. We're liberating the one thing in the world that gives us a fighting chance. The power in that Story Box..." Brer's eyes narrowed to slits as he rubbed his paws together, and I shook my head. That rabbit had problems.

John Henry frowned but was no longer arguing. As much as he hated the idea, I could tell that the constant fighting, defending, leading the charge—it was starting to wear on him. On all of them. I considered Brer's scars, and Miss Sarah's and Miss Rose's burned feathers. The gods were suffering right alongside the Midfolk who were hiding out in the Thicket.

John Henry sighed. "How?" was all he said.

Brer shot up and started pacing around the Warren. "Simple. Well, not that simple, but easier than you might expect. Especially with the butterfly whisperer over here." He pointed at me and I scowled. "Anyway, a Story Box is a vessel for the magic of stories, right? It holds it, ready to bring them to life, much as an Anansesem would, only on a larger and grander scale."

"Okay, so . . ." John Henry prompted.

"So, any stories told in its vicinity would be drawn to it. And vice versa."

I didn't like where this was going.

"If the boy—"

"The name's Tristan," I said, alarm entering my voice. "And I don't think—"

"Yes, whatever. If he spun one of his tales like he did earlier, the magic from it would lead us straight to the Story Box. Then, easy as you like, someone slips in and snags the treasure, and we're out, back home, and waiting for Kwaku Anansi to show up at the bargaining table."

He clapped his paws and gazed around the room. John

Henry looked thoughtful again, while Miss Sarah and Miss Rose seemed skeptical. Ayanna's brow was furrowed. I shook my head, but no one paid me any attention.

Miss Sarah said, "And if someone has—"

"—an issue with us taking it?" Miss Rose finished.

"No one's there anymore. Don't you see? Since that... meeting, I've had the Warren keep track of movements in the Golden Crescent."

John Henry narrowed his eyes, and I did the same. So Brer's tunnels *did* go all the way to the mainland.

"All the citizens left after the iron monsters attacked," Brer continued. "The Story Box is just sitting there, waiting for its next owner to pick it up." The giant rabbit looked at me and frowned. "And you bring it right back here, understand? To me... to us."

"Wait a minute..."

But they ignored me as they all fell silent, weighing the risks versus the potential benefit of having such a valuable treasure to lure Anansi.

Finally, John Henry shrugged.

"I hate to say it, but that may be our only option."

"But who will accompany him?" Miss Rose asked. "It's so dangerous."

"Can I just—?" I began, but the conversation rolled right over me.

"We can't go," said Miss Sarah. "We're already short-handed, and those beasts are going to attack again any day now. Besides, John Henry would be spotted a mile away, and, Brer, you're needed here to oversee the Thicket."

"You're right," John Henry said.

Ayanna cleared her throat. "Chestnutt and I will go with him. Patrols around MidPass have been called off for now, and I refuse to just sit here and wait."

Miss Rose pursed her lips, then nodded. "It would be reassuring to have you go as well. As for Chestnutt..." She trailed off, and her partner spoke up.

"It would get her mind off...losing Brer Fox."

John Henry clapped once, nearly scaring me half to death. "So, Tristan, you ready to be a hero?"

I stared at him.

Ready to be a hero? The words echoed in my ears and pounded in my skull as images of Eddie and Brer Fox came to mind. In both those instances, I'd failed to help anybody. This would be the third attempt, and this time there were even more lives at stake. I might strike out for good. I backed up, nearly stumbling in my haste, and shook my head.

"No."

18
THE ADINKRA

SEND A SEVENTH GRADER TO DO A GOD'S JOB, WHY DON'T YOU.

When I refused to go along with their plan, Brer started pulling his ears and shouting, John Henry rumbled something, and Miss Sarah and Miss Rose took turns cutting each other off. But it was Ayanna's expression that hurt the most. She looked betrayed, and she stomped out of the room, her staff gripped tight.

Finally, John Henry waved both giant arms. "Enough, enough!" He waited until everyone settled down before turning to me with a frown. "Tristan, I know this is scary, but we need your help."

"Why?" I asked, a challenge in my voice.

"Because . . . like Brer said—"

"Then let Brer do it. He's obviously the expert. I'm not going back out there."

Brer's ears went flat and he sneered at me. "Oh, forget it.

It's obvious he's too afraid. He's done pretending to be a hero. Just as well. Fine. Whatever."

If my face got any warmer, my eyebrows would've started smoking, but I refused to look away. Let them readjust their plans. I was tired of trying to live up to everyone else's expectations.

Before I could respond, John Henry cleared his throat. "I reckon I might need to talk to Tristan for a bit. Will y'all excuse us?" He looked at me and nodded at the door. "Let's take a walk."

I studied John Henry out of the corner of my eye as we headed back to the Thicket glade where he liked to think. He reminded me of both my father and Granddad. Proud, silent, stern men. His knuckles weren't scarred and swollen like theirs, but his wrists were marked and the palms of his hands were callused.

Everybody wears life's scars a little differently, I supposed.

The ground began to slope upward, and the tangle of barbed branches we moved through became less dense. Sunlight speared through in angled beams. Green buds could be seen on the vines that crawled up the walls, and tiny white-and-yellow flowers blossomed near the ceiling.

The flowers reminded me of Mom's windowsill garden, and without warning I got hit with a wave of homesickness. I wanted to get back to my world, but the fetterlings and the moaning bone ships in the Burning Sea...they stood between me and home. The thought of trying to get past all that again locked up my muscles. Froze 'em stiff.

And then there was the matter of reaching the tear in the sky. It sounded impossible.

That left me with only one other choice: luring out Anansi. What if he didn't come? What if he *did*?

I didn't want any of this. I'd never asked to become an Anansesem.

All those thoughts grabbed and pulled at my brain, slowing me to a stumbling walk.

"So, you're a boxer, hm?"

The question took me by surprise. I'd expected a lecture, or an interrogation, not idle conversation. After wondering for a moment whether this was a trap, I shrugged.

"Yeah, I guess."

"You guess? You either box or you don't."

"I do."

"You don't sound happy about it. I'm surprised. Heard you gave a pretty good show in the Drowned Forest."

"It didn't help," I said, with a hint of bitterness. "Couldn't rescue Brer Fox. Lost Eddie's journal."

"Is that your friend? Eddie?"

I nodded, and John Henry pursed his lips. "I'm sure he'll understand."

"He's...not here anymore."

I looked down and shoved my hands in the pockets of my hoodie. It smelled like outside, and my sneakers were muddy, and all I wanted to do was worry about what Nana and Granddad would say when they saw how stained everything was. I missed my old problems.

"So, you have any bouts yet?" John Henry asked. I was glad he'd moved on.

I kicked a loose twig. "One. Lost it."

"Oh."

"I wasn't prepared," I said after a second. "Couldn't focus. Didn't sleep well the night before, and I felt tired and couldn't get any energy. So yeah, I lost."

John Henry glanced at me. "Ayanna said you moved like lightning in the forest. Said your fists were a blur."

My neck grew hot. "She said that?"

"Mm-hmm. And that don't jibe with how you say you did in the ring. So you probably ain't as bad as you think. Who holds the bag for you?"

"My dad." I kicked the twig again, sending it flipping end-over-end all the way up the tunnel. "Alvin Strong. Two-time middleweight champion. Boxer extraordinaire."

"Okay, okay. So it runs in your blood."

I shook my head. "Only thing running in my blood is disappointment. Dad was set on me being the next champion in the family. He never lost a professional match. Me? I can't win one fight against a tiny sticky loudmouth."

We walked on and continued to talk about boxing. I stayed away from anything too personal, and eventually we got to discussing favorite boxers.

John Henry whistled in awe. "So this Ali . . . they stripped him of the title?"

I nodded. "Yeah. Disrespectful, right? All for not wanting to shoot anybody in a war. But anyway, he did his stint in the doghouse and came out smelling like roses. Won back his title and did it in style. 'Float like a butterfly, sting like a bee.'"

"That's what he said?"

"That's what he did."

"Well, I'll be. I like that. Like a butterfly, huh? Well, I'll be." As he said that, a few of the colorful insects flapped lazily around his head, almost as if summoned. I stared at my fingers in suspicion.

"What about you?" I asked. "Did you have a favorite? Did they even box back then?"

"Boy, hush. We boxed. Didn't have your fancy equipment, either. Knuckles and heart was all we had, knuckles and heart."

"So who was your favorite?"

John Henry didn't answer. Instead, he held up a hand and eased over to the Thicket wall. He stopped, put his ear as close to it as he could without getting jabbed by thorns, and listened. After a second he moved on, shaking his head.

"Thought I heard something," he said. I began to ask what, but he brushed me aside. "Where were we? Favorite boxer, right? That's easy. Old Man Rawlins, hands down."

I snickered. "Old Man Rawlins? Quit playing—he don't even sound like a boxer. What was his record?"

John Henry stopped walking and held my eye. "One hundred fifty-three and zero."

"No way."

"I'm telling you, he was one hundred fifty-three and zero. No losses."

"How is that possible?"

"Old Man Rawlins was a bit of a story. See, he was never given a choice in the matter. He had to box, plain and simple."

"Sounds familiar," I grumbled.

But John Henry shook his head. "No, sir, you may think it's the same, but it ain't. Not like that. You reckon you were forced into the matter, but at the end of the day, I bet your folks would've let you be."

My folks maybe, but not Granddad. But I kept that to myself.

"See, we worked on the rails, and all of us, we worked for a man we just called Boss."

"Boss?"

"That's it. One word. It's the question and the answer. End and the beginning. Boss wanted you to work a little later, you worked a little later. Boss wanted that mountain drilled before noon, well, you'd better start hammerin' by dawn. And if Boss said you were gonna box for the evening's entertainment, well, you just hoped the other fella was as tired as you were."

"That doesn't sound..." I broke off before I could finish, and John Henry grinned.

"I know you wasn't gonna say *fair*. Is life fair?"

I pictured Brer Fox being hauled away by a fetterling. "No. Life ain't fair."

"Good. 'Cause that's what Old Man Rawlins figured out. But he also figured out a way to get by. Every time Boss told him he had to fight, he just grabbed these thin cloth gloves with the fingers ripped away and went to the middle of camp. Ten minutes later, it'd be over. Another win."

"How?"

John Henry winked and tapped his head. "Let's see if you can figure it out. You the boxer. No rush. Just some brain food for you to chew on."

I ran through boxing tactics in my head. How could a man go 153 and 0? Especially a man named Old Man Rawlins. He sounded ancient. Older than Granddad, probably. Socks-with-sandals ancient. But no matter how much I thought about it, I couldn't come up with an answer.

We reached the entrance to the hidden glade and headed for the hill where I'd been interrogated before. John Henry stayed at the bottom and I climbed to the top so I could face him eye to eye. His hammer was slung across both shoulders, and he draped his arms over it. The head was worn and dented, but John kept it polished, and it gleamed in the warm sunshine.

He saw me eyeing it and smiled. "Must seem silly, me carrying this here hammer everywhere."

I shrugged. "No, it doesn't seem silly. If it means something to you, you should hold on to it." Then I added, "As long as you don't bring it in the shower."

"In the what, now?"

Wow. I started to stammer something, but he cut me off with a laugh. "I'm foolin' with you, boy. And yes, that's a surefire way to find your tools rusted."

I let out a sigh of relief.

"Tristan," John Henry started, then stopped, and started again. "Your friend's book. It meant something to you?"

"Everything," I said right away. I rubbed the side of my pants, feeling the pocket where the journal should've been. "It meant . . . it meant everything."

John Henry nodded, then fished around in the front pouch of his overalls. "One of Sis Crow's brood spotted this—they always got an eye for something shiny, and this little thing glows like you wouldn't believe. Anyway, they found this in the trees, and, well . . . I thought you might want it."

He held out a tattered leather cord, and the breath caught in my throat.

"Is that...?"

"It ain't much, but it's something, and hopefully it helps a little. Doesn't seem right that an adinkra like that should get lost."

He dropped the tassel from Eddie's journal into my palm, and I lost the ability to speak for a second. The charm—Anansi's symbol—was still knotted on the end. I held it up and watched it spin in the light.

"What did you call this?"

"An adinkra. Something else that got carried over from your world. Symbols that held great meaning for the people who wore them. Our people. Kings and queens. If it came off your friend's book, the one all this hoopla is about, I expect you might want to hold on to it."

I looped the cord around my wrist, using my teeth to knot it, and took a deep breath. "Thank you. I thought... Well, thank you."

"Aw, it wasn't nothin'. In fact—"

"Ouch!" I shook my wrist and stared at the charm. The wood was blazing hot, like it was on fire.

Wait a minute.

I brought the charm close to my face, then cupped my hand around it. Sure enough, the adinkra was glowing, a soft green light that confused me for a second.

"Why...?"

A rusty squeal sounded from across the glade, and then another.

John Henry's face went pale, and the hammer was in his hands in a blur.

"It's them iron monsters."

19
ATTACK!

SUNLIGHT WINKED OFF METAL IN THE DISTANCE. A LOT OF METAL.

And then the screeches started.

Iron monsters sprinted in our direction, and though they were still some ways away, I could tell their numbers were greater than before, back in the Drowned Forest. Their collars clacked together like crab claws, and they let out this awful squeal as they ran. Like old car brakes. Or metal on a sidewalk.

"Fetterlings," I whispered.

John Henry's eyes grew big and his head jerked back, like the word was a slap to the face.

Fear.

John Henry, the strongest man I'd ever seen—a folk hero, a god—felt a flash of fear. I saw how it momentarily twisted his face and forced beads of sweat to pop up on his forehead.

He plunged the haft of his hammer into the ground, gripped the metal head, kneeled down, and closed his eyes.

"Brer," his voice rumbled.

My eyes went back and forth between him and the fetterlings, which were splashing across the stream. Then, to my amazement, the bark on the tree roots near our feet began to twist and swirl.

"Brer!" John Henry called again. His voice seemed to echo, and I could feel the vibrations.

I swallowed a scream when a face formed in the dirt around the hammer. Somehow, Brer was looking out at us.

"What is it?" Brer asked.

"Iron monsters have broken into the Thicket." Now John Henry's voice sounded way too calm. "We need help."

"Hold on, hold on, big guy. Let me check. . . . There's no switch for this, you know. Now, let's see."

John Henry clenched a fist as he kneeled there, waiting for Brer to finish whatever he was doing. We just had to trust that it was going to bring help, and quickly, before we were swarmed. I understood the giant man's frustration. God or no god, Brer rubbed me the wrong way.

"Well, I'll be," said Brer. "Something's off—the Thicket isn't talking to me."

I frowned, puzzled, but John Henry's fist clenched even tighter as he pounded his leg softly.

"The Thicket talks to him?" I whispered.

John mumbled, "Brer hears it like you hear that drumming. It's part of the spell he used to build this place. He's been having trouble with it lately, though, and I—"

"Bad news, Johnny Boy," said Brer. "This will take some time. You're going to have to hold them off for a while."

"Brer—"

"No time, no time. Got to get this going. Keep them back. Don't let them reach the tunnels!"

With that last instruction his face disappeared, and John Henry growled. He leaned back, reached into the back pocket of his overalls, and pulled something out. He tossed it—no, *them*—at me. Simple fingerless brown leather gloves. The kind a rail worker might wear. "Put these on," he said.

I did as he said and was surprised to find that they were a perfect fit.

Then he grabbed his hammer with both hands.

"Give me strength," he whispered.

I was confused until I realized it was like a prayer before battle, and I gulped. When gods prayed, things were about to get real.

He stood, pulling the handle . . . and the wood stretched. It grew longer and longer—three feet, five feet, ten!—and my jaw dropped as John Henry's hammer hummed with energy. Symbols rippled up and down the shaft, and the metal head glowed dull orange. He swung it through the air a few times and it whistled past my head, smelling of heated steel and polished wood.

"Follow me."

He took several long strides back toward the valley before I could even begin to follow, and by the time I caught up with him, he was at the sloping trail leading back up to the tunnel entrance. John Henry took two giant steps to the right, then nodded at me.

"Hold up your hands," he said. He brushed each glove gingerly with the hammer, and steam hissed from them. Strangely, I didn't feel any warmth. "There," John Henry said. "I reckon these might do the trick. That is, if you wanna help me defend our home."

When the smoke coming off the gloves cleared, I could see a symbol now branded on the back of each one, just below the knuckles. A hammer.

"You can go back if you want," John Henry said. He kept his eyes on the fetterlings, not on me. "Back into the tunnels with the others."

I swallowed and glanced at the entrance we had come out of. It was dark, yet it looked safe, like when you pull the covers over your head in the middle of the night. I could slip inside there and run as far away as possible....

But then what?

Still no way across the Burning Sea.

Still no way to reach the tear in the sky.

And could you look at yourself ever again? I asked myself. *At Nana?*

When I stood, the decision was made. Taking a deep breath, I moved to John Henry's side. "Maybe we should back up to the tunnel entrance," I said. "Just in case one of them gets past us."

A giant hand patted my shoulder, and he grinned, but his eyes were hard.

"Nothing's getting past us."

The fetterlings stepped out of the stream. Twenty. Thirty. A hundred. They swarmed the hill like locusts.

John Henry and I waited, him holding the hammer in both hands, me with my fists clenched inside my borrowed gloves. My blessed borrowed gloves.

The screeching grew louder. So loud it drowned out everything else. They saw us now—they had a target, and the air filled with their hateful calls.

"Don't let them scare you," John Henry murmured. His fingers tightened on the hammer's carved wooden handle. "You are fighting for something bigger. Something stronger. Trust in that, and we'll be just fine."

I snorted. "You should've been a corner man."

"I was. For Old Man Rawlins."

I stared at him, then at my hands. Were these the

same gloves Rawlins had worn? I wanted to ask, but now proooobably wasn't the best time.

The fetterlings clawed their way to the top of the hill and flooded the valley. Butterflies took flight in a dazzling display of colors, and I tried to focus. The first of the iron monsters ran up to us, only to have its eyeless collar head removed by a single powerful swing of the hammer. The fetterling exploded into bits of metal and that same weird white fluff that floated up into the sky.

"Keep the tunnel entrance at your back," John Henry declared. "The glade is narrowest here—either we repel them, or the Thicket is lost." He took up a wide stance. "If I hold the valley, can you hold the hill?"

I eyed the incline, and how the path narrowed as it got closer to the top. On my left was a Thicket wall, and on my right there was a steep drop-off to where John Henry's hammer awaited. The fetterlings could only come one, two at a time at most.

I pounded my fists together. The gloves felt electric, like I was wearing lightning on my hands.

"Strongs keep punching," I said, and John Henry smiled.

"That's the spirit. The demons won't take another soul, not while we stand here!" He laughed, a great booming sound that rolled like thunder, and when the first wave of fetterlings leaped forward, his hammer was there to greet them.

One swing crashed into a group of three, sending them flying back into the crowd, and the return blow crushed two more. The air filled with screeches and floating white fluff.

But I couldn't just stand and watch. I had my own battles to fight.

A fetterling sprinted up, its collar open wide and its shackles snapping. I ducked one attack and slipped away from another. *Bob and weave,* I could hear Dad shouting. *Then attack!* I feinted, then made a quick jab. I thought it was a decent punch, nothing special, just something to give me more room to operate, but the metal monster shrieked in pain and staggered back like I'd landed a haymaker.

The fetterling and I stopped to stare at the gloves I wore—the hammer symbol glowed an angry orange-red, and the air turned wavy above them, as though my fists were on fire.

The fetterling chittered something.

"You're telling me," I said, and swung a right hook at its head.

It exploded, showering me with broken bits of chain and fluff. Some of it got on my face and lips, and I wiped my mouth.

"Y'all are nasty," I mumbled through my sleeve.

"Tristan, look out!"

The hammer whistled inches from my head, and I ducked just as a fetterling leaped forward. The hammer met it in midair and sent it back in pieces. John Henry pivoted and forced another group to stumble backward.

"Focus!" he rumbled, and I jumped to my feet, embarrassed.

Two fetterlings tried to trap me, but I batted away their snapping manacle-claws, a grin spreading across my face as the arms disintegrated, and a fierce joy exploding inside me as I landed a combination that literally blew them away.

This was nothing like my first boxing match.

Back then I was drifting. I didn't have any purpose.

But now?

Now I had a goal. *Pop*. An objective. *Pop*. One mission, should I choose to accept it, and that was to defend the Thicket. *Pop pop*. Protect this house. *Pop pop*. They—the enemy, the fetterlings, the Maafa, Uncle C, and whoever else—they wanted to win, but I wanted it more.

That must have been why Old Man Rawlins kept winning.

Soon there was no time for thinking. John Henry and I fought side by side (well, not exactly... I kept some space between us, because the hammer scared me). The horde of iron monsters kept coming. I fought the longest boxing round of my life. Swing after swing, punch after punch. When one enemy was defeated, two more stepped up. Eventually, my arms started to get tired and the grin slipped off my face.

The movies, the comics, the stories—none of them mentioned this.

"Johnny Boy, slight problem down here."

Brer's giant face appeared on the hillside again, and the vibrations of his booming voice sent some of the iron monsters tumbling.

John Henry gritted his teeth and kicked a fetterling off his boot, then smashed it with the handle of his hammer. "What is it, Brer? We're a mite busy here."

Brer's face raised its eyebrows in surprise. "That so? Never would've guessed. I put on a pot for tea, but I guess you won't be attending?"

I ducked a leaping fetterling and sent an uppercut into its middle as I rose. The monster exploded and Brer whistled.

"Looks like the coward grew a spine! Well done, champ."

Before I could snap a reply, John Henry spoke up. "Brer!"

"Okay, okay. Just wondered if you'd seen the large iron monster heading your way. Looks like the ones you're pummeling now, only ten times bigger? Maybe gives the orders?"

Hairs rose on the back of my neck.

John Henry swept away seven or eight fetterlings, giving us a second to breathe, and glared up at Brer's face. "No. Why?"

Brer frowned. "Because a little bunny told me it's about to rip its way inside."

20
THE BOSSLING

THE FAR WALL OF THE GLADE EXPLODED IN A SHOWER OF BROKEN branches and fetterlings. More butterflies took to the air as the largest fetterling I could've ever imagined tried to squeeze through a gap like a T. rex. Even though a whole field, a hill, a stream, thirty-odd yards, and a group of trees separated us, the boss fetterling (Bossling? Yeah, that sounds right.) looked huge. It surveyed the glade, then let out a high-pitched roar that made my teeth hurt.

Smaller fetterlings poured in through the breach around it, leaping over the broken branches and thundering across the field.

"John! Tristan!"

Miss Sarah and Miss Rose soared over the glade, their brilliant black wings spread wide.

"Rose, Sarah!" John Henry sounded relieved. "We need to clear the hill!"

Without a moment to lose, the ladies tucked their wings close and knifed toward the ground. At the last second they unfurled them and unleashed powerful flaps. Slicing wind gusted toward the intruders, lifting them up and sending them tumbling backward until they slammed against the rear wall and disintegrated.

But more fetterlings clawed at the hole that trapped the bossling, trying to help it get through. Meanwhile, their leader slammed from side to side, squeezing even farther into the Thicket. Just when it seemed it would pop free, thorny vines shot out of the ground and entangled it further.

"Take that, you blundering cretin!" someone shouted from behind me.

Brer leaped out of the tunnel entrance and landed next to me, finally appearing in the flesh and not as some magical face in the dirt. His fur was matted and twitching, as if his muscles were spasming, and the giant rabbit was gritting his teeth with effort. I heard a strange song in my head, like something was out of harmony, or an instrument was out of tune, and he glared at me as more vines shot out to wrangle the iron monsters.

"Still here? Ayanna and the others are leaving for the Golden Crescent and the Story Box. They need you! Have you two been chitchatting the whole time?"

I punched a fetterling before I turned to Brer, but John

Henry interrupted. "He's right, Tristan! Their mission is fixin' to fail if you ain't with them. Us gods are tied up here."

Literally.

Two fetterlings were trying to clamp themselves around his barrel-size wrists. John Henry flung them into the air, then batted them into a million pieces.

"Go!" Brer shouted to me, just as the bossling forced its way in.

"Please, Tristan," Miss Rose called as Miss Sarah hurtled from the sky, a fetterling in each hand, and dashed them to pieces on the ground. "Do this for us!"

Despite the chaos from the raging battle, now that the other gods of MidPass were here, it seemed like they could hold their own. Brer, struggling with the effort, continued to tangle the fetterlings in vines and thorns. John Henry smashed his hammer down left and right, and Miss Sarah and Miss Rose launched devastating strikes over and over from high above.

They didn't need my help.

But the others did.

I threw my hands up in frustration. "Okay!" A fetterling slipped past Brer, and I nailed it with an uppercut that blew its head off. "Fine!"

"About time," Brer snarled. His left ear pointed at the door. "Now get! They're in the kitchens, stocking up, but you need to hurry. Follow the tunnel to the right, always to the right, and you'll find them!"

The bossling finally emerged. It thundered across the field, stomped through the stream, and John Henry raced toward it, hammer in hand. The winged goddesses spiraled above, preparing for another sweeping attack, and Brer kicked high into the air, trying to close off the hole the monster had made in the Thicket's wall.

"Go!"

I turned and ran.

I sprinted through the Thicket tunnel, turning right whenever I could, and the floor began to slope upward. Gradually the passageway began to widen, until it ended in a circular room with a large hole in the ceiling. Ayanna and Chestnutt stood hunched over a familiar raft, which they'd loaded with bundles of supplies. They both looked up in surprise when I skidded to a stop next to them. Chestnutt grinned, but when she looked at Ayanna and saw the anger simmering on her face, the rabbit's smile quickly faded.

"Thought you didn't want to help," Ayanna finally said.

I clenched my fists, then forced them to relax. I deserved that. Rather than arguing, I picked up the last three bundles of supplies and tucked them on the raft, securing them with straps. Once that was done, I made to get on, but Ayanna stepped in my way.

"Oh no, you don't. You don't get to insert yourself after saying no."

Frustration built up in my chest. "The gods told me I had to!"

"And that's the only reason you're here?"

"Yes! No. Wait." I gripped my skull. If I'd had longer hair, I would've pulled it out. "I have to do this, I think."

"You think?" Ayanna folded her arms and Chestnutt hopped anxiously from foot to foot. "Whatever. Come on, Chestnutt. Let's go."

"Hold on." I reached out but didn't grab her arm. The look in her eyes when she turned around told me that had been a smart decision.

"What?"

"I . . . It's true I don't want to go."

"Well, that's—"

"No, wait. I don't want to go because I'm afraid."

There, I said it. Out loud so everyone could hear it, including me. I'd needed to admit that to myself.

"What, and we aren't?" Ayanna asked. She stepped forward, getting in my face, and pointed back up the tunnel. "You don't think I'm afraid of those things?"

"Not just of them. Of failing. Of letting another person down."

Speaking the words felt like ripping a bandage off—or

getting my chest waxed. (I assume. Saw a video of that online once. Looked really painful.)

Ayanna's eyes softened. "Why? 'Cause of Fox? Tristan, that wasn't your fault. He made that choice. He sacrificed himself for us to escape. You didn't do anything."

You didn't do anything.

She thought I meant Brer Fox, but in my mind it was Eddie's hand I saw reaching out to me. I didn't correct her, though—her words applied just the same. *You didn't do anything.*

I took a deep breath. "I . . . I'm trying to believe it wasn't my fault. So . . . I think I need to do this. I want to help, if you'll have me."

She studied me, then looked at Chestnutt, who twitched an ear. Finally, Ayanna turned back and nodded. "Come on. I guess you might be useful. Besides, I'm pretty sure Miss Sarah and Miss Rose would have my hide if I refused you."

I forced a smile and stepped onto the raft. Chestnutt hopped on beside me. Ayanna murmured a phrase, and the raft began to hum. Symbols flared briefly in the wood, and then we rose into the air. The raft climbed higher and higher, aiming for the circular hole in the ceiling, until we shot out of the darkness of the Thicket and into the red-orange glow of the afternoon sun.

MidPass stretched out below us. It felt weird leaving the

others behind, but they were fighting so we could attempt this heist. Their battle was distracting the iron monsters.

The Drowned Forest lurked like a silent cemetery, and when we rotated the raft to face the curtains of mist and flame beyond, my heart skipped a beat.

The Burning Sea.

"Hold on tight," Ayanna said, and we shot forward, on our way to steal from a god.

21
BRAND FLIES

WE SOARED OVER THE DROWNED FOREST. FROM HERE, THE GAPING wound in the sky looked like a part of the sunset. The farther we got from the Thicket, the more normal everything seemed.

But I knew better.

Soon the raft ascended into a thick cloud that smelled like wet coals.

"Where are we going?" I asked.

Chestnutt huddled next to me but didn't answer. Flying as high as we were, where Ayanna said we wouldn't attract unwanted attention, the air was cold. Chestnutt shivered, and I put her in the front pouch of my hoodie. It was the least I could do.

Ayanna glanced at me, then turned back to guiding the raft. Her staff pulsed with a soft amber light. "We're headed north, to the tip of MidPass. Then we'll cut across the Burning Sea and aim for the top of the Golden Crescent."

"That seems longer than the route John Henry described."

"Yeah, well, John Henry ain't here." She still sounded peeved. I let the conversation die.

Chestnutt poked her nose out of the pouch. "The longer we're in the clouds, the better," she said. Her ears emerged and she peeked up at me. "Brand flies move slower in damp air."

"Brand flies?" I asked. Hadn't Miss Rose said something about those?

"That way, if a scout fly spots us," Chestnutt went on, "we should be able to catch it before it alerts the others."

"Scout fly?"

"Yup, yup." She hopped out of the hoodie and dove into a supply pack. The bunny emerged with a thick pencil in her mouth, and she began to sketch a picture on the floor of the raft.

"Hey!" Ayanna complained.

"Shorry," Chestnutt said around the pencil in her mouth. "I'll cleanishup."

She hopped around as she drew, and I leaned forward to take a look.

"You're pretty good!"

"Yup, yup! Ish the only reashon Mish Sharah allowed me to come."

"Little bunny knows everything about everything," Ayanna said with a roll of her eyes, but she smiled at Chestnutt to take the sting out of her words. "The weak points of every iron monster, schematics of every palace in every region of Alke—you name it, she can lay it out for you, no trouble at all."

I whistled. "That's impressive."

Chestnutt dropped the pencil and stepped on it to keep it from rolling away. "Thanks!" She beamed. Then she tapped the diagram at my feet with her paw. Two diagrams, actually. "Take a look."

"What am I looking at?"

"Brand flies."

"Please tell me the pictures are this big so we can see the details."

"Afraid not. These are almost their actual size—I might have drawn them a bit small. I can redraw them to make it more accurate if—"

"No, that's not necessary!" I yelped. "Those are some big insects."

"Iron monsters," Ayanna corrected me. "Not just insects."

"The one on the right, that's the soldier fly," Chestnutt went on. "Double-winged, it can hover or accelerate to speeds faster than a bird of prey. Two of its six legs are welded into a stinger that injects a poison. If one of those touches you, it will burn and keeps burning until you pass out."

"Then the fetterlings come collect you," Ayanna said, her

voice grim. "The Ma—the brain behind the iron monsters has been sending wave after wave after us. It plays for keeps."

"A one-two punch," I muttered.

Chestnutt nodded and continued. "It took us a while to figure out what was happening at first. We'd be out gathering supplies, then someone would scream, and we'd never see them again."

The grim finality of it all, spoken so simply, boggled my mind. This is what Uncle C was stirring up? Whipping the Maafa into a frenzy, like rabies in wild animals. The more I thought about it, the more appropriate the analogy seemed. Uncle C was a disease, the iron monsters were the symptoms, and MidPass—no, all of Alke—was suffering.

Ayanna spoke up. "I found a victim once."

"And?" I asked, but she fell silent.

Chestnutt hopped closer and whispered to me, "She's never talked about it, but she volunteered to be a pilot soon after that."

I watched Ayanna as she guided the raft, her eyes constantly scanning the horizon for something. Survivors? Iron monsters? I didn't know which, and I wasn't sure how she could find anything in the thick mist.

My foot accidentally smudged the diagram of the scout fly and I shuddered.

"You really don't like them, do you?" Chestnutt stared at me, then examined the drawing.

"I'm . . . not a big fan of insects."

"You're afraid of bugs?" Ayanna asked. She turned her head, and I couldn't tell if she was smirking or not.

"No, I said I'm not a fan," I said. My voice sounded defensive, and I cleared my throat.

"Mm-hmm."

Chestnutt grabbed the pencil in her mouth again and began sketching more flies. "Well, I'm glad you're not afraid—though ish okay if you are—becaush these bugsh travel in shwarms of hundreds."

"Hundreds?" I asked, feeling faint.

"Yup, yup."

"I once saw a swarm of a thousand," Ayanna said.

This time I was sure I saw a little smirk on her face.

"Ish okay to be afraid," Chestnutt whispered to me.

"I'm not afraid, okay? Just . . . *concerned*."

"That'sh all right. I don't like heightsh."

Ayanna winced. "Oh, that's right. I'm sorry, Chestnutt, but I needed to go higher so we wouldn't—"

"Ish okay." Chestnutt continued to draw. "I can't see the ground in thish cloud, so that actually helps. And if I keep focushing on something else, that helps, too."

"That's why you're drawing," I said, feeling sorry for the little rabbit.

"Yup, yup."

"If it makes you feel better," I whispered, "I'm not that fond of heights, either."

The bunny looked up and twitched her nose hopefully. "You aren't?"

"Nope. Gives me the willies. And the Freddies."

Chestnutt grinned at me, and I watched her sketch a picture of a fox and a tiny rabbit walking side by side. After a while she smudged it out and started on something else. Ayanna stared straight ahead, and I cocked my head and studied her.

"What are *you* afraid of?" I asked.

She raised an eyebrow without turning to look at me. "Me? Nothing."

"Nothing?"

"Not a thing."

"Okay. You're not afraid of anything. Well, what are you not a fan of?"

She rolled her eyes. "Pointless conversations."

"And..."

"And loudmouths who want attention all the time."

I ignored that. She just wanted to get under my skin so I'd leave her alone, but instead I pressed her some more. "Come on. Chestnutt and I shared our fears. And this is a team, right? Besides, if you don't answer, I'll sing that song Gum Baby likes to hum."

Ayanna stiffened.

I cleared my throat and hummed a few bars. Ayanna flinched and shot me a death glare. Chestnutt waited for her to answer, too, and finally the pilot threw one hand up in the air.

"All right, fine!" Ayanna shook her head at both of us and then turned to keep an eye on our flight. "Surprises. I don't like surprises."

"Like preshents?" Chestnutt asked.

"No, like . . . I don't know. Like people jumping out at me."

"Ambushes," I said quietly. "You don't like being ambushed."

She stayed silent, and I started to ask another question, when one of the supply bags began to rustle, scaring me half to death. Ayanna jerked back and the raft wobbled, and my stomach flipped.

"Fetterling!" I shouted, ready to kick the whole bag overboard.

The bag shifted, then lifted, and a face emerged.

22
LEGEND OF THE BOTTLE ROCKET

"FETTERLING?" THE VOICE THAT CAME FROM THE BAG WAS MUFFLED, but there was no mistaking that high-pitched voice. "Where? Gum Baby need to work off some energy anyway."

"Gum Baby!" Ayanna shouted. "What are you doing here?"

A lumpy leather-wrapped bundle stood up in the middle of the supplies. Two short, stubby legs poked out from the bottom, and the weird creature stomped indignantly out to the middle of the raft.

"What's Gum Baby doing here? *What's Gum Baby doing here?* Being insulted. How dare you leave on a mission without Gum Baby! That's like leaving sand out of a sandwich. Or toes out of tomatoes. Or—"

"Okay," Ayanna interrupted. "First of all, none of that makes any sense."

"You put sand in sandwiches?" Chestnutt whispered, and I shook my head.

"Second of all," Ayanna continued, "we're over here."

Gum Baby was standing in front of a sack of carrots Chestnutt had brought along. The leather bundle stuck to the doll's face swiveled left and right. Then, with a grunt and some pulling and a whole lotta sap, off it popped. Her curly hair stood straight up, and she wore miniature overalls that were rumpled. They'd been dyed black, and she had two black feathers glued to her back. It almost looked like . . .

"Are you . . . dressed like Miss Rose?" Chestnutt asked.

That was it! The black outfit, the feathers. . . . Gum Baby had a new mentor, it seemed.

"No," Gum Baby said. "Just thought feathers made Gum Baby look fierce." She struck a pose, flexing her biceps and shaking her back so the feathers wiggled.

Chestnutt, Ayanna, and I looked at each other and tried not to smile.

"Okay," Ayanna said, "but what are you doing here? I thought you were on kitchen duty."

Gum Baby sank to the floor of the raft and fiddled with the empty supply sack. "Gum Baby thought if she got another chance, she could prove she could be a part of the team."

Ayanna's face softened. She bit her lip, then sighed. "You can't just insert yourself, Gum Baby. You have to give it some time. Miss Rose and Miss Sarah and the others will come around. But sneaking off on a mission you're not supposed to be on isn't going to help. You know that."

Gum Baby slumped even lower. Any farther and her face would be on the floor.

"What does she want to do?" I whispered to Chestnutt.

At least I thought I had whispered. Ayanna looked up with a frown. What had I said wrong this time?

"She wants to be a pilot," Chestnutt answered. "Like Ayanna."

Gum Baby sighed and stared at her wooden hands, then reached behind and pulled the feathers from her back. She crumpled them and tossed them away, then drew her little knees up to her chest.

"Gum Baby thought she could do it. Go on adventures, find others, lead them home and be a hero, yay. Gum Baby worked so hard. She trained. She studied. She thought she was ready. Gum Baby begged and pleaded. But no, they said. She was too small, or too sticky."

We all watched her—even Ayanna turned toward her. It wasn't normal to see Gum Baby like this. She was always energetic, never sad.

I thought *I* was the sad one.

Turns out other people—even dolls, I guess—have issues, too.

"What happened?" I asked.

She looked at me. "Finally, after Gum Baby stuck herself

behind John Henry's ear and whispered for a few days, they agreed to give Gum Baby a test. Said if she passed, Gum Baby could go on a 'frobation as a pilot." She patted her curls and sighed. "Even had Miss Rose work on the hair."

I winced. "You mean...*pro*bation, right?"

Gum Baby's eyes grew wide, then she dropped her face into her hands and started wailing. "Gum Baby got this 'fro for nothing? Do you know how hard it is to get sap out of an afro? Do you? DO YOU?"

Chestnutt patted her on the back as Ayanna gave me an exasperated look.

I raised my hands defensively. "I'm sorry! I just thought she should know!"

"You could've said it later," she muttered.

After a few moments Gum Baby calmed down and sniffled. I handed her a paper towel and she blew her nose. Have you ever seen a doll full of sap blow her nose? Um...trust me, you don't want to.

"So, Gum Baby," Chestnutt said, trying to change the subject, "what mission did they send you on? How'd you do?"

Gum Baby shrugged. "Ask him," she said, pointing at me. "He was there, too."

"What?" I said. "What did I do?"

Gum Baby sniffled again. "You didn't let Gum Baby have the book!"

I gawped in disbelief. "You're mad because I didn't let

you *steal* my best friend's journal? You're the whole reason I'm stuck here!"

"No, *you're* the reason you're here. Nobody told your big head to chase Gum Baby. You could've let her have it. You were just being selfish."

"Of all the— I mean, how—? I can't even begin—" I spluttered in frustration. Chestnutt and Ayanna looked back and forth between the two of us.

"I never heard the full story," Ayanna said thoughtfully. "How *did* you and Gum Baby end up destroying the lives of everyone in MidPass and possibly Alke as well?" I winced, and she shrugged. "I call it as I see it."

Chestnutt hopped up and down. "Oh, a story, a story!"

Gum Baby started jumping up and down as well, and I wrinkled my forehead at her. "You know the story. You were in it."

"Gum Baby just likes stories," she said.

"Well, I'm not telling one."

"Why?"

"Yeah, why?" Ayanna said, and she grinned when I rolled my eyes.

"Because weird things happen when I tell stories, remember?"

"Mm-hmm. But you're an Anansesem, right? Isn't that what Brer and John Henry and Miss Rose said? You're supposed to be superspecial when it comes to telling stories. Are you saying you're really not that special after all?" She smiled and raised her eyebrows.

I gritted my teeth and tried to ignore her.

"So...you're not going to tell a story?" Chestnutt's voice sounded smaller than normal. When I looked up, both she and Gum Baby looked disappointed.

I sighed. Maybe nothing bad would come of it. And if it did, well, then at least I'd be diverting iron monsters from the Thicket. Yeah. I'd be doing the gods a favor....

To be honest, I *did* want to try out the Anansesem powers again, just so I could get into the rhythm of telling stories to groups of people. If was going to help, I needed to practice.

"Fine. I'll tell a story—but not the one about how I met Gum Baby. I saw what happened when I talked about that."

"Oh? Then what *are* you going to share with the class today?" Ayanna pitched the raft upward slightly and we popped into clear sky. The cloudbank drifted beneath and we floated on a sea of white.

I stuck my tongue out at Ayanna before turning to Chestnutt and Gum Baby, racking my brain. What story would be safe to tell?

Another pocket of mist and clouds drifted up past the raft and over our heads. Chestnutt giggled as a white sphere settled between the tips of her ears, then yelped as Gum Baby popped it.

I could feel a rhythm in the raft.

More cloud bubbles rose, floated around us, and burst into joy. Laughter and shouts. I heard children calling and playing. I grinned.

"Okay," I said in a loud voice, clapping my hands. I could sense energy in them, like when I made the butterflies tell the story in the Thicket glade. It was still a bit strange, but the feeling was lighter this time, less like needles and more like a buzzing.

Everyone looked at me, then settled down and waited. Even Ayanna seemed curious.

"One time, Eddie and I made our own super soda."

The rhythm was in my fingertips now. It felt like I could shape the story, work the words like clay and sculpt a tale for everyone to see.

"It started as a dare. A prank, really."

The story materialized with little effort this time. Maybe because I wasn't angry or threatened. Either way, everyone on the raft oohed and aahed as the bubbles of mist surrounding us swirled and stretched into a diorama. Two cloud boys—one slightly larger than the other—crept into a large nimbus of a building. We entered, too, and watched the mischievous boys as they laughed and huddled together in a fluffy white cafeteria.

I felt a tug of sadness—I'd nearly forgotten this memory.

"Our heroes thought they were alone in the building. It was a Saturday, nobody was at the school, and the lights were off. Little did they know..."

A tall woman with silver-stratus dreadlocks and wearing a cirrus-cloud dress marched down the hallway to the cafeteria. The larger boy didn't hear her—he was buried in chemistry, mixing sparkling water and food coloring and fizzy candy in six different sports bottles, and his back was to the door. At the last second, the smaller boy sounded the alarm—someone was coming! The boys hid, their delicious project perched precariously on the edge of a tabletop. The bottles started bubbling, gently at first, but then they began to shake faster and faster until the whole table jitterbugged.

The woman, with a cumulonimbus frown that grew darker and darker, investigated the commotion. While her back was turned, the boys snuck out, their little legs churning and kicking up puffs behind them.

I closed my eyes, remembering the breathless laughter, the whispers, the anticipation. I could hear Eddie hissing at me to slow down and wait for him, feel my ribs splitting with laughter as I ran.

I didn't have to open my eyes to see what happened next. It unfolded in my mind.

The soda bottles launched into the air and sent sweet suds bursting out of every window in the cafeteria, and one bottle zoomed down the hallway and out the front door. Kids playing blocks away said they saw it whiz by, and legend has it that people fighting in the burger joint parking lot stopped to watch. By the time all the soda had fizzed out, the two sides couldn't remember what they'd been fighting over.

When I opened my eyes, a cloud bottle streamed across the sky. Chestnutt, Gum Baby, and even Ayanna watched it. It flew toward us, soaring just above the raft before bursting into twinkling vapor and misty streamers.

But my attention stayed on the diorama. On the two boys and the way the smaller one clapped the larger one on the shoulder. Even if no one else could hear them, the words he spoke still rang clear in my mind.

I got your back.

A flare of anger spiked through me.

Eddie wasn't around anymore. He couldn't have my back. He wasn't there to get me in trouble, or get me out of trouble, or do anything. The memory was just a reminder of something that could never be again.

"Hey, what happened?"

Chestnutt's voice broke through my thoughts. I realized that the diorama had frozen—the boys were in mid-stride. I struggled to recapture the rhythm, to get the feeling of creation in my fingers, but the anger had disrupted everything.

"Nothing," I said.

"Is that it? Did they get away?" Gum Baby hopped up and down in frustration. "You can't leave Gum Baby hanging like this. Stupid cloud people! Never can tell with them."

Ayanna studied me. "You okay?"

I didn't answer. The drumming had stopped, and my old anger and resentment had returned. But this time, the tingling remained in my fingertips, like that sticky feeling you can never get rid of after touching honey or syrup.

Just to see what would happen, I conjured an image of Eddie in my mind. I squeezed my eyes shut, reached out toward the mist, and tried to bring the little cloud boy back.

Nothing.

I let my hands drop in disappointment.

Concentrate on what you're speaking about, and learn control.

Miss Sarah's words echoed in my ear, and I frowned. Concentrate and control....

I hesitated, then reached out again. This time I kept my eyes open, and I whispered to myself, *"Once I had a brother and friend...."*

My fingers buzzed, and then the small boy made of mist and mischief climbed out of the clouds.

I smiled.

"Heads up, everyone," Ayanna called. The solemn expression on her face wiped the smile off mine. "We're here."

Gum Baby rushed to the edge of the raft. Chestnutt and I

stayed put. My stomach flopped as we tilted. Ayanna, steering from the rear, nodded toward the front.

"Go look," she said.

I shook my head. "I'm good right here."

"Aw, don't be like that. Trust me, this is the best view you'll ever see." She studied my expression, then raised an eyebrow. "Wow, you weren't kidding about your fear of heights, huh?"

I hesitated, then gave her a few short, jerky nods and waited for her to laugh at me. But she didn't say anything else. She just turned back to her glowing staff, made minute adjustments, and stared at the mist like a psychic reading tea leaves.

As we descended, Gum Baby rejoined Chestnutt and they whispered excitedly to each other.

"Last chance, flyboy!" Ayanna called. She didn't turn around. "If you miss this, you'll never forgive yourself."

"If I fall, I won't forgive myself," I muttered.

But as I spoke, the mist took on a golden sparkle, as if the bottom of the clouds had been dipped in glitter. Pinpricks of light speared up from the ground like miniature searchlights guiding us in for a landing. The raft swam in a golden pond for several seconds. Chestnutt started hopping back and forth—so fast that Gum Baby had to tell her to settle down.

"Calm down, bunny, this ain't hopscotch!"

The anticipation was contagious, and my curiosity

eventually outweighed my allergy to plunging to my death. Barely.

I scooted to the rear edge on the seat of my pants, ignoring Ayanna's mocking look as I eased up next to her.

"About time," she said.

"View better be worth it," I grumbled.

She snorted. "Oh, it will be. And when we land, you gonna apologize for doubting me."

"Yeah, we'll see.

But as I spoke, the final remains of the glitter-dusted clouds faded, and my jaw dropped so far I thought I'd have to duct-tape it back to my face.

"Holy—"

"We're here!" Gum Baby and Chestnutt shouted.

Ayanna smirked.

"Welcome to the Golden Crescent," she said.

23

THE GOLDEN CRESCENT

WATER AS BLUE AS A SUMMER SKY STRETCHED BENEATH US, AND giant ships dotted the sea. Yachts and super-yachts. Ocean liners and huge oval hoverships with domes that sparkled and rippled like bubbles in the sun—every single one of them large enough to make the *Titanic* blush. Ruby-red symbols on their sides blazed when the sunlight reflected off them, but they were too dazzling to make out.

And that was just the driveway.

"Are those palaces?" I asked. My voice came out in a whisper, as if I didn't want to interrupt the painter who was creating the scene below.

"Yep." Ayanna's voice sounded grim for some reason, but I didn't ask why. I stared greedily, drinking in the glamorous world we were descending into.

The Golden Crescent wasn't a place. It was a spectacle. The coastal city was shaped like an arc that grew thinner on both ends until the tips stabbed into the sea. Two pearl lighthouses with massive crystals on their tops stood at the end of each crescent point.

Dark mountains rose out of the horizon—angry, sharp peaks that chewed at the sky, a mouth threatening to devour the glistening jewel in front of it.

And I mean, this town glistened.

Rose-gold sand met the turquoise sea in a clash of vibrant fury. In the distance, near the city center, spires of midnight black and dream silver stood proudly next to ivory domes and marble castles. Massive homes, bigger than any mansion I'd seen along Lakeshore Drive at home—bigger, in fact, than the museums we traveled to on field trips—lined city streets so wide you could play football from curb to jewel-encrusted curb.

The streets curved up and around as the ground rose away from the coast like a spiral. And there, at the top of a hill, the grandest palace of all awaited.

We angled down toward a giant marina, where more yachts of weird shapes and sizes floated. One had two stories, like a double-decker bus, except the windows were see-through bubbles. Inside, a waterfall splashed in a grotto, while a spiraling waterslide connected it to the bottom level, where a miniature beach awaited.

"That's so cool," I said as we passed it. "If I had that, I'd never leave Lake Michigan."

A winding road led from the marina to a huge square of polished marble, and that's where Ayanna steered the raft. More symbols, like those painted on the sides of the ships, were carved into the ground. I gulped as I recognized one—an adinkra, the same as on my bracelet, and on Eddie's journal.

The raft settled down in the middle of the landing space with a gentle bump.

"Let's go," Gum Baby said, but Ayanna shook her head.

"Not yet."

"But—"

"We're not dashing off anywhere. You could get lost, or something even worse might happen."

Ayanna passed out gear as we waited, and I raised my eyebrows as Gum Baby scampered behind a pile of supplies. Ayanna nudged my arm and handed me an empty satchel.

"What's this for?" I asked.

"For the Story Box. I'm not carrying that thing."

I crossed my arms. "Oh, so *I* have to carry the stolen goods? Nice. Real nice."

"Well, Gum Baby ain't doing it, Bumbletongue," the doll said, popping back into view, "so don't even fix your mouth to suggest it."

I began to snap at the little loudmouth but stopped when I saw what she was wearing.

Ayanna noticed it at the same time. "Um, GB . . ."

"What?" Gum Baby was now in a black cape over tiny

black pants and a thin black blouse. Her hair was pulled back in a tiny bun, and she posed dramatically with the cape extended.

"Don't let Gum Baby scare you," she said. "It's just for stealth. Gum Baby gonna be the wind. No, lightning! Wait, is lightning stealthy? Wind makes a *whoosh* sound, but lightning sorta cracks, don't it? Yeah, Gum Baby is wind lightning. Gonna *whoosh-crack* all over the place."

She ran around the raft making *whoosh* sounds, and I sighed.

Chestnutt stood on her hind paws and dropped the pencil she had been using to sketch on the raft. "Okay, I'm ready."

A map of the city covered the wooden planks, and I whistled silently at the amount of detail Chestnutt had managed to fit in. Palace-lined streets, parks and fountains, spires and towers—all were labeled in neat and legible handwriting. Arrows pointed toward one palace, larger than all the others, so large it took up half the map, and I gulped.

This was becoming too real.

We actually planned on stealing a god's treasure. Nyame, the sky god. The one who first created stories, and who'd awarded them to Anansi after the Weaver had completed three seemingly insurmountable tasks.

I rubbed my forehead and took a deep breath. Man oh man.

Ayanna slipped on her backpack, then stepped on Gum Baby's cape to stop her zooming. Ayanna wagged a finger at her and said, "Hush. Time to plan our attack."

Chestnutt looked at each of us and twitched her nose. "Okay, listen up. This is how it's going to go...."

The plan went down the drain fifteen minutes in. Our group split up, with each pair taking one of the two main avenues leading to Nyame's estate. I got partnered with Gum Baby.

Typical.

Instead of creeping stealthily down an unfamiliar street surrounded by unfamiliar buildings while trying to steal the most valuable treasure in an unfamiliar city, guess what I was doing?

Yep.

Arguing with a ten-inch doll.

"No, you cannot leave a sap trail!" I hissed as she moped behind me. "Now come on."

"But what if monsters chase us through the city and we need to find our way back? Huh? What then? You ain't heard of precoffinary measures?"

"First off, it's *precautionary* measures—"

"First off, sap attack, Gum Baby know the phrase, but if you don't wanna die, it's precoffinary. Fool. Gum Baby know what words she wanna use."

I gritted my teeth and wiped off the ball of sap she'd flung at my face. "Just . . . come on. We're almost there."

We walked up a slight hill, following a simple map Chestnutt had drawn on a scrap of paper. We'd passed several palaces, each grander and more luxurious than the last. But it was all very eerie.

The streets were deserted.

No people poked their heads out of their massive homes to investigate the intruders.

No kids ran along the streets playing with their friends.

No gossip or chatter or movement in the streets or market-day traffic or block party or any other community-based event. Nothing.

Gum Baby's voice broke the silence. "Hey, look at this."

She had climbed the stairs to a vine-covered palace across the street and stood peeking through the towering front gate. A small copper statue of a girl stood on a tiny ivory column, both hands frozen on her hips. I know it didn't make sense, but I felt eyes on me as I walked up the steps, and I looked over my shoulder uneasily.

"Gum Baby," I said, from several feet away, "I don't think we should—"

"Too late," she announced loudly, and she rapped the base of the statue. "You too scared, Bumbletongue."

"WHO GOES THERE?"

Gum Baby squeaked, scrambled up the statue, and hastily

clapped a sticky hand over its mouth, shushing the indignant copper girl doorbell.

"*Shh!* Sap attack! You gonna get us in trouble. Two sap attacks!"

The statue seemed to glare at us from behind a layer of sap covering her face.

"Gum Baby, get down from there," I stage-whispered.

She flapped a hand at me, sending sticky drops of sap everywhere. "Come over here," she said impatiently.

I growled something I probably wouldn't say anywhere near Nana and stalked up the rest of the steps. Two more statues posed on either side of the gate, and they made my neck itch—I felt like they were watching me trespass. I crouched down beside Gum Baby and tried not to gawk at the size of everything around me. The entry arches, which stood as tall as John Henry, were copper trees with silhouettes of tiny people in motion on the top.

"Look." Gum Baby pointed beyond the arches to a courtyard, where there was a small grove of real trees. A monstrous sycamore stood in the middle, so large that it shaded the entire grounds.

I cocked my ear. "Do you hear that?"

"Hear what?"

Faint whistling sounded from deep within the tiny forest. A lot of whistling. It was like birds calling back and forth and then joining together in a loud, trilling chorus.

"That," I said.

Gum Baby shook her head. "Nope. Clean your ears, Bumbletongue, and maybe that'll fix it."

The whistling grew louder and closer, and I licked my lips nervously. "Something's coming."

Then Gum Baby did look around uneasily. "What is it?"

"I don't know—maybe we should go."

"Don't worry, Gum Baby will protect you." But as she said that, she tried to hide behind my legs.

I was already backing away. That forest felt ancient. Neither good nor bad—but powerful. I wanted no part of that right now, not with everything else that was going on. My feet were turning to the street on their own, and who was I to stop them?

My name was Tristan Nope-I'm-Gone.

"Bumbletongue, quit being such a scaredy-cat! Bumbletongue! Ooh, Gum Baby gonna get you! Don't you leave Gum Baby alone in here!"

We met up with Ayanna and Chestnutt at a giant plaza filled with fountains disguised as statues, and flowering bushes shaped to look like animals. Gum Baby was still fuming, but I felt nothing except relief. A boy can only take so much.

The air was filled with the aroma of springtime, and if it weren't for the overwhelming silence, it would've been peaceful. Our footsteps echoed as we met in the middle of the open space.

"Guess we didn't need to split up," Ayanna admitted.

I'd like to say a smug smile didn't appear on my face, but you take the wins you can get.

"Finished marking the trail back to the plaza," Chestnutt said. "Just in case we're chased and get lost."

"Oh, did you?" Gum Baby said in an extra loud voice. "Would you call those . . . *precoffinary measures?*"

Chestnutt paused, then started to giggle. "Yup, yup, I guess I would."

I could feel Gum Baby's eyes lasering the back of my head. "Okay, so what's next?" I asked, trying to move on quickly.

"That's the entrance to Nyame's estate over there," Chestnutt said, flicking her ears toward the far end of the plaza, where two towering marble pillars marked an exit. Between them—

"Do y'all see that?" Gum Baby asked.

"It's a gate," Ayanna said.

"Gum Baby knows what a gate looks like. She's very familiar with them. *That* ain't no gate."

"It's Nyame's gate," Chestnutt said. "And that's where we're heading."

Between the pillars, the air shimmered, gold flecks occasionally winking into existence like jeweled fireflies. The palace grounds beyond looked distorted, as if we were peering through frosted glass.

We stopped in front of the pillars. Ayanna looked at me, and I rolled my eyes and sighed.

Leadership is tough, man.

I hefted the empty satchel around my shoulders, took a deep breath, and stepped through the twinkling gate.

24
NYAME'S PALACE

NYAME'S PALACE GROUNDS BLEW MY MIND.

My brain was toast—burnt toast that your mom scrapes so you can still try to eat it for breakfast, but there is no saving it.

"That is one giant driveway," I said.

The paved road in front of us, lined with glittering ivory bricks on one side and edged with golden stones on the other, curved around ripe orchards stuffed with fruit trees I never knew existed. It skipped over hills greener than fresh twenty-dollar bills.

Sunlight splashed in from overhead, bright without being too glaring, and my tension drained away. A gentle breeze carried the smell of spring turned to summer—fresh-cut grass, the ocean, and wildflowers newly bloomed.

"This place is incredible," Chestnutt whispered.

Ayanna nodded but kept her eyes on a swivel. Always the pilot. Her eyes met mine and we exchanged a look of disbelief. This paradise felt too good to be true.

Gum Baby ran up a slight hill before the rest of us and froze.

"What is it?" I asked, following.

Gum Baby shook her head and backed up. My fists clenched and Ayanna reached for the staff slung across her back. Chestnutt dropped behind us as we crested the hill.

Everything we'd seen so far had been impressive. Clearly the palace estate had been designed to draw in visitors and astound them with the splendor and glory of the Golden Crescent. Nyame knew how to wow a crowd.

But after those appetizers came the main course.

Massive statues of people I didn't recognize lined the path leading to an enormous golden domed palace. Some pointed at the horizon, or lifted children high into the air, and others carried spears and shields. The closest one was a woman with a stern face and a golden stool under one arm.

As we walked by, I swear her eyes followed us.

Ayanna raised an eyebrow as I quickened my pace, but she didn't comment. Nobody wanted to talk near these statues that seemed to be watching our every move, so silence fell over us until we reached the entrance to Nyame's palace.

And what an entrance it was.

"A waterfall," I mumbled to no one in particular. "The

entry is a waterfall. What is with this city and its weird front doors?"

The doorway, which looked large enough for one of the statues to walk through, was framed with stone that had been carved with symbols—more adinkra. A curtain of water streamed out of a slit on the top, falling in a perfect sheet like a single pane of glass, and the same winking flecks of gold from the front gate appeared here. I couldn't see inside.

I took a step forward, and a seam appeared in the middle of the waterfall.

"Wait, wait," Ayanna whispered. "What is that?"

"I don't know," I said. I took another step and the seam widened at the bottom, like a curtain being drawn at the start of a play. "I think it has a motion sensor? Alkean smart-home technology. Who'd a thunk it?"

Ayanna rolled her eyes. "Just be careful, flyboy. You're our ticket out of here."

"I'm touched by your concern."

"Gum Baby gonna touch up your chin if you don't get a move on." The little loudmouth used my legs as cover, peeking out from one before diving behind the other.

"Okay, okay." I scooted closer and the seam in the waterfall opened even farther, so I could peek through and check the ground ahead. No immediate sign of a trap. *I can do this*, I thought. I took a deep breath and leaped through the doorway with a holler.

"HAH!"

Nobody jumped out at me. No monsters, no weird statues, nothing. Instead, I stood in a massive rectangular room— an audience chamber, from the looks of it. Polished marble floors reflected the golden plaques hanging from the walls.

Gum Baby came in behind me. "Where's the ceiling?" she asked in a hushed whisper.

White marble pillars towered over us. They ended high above where the ceiling should have been, as if they held up the sky. Each had an image of life in the Golden Crescent painted on it—families sailing in the bay, children playing in the palace gardens, men and women in formal dress in this very hall. All of them with deep brown skin like mine. All of them happy.

None of them anywhere to be found in real life.

The pillars lined both sides like sentinels all the way to other end, a full football field away, where a statue sat on a golden throne. More waterfalls spilled out of holes in the walls, and they splashed into oval pools as blue as the sky. Silver lily pads with ruby-red flowers floated on the surface of the water.

Everything looked so . . .

"Beautiful," I said out loud. Ayanna, who had entered after Chestnutt, moved to my side. "Where are they?" I asked her. "Where did all the people go?"

"Brer said the Golden Crescent was the first to be ravaged

by the iron monsters," she responded. "Maybe they're all in hiding. Or..."

She didn't finish, but she didn't have to.

Maybe they'd all been taken.

"Hey, these statues are different."

Gum Baby's voice echoed from the other end of the hall. She stood near the statue on the throne, her silly cape fluttering in a gentle cross breeze, and pointed at the two figures flanking it—one of a large leopard in mid-leap, the other of a python lashing forward. I joined her in examining them. Both looked so fierce, so lifelike, that I could almost hear their snarls and hisses.

"Freaky," I mumbled.

I moved closer to the throne, eager to get away from those creatures. The statue in the huge chair was just as detailed—a man staring straight ahead, his hands gripping the armrests, with bracelets on his wrists and anklets above his bare feet. His head was balding, and around the detailed crown of curls, he wore a circlet studded with large jeweled insects.

I could feel it again—that weird energy, like an electric bass line trying to get out of my skin. The waterfalls splashed in time, keeping the beat. There was a story here, somewhere, itching to be told.

My eyes fell to a circle in the floor right in front of the throne. "Hey now. What's this?"

The others crowded around as I dropped into a squat and

stared at faint indentations that were covered with sandy-brown dust. I blew gently across the surface, then leaned back in satisfaction.

"It's a door," Ayanna breathed.

"Do you think—?"

"It has to be."

Could the Story Box really be under there? This was almost too easy.

I looked for a latch I could pull to lift the circular trap-door, but there wasn't one. We had nothing to pry it open with, either.

Ayanna turned to me. "Remember what Brer said? When the Anansesem tells a story—"

"It will be drawn to the Story Box."

"And vice versa," said Ayanna.

"Yeah, I remember."

"Well?"

"Um, right." Story, story. Needed a story. I could hear the faint rhythmic beating in the background. But what story would be appropriate for summoning a magical treasure chest?

My eyes flitted around the chamber, seeking inspiration. Finally they landed on the figure seated on the throne. An old man, almost larger-than-life, presiding over the room like a king. Or a god...

"I got it," I said.

"'Bout time," Gum Baby grumbled.

Ayanna shushed her and motioned for me to continue. Chestnutt hopped closer.

Concentrate on what you're speaking about....

I took a deep breath, stared at the circle in the floor, then began to talk slowly, shaping the story with my hands as the words gave it form.

"What if I told you stories didn't always exist?"

The light in the room faded. The grooves of the trapdoor began to glow, illuminating our faces. Sand swirled gently as I spoke, spinning into pillars, walls, and waterfalls, until a small replica of the throne room appeared in front of us.

"Once, Nyame, the sky god, owned all stories. He kept them in a magnificent chest, woven from light and dreams. He kept them in...his Story Box."

I twirled my fingers, and a small figure stepped out of the whirling sand and took his place on the miniature throne. He pointed at the floor, and the circular door slid open. A glimmering chest rose into the air, spinning slowly and opening to reveal an emerald-green glow.

The same glow that had come from Eddie's journal.

"But Kwaku Anansi, the spider god, wanted—"

A scraping sound interrupted me. At first I thought Gum Baby had fallen, but...no, there she was, sitting on my foot and staring intently at the sand.

The scrape came again.

This time Ayanna heard it, too. She frowned and looked around. "What was—?"

A groan filled the hall, and every muscle in my body locked up. Dust fell off the three statues—the leopard, the snake, and the god on the throne. The bracelets on his wrists and ankles jangled.

The statue's head swiveled in my direction. Its eyes narrowed in anger, and a booming voice echoed in my skull.

LEAVE!

25
THAT WAS NO STATUE

I STAGGERED BACK. THE VOICE HAD SOUNDED LOUD ENOUGH TO shatter stone, and yet no one else looked concerned.

"Everything okay?" Ayanna asked.

I opened my mouth, but nothing came out. Gum Baby and Chestnutt paid me no attention—they were still fascinated by the whirling sand story. Ayanna cocked her head, but before I could try to speak to her again, the booming voice echoed.

They cannot hear. But you can. Why? Why are you here?

I gulped and turned to the statue on the throne. Dust and sand blew off of it in spiraling streams to reveal...

"Gaaaaah," I spluttered.

That was no statue.

Brown skin. Fuzzy graying hair. Piercing brown eyes flecked with gold. A chain necklace with a symbol I'd seen before. Not Anansi's symbol, but another adinkra even more familiar. Nana used to knit it into her quilts all the time.

"N-n-nah," I stuttered. "It's ... You're ..."

Speak! Have you come to torment me further? Does your master need more of my pain? Were my people, my heart, my home not enough?

I licked my lips. This was going all wrong. One, Nyame wasn't supposed to be here. It was just an in-and-out mission. Grab the Story Box and go. No one had said anything about having to convince an angry god you weren't here to destroy his culture.

Two, how do you address the sky god?

"Your Honor—"

That didn't seem right.

"I'm not here to hurt you."

LIES!

I staggered back from the verbal assault. Ayanna grabbed my arm before I could fall.

"Tristan? Are you okay? Who are you talking to?"

I shook my head at her. One conversation at a time.

"My Lord, we're here—" I broke off. What could I tell him? We were here to steal from him? That much was true, no matter how worthy our cause might have been.

Nyame swiveled his head, and this time Ayanna noticed. "By the wings," she said in a breathless whisper. "Is that—?"

Take what you will, usurper, but your time will come. You cannot hold us here forever.

I blinked. Who was this "us" he spoke of? For the first

time, I took a longer look at the two statues on either side of the throne. The lifelike leopard and python...Could it be? Were they—?

Ayanna had stumbled back, clutching her head in pain, but now she moved forward again, nearly collapsing against my shoulder, and pointed. "The...bracelets!"

I followed her finger and my hands curled into fists.

Of course.

Nyame's bracelets and anklets were fully visible now. They weren't made out of gold, like most of the Golden Crescent's beautiful creations. They were made of iron and connected to—

"Fetterlings," I said in a growl.

The iron monsters behind the throne were unanimated and camouflaged to look like part of the statues. They were bigger than the bossling in MidPass, but still I wondered how they had managed to overcome Nyame.

"How can they hold back the sky god?" I whispered to Ayanna.

"I don't know, but— Look! The crown!" She pointed to Nyame's circlet, and at first I didn't notice anything unusual.

"What?"

"Just wait.... There, did you see it?"

I did. "The jeweled butterflies. They're moving, flapping their wings, right?"

"I don't think those are butterflies."

The trace of fear in her voice sent a shiver through me.

"Ayanna—"

"Those are brand flies, Tristan."

"Wait, what?"

"They're poisoning him. He's too powerful to be killed by their stings, but their poison is keeping him paralyzed. He couldn't do anything when they came and took his people. He could only watch." Ayanna was on the verge of tears, and, seeing the brand flies pressing against Nyame's forehead, I could understand why.

Can you imagine being forced to watch as the people you loved and protected were hunted down and dragged away, never to be seen again?

A tear welled up in my eye, too.

Anger welled up in my heart.

"Not anymore, they aren't."

The rhythm inside the hall got louder and faster. It swelled into a thumping beat that sent needle pricks down my arms, like they were recovering from falling asleep. My little story reenactment stopped, the sandy scene falling to the floor.

"Hey!" Gum Baby protested, before realizing that something else was going on. But I ignored her.

Finally, something I'd learned in this world was going to come in handy.

I stalked up the three steps to the throne. Nyame's eyes glittered with rage, and beneath that, pain.

I lifted my chin. "I've come to help, Sky God."

He scowled. *Have you not done enough?*

Not yet, I thought. It was time for a bigger, louder story.

I drove my right fist into the palm of my left hand. *"What if I told you, Nyame, that you gave Kwaku Anansi your stories after he did the impossible?"*

I willed that story into the throne room. Nana loved telling it, and it was the first one Eddie had written in the journal. Grains of golden sand and dust bounced on the floor before rising and swirling in the air. The waterfalls on the walls stopped flowing into the pools—instead, droplets began flowing upward, sparkling like diamonds as they joined the story above our heads.

"Anansi visited the sky god and asked to buy his Story Box, with all the stories inside. Nyame, humoring him, agreed. But only if Anansi brought him Leopard, Python, and one of the Mmoatia, the forest spirits."

Out of the whirling sand and water drops a scene appeared. Anansi—sometimes a smiling man, other times a large spider—strolled through a forest. He stopped in front of a tree, where a giant leopard slept in the branches. He bowed, and the leopard raised its head, then hopped down. Anansi pointed at a pile of leaves beneath the tree, and when Leopard prowled over them, the great cat fell into a hidden trap.

"Anansi tricked Leopard, then brought him to you, Sky God. But he wasn't done."

As I spoke and pulled the story out of the sand, I kept an eye on the giant fetterlings. Their chains began to rattle.

Anansi continued to walk through the forest, this time carrying a long staff. He stopped at a giant boulder beside the trail, where Python lay in the sun. Anansi bowed, then studied the snake and the wooden pole, comparing the two. He shook his head, saying *Surely the staff was longer?* Python hissed, insulted. His length was his pride, and no mere walking stick was more impressive than he! Anansi looked unsure but laid his staff on the ground. Python flicked his tongue out, slithered off the rock, and stretched out beside the pole. Quick as a flash, Anansi tied the great snake to the staff and carried it away.

"Anansi tricked Python, then brought him to Nyame. But he wasn't done."

Now the bosslings were clearly agitated. Their chains lashed like angry snakes. The brand flies buzzed in irritation, and a few peeled off from the sky god's head like wet leaves and fluttered weakly to the ground. Ayanna dashed forward and hammered them with her staff.

Nyame turned his head. *What are you doing? Your actions confuse me, usurper.*

I ignored him. I was starting to understand.

Iron monsters didn't just react to stories about them. They reacted to stories, period.

When I told a tale, something pulled at the creatures.

The knowledge, the history, the culture—it drew them like magnets. Tell a story, or, if you were an Anansesem like me, bring a story to life in their presence, and they'd drop whatever they were doing to get at it.

Now I just hoped the second part of my idea would work.

A series of loud clicks echoed around the throne room, and I swallowed. The bosslings released their grip on Nyame and shuddered. Four large iron monsters spread out in front of us.

No, six. Two more had disengaged from Leopard and Python and joined the group.

Nyame slumped down in the throne behind them. Leopard and Python collapsed to the ground.

Okay, yep, I really needed to start on the second part of my plan.

"Tristan," Ayanna said. "What do we do now?"

She held Chestnutt, and Gum Baby scrambled up into my hoodie. Together we all backed up as the huge bosslings stalked forward. I eyed the story swirling in the air, felt the itch to continue in my palms, then took a quick glance behind me.

"Gum Baby, do you remember the statue that talked to you?" I asked.

She wriggled in my hood. "Gum Baby does not want to hear about that again. Why you always living in the past?"

I winced as two of the fetterlings squealed. "Well, I'm

sorry, but times are hard. When I give the signal, everyone run back out and touch the first giant bronze statue you see. The big one, right in front."

Ayanna shook her head. "You want us to *what?*"

"Trust me. Just do it!"

"But—"

All six bosslings screeched, and they lunged forward. I severed my connection to the sand story above our heads and shoved everyone toward the entrance. "Go, go!"

26

BRONZEY TO THE RESCUE

A LOUD *WHUMP* SOUNDED BEHIND US AS THE WET SAND LANDED directly on the bosslings. They collapsed in a cacophony of grinding metal and shrieks as they struggled to extricate themselves.

"Nice," Gum Baby said, peeking out over my hood. "Gum Baby taught you some good strategy."

"Whatever," I said, gasping as we sprinted for the waterfall exit. "Just get ready."

"Get ready for what? Gum Baby staying right in here."

The seam in the waterfall opened, and we dashed out into the plaza. I headed for the path at the opposite end. Rumbling sounded from the palace behind us, and stone and water exploded outward as the stampede of bosslings burst into the sunlight. They quickly gained on us—we weren't going to make it.

Desperate times call for desperate measures.

I reached behind me. "Sorry," I said in advance.

"What? What are you—? Hey! Unhand Gum Baby! This ain't no party! Hey!"

I grabbed her out of my hood, aimed at the giant bronze woman in the courtyard, then threw the best spiral I'd ever tossed in my life. Like, fifty yards, easy. I should've played football. And I hate football.

Gum Baby soared through the air, shouting insults as she flew.

"You gonna regret this day, Bumbletongue! Gum Baby gonna kick your—"

Splat!

She landed just below the statue's knee and stuck there. Her little arms and legs flailed helplessly, but I couldn't watch her anymore.

"Tristan, look out!" Ayanna called.

I skidded to a stop as a bossling lunged in front of us. Ayanna moved next to me. She held a quivering Chestnutt in one hand and her glowing staff in the other. Iron monsters stalked around us, snapping their collars and screeching.

"What now?" Ayanna asked, but I didn't answer. "Tristan," she said again, almost pleading, "you have a plan, right?"

"Just wait," I said.

Chestnutt peeked up at me and I couldn't meet her eyes. If I was wrong...

All six bosslings shrieked at once, and one of them lunged forward, reaching for my throat.

A bronze foot the size of a compact car smashed it to pieces.

Chestnutt screamed, and Ayanna brandished her staff, but I raised my hand. "Wait."

"But—"

"Look," I said, pointing.

The ground trembled as the giant bronze woman stepped down off her pedestal and twisted her foot, grinding the bossling into dust. The remaining iron monsters screeched at this new enemy, and they thundered past us to attack her.

Gum Baby straddled the statue's big toe like a horse and whooped with joy. "Stomp these fools, Bronzey! Look, that one's feeling froggy! Aha-ha-ha-ha, squish that chump. Yeeeeah. Y'all don't want none of this. Oh, where you going?"

She pointed at a bossling trying to sneak around the statue's foot. It looked like a mouse creeping around an elephant, and I grinned when the statue kicked it so hard it flew into the sky and disappeared.

"Aha-ha-ha-ha! Did y'all see that?" Gum Baby slapped her knee and howled with laughter. "Bronzey chucked that thing into the bratosphere!"

"You mean the *strat*osphere," I said, rolling my eyes.

"Yo, why you always correcting something? You Professor Bumbletongue or something?"

Ayanna kept a firm eye on the remaining bosslings. "Can you two put off the bickering until after we're safe?"

The statue leaped high in the air, so high the sun framed her and gave her glaring angel wings.

SMASH!

When I opened my eyes, four oversize fetterlings were writhing beneath both of her heels, like roaches being smooshed on a kitchen floor. She twisted her heels again, then took two ground-shaking steps back.

I looked around. That was the last of them. "Well...I think we're good now."

Gum Baby peeked over the big toe and sucked her teeth at the sight of the defeated iron monsters. "Y'all should've been raised better," she said to their remains. "Ain't got no home training."

"Kumi!" Nyame's voice boomed out of the palace, and we all flinched. His voice wasn't only in my head anymore. "Bring the usurpers to me."

The bronze giant reached behind her back, pulled out a giant spear with a broad-leaved blade the size of a windshield, and leveled it at us.

Ayanna stared at me, and I cleared my throat. I'd thought we were safe.

Gum Baby crossed her legs and shook her head. "Y'all in trouble now."

"You have come for the Story Box."

It wasn't a question. The four of us stood in front of the throne, where Nyame slouched to one side. It seemed the effect of the brand flies' poison still lingered in the sky god's system. Yet his eyes were alert. He gathered us all in his gaze, the gold flecks in his eyes glinting in the setting sun. Leopard and Python were curled on either side of him, staring at us with distrust.

"Yes," I said.

"With the hope Anansi will aid you."

I nodded.

"And you think I should help you . . . why? For your efforts just now? You have my thanks, but my support?" He shook his head.

"MidPass is dying, Lord Nyame," Ayanna said. She still held Chestnutt in both arms. "The iron monsters are tearing our families apart."

"The monsters tore my *country* apart!" Nyame accused.

"Yes, but—"

"They attacked my people. The monsters chased them and captured them and stripped them from their homes and lives and families!"

"Mr. Nyame—" Chestnutt squeaked, but the sky god's words rolled right over her.

"The monsters took them off to die!"

His eyes flashed as he gripped the arms of his throne, daring us to speak. Ayanna bit her lip. Chestnutt buried her head in the crook of Ayanna's elbow. Gum Baby hurled little balls of sap at Leopard's tail as it swished in agitation.

This was getting us nowhere.

I ground my teeth, ignoring Nana's warning that I'd wear them down to the gums eventually.

I knew what had to be done. I didn't want to do it—not at all—but I had no reason to keep my secret anymore. When I revealed it, each word felt like a hot iron hook being ripped from my flesh.

"They're not dead."

Leopard's tail went still. A ball of sap landed right on the tip. ("Got 'im!") Ayanna turned and stared at me, and I did my best not to meet her eyes. They burned a hole in the side of my face, and I didn't want to deal with that problem just yet.

"Not dead?" she hissed.

"Not dead?" Chestnutt asked, her ears flicking up in hope.

"Not dead?" Nyame whispered.

I sighed. *Out with it all, Tristan.* "I saw them. Before we left MidPass, I saw them, in a dream or a vision. They were alive inside . . . something." Now I did look at Ayanna, and I flinched at the anger and the betrayal in her eyes.

Her nostrils flared and she shook her head. "You knew? This whole time, you knew?"

I winced. "I'm sorry, I—"

"No! You should've told me. You should've told *us*."

"I wasn't sure it was real, and I didn't want to get your hopes up, and—"

I broke off, because no excuse was going to cut it. I had no right to decide what they were or weren't capable of handling. Adults were always doing that to me, and I hated it.

"I'm sorry. You're right, I should've told you—I should've told you all."

Ayanna shook her head and looked away as I notified the sky god about the visions I'd been having, the haint with the white flowers, the captured Alkeans and Midfolk in the walls.

Nyame drummed his fingers on the arm of the chair. "You saw them in a dream? And I am supposed to believe this?"

I started to protest but stopped, surprised, when Ayanna beat me to it. "I believe him, Lord Nyame. He wouldn't lie, not about this." She glared at me. "If he says he saw it, then it's true. You have my word as a pilot."

"Hmph. The word of a pilot."

His fingers beat at a faster pace, and some of the sand began bouncing on the floor.

"And my Story Box will aid you in the fight against this ghost and the Maafa? It will free my people?"

"Yes.... At least, we think so," she answered. "If we have it, Anansi might come out of hiding and accept it as payment, since, you know..."

"He wanted it badly enough before," I finished.

"As in your story, Anansesem." Nyame watched me carefully. "But what do you mean by 'payment'? Payment for what?"

I straightened. "We need the Weaver to close the tear in the sky. If he does, it will cut off the iron monsters' power. Then we might stand a chance in defeating the Maafa once and for all."

My words spilled out of my mouth at a breathless pace, and we all clenched our fists and waited for the sky god's verdict. Nyame looked at Leopard, then at Python, before rubbing his forehead where the brand flies had been fastened.

Nyame's hand stopped, and then he waved toward the circle in the floor. "The Weaver is still in Alke. That I can assure you. Where he is, I don't know, and whether he will accept your bribe is another question. But go ahead, Anansesem.... Fulfill your mission."

I gaped in surprise. "For real?"

Nyame raised an eyebrow and I walked toward the trapdoor. I'd expected more resistance from him. I mean, we had originally intended to steal the Story Box, and now Nyame was just going to give it to us.

What were the odds?

The background rhythm of the story still beat in the throne room like a pulse. Once again I willed the sand to come to life above the circular door, and I barely had to pull the figure of Anansi into existence before the grooves in the floor blazed to life. The sound of stone grinding on stone echoed through the space, and the panel slid open. My friends and I gasped simultaneously.

A polished pedestal made of gold-tipped wood rose from beneath the floor. Detailed carvings decorated every inch. More adinkra—some I recognized, but many that I didn't. The panel closed under it and the pedestal settled gently on top.

Our gasps turned into groans.

Nyame waved his hands and a bitter smile crossed his face. "Tell me, did none of you think your plan too obvious?"

I squeezed my hands into fists so tight I may have drawn blood.

Ayanna bit her lip again.

Chestnutt buried her head in her paws and shivered, and Gum Baby's jaw dropped.

"You are not the first usurpers, nor the second. I am sorry, little ones, but you will need a new plan."

The pedestal was empty.

The Story Box was gone.

27

NYAME'S CHARM

"YOU KNEW ABOUT US," I SAID. "YOU KNEW, WHEN WE ARRIVED, what our plans were."

"I did," said the sky god.

A whisper of wind brushed through the palace's rooftop garden. Nyame stood in front of me, hands clasped behind his back, as he stared at the sun setting over the city. I was sorry my friends were missing out on the view, but the sky god had asked for a private consult with me.

Nyame had shifted to a normal size now—a bit shorter than Granddad—and he wore a cream-and-dark-brown-striped tunic and loose cream pants. If I didn't know better—if the gold-flecked eyes didn't brim with many millennia's worth of knowledge—I'd swear he was just one of the chess-playing old heads at my apartment complex in Chicago.

"You used the statues," I said. "You looked through their eyes."

He nodded. "Yes. That is how I witnessed what happened to my people. If only I had foreseen what was to come, I might have been able to prevent it. To save at least some of them . . ."

"Some did get away," I said. "They fled to MidPass. But now they and the Midfolk both face the same trouble there."

Nyame glanced at me, and I swallowed at the intensity of his gaze. It was like being held in place by a huge magnet.

"The monsters still lurk here, too," he said. "I'd hoped that their appetite would be sated by now, that my people could return . . ."

"But can't you help them? You're the all-powerful sky god. Can't you defeat the Maa—er, you-know-what? Can't you fix the tear?"

Nyame sank down on a stone bench and put his head in his hands. "I wish I could. I do not have the strength. My powers have been sapped."

"So we should all just suffer? There's nothing you can do?" He shook his head.

"What about those statues? The sentries? We could take a couple to help fight."

"Only Kumi could stand up to this threat, and her strength is tied to mine. The rest . . . they are barely enough to protect the Golden Crescent," Nyame said sadly. "Even if they were stronger, I cannot spare them now, not when I'm so weak."

I sank down next to him on the bench. "So we're doomed, then?"

The sky god turned back to the view. The sun winked behind a bank of low-hanging clouds, turning their undersides rosy pink.

He sighed. "Not yet. I may not be able to give you the help you seek, Anansesem. It will be some time before I am myself, but I can give you something else. It may increase the chance that my people will eventually be restored to their homes . . . to their lives, their happiness."

I watched, confused, as Nyame stood up and plucked a rosy cloud from the sky.

Yeah, that's right.

He plucked . . . a cloud . . . from the sky. Like it was a flower from one of the trees in the garden. He rolled the wisp between his two palms. Then he pressed both hands together and whispered something between them.

He extended his hand. "Your bracelet, please."

I clutched the tassel from Eddie's journal, not wanting to part with it.

Nyame smiled, and this time it reached his eyes. "No harm will come to it. I may be suffering from brand-fly poison, but I can still imbue a charm or two."

I untied it and passed it over. Nyame took the tassel and tied a small charm onto it. When he handed it back, I gawked at the rose-gold adinkra resting next to Anansi's symbol. It matched what was painted on the yachts in the marina, on the front of the palace, and on the arms of the statues.

"Gye Nyame," I whispered, and the sky god nodded.

"You already have Anansi's adinkra, which brings power to your stories. That is important—Alke is woven with stories, and the threads exist all around us. You can hear them sometimes. Music. Chanting. Rhythm."

I inhaled. "I thought I was hearing things."

"You were. The heartbeat of this world. If you concentrate, the sound can become so vivid you can almost see it." Nyame sighed wistfully before pointing at the adinkra he'd just bestowed to me. "I cannot give you one of my sentries, Anansesem. But I can give you this charm. It will bring focus to your surroundings, and help you gain clarity. You'll find the mysteries of Alke a bit . . . easier to solve."

I looped the bracelet around my wrist and studied the silver and gold charms. They looked nice together. But how would they help us repair the hole?

"You're wondering what good a little charm will do." Nyame clasped his hands behind his back and tipped his head for me to join him. "Come, walk with me."

We strolled around the garden. On the opposite side of the roof, facing southeast, Nyame stopped and stared at the dark, jagged mountains ringing the Golden Crescent.

"Alke is a land divided," Nyame said after a moment. "The great cities do not share as they once did. The iron monsters only pushed a wedge into a fractured landscape that already existed. We used to meet every season, to swap ideas and music and stories. To exchange culture. Our sons danced with their daughters and their sons danced with ours. Our mothers taught their children and their mothers taught ours."

"And with the tear and the iron monsters," I finished, "you can't make things better. MidPass and the rest of the Alkeans will always be divided, even if we huddle together, hiding from the same threat." I shook my head. "It really needs to be fixed now."

"It does. And I agree with your goal, if not your plan. Anansi, if he can be found and bribed, could weave the hole shut and greatly diminish the power of the iron monsters. But after that they'd still need to be defeated once and for all. Them," he added grimly, "and this haint that's tormenting you."

At this Nyame's face twisted into anger for a brief moment. Then he exhaled and pointed to a palace with seven towers, off by itself in the foothills of the soaring mountain range.

"That is Anansi's palace. If you want a clue about the Story Box's whereabouts, I would start there. Do not mistake me, Anansesem—this will be no easy quest. If you continue, you will be risking your life and the lives of your friends. But you must try, and so I give you these words of advice."

I stood up straighter, ready to receive some profound words of wisdom.

"Those who help you may not be on your side, and those who oppose you can be your greatest allies."

I waited for more, but Nyame just clasped his hands again and stared out, wise and all-knowing, like he'd just dropped some crazy freestyle bars and the crowd was going wild.

Nah.

I cleared my throat. "Um . . . is that it?"

He turned, surprised. "Yes. Do you need me to repeat it?"

"No, but, like . . . can you elaborate?"

"I don't understand."

"I mean, why does everything gotta be so mysterious? Can't I get a clear instruction or something? A manual? A step-by-step guide to being a hero?"

"But . . . that's not how this works." The sky god looked confused.

"But you're a god, right? Can't you just abracadabra me a quest translator so I can make sure I'm doing the right thing?"

"No! Heroes don't—"

"I'm not a hero. I'm a boy with a crew straight out of a dusty fairy-tale book, and everybody expects me to confront beasts and monsters and fly around on a raft. I don't even like flying. I'm scared of heights. There, I said it."

"But—" Nyame looked worried now.

"And I don't even get a sword or a spear or a magical slingshot?"

"You've got the adinkra of the gods! What more—?"

"Man, you gave me a charm from the department store.

Dad gives those to Mom when he forgets her birthday, and you expect it to make me clairvoyant against evil. Okay." I shook my head. The confusion in Nyame's golden eyes as he watched me walk away nearly made me laugh.

It would have been funny if my life wasn't on the line.

28
ANANSI'S LAIR

EVEN FROM UP HIGH AND AT A DISTANCE, ANANSI'S PALACE LURED your eyes. Partially hidden in a valley on the outskirts of the Golden Crescent, near the intimidating mountain cliffs of what Chestnutt called Isihlangu, it was surrounded by seven spiraling towers made of ivory and gold. Ayanna had to circle a few times to find a place to land the raft among the foothills. If Nyame's magnificent home displayed the sky god's wealth and power, Anansi's emphasized his cleverness.

"How do we get in?" Ayanna asked when we were on the ground. She whispered a soft, musical phrase and the raft shrank down to a size she could carry on her back.

Chestnutt spread out some papers she'd brought from the Warren to study, while Gum Baby snoozed under a blanket on the grass nearby.

Anansi's adinkra was front and center on each tower, painted in a shiny gold that drew your attention. But the most amazing feature was the braided silk that linked each tower in a glittering web. If you looked at them from one angle, the threads were invisible. Turn your head a bit, and suddenly they—and white fuzzy lumps scattered along them— popped into view.

And, at the center of the web high above us, in the middle of all seven towers, sat the palace.

I mean, Chicago had some impressive skyscrapers, but this was incredible.

"How *do* we get up there?" I asked Chestnutt.

The little bunny continued to rifle through her notes, but she kept shaking her head.

"I don't know. The only thing I see mentioned is that no one has ever gotten inside. Ever." She looked up and rubbed at her whiskers in frustration. "The Warren rates this place a five-out-of-five-paws difficulty."

I glanced at Ayanna. "Can we just fly up there on your raft?"

"I don't know." She chewed her lip. "Something about this bothers me."

I studied the courtyard, with its marble flagstones, several of which were broken. Giant scars sliced through one spot, as if an oversize claw had ripped the earth. More of those weird lumps were scattered here and there.

The obvious treasure dangled just out of reach. A desperate

person—say, someone trying to get the spider god to fix a mistake that had stirred up monsters—why, that person might try anything to get to Anansi in the palace above. If someone tried just a little harder, maybe attempted to climb the towers, or use a magic raft...

"It's a trap," I said slowly. "That palace is bait. I bet...I bet if we looked carefully, we'd find more of those threads all around the clearing. And that means those lumps—"

Ayanna's eyes widened, then she wrinkled her nose. "Oh, gross. Are those...?"

I nodded. "People who tried to find Anansi, got wrapped up in the web, and..."

"People...or iron monsters."

"Those, too."

As if on cue, one of the lumps on the ground wriggled, scaring the mess out of me. I might've squealed. But it was only Gum Baby throwing off her blanket. She sat up and hurled a sap ball at my head.

"SAP ATTACK! Who need hurting? Who dead? What happened?"

I rubbed the stinging, sticky spot near my ear. "Nobody. Go back to sleep."

"Shoot, you ain't gotta tell Gum Baby twice. Y'all boring anyway." Sure enough, three seconds later the little loudmouth was back to snoring.

Ayanna chuckled, then sighed. "Okay, so now what? I don't see any way we're getting in."

"Yeah, I don't—" I stopped and stared at her, then held up my wrist.

Nyame's adinkra dangled from my bracelet, and the sky god's words echoed in my ears.

It will bring focus to your surroundings.

"I think I have an idea." I took a deep breath and closed my eyes. Anansi's palace had hundreds of stories whispering all around it. I could hear them, feel them, and more important, when I gripped the Gye Nyame adinkra tight and opened my eyes, I could *see* them.

"Sweet peaches," I whispered.

Anansi's threads crisscrossed the valley, and they were anchored everywhere. I mean, *everywhere*. Boulders, bushes—some smaller strands even clung to our clothes. They shimmered and rippled, and when I looked closer, I realized that the threads were fragments of stories—actual lines from tales I vaguely remembered—spun into golden silk.

"Tristan!" Ayanna's eyes widened when I turned to her, and Chestnutt squeaked in surprise.

"What?"

"Your eyes... They're glowing!"

I began to splutter in protest, but something shiny caught my attention. Behind them, a giant cylindrical boulder was gleaming as brightly as the towers in the valley. As if...

"That's no boulder," I said, realization smacking me in the face.

"What are you babbling about, Bumbletongue?"

Oh, no, that wasn't realization. That was Gum Baby whacking me upside the head as she climbed onto my shoulder with a yawn.

I rolled my eyes. "I said, that's no boulder. It's another building." I ran up to the half-buried structure, and after a quick search, found a hidden door that we'd walked right past, except now it shimmered like sunshine on water. "Follow me," I said, and stepped into Anansi's home.

The descent into the underground lair took longer than I thought it would, partly because the curving staircase was covered in invisible booby traps. If it weren't for Nyame's gift, which enabled me to see them, we would've been splattered across the stone walls several times over.

Also, every ten seconds or so, Chestnutt wanted me to stop so she could take notes. "They're sure to let me into the Warren Society after this," she said when I asked what she was doing. Even though I was impatient to find out if Anansi was hiding below, I bit my tongue and let her do her thing. There really wasn't any reason for Chestnutt to be excluded from Brer's army of bunny spies—from what I'd seen, she was more than capable. He was just being his typical annoying self.

We reached the bottom of the stairs like a slow-moving train of caution. I clutched the Gye Nyame adinkra, Ayanna clutched my arm, Gum Baby rode in my hoodie, and Chestnutt brought up the rear. A thick wooden door awaited, covered in cobwebs and dusted with golden Alkean greetings, and I eased it open, flinching as something tickled my head. I peeked inside, yelped, and quickly shut it again.

"What? What is it? What did you see, Tristan?" Ayanna whispered.

"An iron monster!"

"What?"

I hid behind the door, my heart thumping in my chest, as Ayanna and Chestnutt huddled next to me. Gum Baby crawled carefully out of my hood and put her ear to the door.

"Why ain't it trying to attack?" she asked.

I looked over my shoulder at Ayanna. That was a good question. There was nothing but silence inside. I cracked the door open and peeked in again.

Nyame's adinkra gave me the gift of sight, but it framed everything in golden words that told Alkean stories. Anansi's table was outlined by a snippet of a fable. A bed was covered in a spread made of lullabies. The cooking pots and the kettle were rimmed with opening prayers.

But the object that had frightened me half to death, standing right in the middle of the room, was the golden silhouette of a fetterling, poised to attack, with legends coiling around its chain body.

We tiptoed inside, and I found a torch lying on the floor. Ayanna lit it, and light flickered in the abandoned tower.

"Sweet peaches," I breathed.

Ayanna pursed her lips and didn't speak.

Chestnutt started scribbling furiously.

Gum Baby hopped down and stomped across the floor. "Is this what Gum Baby thinks it is?"

I let go of Nyame's adinkra—the strain of seeing so much detail was giving me a headache. My vision slowly returned to normal. "If you're asking me *Is that a fetterling tied up in a spider's silk*, then yes. If you're asking *Are those more fetterlings tied up next to the table, with what looks to be notes*, also yes."

Ayanna moved farther into the room, carefully. "Anansi was studying the iron monsters? Why?"

The fetterling in the center of the room looked like it belonged in a museum. The Weaver's silk held the monster tight, its manacle-hands in mid-attack, its collar-head in mid-snap. Several others were in various stages of dismantlement in the corner, and bits of chain were scattered across the table.

"I don't know," I barked. "But he's not here. Which means we're stuck. Again." A wave of anger boiled in my stomach, and I slammed a fist onto the table, scattering papers and chains onto the floor.

Chestnutt started rustling through Anansi's notes while Ayanna sighed.

"What do we do now?"

I threw up my hands. "I don't know! This whole trip has been one failure after another. That stupid haint has my friend locked up in ghost prison, and I'm never gonna get him back. And I'm also never getting home at this rate!"

"Hey—" Chestnutt began, but Ayanna cut her off.

"It's not all about you, flyboy! We're losing our home as we speak!"

"I know that—"

"Well, then think of others before you start complaining."

Chestnutt hopped closer, holding some papers. "Um—"

I gritted my teeth and glared at Ayanna. "How about you get off my back?"

Her hands went to her staff, and I gripped the gloves in my pocket, just as two large balls of sap pelted us both between our eyes.

"Y'all being rude!" Gum Baby aimed another glob at us. "Gum Baby always gotta be the mature one. Chestnutt is *trying* to educate your ignorant butts. Now stop fighting and apologize."

Ayanna and I eyed each other. Gum Baby raised her sap balls higher, and I sighed. "I'm sorry. You're right, I'm not the only one who's lost something."

Ayanna grunted. "Yeah. I'm sorry, too."

Gum Baby lowered her arms. "Good. Now sit on the floor, crisscross applesauce."

I frowned. "What?"

"You heard Gum Baby!"

Ayanna shook her head. "I'm not sitting in this—"

"GUM BABY SAID SIT CRISSCROSS APPLESAUCE, SO YOU DO IT, OR GUM BABY'S GONNA TURN THIS WHOLE TRIP AROUND! NOW SIT!"

Somehow Ayanna and I were sitting, hands in our laps, and Gum Baby sniffed. "Good. Chestnutt?"

Chestnutt looked embarrassed, but she stood on her hind paws and held up a note. "I . . . I think I know where the Story Box is."

I gawked, and Ayanna choked on air. "Where?"

"It looks like Anansi was studying how and why the iron monsters are drawn to stories, and he even managed to capture a few, but . . . I think something went wrong. More of them came and attacked him."

A chill went down my spine, and I examined the room as Chestnutt continued. It looked like a meeting had taken place there. Several dishes and cups were knocked over. Whatever had happened, Anansi and his guest had been interrupted, and judging from the mess, a great struggle had occurred. But who—?

The answer struck like lightning.

"Brer Rabbit," I whispered.

"What?" Ayanna looked around. "Where?"

"No. He said he and Anansi were working on a project for the Story Box, and then iron monsters attacked."

"According to this entry here," Chestnutt said, "something stronger than fett—those things over there came along, and Anansi fled. I guess Brer Rabbit did, too. But before they did, it looks like Anansi sent the Story Box somewhere impenetrable. Where no one could get it until he was ready to retrieve it."

"Okay," I said, impatient. "So where is it?"

Chestnutt gulped, and instead of replying, she turned over the note. Everybody gasped.

The schematic of a dark, foreboding mountain range was scrawled on the paper, showing tunnels, access points, and exits.

The same mountain range rising in the distance beyond the Golden Crescent.

"I think he hid it in the Ridge."

29
ROCK LASERS

GUM BABY SCRAMBLED UP TO HER FAVORITE PERCH IN MY HOOD
and propped her elbows on my shoulders as we left Anansi's
home. "The Ridge, huh? Gum Baby heard some crazy things
about that place."

In Ayanna's arms, Chestnutt nodded. "Yup, yup. A mountain fortress. Nothing gets in or out without going through
twelve levels of inspection. They're very territorial."

"Yes," Ayanna agreed. "MidPass and the Ridge have never
gotten along. Something to do with the stories of Alke, and
which belonged to whom." She pulled the raft from over her
shoulders, laid it down, whispered something, and the raft
grew to its normal size. She stepped on, set Chestnutt down
in the middle, then raised an eyebrow. "Well, are you coming?" she asked. "We've got floating rock lasers to sneak past."

"Wait, wait. Run that by me again?" I said.

"You heard me," Ayanna said as she went through her checks.

"No, I don't think I did, because it sounded like you just said we'll have to dodge rock lasers."

"I did."

"Aaaaaaaand that's where you lost me."

Gum Baby climbed down my back and stalked around the raft with tiny footsteps, muttering to herself. Chestnutt began sketching something on the floor of the raft.

"Rock lasers shouldn't be a thing," I said. "Why are they a thing?"

Ayanna opened her mouth, closed it, then spoke in a rush. "Remember Kumi? The statue sentry from Nyame's palace? It's like that. The first line of defense."

"That's supposed to make me feel better?"

She threw up her arms. "What do you want me to say? The Ridge people don't like visitors. And if they sense for one second that their homes are under attack, they'll send out every warrior they have." In a sudden fury, she stabbed the air with a finger like she wanted to pin me to the raft. "So you'd better be absolutely sure about this. Because it's . . ." Some of the heat faded from her eyes as she turned to fasten her staff to the back of the raft. "This is going to be hard."

Chestnutt hopped over and nuzzled Ayanna's leg, and the pilot stooped over, picked her up, and buried her face in the bunny's fur. Then she set Chestnutt down, cleared her throat, and nodded. "Let's go over the plan. Maybe this time something will go right for once."

Chestnutt sat back on her hind legs and pointed at the map she'd drawn on the raft floor. "This is our target. The Ridge. A heavily defended, fiercely guarded, fortified city high up inside Isihlangu."

"Isihlangu?" I repeated with a frown. "Does that name mean anything?"

"It means *shield*."

A shiver rippled down my spine. I squinted at the thick black section Chestnutt had drawn as she continued.

"But Isihlangu isn't just any mountain. It's a wall of rock so steep and high that its peaks are hidden in the clouds. The people used to come down and trade—at least that's what the records in Anansi's palace said—but ever since the iron monsters started boiling out of the Burning Sea, they've stayed behind their gates."

Chestnutt paused and I looked at Ayanna. "Having second thoughts?" she asked me. "Just wait, it gets better."

I ignored her, then turned pointedly back to Chestnutt. "Okay, it's a tough walnut to crack. But it can be cracked, right? We can get in there somehow."

Chestnutt cleared her throat. "Yup, yup. Well, sort of. Maybe."

"Maybe?"

"I mean, I think it'll work. Hopefully."

"Hopefully?" My voice started to rise, and Chestnutt hurried to continue.

"See, look at these." She tapped a paw on a section of the drawing where it looked like a series of trails went up the mountain. "They need some way of getting food from the farms at the bottom of the mountain to the city at the top. So they built these trams. They even carry passengers."

"Like trains," I said. "So we'll ride with the other passengers?"

"Oh no. They'd see we're strangers. We're going to hide in the back, with the trash."

I stared at her.

"With the trash?"

"Yup, yup! Only for a little bit, and then, before we're discovered, we'll slip off into a ventilation tunnel. Hopefully."

"Assuming that works," said Ayanna, "what do we do once we get to the top?"

The bunny took a deep breath before saying, "According to my cousin Lily, who heard it from her sister Apple, whose best friend's mother's second cousin, Tulip, traveled there with a trading party one time, the people of the Ridge have a vault where they keep their most valuable items. They call it the Atrium. Anansi circled it on this diagram." She pulled out a page she'd taken from the Weaver's workroom.

I squinted at it. "The Atrium, huh?"

"That's gotta be where the Story Box is. Yup, yup," said Chestnutt, hopping excitedly.

"All right." I looked at my squad. "So we catch the tram, make our way to this Atrium, snag the Story Box, and high-tail it out of there. Sounds easy enough."

Ayanna didn't look convinced. "But first, we have to avoid those floating rock lasers. Everybody, hang on tight—I need to be sure you're not rolling about, getting sick over everything."

My stomach lurched at the thought.

"And, Gum Baby?" Ayanna said. "Get ready for some pre-coffinary measures."

"AAAAAHHHHH!"

Have I mentioned that I don't love heights? If it weren't for the fact that the island of MidPass, hundreds of Midfolk, and the spirit of my dead best friend depended on me, I would've called it a night.

"AAAAAHHHHH!"

Silver and black lightning bolts were being hurled at us by giant black stone towers with jewels at the tops, but that was no reason to panic, now was it?

"AAAAAHHHHH!"

I lay on my back on the raft, spread-eagled so I looked like a brown X, my hands and feet stuck in mounds of sap. Why? Well, flying rafts don't come with seat belts, and the rock lasers were all riled up.

"Will you stop screaming!" Ayanna yelled at me.

She stood in a crouch, both hands on her staff as the wind whipped her braids behind her. She flinched to her right, and all of a sudden the raft tilted sharply, and, regrettably, I was unable to follow her instructions.

A blast of night-dark lightning (Nightning? Did I just make up a word? IT'S TRADEMARKED, CHUMPS, HANDS OFF!) whizzed by and scorched the earth below. I could smell burning grass and dirt.

"Make them stop shooting at us!" I hollered.

Chestnutt huddled in a corner, the straps of my backpack— which Ayanna had secured to the raft—crisscrossed over her little body like a harness. She squeezed her eyes shut and her ears lay flat against her head.

Ayanna gritted her teeth. "Oh, I'm sorry. Allow me to make that request."

Another blast barely missed our heads. I opened my mouth to scream, but Gum Baby's voice cut me off.

"We're almost clear, Ayanna! Just one more! Ready?"

I looked up, pressing my chin to my chest to focus on the doll at the front of the raft. She stood with her legs spread wide, her hands on her hips, and her miniature braids pulled back in a ponytail.

"Ready for what?" I looked back at Ayanna. "Ready for what?"

She grimaced. "Something I hoped we wouldn't need to

do, but if we don't shut down these lasers, reinforcements will be all over us."

"Um—"

"GB!" she yelled, talking right over me. "Here we go!"

Gum Baby nodded. Ayanna tightened her grip on the staff and glanced at me. "Hold on tight."

I tried to crane my neck as far up as I could. "But I'm already stu— OOOOOHHHHH!"

The raft jerked to the right just as a polished rock tower the size of a skyscraper appeared in our path. Perfectly smooth, like a cylinder of black glass, it stretched way above us. As we circled it, rising in a spiral, the sheer height of the thing blew my mind. Jagged blue sapphires and purple amethysts floated in a space cut way at the top, and they flashed in warning, like a lighthouse. The hairs on my arms stood up straight, and then, with a crackling burst, another blast of nightning shot out of the precious stones. The raft swung sideways to avoid it, and Ayanna yelled.

"Now, Gum Baby!"

But our fearless little marksman—markswoman (marks-doll-baby?)—was already taking aim and screaming at the top of her lungs.

"Sap attack! Sap, sap, sap, sap attack! Super sap attack!"

Glob after sticky glob of sap landed right in the center of the blinking gems, dousing the beams of light, and Gum Baby waved her hands urgently.

"Go, go, go!"

Ayanna pulled back on the rudder, and the raft peeled away, diving toward the rocky slope far below. The shiny tower whizzed by as we dropped, and then a rumble sounded high above us. The sap must have gummed up the works, because a deafening *crack* echoed down the mountainside.

Chestnutt squealed in fright, and I clenched every muscle as the tower began to lean to one side. Its top was gone—a smoking crater was all that remained. The structure continued to topple until it hit the mountainside with a thunderous *boom* and rolled down the slope in pieces.

"So much for stealth," I muttered. "Can someone un-gum me now?"

Ayanna ignored me, focusing on keeping the raft low to the ground. Gum Baby hopped on my chest. She squatted and patted me on the jaw.

"Gum Baby would help, but she don't do 'un-gum.' So sit tight, big boy. Enjoy the rest of the flight." She sat on my chest and leaned back, rolling her little head like she was stretching her neck, and sighed. "This is nice. We should do this more often."

I growled. "I'm gonna—"

"I see the tram!" Ayanna called.

A long dark trench sliced through the steep slope of Isihlangu, stretching up into the clouds, where it disappeared.

At the bottom was a gleaming silver train, its line of cars nearly vertical as it waited to travel up the mountain.

A piercing whistle sounded, and Ayanna's face grew worried.

"They're about to leave. Hold on!"

She aimed the raft straight down, and we dropped like an anchor. The wind pulled the scream from my mouth, and my lips flapped like I was blowing a thirty-second raspberry. The train grew bigger and bigger, and Gum Baby cackled louder and louder as we got closer and closer.

"Ayanna," I tried to say calmly as we flew at full speed toward the rear of the train. The lip of the canyon zipped past in a blur.

"Ayanna?"

The last car on the train had an open door, wide enough to hurl garbage in and out of, I guessed. That's where the raft was heading. That itty-bitty entrance.

"Ayanna!"

I looked back and my heart skipped a beat. She wore a grim, determined expression and I swallowed, then squeezed my eyes shut tight. The last thing I heard was Gum Baby's shrieking in my ear.

"Aha-ha-ha-ha, y'all ain't ready for this! Gum Squaaaaad!"

Whump!

30
INTO ISIHLANGU

IT WAS DARK, AND SOMETHING SQUISHY PRESSED AGAINST MY ARM.

"I . . . want to go home."

My hands were still glued, or gummed, to the raft, which had landed. Something else—slimy and cold—touched my face, just above my mouth, and I couldn't free my arms to brush it away. I kept my lips very still as I spoke. "I really . . . really . . . want to go home."

The floor of the tram vibrated, and it felt like we were aiming straight toward the sky.

Something rustled next to me, and then the darkness disappeared as whatever was lying on top of me was pulled off. Ayanna held on to a metal pole that ran from floor to ceiling, an exasperated look on her face.

"This," she said, waving her arms up at the front of the tram. "This was all your idea. You don't get to whine, flyboy."

She touched her staff to the raft, and the wood warmed

beneath my wrists and ankles. The gummy restraints loosened and I dropped down, crashing into the back wall.

"Oof!"

Ayanna snorted. "When you're done being goofy, you should take a look at this."

As I watched her use some handholds to climb to the top—or front of—the tram car, I made a face at her back. When I sat up, my face froze that way.

I was sitting in Alke's version of a subway. Chicago's L train was nothing compared to this.

I mean, the rear half of the train car was disgusting, but it was all our fault. It was the trash car, after all. When we landed, we'd knocked over thin, papery containers filled with garbage. Old clothes were strewn across the floor, and bags of rotten food had splattered the walls. I shuddered. It was like we were riding in the loader of a garbage truck. Ever smelled the nasty trash water they drip behind them? Yeah, I needed a bath. Two baths. With a shower in the middle. A clean sandwich.

I groaned as I pulled myself upright. I slid closed the door we had entered so the trash wouldn't fall out and give us away. Then I scrambled to join the others.

A shimmering curtain of light separated the rear half of the car from the front. When I passed through the divider, I felt a tingling sensation from head to toe, and the scents of lemon, ginger, and fresh air washed over me. I closed my eyes. When I opened them, all traces of our nasty landing had been removed.

"Man," I breathed. "I need one of those curtains in my bedroom."

This part of the tram car had a soft silver glow. Ayanna and Chestnutt sat in slightly inclined bucket seats that were beaded in beautiful patterns. Gum Baby stood on the back of Chestnutt's chair. They stared at the scenery out of floor-to-ceiling windows.

As I approached Ayanna—very slowly and carefully—she nodded toward the outside. "Look."

I collapsed into a seat next to her, whispering a prayer of thanks for the harness I strapped on, then gazed out the window—

—and gasped.

I had seen the train's vertical position from the air, but it was even more intense when you were actually inside it. We were climbing straight up the side of Isihlangu. The walls of the trench we were moving through had dropped, and the view beyond stretched for an eternity. The valley of the rock-laser sentinels lay far below. The mountainside was streaked with sparkling black and blue lines, like the veins of some giant we little insects were inching across. When I pressed my face against the window, I could see the mountain peaks disappearing into the clouds.

"Look." Chestnutt pointed out tiny turret-like rocks with

the same gems rotating in them. The tram zipped past a series of them, and suddenly hitching a ride in a trash train didn't seem so bad.

Between the rock lasers, the sheer mountain face, and its completely obscured city on top, the Ridgefolk really did seem to discourage visitors.

Yay.

Ayanna nudged me. "This is our stop."

Gum Baby scrambled back behind my head and into my hood, and Ayanna picked up Chestnutt. I frowned. "But we're still moving."

"And we don't want to be on board when it stops," said Ayanna. "Unless you want to introduce yourself to a group of angry guards."

"Ah. No. No, I do not."

Ayanna expanded the raft, we all stepped on board, and we floated through the cleansing curtain and back into the trash compartment. The bits of nastiness whirled around when I slid open the door, and I flinched as something wet splashed against my bicep.

Chestnutt poked her head out of the crook of Ayanna's arm. "Wait for it. A service entrance should be coming up in three . . . two . . . one—now."

The raft shot out of the tram, through a small cloud of mist that felt cool on my skin, and into a hole cut into the smooth exterior of Isihlangu. Ayanna set us down just inside the entrance, and more veins of blue silver lit the passage beyond.

Chestnutt hopped down and her ears twitched forward. After a second, she turned around. "I don't hear anything."

"Something went right for a change," Ayanna muttered softly. "The guards must've been distracted by the laser-tower explosion. Well, let's not waste the opportunity. They know something's wrong. We need to get in, grab the Story Box, and get out."

Gum Baby nodded and leaned forward by my ear. "Don't touch any strange statues this time, Bumbletongue," she whispered.

"Me? You're the one who—"

Ayanna hissed and glared at us. "Hush!"

"But—"

"Quiet! You're going to get us caught."

I shook my head as Gum Baby cackled softly in my hood and followed the others deep into the mountain.

The tunnel twisted and turned for several hundred feet. As we moved farther inside, the vibration I'd felt earlier grew stronger.

"What is that noise?" I whispered.

Ayanna shrugged. Gum Baby ignored me and hummed a few bars from the song she'd been making up. She called it "The Ballad of Gummy." It was catchy.

Chestnutt glanced back. "The Warren doesn't know about

this. It's one of the few places we can't get into. My aunt's best friend's cousin said they've caught every kit sent here."

My eyes grew wide. "You mean baby rabbits? What happens to them? They don't..."

Chestnutt shook her head. "Nope, nope, nothing like that. They just send them home with an insult. *Better luck next time*—that sort of thing, only ruder."

"Oh."

"That's why this is so incredible. If I can bring new information back to the Warren Society, they'll have to let me in. They just have to."

I heard the same longing in her voice that Gum Baby had when she dreamed about becoming a pilot. Ayanna and I exchanged glances. We all had something to prove to someone, even if it was just ourselves.

The tunnel widened and brightened, and the exit appeared around a curve. Chestnutt and Ayanna peeked out first. They gasped.

"What? What is it?" I whispered.

Ayanna muttered something that sounded suspiciously like a prayer, then motioned me and Gum Baby forward. "Come on, we're wasting time."

I stared at her as I stepped out of the tunnel. She was so confus—

My stomach flipped and flopped as I saw that I was on a very thin ledge with a steep drop-off.

"I hate heights."

Gum Baby leaned over my shoulder and whistled. "Boy, you in trouble. Let Gum Baby know if you scared. If you scared, say you scared. Ain't no shame. Gum Baby got this."

I swallowed and crept out a little farther.

Isihlangu was almost completely hollow. I don't know what I expected, but there really was a city inside a mountain. Obsidian towers and spires rose out of the walls at an angle. Thousands of homes had been cut into the rock, and each had a single large gemstone embedded above its entrance, like a diamond porch light. Glimmering tracks of blue-black amethysts crisscrossed the vast open space, connecting one side of the underground city with the other.

I gripped my chest. "Are they . . . are they *skateboarding* across?"

A trio of Ridgefolk—I couldn't tell their ages from here—rode across the chasm at breakneck speed a few levels down. They stood on wide, flat oblong slabs of obsidian that hovered over the amethyst rails. My eyes widened at the vicious club-like staffs strapped to their backs. I could hear them laughing from here. Kids? They disappeared beneath the ledge we hid on, and Ayanna hissed at me.

"Hurry up, flyboy, unless you want to get caught!"

After one more stomach-tightening glance over the edge, I followed Ayanna and Chestnutt up the winding path.

The ballad of the gummy, ballad of the gummy.

Strongest and the fiercest, and her nose is never runny.

Sap attack, back it back, the hero of the hour.

Riding on her bumbly steed, who needs to take a shower."

I rolled my eyes as Gum Baby hummed the rest of the song under her breath. *Bumbly steed.* The nerve!

"There it is," Chestnutt whispered. She pointed near the ceiling. "That has to be it."

What I'd thought was the ceiling was really the bottom of a giant room carved into the mountain peak. The ledge we stood on curved around several more times before it disappeared inside.

A booming sound shook the mountain, throwing me flat to my stomach.

"What was that?" Ayanna asked. Her voice trembled just a bit—I didn't blame her. Mine came out in a high-pitched squeak as I peeked over the edge.

"Don't know." I cleared my throat. "Wait. Something's happening down there."

The large main doors were opening. A group of Ridgefolk floated in on obsidian hoverboards. They slowed to a stop for just a second before spreading out and taking off in different directions.

I looked up. "They're searching for something."

Ayanna met my eyes, then nodded. "Us. That boom must have been an alarm signal. We need to hurry."

We scurried up the ledge, trying to keep low, and, after

several nerve-racking minutes, we reached the final curve. The Atrium. Two giant doors stood ajar and I breathed a sigh of relief. It was unlocked. Ayanna looked at me, and I swallowed and moved to the front. Gum Baby bounced up and down in my hood.

"Game time, big boy."

"Yeah, yeah." I thumbed the adinkra on my bracelet. Eddie's Anansi symbol was cool to the touch, as was Nyame's. No iron monsters or booby traps here.

Just a mountain full of angry Ridgefolk.

"Strongs keep punching," I muttered. Then I took a deep breath and darted inside, ready with my empty sack for a snatch-and-grab, a dine-and-dash (not exactly the same, but you get the concept). The only thing missing was a dope soundtrack to this epic heist we were about to pull off.

Ayanna pushed in behind me and jabbed me in the ribs. "Why are you humming? You want to get us caught? Idiot."

My face flushed as we stepped into the room. "Don't poke me! And we won't get caught. I"—we both froze as the wickedly sharp tips of three spears were leveled at our faces—"promise."

31
THE ELDERS

THE SPEARS DIDN'T WAVER. I SWALLOWED AND LOOKED PAST them to the people—guards, I guess—holding them. They wore long blanketlike cloaks with mesmerizing stitched and beaded patterns. The material seemed to absorb light, and if I gazed at the beads too long, they started to glow and burn my eyes, like I was staring into the sun. Their faces were wrapped in cloth so only their eyes could be seen—bright, glittering eyes that watched my every movement. Two of them wore beaded headwraps, and the third had bead bracelets around the wrists and ankles. When I flinched from the glare of a bracelet, the guard in front glowered at me even harder.

All in all, they were beautiful, and I could've stood there for hours gawking, but I needed to do something.

I cleared my throat and stepped forward with my hands up. "My name is—"

All three cloaks were thrown aside as the guards dropped into fighting stances. Chestnutt squeaked in alarm.

"Tristan," Ayanna whispered.

I swallowed and backed up.

The spears were about as long as Ayanna's staff and had wide leaf-shaped blades the size of footballs. And now, in addition to those, each guard produced one of those polished clubs the patrollers had been carrying.

Okay. Yeah.

"You will come with us. You will speak before the council." The guard in the front spoke through her face covering in a soft but clear voice. "Or you will speak to my kierie." She twirled her club in her left hand, and my eyes followed the wicked head of the weapon.

I gulped. "Yep. Yes. Yes, we will, that's what we'll do. Right, y'all?"

"Yes!"

"Yup, yup!"

"Gum Baby ain't going nowh—*uuurgghh*—"

Ayanna had grabbed Gum Baby and covered her mouth. The lead guard's eyes narrowed, but she nodded to her comrades.

"Take them."

One guard picked up Gum Baby and Chestnutt by their necks. The other guard tied Ayanna's and my wrists in front of us with strips of cloth. They marched us out of the Atrium and into chaos. The guard nearest me slipped the cover down off her face—it was a girl just a few years older than me—and she grabbed me by the collar and hissed, which I guessed was supposed to be a warning.

Outside, the entire population of the Ridge seemed to line the walkway that spiraled down the interior of the mountain. Apparently, everybody in Isihlangu had come to witness the commotion, and all of them were armed. Men, women, and children gripped clubs and scowled as we passed. Nobody spoke.

Well, nobody from the Ridge.

"Get your hands off Gum Baby! This ain't no hug-fest. Who you frowning at? Better send those looks that way— Gum Baby ain't the one."

I gritted my teeth. "Gum Baby," I muttered, "maybe you can, I don't know, *not* harass our captors?"

"Gum Baby ain't caught," she said, sniffing in contempt. "She's escorting y'all for your own protection."

I started to say something else, then shut up when my guard waved at me to hush. The other guard dangled Gum Baby and Chestnutt. "What about them, Thandiwe?"

My guard—Thandiwe—pursed her lips, then shrugged. "Bag them" was all she said.

Chestnutt whimpered as she and a now-gagged Gum Baby

were stuffed in a sack. I grimaced—assuming we all survived, I'd never hear the end of it. Thandiwe pushed me toward the edge, and I resisted.

"No, wait—"

"Keep quiet and move," she snapped. "Step down, now."

I tossed a nervous look back, then inched forward to peer over the edge. One of the floating obsidian hoverboards waited, bobbing up and down above a rail. From this close I could see it was bigger than I'd assumed. It was shaped like a wide trapezoid, and there were two indentations in the middle. Two more hoverboards floated on either side, and I realized the guards must've ridden the rails up here—that's how they'd arrived so fast.

Man, that board was really big. Big enough for two people to stand on.

Oh, crap.

"Nope." I shook my head. "I'll walk down."

"What's the matter, thief? Scared?" The girl slipped her kierie into a holster behind her back, so it could join her spear, and folded her arms beneath her cloak. "Having second thoughts?"

I mumbled something.

"What?"

"I don't do heights," I muttered. Ayanna winced.

"Speak up, boy."

"I DON'T DO HEIGHTS!"

The shout echoed throughout the entire mountain. A second passed, and then all the Ridgefolk burst into laughter. And I mean every single one. Even a baby, wrapped behind his mother's back, flashed a gummy grin and drooled at me.

The nerve.

Thandiwe wiped a tear from her eye and gasped for air. "Get on the forebear before you embarrass yourself further." I opened my mouth to protest and her smile disappeared. "Now."

I shut my trap, then took a deep breath and stepped off the edge onto the glass skateboard—the forebear. It sank a little like a boat would in the water, and I held both hands out for balance and shut my eyes.

"Move to the middle, near the back."

I did as I was told, and she smirked and held up two metal loops tied to her belt.

"Hold on tight, or you might fall. That would be a shame."

I took them, squeezed them in my fists, and waited for her signal that we were going to take off. Which is why, when all of a sudden we leaped forward onto the black metal rail and zoomed toward the ground miles below, I screamed at the top of my lungs.

Everything was a blur. The metal hoops bit into my palms as I gripped them harder each time we swerved or dipped or dove. I swear we took the scariest way down. The forebear flicked up and down, left and right, jumping from rail to rail with the slightest movement of the girl's feet. The kids who skated the handrails at the park back in Chicago would've been impressed. Me, too, if I hadn't had to close my eyes every few seconds.

"Are you that scared, thief?"

Thandiwe's voice whipped back to me. I gritted my teeth and didn't answer.

"You brave the wrath of Isihlangu by breaking in, but some wind in your face terrifies you? You are the most pathetic of thieves. I hope the council sends you to the mines for the rest of your miserable life, once you answer for your other crimes."

I opened my eyes again and focused on the beaded wrap on her head. "What other crimes?"

"Don't treat me like I'm stupid," Thandiwe snapped. "We've been hunting for you and the others. You'll talk soon enough. Isihlangu is angry. You'll face the council now."

She tipped the forebear forward and we hurtled down some more, and whatever protests I was going to make died in my throat. I didn't scream again, though. Wasn't going to give her the satisfaction. But as the ground approached and we slowed, questions bounced around my head.

What other crimes?

How can a mountain be angry?

What council?

The forebear stopped on an elevated platform right in the middle of the mountain floor. Great, another stage. Ridge-folk streamed out of their homes carved into the mountain to gather around. They rode their own forebear or doubled or tripled up on someone else's. Ayanna arrived with her guard, a middle-aged woman, and the third guard dumped Chestnutt and Gum Baby next to us. In the process, Gum Baby's gag slipped off, which I was very sorry about.

"Gum Baby gonna act a fool in a second," she promised me, and I shushed her.

The crowd surrounding us filled the cavern, and more zipped around on rails above our heads. Beads of sweat gathered on my forehead. "This isn't an interrogation," I whispered to Ayanna. "This is a trial."

Shuffling sounds came from behind us. An elderly woman, with graying dreadlocks peeking out of a bright yellow head-wrap and wearing a brilliant gold-studded blanket draped over her shoulders, stepped barefoot onto the stone stage.

A hush fell over the crowd.

I gulped. "I guess she's our prosecutor."

A sharp jab in the back cut off my comments. Thandiwe glared at me and took out her kierie again. "You will show the diviner some respect, thief."

Diviner?

I kept my mouth shut, though, and turned around.

"If this is a trial," Ayanna whispered, "where are the judge and jury?"

The old woman raised her arms, and then, in a voice that surprised me with its deep strength and volume, shouted to the top of the mountain.

"Ancestors! Lend your children your guidance and wisdom. We have need! Please, descend from your thrones on high!"

Ayanna and I exchanged confused glances. But before I could say anything, a million pencil-thin beams of light radiated out of the gemstones above every house. They blazed brighter than any sun, and a giant flare exploded silently just above the stage.

I flinched and, with my eyes closed, felt Ayanna do the same.

When I opened them again, a group of men and women sat on stools at one end of the stone stage. I looked around, confused as to where they had come from.

My hands were still tied, but I was able to reach out a finger to touch Nyame's adinkra charm on my opposite wrist. As I did, I peered more closely at the newcomers.

I held back a gasp. I could see *through* them.

"They're spirits," I mumbled, and my knees went limp. "The ancestors."

The ancestor in front was a thin older man, with a heavily

beaded blanket across one shoulder, short curly hair, and a stern expression. The way he sat with one leg crossed over the other reminded me of Granddad. That didn't reassure me.

He nodded at the crowd and bowed to the diviner, who returned an even deeper one.

Finally, he looked at me and my crew, and his eyes narrowed.

"And at last...here you are. I must confess, I am deeply disappointed. You've taken much, boy. You and the others have stolen your last piece of our culture. No more! We will make an example out of you."

I shook my head. "Sir, we didn't—"

"You will not lie to my face!" He stabbed a ghostly finger at us. "You were caught in our trap, plain as day. We knew the trickster would send someone, but children? He is truly desperate."

Gum Baby blew a raspberry. "This is the worst heist Gum Baby has ever been a part of."

"How many heists have you gone on?" I muttered out the side of my mouth.

She counted on her tiny fingers. "Two."

"Not including stealing Eddie's journal?"

"Oh. Um, one. This one."

I snorted, then froze. *Eddie's journal.* An idea tickled the back of my brain. Maybe...just maybe. If I—

The elderly spirit leaned forward, and the others around him floated closer on their stools, until a semicircle of ancestors hemmed us in.

"What's this? Conspiring? No plan will save you and your band of culture-ravagers!"

I licked my lips. This didn't look good. But I couldn't go out like a loser. Somehow, they thought we were a part of some grand circle of thieves, but we were innocent. At least up to that moment. But who would try to break into a fortified mountain, unless they were desperate, like us?

"Speechless!" The spirit pounded his ceremonial stool with the palm of his hand and shook his head. "You have no defense. First you take our people, then our—"

My head snapped up.

Ayanna said, "What?"

"Wait," I interrupted. Thandiwe shifted behind me, but I ignored her and stepped forward. "What do you mean, 'take your people'? You've had people taken, too?"

The elder's eyes narrowed. "Do not play the fool, boy. This is no game. This is the life, the history, and the future of my people! You think you can dance your way into this mountain and slip away with our children's inheritance? With their parents, their brothers, and their sisters?" He slapped his stool again, and when he pointed at us, his finger quivered. "You will tell us why you took them and where they are. One way"—he looked at Thandiwe, who stepped forward with spear and kierie in both hands—"or another."

Chestnutt buried her head in Ayanna's feet, and even Gum Baby gripped my leg tightly. I couldn't let them down. I had led them here—it was my responsibility to get them out.

"Fine," I said.

Go-time.

I stepped forward again—only to stop when the edge of a spear gently touched my neck.

Maybe *not* go-time, then.

"Make your next move very slowly, thief." Thandiwe spat her words out like poison.

Okay, slow-time.

I raised my arms very deliberately, keeping my tied hands outstretched, and prayed that—for once—I knew what I was doing.

"What if I told you I know who took your people? They also took friends of ours and are hunting us even now."

The elder ancestor narrowed his eyes. "You—"

"What if I told you . . ." I said, riding right over his words and the gasps of the audience. "What if I told you that the other lands of Alke are under the same threat? That because no one talked with each other, and"—I pointed around the room, ignoring the spear at my throat—"because you all closed your borders and refused to come out, you and Nyame and everyone else, you failed to protect everything that you loved."

"Be careful, boy," Thandiwe hissed. "Be very careful."

No pressure, then.

I smiled and, keeping my arms raised, wiggled my left wrist. The Anansi adinkra charm caught the light, and a murmur swept through the crowd surrounding the stage.

"Let me tell you a story."

32

SPIRIT OF THE IMBONGI

"A STORY?" THANDIWE STARED AT ME, INCREDULOUS. SHE TURNED to the ancestors. "Honored ones, let me take this...this *pretender*, this prince of thieves, to the mines, where his words will be the only ones he hears in a long time."

Prince of thieves? That was actually pretty cool.

The mines, not so much.

The elder ancestors floated in silence. Finally, the leader scratched his chin—so spirits itched?—and gestured at the diviner standing nearby. "What say you, my Amagqirha?"

The old woman never looked up. She sort of did this thing where she spoke and sang at the same time. If you've ever heard a preacher get excited in the middle of a sermon, you know exactly what I'm talking about. Her voice rang clear and high, surprising me—then again, Nana could seem small and weak, too, until she decided to tell you about yourself.

But this woman, this Amagqirha, she never stopped moving to her own rhythm.

"This one has the blessing of gods and the spirit of the imbongi, Elder Fezile," she said. "I can feel it. If he speaks, Isihlangu should listen."

Murmurs went through the crowd of onlookers as the Amagqirha lifted her head and stared straight through me. Eyes as black as the obsidian dangling above our heads pinned me where I stood.

"Speak, imbongi. Speak."

Her voice tumbled around inside my head as she slowly circled the ghostly ancestors, humming and rattling her beads. Every footstep kicked up a little cloud of dust that flashed silver above the stage. Shadows moved to her beat.

And then... then I felt it.

The story I needed to tell—she was humming it. My fingers started twitching and my foot started tapping.

The ancestors leaned close to one another and talked before coming to some decision.

Chief Elder Fezile looked at me. "Proceed" was all he said.

"May I...?" I asked, holding up my tied wrists. "I can't tell a story without them. I promise I won't hurt anyone."

The chief gave a curt nod, and, with one swipe of her spear, Thandiwe cut my bonds.

I couldn't help it—I grinned as I turned to the crowd.

Ayanna took one look at my face and groaned. "Don't do too much," she whispered.

"Naw, do the most, Bumbletongue," Gum Baby said. "Gum Baby gonna just sit here and watch, but you go ahead and do the most."

Their advice disappeared as the rhythm of the story swelled in my ears. What's a song but a story told to a beat? I waited until the Amagqirha had made a full circle around the gathered ancestors. When I was sure of the rhythm, I joined in.

She hummed, and I stomped. She rattled, and I clapped.

A familiar buzzing grew in my fingertips, the sign that a story needed to be let out. I took a deep breath and concentrated, trying to make sure I got this right. When I couldn't take it any longer, I reached out and grabbed some of the dust the Amagqirha had kicked up, and some of the shadows stretching across the stage. I pulled them into my fists and held them tight.

"Let's say there are monsters," I boomed into the near-silent mountain city. My eyes swept the crowd. The rhythm had caught on, and they were now clapping along.

That's the power of the Anansesem, I realized. Giving the story to the listeners, so they can pass it on to others.

Anansesem shared not only the stories, but also the story-telling experience.

I smiled. "Let's say there are monsters. Let's say they exist. We say this because it's true. Is it true?"

"Yes!" a child yelled before being shushed.

I pointed in the direction of the voice. "Of course it is! Monsters exist all around us. I say Abiyoyo . . ."

I threw some shadow and dust high into the air, and the crowd gasped. The clapping stopped, children shrieked, and more than a few adults backed away as a ten-foot giant appeared. Hulking, menacing, with eyes of blazing silver, Abiyoyo stomped around the stage, roaring silently at children he spotted.

"Listen to your parents, young ones," I called, "or Abiyoyo will come for you. Or maybe the Evil Ones who chased Demane and Demazane!"

The giant faded into a corner, and I threw a little more story into the air. A boy and a girl sprang out of the dust cloud and raced through a forest of inky-black trees. Behind them, shadowy two-legged creatures gave chase, their mouths filled with shiny, razor-sharp teeth. The girl and the boy hid in a cave, and the hungry creatures ran on by, leaping off the stage and into the crowd.

More shrieks rang out, and then nervous laughter rippled through the audience as they realized the conjured creatures had disappeared.

"Yes," I continued, "let's say there are monsters."

I swallowed a lump in my throat. This next part was going to be difficult.

"Let's say there's a *new* monster. Something...something that doesn't want your money or treasures. It doesn't want to eat your children or dreams. No."

I tossed a giant fetterling into the air, and the crowd went deathly silent.

"It wants it *all*."

Thandiwe took a step forward and her arm trembled as she raised it to point at the iron monster. "I've seen this... this thing!" She looked at the ancestors on the stage. "I've seen it."

"It hunts us," I said, turning and stepping up next to her. "It doesn't care if you're from the Golden Crescent or from MidPass. It doesn't care if you're holed up in a thicket the size of Lake Michigan, or in a fortress inside the heart of a mountain. It will find you, your children, all your loved ones, and drag them back to where its boss awaits."

"Its boss?" the elder ancestor said.

I nodded, then tossed the last—and biggest—fistful into the air.

An undefined shape, larger than John Henry, swirled above the stage. Shadows slipped toward it, as if it were a black hole of pure evil. As the form fed, it grew and grew, until it nearly covered the entire stage, and when it had gorged on all the shadows it could find, it turned and floated toward the crowd. At the last moment, just when it looked as if it would descend and begin ravaging the Ridgefolk, I stomped my feet and shouted at the same time:

"THE MAAFA!"

The monster burst into shadows that fled into the corners. Someone screamed. When I looked around, I saw Gum Baby lying on the floor as if she had fainted. Chestnutt was fanning the little drama queen with her ears.

"But what is it? Why does it hunt us?" Another spirit, a woman with a large headwrap, leaned forward on her cane.

"How can we stop it?"

"What can we do?"

I raised my hands and the ancestors grew silent. "This thing hunts you . . . because of me."

Rumbles of anger and confusion swept the space, but I pressed on. "I come from a place far from here called Alabama. I ripped a hole between our worlds when I damaged an old, powerful Bottle Tree. When I fell through the hole, something came with me. Something old. Something evil. A haint that I freed. Now it's looking for me, and it's riling up an old enemy of Alke from the depths of the Burning Sea—the Maafa."

The ancestors gasped. From the looks on their faces, some—if not most—had been around to witness the battles between the gods and the Maafa. They whispered among each other, and I held up my hands.

"We have to stop these iron monsters—more and more are appearing in Alke, each bigger and eviler than the last, and if we don't find Anansi and get him to fix the hole in the sky, they will overrun us. There will be no place any of us can hide."

I dropped my hands and took a deep breath. The crowd murmured while the elders conferred with each other before the chief, Fezile, finally nodded and looked at me. "We've seen this hole in the sky. If it is indeed fueling the violent energy that is coursing through these 'iron monsters,' we would do well to continue as we have been recently. Remain hidden in the mountain. Lock our doors to all outsiders. Protect our children."

A murmur swept through the crowd, with many nodding. Not all, however. Thandiwe looked unconvinced. But she didn't challenge the chief. My shoulders slumped. This had been a long shot, trying to get the Ridgefolk to help. And I couldn't really blame them.

"I understand," I said. "Believe me, I do. But please listen to me—there is no hiding. These things will find you—all of you—even here." I turned in a circle with my arms up, indicating the entire cavern.

"They even found us in the Thicket!" Chestnutt piped up.

"If you don't want to lose more of your people, we must try," I pleaded. "Please. This—everything, it's . . . it's my fault, and I have to fix it."

When my voice cracked, Ayanna took over. "Nyame's Story Box is the key. We think it's here, and it's the way to lure Anansi . . ."

Fezile looked as if he thought that was a foolhardy plan.

"It has to work," I said, trying to put conviction and confidence into my words. "It just has to." I don't know if I was trying to convince the Ridgefolk or myself.

The elders remained silent for what seemed like forever. I had just about lost any hope of their helping us, when someone spoke up next to me.

"He gave it to us," Thandiwe said quietly.

When I looked over, anger was written all over her face. "Anansi. He waltzed in here, with his charm and his compliments, and presented the Story Box to us. 'A gift,' he said. 'For better relations,' he said. It was a trick!" She spat the words out with a scowl. "Coward. He was running away!"

Thandiwe glanced at me, then turned to the elders. "Honored ancestors, we must return Nyame's Story Box to its rightful place. Let the warriors of MidPass take it back, find Anansi, and make their homes safe again. We would want the same for ourselves."

Shouts of agreement echoed throughout the mountain, growing louder as more children and adults yelled their approval. The chorus grew to a rolling thunder of support, and it felt as if Isihlangu was shaking beneath our feet.

The chief elder turned to the other spirits of the Ridgefolk and conferred. I stepped back next to Ayanna and Chestnutt, and Gum Baby sat up groggily and peered up at me.

"Wha—what happened? What's all the noise about?"

I smiled. "Because you're awesome, that's what."

"Oh." She yawned. "Tell Gum Baby something she don't already know."

I snorted, and Ayanna and Chestnutt laughed. Thandiwe overheard and rolled her eyes as well. She started to say something, but the ancestors broke their ghostly huddle and returned to their floating semicircle.

"It is decided." The chief elder held up his hands for complete silence, then nodded. "We will—"

A chest-thumping roar shook the mountain, sending dust trickling down on everyone's heads.

We all froze.

Then a little girl sitting on her father's shoulders pointed at something above us and screamed. More people in the crowd began shouting and gesturing as well.

Ayanna's eyes grew huge. She grabbed my shoulders and shouted, "Tristan!"

I whirled around, ready for anything.

Well, almost anything.

33
ABIYOYO

"HOW...? WHAT...IS THAT?"

Ayanna shoved me forward. "Stop yammering and fix it! You called him, you send him away!"

The giant shadow of Abiyoyo was stomping around the back of the stage. It swiped at the ancestral spirits, trying to claw their shimmering forms.

"Don't worry!" I called out. "It's just a—"

An arm slashed down viciously, and Ayanna barreled into my shoulder, sending us tumbling.

Deep claw marks gouged the obsidian stage where we'd just been standing.

"Just a what, flyboy?" Ayanna grunted as she stood up. "Just a story?"

I shook my head in disbelief as Abiyoyo roared another challenge. The elders tried to flee, but they seemed tethered in place. The Ridgefolk surrounding the stage scattered left and right, fleeing back to the safety of their homes.

"Tristan!" Ayanna shouted. "Do something!"

"Do what?" I yelled back. My hands felt like they'd fallen asleep with the story still tingling inside of them, and I shook them as I searched for a solution. The charms on my bracelet jingled. I could definitely use their help now....

Wait. Anansi's story thread. I could still feel it—the rhythm. Normally, it faded after I finished shaping a story. But now...electric energy still pounded up my spine and down to my fingertips. Abiyoyo's story wasn't complete.

"Gum Baby, let's go!" I shouted, picking her up and setting her on my shoulder. Then I sprinted across the stage toward where Abiyoyo stalked the Amagqirha.

The Amagqirha held her beaded skirt off the floor and circled the stage in a half-run, keeping the ancestors connected to us as Abiyoyo chased her, stomping and clawing as he went. I dodged between ancestors, apologizing as I ran through their ghostly chairs and stools.

Someone joined me, and I glanced over to see Thandiwe joining the pursuit, her spear drawn.

"Why doesn't she break the connection?" I shouted. "Can't she, I don't know, hang up the spirit phone?" The Amagqirha continued to speak in her humming voice, naming the elders and their lineages. She hopped over one of the guards' kieries and dashed to the other side of the stage, all without losing concentration.

Impressive.

"Gum Baby," I shouted, still running. "I have a plan! Can you slow down the monster?"

"Gum Baby ain't—"

"The feet—throw sap at its feet!"

On cue, the giant tried to stomp on the Amagqirha. Gum Baby made an *Oh!* face, then saluted, flinging sap everywhere.

"Ooh, Gum Baby understands. Gum Baby picking up what you're putting down. She smells what you're cooking. Gum Baby hears—"

"Gum Baby! Just do it!"

"Oh, right!" She hopped off my shoulder and cupped her hands around her mouth. "Hey, dusty feet! Down here. Yeah, right here, big boy. You like stepping on folks? Step on this. Sap attack!"

Sap splattered across the stage, and Gum Baby cartwheeled away. Abiyoyo slowed to a stop, frustrated by the Amagqirha's surprising nimbleness, and his beady eyes swiveled toward the tiny loudmouth. He lumbered after her, but when a blurry foot stepped into one of Gum Baby's sticky traps, he was caught fast. I saw my chance.

"Hey!" I shouted. The rhythm tingled as I pulled small toddler-like shadows from the corners of the mountain. I dressed them in glittering clothes made of silver dust and sent them skipping around the giant's ink-black feet.

"What are you doing?" Ayanna shouted, cowering under a rocky ledge and cradling Chestnutt. "Children? You're sending children against a giant?"

"Trust me," I said. "Do you remember how to keep him away?"

"Tristan—"

"I'm serious!"

Abiyoyo strained, and with a wrenching twist and another roar, he pulled free of the sap.

Thandiwe stopped short behind me. "Um, it was—oh elders, help us—it was . . . the lullaby!" She snapped her fingers. "We sang it every night."

"Right!" I said. More and more shadow children danced out of the corners of Isihlangu. They pranced and whirled in circles around the stage. I gasped from the effort and dropped to a knee. "We need everyone in the mountain to help. It's the only way."

"Everyone?" Thandiwe asked.

"Everyone. You all spread the word. I'll keep him distracted here." Before Ayanna and Thandiwe could argue, I ran to the center of the stage. The little shadow children parted before me and then followed, skipping along.

I hoped this would work.

"Abiyoyo!" I shouted, my hands cupped around my mouth.

The giant paused his efforts to scoop the shadow children into his mouth.

"Abiyoyo!"

Every time I shouted his name, he flinched, like hearing it caused him pain.

Abiyoyo's story is pretty simple. Parents make their children sing his name softly over and over every night before they go to bed, and then it's lights-out, don't make a sound. If you don't obey and go to sleep, the hungry giant will stomp to your house and steal you. And he won't be taking you to play hide-and-seek.

More like fry-and-eat, you get me?

I was betting everything on that lullaby.

The shadow children linked arms and danced in a giant circle around the stage, with a second circle and then yet another inside of the first. Each ring moved in a different direction until a dizzying black-and-silver spiral swirled around us. It left the two of us, the giant and me, face-to-face. Beady silver eyes to handsome, intelligent brown eyes. Super-sharp silver teeth to... well, I brushed my teeth pretty well. Most nights.

ANYWAY...

Abiyoyo spun around with a confused roar. He probably couldn't choose which kid to snack on first. Before he made up his mind, I had the shadow children cup their hands around their silent mouths.

"Now, Ayanna!" I shouted.

High above us, Ayanna clung to Thandiwe's back as they rode up through the mountain on the warrior girl's forebear. At my signal, Ayanna waved frantically at people's doors, and Thandiwe called to them.

None of them opened.

Abiyoyo roared a challenge and stomped toward me. His silver claws scraped stone as he stretched out to grab me, and drops of black drool sizzled as his mouth opened wide to swallow me whole. I flinched out of reach.

"Abiyoyo!"

Claws the size of my arm barely missed slicing me like a loaf of bread. Abiyoyo jerked away as the mountain echoed with his name. The shadow children continued to spin in circles, and as soon as I realized I was still in one piece, I sent them twirling faster and faster.

"Abiyoyo!"

This time my call was echoed above me. Boys and girls stood in their open doorways and shouted at the giant. Even some of their parents and grandparents got into the act.

"ABIYOYO!"

The giant backed away, but my shadow children kept him hemmed in so he couldn't escape. They leaped onto one another's shoulders and swarmed him as now the entire mountain—ghostly ancestors, Ridgefolk, Midfolk, and a boy from Chicago—shouted the giant into submission.

"ABIYOYO!"

With a final roar, the giant splintered into a million tiny fragments of darkness. The mountain folk erupted in a giant cheer. I sagged onto the stone stage floor. The shadow children scampered like kids chasing bubbles, hunting down every last piece of the monster and clutching it tight. They bounced over to me, hopping up and down with pride, and I chuckled wearily.

"Yeah, all right, y'all did good."

"No," a voice said behind me. Ayanna leaped off the forebear as Thandiwe came to a stop. They both ran over, whooping and hollering along with the rest of the Ridgefolk. "*You* did good," Ayanna said. "That was amazing!"

Thandiwe smiled and punched my shoulder. "Not bad, thief."

I smiled and pretended my shoulder didn't hurt. "Thanks."

"Ahem." Someone cleared their throat, and we turned to see the elders gazing at the shadow children.

"Oh, right," I said. I closed my eyes and concentrated, willing the children back to their homes in dark corners and under the moonless sky. With a rush of air, like a balloon released from your hands, the tiny silver-and-black toddlers skipped away, until only one was left. It waved at Gum Baby then dove into the shadow of my leg.

"That was great, Tristan," Gum Baby crowed. "Did you see that giant fall back? He was like, *Oh no, don't, y'all too strong, especially you, Gum Baby, you're really talented and should be cheered, raaaaahhhhhh.*"

I grinned and Ayanna shook her head. Chestnutt hopped over and she and Gum Baby excitedly recounted what had just happened.

The elders and the Amagqirha gathered around, and everybody grew silent.

"Your efforts were admirable," Fezile said. "You have proven yourself to be a true Anansesem. Perhaps…a bit more than was necessary. But, because of this, it is clear to us that the Midfolk need Nyame's treasure." The chief elder stared grimly around the chamber. "If childhood stories can be corrupted even here, at the top of Isihlangu, that gash in the sky is indeed a threat to us. Bring the Story Box!"

At his command, two guards zoomed upward on their hoverboards.

"Thank you, honored ancestors," I said, bowing low. "I won't let you down."

As we waited for the guards to return with the Box, I rocked back and forth on my feet with excitement. Finally, after searching for so long, we were close to being able to fix the damage I'd caused. Once we snared Anansi and convinced him to close up the tear in the sky, the gods and heroes could work together to defeat the iron monsters once and for all. Then it was back to my world.

Within just a few minutes the guards emerged from the crowd, gliding on their forebears, carrying something covered in cloth between them on a little stretcher.

The chief elder nodded, and the guards set the object down in front of me. "Well, go on, Anansesem," he said. "Behold your prize."

The Story Box awaited.

I grinned and reached for the cloth—

—and a sudden electric spike shot through me.

I whirled around. Something had just stepped onto the stage. No, some*one*.

"Tristan? What's wrong?" Ayanna scrunched up her forehead in confusion.

But I couldn't explain it. A person had stepped *out of nothingness* and stood behind the ancestors, watching us.

Watching *me*.

His face was obscured by the hood of a long cloak, and I swallowed as he began to make his way over to me. Who was this? Another story I had forgotten to dismiss? I racked my brain, trying to imagine who I might have called into this world.

"Tristan? Aren't you going to—?"

"I'm afraid he can't rightly do that, Miss Ayanna. Not at all."

The smooth voice had notes of sadness and joy. Like someone getting ready to laugh or cry or both. It made me want to dance and shout, and I could hear tinkling instruments somewhere in the distance as the man stepped into view. He was large—taller than me, but not quite John Henry's size. Once he pushed back his hood, I saw that he had a smooth brown face, dimples that threatened to pull out a wide smile, and tight curly hair so black it shone.

He winked at Ayanna and said, "But I'll take it, sure enough. I'll take it and be on my way, if it pleases you."

The energy rippling off this dude was jaw-dropping. The tingling sensation I normally got in my fingers now stormed through my whole body, like just being near him would make every story funnier and more memorable.

"Who are you?" I squeezed out through gritted teeth. Powerful or not, I wasn't giving up that Story Box. Not now. Not after everything the crew and I had been through. No way, nohow.

"Oh." The man actually had the nerve to be surprised, as if I should know him already.

And . . . everyone *did* seem to know him already. Ayanna's mouth was open so wide I thought I might trip over her chin. Chestnutt trembled as the man walked to center stage to grin cheekily at me. And Gum Baby . . .

"Well, sap Gum Baby down and stick her to a wall. Is that who I think it is?"

The man laughed, a bright and contagious sound that had me smiling along before I could catch myself. "Well, if it ain't GB. How's it flowing?"

"Wait," I interrupted. "You all know this guy?"

Ayanna nodded, but it was Gum Baby who answered.

"Sure do! One of Gum Baby's best students. This is—"

"My name," the man said, "is John, but"—he held out a hand—"you can call me High John."

34
HIGH JOHN

WHEN SCHOOL FIRST STARTED, I ATE LUNCH IN THE LIBRARY ALL
the time. Monday through Friday you could find me huddled behind a large stack of science-fiction novels, scarfing
down a turkey-and-cheese sandwich. I didn't know anyone
well enough to sit with them, and lunchtime was a loud mess
of cliques and conflicts. No slick comments meant no quick
tempers, which meant no even quicker fists. It was best for
me to avoid all that.

So I went to our library. The librarian was cool—Mrs.
Timmons. She would even let me borrow more books than
I was supposed to, because we both loved mythology stories.
Gods or demigods or heroes? Sign me up. Funny, right?

One day I devoured my lunch so I could spend the remaining eighteen minutes devouring the latest graphic novel about
some caped superhero—can't remember which one—when

a reedy voice interrupted me in the middle of a full-battle spread.

"That book is dumb."

The voice came from behind the stack of books on the table. I leaned to the side to see, sitting across from me, a short, scrawny Black boy with a do-it-yourself haircut, thick red-and-black-framed glasses, super-baggy cargo shorts, and a Malcolm X T-shirt.

"Yeah, okay," I said, and went back to my book.

This kid had the nerve to keep talking. "I'm serious. Gimmicks and overpowered, square-jawed jocks. Miss me with that. And the villains are so over-the-top!"

Mrs. Timmons glanced over at us with a frown and I glared at the boy. "Okay, cool." Then I stuck my nose in the book and tried to ignore him.

He was rude enough to scoot his chair around so he could look over my shoulder. I was too flabbergasted to get angry. You know what Nana calls people like him? *Space invaders.* Continually pushing into your personal bubble until you pop. But before I could put him in his place, he held out his hand.

"Edward Garvey. Like Marcus Garvey, except Edward. But everyone calls me Eddie. I just started here this week."

Oh. I mean, what are you supposed to do with that?

I shook his hand. "Tristan," I muttered.

"Cool. But, yo, seriously. That book is dumb."

I sighed, marked my place with a piece of scrap paper, then leaned back in the chair and studied the kid. He had an earnest, honest expression, like he really expected me to debate him on this, when all I really wanted to do was tell him to scram. But . . . I didn't for some reason.

Maybe it was the look.

You know what I'm talking about. That look kids have when they're trying to make friends and aren't sure how they're being received. Hopeful. Anxious. Nervous.

He fiddled with the straps on his book bag and stared at me.

Everybody has a story, Nana used to say when I was younger. *Listen to it, and they'll be friendly. Engage with it, and they'll be your friend.*

Fine.

"So this is dumb," I said, nodding at the graphic novel.

"Yup."

"And I guess you got something better?"

Eddie's eyes lit up. "Only the strongest, smoothest, wildest hero ever. Rides a crow the size of a Cadillac truck—no, a stretch limo! He even has his own walk-up music—they say drums play when he walks."

He started tapping a rhythm on the desk and I started nodding along before I could stop myself. This kid wasn't so bad. He could lay down a pretty solid beat, and besides, I knew where he was heading.

"He used to be a prince," Eddie continued. "In Africa. But he got captured and was forced into slavery. His name—"

"—is High John," I said, cutting him off. "High John the Conqueror."

Eddie's eyes nearly bugged out of his skull. "You know the stories?"

I shrugged. "My grandmother used to tell them."

"Yo, that's so cool! You know those aren't really written down anywhere? They were passed along by word of mouth. Does your grandmother know any other stories?"

"She knows *all* the stories. Trust me. I've been hearing them since I was a baby."

Eddie basically dove into his backpack—while still wearing it, which was impressive—and pulled out a battered leather journal. I wrinkled my nose. It smelled like old hot dogs that had been left in the sun. A strange tassel hung from the top of the book—a worn leather cord, frayed and tied back together in several spots.

"You think she'd tell me some?" He stared at me with a serious look, biting his lip while opening and closing the cover of the journal.

"What?"

"Do you think, if you asked her, your grandmother would tell me some? I collect old folktales and stuff like that."

"Why?" I asked. That didn't seem like the sort of thing a normal seventh grader would do.

"Because. Someone has to. Why not me? I like them. I even got a few drawings of some of the heroes. See? Here's High John. And here's John Henry. He's cool, too, but mostly I love his hammer. And this..."

His drawings were pretty good, I had to admit. Soon we were both huddled over his journal, arguing over what-ifs and team battles. We were both late to our next period, but somehow it didn't matter.

That was the day I'd met my best friend.

High John or High John the Conqueror or John de Conquer.

All names for one of the most fascinating folk heroes I'd ever heard of. John Henry may have been powerful, but High John was power personified.

Now the legend himself—Eddie's favorite—stood there, dressed like the uncle who's always the loudest at the family picnic. Pants a little too short to reach the top of his high-top sandals. Butterfly-collar shirt only halfway buttoned, and peeking out from beneath it was a small drawstring pouch hanging from a cord around his neck.

High John noticed my eyes and smiled, then tucked the pouch back inside his shirt. He stretched and cracked his neck. "We ain't got time to chew the fat. Grab that Story Box for me, will you?"

Ayanna bit her lip. Chestnutt's ears drooped so low they covered her eyes, and Gum Baby looked confused. No one wanted to say anything, and you know what that meant.

Yep.

I had to be the one.

"Mr. High John—"

"Just High John," he interrupted with a smile. "Only Mister I knew cracked whips, and I ain't him."

"Right," I said, flustered. "High John—"

"But we ain't got time for chitchat right now." He walked over and threw an arm around my shoulders, flashing a wide grin at the others on the stage. "Young Tristan here has done a great job so far, but I reckon it's time to put a little hot sauce on the wheels."

He waited, but when everyone—including the elders, still sitting on their spirit stools—stared at him blankly, I sighed. Adults and their strange figures of speech. "He's saying he wants us to hurry," I explained to the room before turning to High John. "But that's what I'm trying to tell you. I got this. Nyame told us—"

"Nyame?" High John snorted. "He still ain't right, is he? Still got the bug juice in his veins."

Thandiwe frowned. "Bug juice?"

"Brand flies," I said, slightly distracted. High John's comment bothered me, but I tried to push past it. "And I'm sorry,

High John, but we're taking the Story Box back with us. It's the only shot we have at saving MidPass!"

"MidPass?" High John looked around in disbelief. "Y'all think...? Oh, no, no, no." His arm slipped off my shoulder and he moved to the center of the stage, one hand on his hip and the other pinching the bridge of his nose. "Ain't no saving MidPass—y'all might as well get that outta your heads. It's gone. Done for. If not today, then tomorrow. Them monsters done surely chewed through that place by now."

His words hit me like a jab to the chin.

"What do you mean, *gone*?"

"I mean gone. Them folks either packed up or they dead. Ain't nobody moving in MidPass now except for fetterlings."

An icy chill swept through Isihlangu, and nobody spoke for several heartbeats. Chestnutt broke the silence with a sniffle, and she collapsed against Ayanna's legs. Gum Baby tried to form a sentence, but nothing came out. Thandiwe and the Amagqirha pressed their lips tight together.

"So," High John said, staring at me, "what we've got to do, if we don't want the same thing that happened to the Golden Crescent and MidPass happening here? We've got to take the fight to them."

"But—"

"But nothing, boy, I'm trying to save lives! What? You still fixed on the words of one Alkean god?"

A wave of despair washed over me. The division between the countries was going to destroy everyone before the iron monsters could! High John was one folk hero god who maybe could've bridged the gap. But he didn't seem to respect Nyame or care about MidPass.

It was just so *frustrating*!

A small crowd of onlookers had gathered again, and they muttered among themselves, but I ignored the mounting tension. A growing, wiggling tentacle of doubt wouldn't let me completely believe High John's words. MidPass gone? No way. John Henry wouldn't let that happen. We were just there yesterday. Yeah, okay, the Thicket had been under assault, and yeah, things had looked bad, but Miss Sarah and Miss Rose, and Brer and John Henry, they wouldn't allow Midfolk to get taken.

Not unless...

A sharp inhale sounded next to me. I looked over to see Ayanna holding a hand over her mouth. She'd arrived at the same thought.

"They're okay," I assured her. "They've gotta be okay."

"Perhaps," the chief elder broke in, "it would be best to move this discussion and—"

"Naw, ain't no need to move, 'cause there ain't no discussion." High John shoved both hands in his pockets and rocked on his heels. "Is there, Tristan?"

Everyone looked at me. High John raised an eyebrow and waited, and a flush of hot anger burned my face. I hated being put on the spot.

Bad things always happened when I got put on the spot. Hardheaded things.

I was just about to snap off a remark Nana would have something to say about (you know they can hear you across the street, city, or world, no matter where you're at) when the wiggling little thought that had been bothering me this whole time finally wriggled free.

"How do you know everyone in MidPass is gone?" I asked slowly.

High John groaned. "We ain't got time for—"

"No. How do you know they're gone?"

"I just know."

Chestnutt poked her head up. "Tristan, what is it?"

I pointed at him. "This dude comes out of nowhere saying it's over for MidPass and there's no need to go back there. How do we know? Y'all just trust him? He could be—"

"I could be what?" High John said with an easy smile that didn't reach his eyes. "Lying? Pulling a fast one? That'd be a mighty low thing for me to do, wouldn't you say?"

I glared at him. Ayanna started to interject, but I ignored her. "All I know is I haven't seen you at all before now, but as soon as Nyame's Story Box comes out of hiding, you pop up. Nah, I don't like it. I don't like it one bit." I turned to Ayanna and jerked my head at the door. "Come on, let's go. We've got a country to save."

Her eyes widened. I turned to see High John stalking over. Before I could say anything, he had crossed the stage in three steps and grabbed the front of my collar in his fist.

"Hey, get your hands—"

But he yanked hard, and I felt something rip. My chest— he was ripping my chest. Wait, no, he was pulling me out of my . . . What in the . . . ? Everything looked blurry and upside down. A wordless scream spilled out of my mouth and the world went black.

35

A DIFFERENT PERSPECTIVE

AIR WHISTLED PAST MY FACE.

Before I even opened my eyes, I knew we were moving. I lay flat on my back and the rushing winds tugged at the adinkra charms on my wrist. I rolled over to cover them with my other hand, but the floor felt weird. It was soft. Not like a carpet or that fancy rug Mom didn't let anyone step on. No, it felt like fur or...

I opened my eyes and immediately closed them again.

Sweet peaches.

"If you're gonna empty your stomach, best to turn outta the wind," High John said from somewhere off in the distance. "Otherwise you gonna get a face full of nasty."

"I'm not going to throw up," I said, gritting my teeth. "I just... need a second."

"Take all the time you want, boy. Ain't going nowhere but in circles."

He sounded sincere, which only made me more determined to get up. I swallowed the lump of sour fear in my throat and forced my eyes open. Glossy black feathers the length of my forearm fluttered in the wind, and I glared at them, then got up on wobbly legs.

I stood on the back of a giant bird—a crow, I think—as big as a private jet. Its wings moved up and down with long, massive flaps that swept away the clouds we were flying through. I couldn't even see the tips of each wing. Every now and then it cawed, a loud, shrill cry that made me flinch.

"There he is, right as rain."

I turned—slowly—to find High John watching me from near the bird's head. His hands were in his pockets, and he smiled, all traces of his earlier anger gone. "Surprised me, boy," he said. "Most don't take to Old Familiar their first go-round."

"Familiar?" I asked, while inching closer. Baby steps. Itty-bitty baby steps.

High John squatted and patted the crow's neck feathers. "This old man right here. Been with me for . . . Shoot, I don't rightly know anymore. But he's carried more souls than there are stars in the sky, and he's still going strong. Ain't that right, sir?"

Familiar cawed again, and I swallowed.

"Souls? Am . . . am I—?"

"Shoot, no. You just stepped outside."

"Outside?"

"Of yourself. I had to give you a little tug, but that happens."

"What do you mean I'm outside of myself?" I asked, once Familiar leveled out. "Where are we? Last thing I remember is you getting mad and yanking my collar."

High John's face grew serious. "Had to do something. Some things ain't meant to be heard by everybody. Too many people hear a thing, and that thing takes on a life of its own."

I shook my head. "You're not making any sense."

High John pursed his lips. "You called me a liar. I may be many things, boy, but a liar? Not High John. No, sir."

"I'm sorry I said that. It's just that—"

He ignored me and kept on talking. "You the one who's lyin'. You supposed to be a master storyteller, right? Got all these Alkeans in a fuss 'cause of some tales you can bring to life."

"So?"

"So you know how stories can grow and change over time. Guesses can become rumors can become legends can become reality. Let a few people think there's hope, and all of a sudden a bad situation gets worse." High John stabbed a finger at me, then pointed down. "Them folk, all of them on MidPass, they're done for, boy. You've been blessed. Several times. Got gods over here and gods over there giving you protections and charms. Well, I'm gonna give you something, too. I'm gonna give you two gifts. The first is advice: Quit living in the past. Ain't nothing back there that you can save."

He looked me in the eyes as he said that, and somehow it felt like he wasn't just talking about the Midfolk. He was talking about Eddie, too. I swallowed and looked away.

"Now, for the second."

High John waved his hand, and like fog lifting when the sun rose in the sky, the clouds faded away into nothing. He motioned me forward, and I reluctantly inched closer and looked over the side of the giant crow.

"Sweet peaches," I gasped.

High John grinned. "Gets me every time. Welcome to Alke, boy."

The last wispy cloud disappeared as the world of Alke emerged like a jewel beneath us.

We were high in the air—so high my heart climbed into my throat and stayed there—and yet the different lands appeared sharp and focused, like I had zoomed in on a map. I asked High John about that and he laughed.

"That's Old Familiar. It's amazing what you gon' see when you step outside yourself. Old Familiar helps with the perspective, yes he do." He pointed at a shining golden sliver of land. "See that? That's the Golden Crescent. Now, right behind it is where we just was, the Ridge, or Isihlangu, as they say. That thang glitters like black diamonds, boy, it sure do. Now, behind that—"

"Why'd you bring me up here?" I interrupted. My eyes were glued to an island hidden beneath charcoal-gray clouds of smoke. Every so often I thought I saw flashes, like lightning jumping around during a thunderstorm.

High John grunted. "Like I said, boy, perspective."

"Is that MidPass?" I already knew the answer, but I needed to hear it.

"Sure is."

"Can we get closer?"

"I ain't bring you up here to watch them folks get harassed and stripped from their homes. I brought you here 'cause you asked how I knew. You look at that and tell me that place ain't finished."

My fists clenched, but I forced them to relax, and as much as I wanted to snap, to point at the burning land and scream, I didn't. It took some effort, but I did it. Mr. Richardson would've been proud. "You know, Nana—my grandmother—used to tell me stories about you."

High John preened like a peacock. "Oh yeah?"

"Yeah. She told me that you were the strongest of all the folk heroes, and you were a man of the people. Anytime one of us suffered, you could feel it and would be there in an instant. Comforting. Helping."

I turned and faced him, looking him in his eye. The smile froze on his face.

"So," I asked, "why aren't you helping them?"

"Now look, Tristan, it ain't that simple...."

"Are you a god or aren't you?"

"I can't just—"

"Are you a god or aren't you?"

"I need to be called upon. I can't just show up like—"

"Are you. A god. Or not?"

In a blur of motion he was standing in front of me. My shirt was in his fists and I was hoisted high in the air. "Do you think I want to see my country die?" he exploded.

His voice was crashing ocean waves and shaking earth. Old trees and Mississippi suns. Auction houses and Congo landings.

I didn't recognize any of the images and yet I knew them all.

Old Familiar cawed at the waves of energy coming off High John's fury. I swallowed but didn't look away. He held me there for a second longer, my feet dangling a mile above Alke, and I didn't doubt for a second that—outside myself or not—if he dropped me, I wouldn't be waking up again. Then something in his face changed, and High John sighed and set me down.

"Those are my friends. You think I want to see them dragged off? My home burned and desecrated? I don't. But if I go back there as I am right now, I don't have a burp's chance in a whirlwind of making a difference. You know that. Those monsters want us to fight. They snatching folk up left and right, no matter how hard John Henry swings that hammer or how many Rose and Sarah try to save. They too strong."

He gripped my shoulder and stared at me. "That's why I need that Story Box, Tristan. With it, I could get stronger. Way stronger."

"How?"

"The Story Box is power, Tristan. All them tales, they're the strength of gods. They feed us, give us energy. Why do you think Nyame hoards them? Why you think them iron monsters is hauling us all back into the belly of that monster? Power, boy! It's all about power. You control the story, you control the narrative, you control power."

Anansi's research flashed in my mind. The dismantled fetterlings. The notes. The diagrams. "That's what he was looking for..." I said slowly.

"What?"

"Anansi. He— Never mind. If these Story Boxes are so powerful, why doesn't MidPass have one?"

High John let go of me and made a disgusted noise in his throat. "'Cause we're the new kids 'round town. 'Cause we're different. 'Cause the sky is up, who knows? But we don't, and now that we have the chance to get our hands on one, I'm not giving it up."

I shook my head. "We need it to lure Anansi—"

He grunted. "Anansi? You pinning our lives on one Alkean god? What makes you think he gonna help? What has he done so far? He down there putting out flames or fighting?"

"Are you?"

"Aw, here you go. I see." High John took a step back. "I see. Am I helping? I *AM* HELPING!" He pounded his chest. "I'm trying to become as strong as them iron monsters, so I can do some snatchin' of my own."

I huffed impatiently. What more could I say to convince him to do the right thing?

High John snorted. "You wanna get closer? Okay, let's get closer. Let's have us a little look-see, boy."

He snarled something I didn't quite catch to Old Familiar, and the crow cawed once and began to turn. I thought we were going to glide down, but High John grabbed my collar again, and without another word, he stepped off the crow's back, pulling me with him.

36
THE MAN OF FIRE AND SMOKE

MY STOMACH ROSE INTO MY THROAT TO JOIN MY HEART IN A town house of terror, and I closed my eyes, but before I could scream, I felt solid ground beneath my feet. I opened my eyes, stumbled a little, and almost choked.

The Thicket was burning in a bonfire the size of a mountain.

We stood in the middle of the forest glade where I'd first met John Henry. But instead of peace and tranquility, chaos and mayhem greeted us. Midfolk ran screaming left and right as patches of the thorny ceiling fell to the ground in explosions of heat and sparks. A mother was fleeing with one child over her shoulder and another holding her hand, and they zigged around a burning section of grass and came right at us. Before I could shout a warning, they dashed through me like I wasn't there and headed for an exit in the back wall.

"What . . . what happened?" I asked, shaken and confused.

"You ain't really here," High John answered. He sat atop a fallen tree that still smoldered, studying his fingernails. "Stepped outside yourself, remember? But you wanted to look, so go ahead. Get a good look."

"Aren't you going to help?" I asked. Misery filled me as a group of Midfolk hustled away from the flames and into the glowing night.

"I am, boy." He pointed high above us, where flames and smoke were being drawn through a hole in the glade ceiling. "Old Familiar is sucking up them flames as we speak. But that's about all I got. Can't do much in this form, and I can't step back into myself here, 'cause that would leave you untethered. You already ain't got much time—if you humans spend too long outside yourselves, you liable to stay that way. You don't wanna be a haint forever, do you?"

A shiver rippled down my spine. "There's got to be something we can do to help them," I said. I jogged over to the people and animals crowding around an exit. A little boy dropped a cloth bundle and scampered after it, and I stooped to pick it up at the same time he did. His finger slid right through mine, and he paused to look around. Someone called him, and he snatched the bundle and scampered back to his place in line.

"Everyone out the back!" A familiar voice boomed above the chaos. John Henry strode by, the ground shaking as he cut a path through the glade. His hammer pointed toward the back wall. The symbols on its handle—adinkra, I realized with a surprise—glowed almost as bright as the fire.

"Out the back and stay with your groups!"

A faint scream cut through the night.

I looked around. There were more shrieks, and I waited to see someone rush off to help them, but no one did.

"Nobody can hear them," I whispered. I turned around and started running before I remembered my body wasn't physically there. The cries came again, and nobody seemed to hear them but me, not over John Henry's roars, so I kept running.

I left the glade and plunged into the winding tunnels of the Thicket. Smoke and heat didn't bother me in my ghostly form, so I ran on. I couldn't see, but the screams were coming faster now, from the direction of the auditorium. When I arrived, I lunged through the wide doorway and skidded to a stop.

Two rusty fetterlings, screeching and clanking, had cornered a group of older children, like foxes herding chickens. The biggest girl was valiantly trying to ward off the monsters with a straw broom while the rest of the kids cried or screamed.

One of the fetterlings dashed forward, the shackles on its arms snapping for a boy, and I shouted, "NO!"

Before I thought about what I was about to do, and if it was even possible, I was doing it. I pulled smoke and flame from outside the hallway and shaped it into a tall man. The movements were hard to do in my current condition, like trying to walk through water. Several times I thought I'd lose the thread of the story, and only sheer effort kept it going.

Once there was a prince from Africa.

The man of fire and smoke stalked forward. The kids saw him first and begin to scream even louder. The iron monsters rattled when the man got between them and the children.

His walk was rhythm and his words were pride.

The fetterlings snapped in vain at my creation. I made him point at the children, then at the door, and the letters *G-O* appeared in smoke above his fingertips. A few kids recognized the word, and, with some convincing, got the rest of the group up and moving. The oldest girl kept her broom up as she hustled her companions toward the door.

The fetterlings hissed in anger, and I could barely control my movements now, but I had enough energy left for one last command.

Sold into slavery, he helped those who couldn't help themselves.

The man of fire and smoke took two large steps forward and exploded into a vortex of heat and wind. The fetterlings were swept up and carried the length of the auditorium, until they smashed against the thorny back wall.

My legs trembled beneath me, and I began to fall over sideways, and suddenly High John was there. "Time to go, stupid boy."

"No," I said, shivering uncontrollably. "There's more... we can do."

"Come on. Any longer and you fixin' to fade away. Look." He pointed at my hands as he dragged me out toward Old Familiar, and I watched with growing horror as their dark brown color slowly turned transparent.

And yet...

"One... more thing," I gasped.

John Henry was still ushering people out of the burning Thicket entrance, and I concentrated as hard as I could. I needed to get this right. I needed to...

The man of fire and smoke appeared again, and several people screamed. John Henry flinched and whirled around, hammer raised. Then he paused at the sight of the apparition floating in midair. "High John," he muttered.

The fire man pointed at an adinkra swirling out of the flames next to him—the Gye Nyame. John Henry's eyes narrowed at the symbol, then he nodded sharply, and I let the image disappear. I hoped he'd gotten the message.

My arm was nearly invisible now. High John picked me up and climbed into the air as if on hidden stairs. Then we were back on Old Familiar. High John spoke again in that language of dancing slaves and hidden meanings, and the giant black crow cawed and flapped into the sky.

I was colder than I'd ever been, even during the most brutal Chicago winter. My shivering wouldn't stop, and my bones rattled. I couldn't feel my toes or my hands, and I just wanted to lie down and sleep. My eyes closed.

"Tristan?" High John called.

"Yeah?" I mumbled.

"That man you conjured out of fire and smoke . . . is that how I look? Is that . . . is that how you see me when you tell your stories?"

I tried to answer. I tried to tell him about Eddie and how he could spin a High John tale that would rival any superhero story. About fighting injustice, and doing it with a laugh and a dance. But all I could do was close my eyes.

"Tristan? Tristan!"

37
MISSING MEMORIES

"I'M DISAPPOINTED IN YOU, TRISTAN."

I was back in the dark, moldy hallway with two torches floating alongside me. My feet walked forward automatically, and a voice slinked out of the shadows.

"Real disappointed."

"Yeah, well, get in line," I muttered. "Disappointing people is kind of my thing."

More victims were chained against the walls now. Midfolk and Alkeans. They were crammed against one another and, just like last time, I couldn't stop to try to help them—my feet moved me past until finally I arrived at that same rotted wooden door.

Inside, the old lantern hissed before the flame flickered to life, just barely. More of those blurry, shriveled white flowers recoiled out of the thin light, rolling to the far corner, where something moved. It was like seeing something out the corner of your eye and never quite getting a good look at it. Just a shadow, and yet something more.

Uncle C.

"I told you I'd come for you," the haint said. He almost sounded apologetic. "I told you, and you didn't listen. Now your precious hideout is burning, and I'm gonna hunt down all your little friends and put all their miserable hides with the rest of my collection."

His voice lowered to a hiss that merged with the lantern's struggling flame. "I asked for *one* thing. One! And you trying to play me like I can't take everything you love. You think it's a game? Maybe I been too lenient. Maybe you need some *inspiration.*"

The lantern flame finally sputtered out, and darkness flooded over me, carrying the sound of rustling and the smell of death. The hairs on the back of my neck stood up, and an invisible rope snaked around my arms and legs. I couldn't get away, or move at all, and a violent wind ripped past me, snatching and grabbing at my clothes. It whipped into my eyes and swirled around my head and...

An image of Eddie scribbling in his journal popped into my mind.

Another followed—this one of him laughing at some joke I'd just made.

More scenes appeared, and they swirled around my head, just like the wind, and...

And then...

They were out of reach. I could remember...something. I could feel the empty space where the memories used to be, but everything else, the specifics...they were gone.

Except for one.

A bus crash, a feeble hand reaching for help...

"What did you do?" I whispered.

"I will *end* you, boy," Uncle C hissed. "But before I do, I'm gonna make you suffer. I'm gonna rip away everything you hold dear. All the memories of your little friend? Mine now. The only picture you can cling to is of you *failing* to be a hero. And all them friends you made, all them gods with all their powers, they ain't gonna help you. I'm gonna pluck your recollections out, one by one, and leave you with nothing but dusssssst."

The hiss grew into a shout by the time he was finished. A great pressure, like the weight of the entire world, landed on my shoulders, and it took every ounce of my strength not to buckle under it and sink to the floor. It grew heavier and heavier, and just when I thought I couldn't take it any longer, Uncle C sighed and the weight disappeared.

"Unless...you give me what I want."

"What...is that?" I asked, exhausted.

"Aw, do I really gotta spell it out for you, boy? That fancy box everybody's all in a tiff about. You bring that to me, and I'll give back your precious little book, and nobody's gotta get hurt. You hear me? It's on you now, Tristan. Give me what I want, and you can save everybody."

The Story Box? Everyone wanted the power of that thing. But why—?

Before I could respond, the invisible rope yanked at me again, and I was dragged backward out of the room, Uncle C's last words following me into the hallway:

"You want to be a hero, right?"

And then I was back at the entrance, staring into the dark, two torches floating alongside me. I took a deep breath, then another, just as I heard an exasperated sigh.

"Hey, genius," somebody said sadly. "You're still talking to the wrong one."

I squeezed my eyes tight. That voice sounded familiar. I knew it. I *knew* it. I . . . Eddie. It was Eddie's voice. The haint had taken some of my dearest memories, but I clung to what I had left.

"I don't know what that means," I whispered. "Uncle C? Who? Who's the wrong one?"

"You're still talking to the wrong one."

"I DON'T KNOW WHAT THAT MEANS!" I shouted into the darkness.

The only answer was silence.

"Tristan?"

I opened my eyes to see Gum Baby's head inches from

mine. She held my face in one sticky hand, and the other was stretched behind her, as if she were seconds away from smacking the taste buds out my mouth.

I narrowed my eyes. "Don't you dare—"

SMACK!

"Ow!" I yelled. "What was that for?"

"You wasn't moving." Gum Baby shrugged. "Ain't no time for sleep, Bumbletongue, Gum Baby got missions and stuff."

I slowly became aware that I was back on the polished stage inside Isihlangu. Not watching the Thicket burn. Not being threatened by Uncle C in a nightmare. I was in the Ridge.

Everyone was staring at me. The elders, the Amagqirha, Thandiwe...even Ayanna and Chestnutt were looking at me weirdly. High John stood apart from us with his arms crossed, in the same position he'd been in before, but now, instead of a smile, he wore a scowl. He met my eyes and I recoiled from the centuries-old fury roiling in his gaze. But just for a second, something else flickered there.

Confusion?

"Tristan, you all right?" Chestnutt asked.

I shook my head and tried to catch up mentally. My mind was foggy. I'd had a best friend once, back home.... What was his name again? Eddie? I vaguely remembered letting him down somehow. There'd been a lot of pain....

"Tristan?" Ayanna called.

I took a breath and pulled myself together. Apparently, no one had noticed that High John and I had disappeared for a while. In the stories, he took slaves' spirits on trips of happiness and joy and wonder, all while their bodies remained on the plantation and continued to work.

I guess that's what he'd done to me, though I couldn't say the trip was a happy one....

"Tristan!" Gum Baby shouted.

"What?"

"You standing there drooling, that's what! They about to hand over what we came for, and you like a frog on a log. And Gum Baby hates frogs. Are you even listening?" Gum Baby scrambled to my shoulder and grabbed my ear. "Can you hear Gum Baby? Oh, no wonder—you really need to clean your ears out."

"Hey!" I brushed her off and she slid down to the floor and folded her arms. I cleared my throat. "Sorry. I just . . . Sorry. Continue. I'm here—I mean, I'm listening."

Two Ridgefolk guards flanked a large, cloth-covered object. My throat tightened.

The chief elder stood, and so did the rest of the ancestors, the Amagqirha's humming chant still powering their ghostly presence. "As I was saying," Fezile said, "High John has relinquished his demand for Nyame's Story Box."

I gawked. High John shrugged, but anger still lined his face. Anger and embarrassment.

"Before we hand it over to you, champions of MidPass, a request must be honored. Thandiwe, step forward."

The tall girl moved to the center of the stage and extended her hoverboard to the Amagqirha. The diviner tied something to its middle, all the while stepping from foot to foot and humming. When she was done, the older woman gave the forebear back to Thandiwe, slipping it on her arm like a—

"A shield?" I asked out loud. "Wait, why a shield?"

The answer hit me just as Thandiwe grinned and tied a beaded wrap around her head. "I shall be coming with you. Anansi owes all of Isihlangu an explanation." She sniffed. "And to show you Midfolk how to fight, of course."

Gum Baby rolled her eyes. "Girl, please."

"Hush, Gum Baby," Ayanna said, then she smiled at Thandiwe. The two had become fast friends since our arrival. Which made sense, 'cause they were a lot alike. "We need all the help we can get."

"Then take the Story Box," the chief elder commanded. "I hope your plans succeed. For all our sakes."

The tone of the spirit's voice caught my attention. It seemed like there was something he wasn't telling us. Before I could ask any questions, however, the Amagqirha stopped moving and humming. The elders began to fade away. The oldest leaders of the Ridgefolk, still guiding and inspiring their people even after death, had stared at me with such intensity that it was almost a relief when they were gone.

"Well, y'all gonna open it?" High John's drawl broke the spell.

I cleared my throat and nodded at Thandiwe. "Why don't you do the honors?"

She shrugged. With an unceremonious yank, she pulled off the covering and tossed it aside.

Everyone gasped.

I'd expected a shining golden treasure chest, like the one in Chestnutt's drawing.

Or a diamond-encrusted, velvet-lined case.

Even a fake leather trunk would've been acceptable.

High John gave an angry little snort and shook his head. He shoved his hands in his pockets and hopped down off the stage. "Yeah, y'all can keep all that."

Gum Baby threw her little hands up with so much anger, sap flew across the stage. "What sort of soggy garbage is this mess?"

An old brown crate covered in layers of dust, with sagging hinges and a partially splintered lid, sat there. Thandiwe looked at each of us, puzzled. "You didn't know? This is how Anansi brought it to us. It's empty."

38
THE STORY BOX

"WHAT ARE WE GOING TO DO?" AYANNA WHISPERED TO ME.

We were at a long table—me, Ayanna, and Thandiwe. Gum Baby and Chestnutt sat on the surface and shared a plate of steaming carrots. They seemed oblivious to our disappointment. The sound of drums and singing and clapping kept our conversation from being overheard.

Why so loud?

Oh, well, turns out whenever the elders were summoned beneath Isihlangu, a feast was in order—never mind that it was because we had arrived as thieves in the night. I found myself staring at a plate of food I had no desire to eat as the entire mountain population celebrated around us.

And if you know me, you know a plate of food lying untouched in my presence is weird.

"Tristan?" Ayanna repeated, and I shook my head.

"Don't know."

Thandiwe watched both of us with a confused look. "I don't understand. How did you not know Nyame's Story Box was empty?"

I looked at Ayanna, who shrugged and sighed. "We never thought to ask," I said.

"It's not like we *could* ask," Ayanna said, looking at Thandiwe and frowning accusingly. "You wouldn't speak with us. You treated us like beggars and thieves."

The warrior girl pointed a stew-covered spoon in our direction. "One of those labels is accurate, don't forget."

"Okay, okay," I cut in, not in the mood for another territorial fight. High John had done enough of that already. "The question is, what do we do now?"

"I think we should take it to Brer anyway, like we're supposed to," said Ayanna. "Maybe it will still bring Anansi...."

"You think Anansi will barter for a broken, dusty old crate?"

But Thandiwe didn't seem fazed. "What if you had it repaired?" she suggested.

Ayanna scoffed, but I ignored it. "What do you mean?"

"I mean, bring it back to Nyame. It was his creation in the first place. Surely he could restore it. Maybe even refill it with stories. Then you take it on to MidPass and summon Anansi."

I chewed that over for a few seconds. "Brer did tell me to bring it right away, but..."

"But, like you said, there's no point in bringing an empty, broken Story Box," she finished.

I nodded. "Okay. Yes, let's get it fixed. Nyame owes us one, anyway."

"He does?" Thandiwe raised an eyebrow. "Why?"

"Because we—"

"Tristan freed him from iron-monster control," Ayanna interrupted. I straightened an imaginary tie and she snorted. "But don't talk about it around Tristan or his head will get even bigger."

"Who's got a big head? Bumbletongue?" Gum Baby shouted. She was out of her little chair on top of the table and was dancing around my plate to the celebratory drumbeat. Sticky purple drops of syrupy sap splattered my food. I groaned and pushed it away. Now I definitely didn't feel like eating.

"Gum Baby been saying that. Boy's head is so big, we could use *it* to plug up the tear in the sky. Little bit of sap and a big ole head sounds like the answer. Gum Baby'll do it. Shoot, won't even cost you much. Just a new pair of boots and a smile."

"You don't even wear boots," I said, rolling my eyes as Thandiwe, Ayanna, and Chestnutt laughed at me.

"You don't even wear boots," Gum Baby mocked. "Oh, look, Gum Baby is Tristan. *Gaaaaah.*" She quickly rolled sap on her head until a giant wobbly ball rested on top of her braids. I

guess that was supposed to be my head. She strutted around the table, shouting and throwing a few punches. *"Gaaaaah. Look out, Chestnutt, Tristan is gonna get you. Gaaaaah."*

Chestnutt laughed so hard, chewed-up carrots came out of her nose, and then we all collapsed. It had been a rough few days, so laughing with friends—no matter how weird or small or irritating they were—felt good. It felt real good.

I saw something move out of the corner of my eye and turned to spy the Amagqirha standing in the shadows. She beckoned me, and I frowned. What had I done now? She gestured again, putting a finger over her lips, and I turned to the group and cleared my throat. "I, uh, gotta go use the bathroom. I'll be back."

"Boy, nobody cares," Gum Baby shouted. "Go do your thing and leave us cool kids alone." She strutted again. *"Tristan needs to go—"*

"All right!" I yelled, trying to keep a smile off my face. I trotted over to the Amagqirha. She headed up the sloping ramp that curled around Isihlangu's walls. We climbed in silence, and I watched as the feast carried on below us, with the dancers dancing and the singers singing. It was a beautiful sight, and the fact that people from MidPass and the Ridge were enjoying it together made me feel like they were going to be okay. For now, anyway.

All of a sudden I realized just how high we were climbing. "Um, where are we going?"

The Amagqirha pointed up, to the Atrium above us, and stared at me. "There is something I must show you."

We finally reached the heavy stone door of the Atrium, which was now closed and flanked by two guards. They slid aside the complicated series of magnetic locks and pushed it open, allowing the diviner to enter. She waved me in behind her.

I contemplated heading back to the feast, but I'm not built to be rude to elders. (Thanks, Mom.) I stepped inside, and the guards closed the door behind me, leaving us alone. I let my eyes adjust.

"Sweet peaches," I said in a low whisper.

We stood in a perfect cube of polished stone. Black obsidian walls reflected the dim silver glow leaking out of a closed clamshell-like container atop a pedestal. Whatever was inside was the only thing lighting the room, and it gave the Amagqirha's face a haunted look as she stepped up to it and whispered a command. The light inside flared as the clamshell popped open.

"You may approach," she said to me. Tufts of gray hair escaped from the braids beneath her beaded wrap, and more wrinkles than I thought humanly possible lined her face.

She grunted a few times, and I realized she was chuckling. "Think I'm too old, boy?"

"No, ma'am," I said right away, trying not to stare.

"Liar."

She stirred her hands in the air above the pedestal, then motioned me closer. "Look."

I climbed three steps, peered down into the container, and my jaw hit the floor. "Is that what I think it is?"

"That depends on what you think it is."

"A Story Box?"

She nodded. "The Story Box of the Ridge people."

A gleaming silver-and-black chest sat on a pillow of black satin. It was a perfect octagon, the eight sides joined at the corners by rippling seams of silver. Patterns etched into the top and sides flared with light every so often, as if it held energy too powerful to be contained.

The Amagqirha went on. "When the sky god bartered away his golden Story Box, it made his tales available for all to consume. But soon the different lands of Alke discovered that some stories are too potent to be exchanged freely by ordinary people. The tales' meanings can be distorted if they are shared without guidance. Anansi realized this when he received his prize from Nyame, so he created the Anansesem, his champion orators, like you, to carry his fables far and wide. The other realms, they had no such champions. So they built Story Boxes in the image of the original one to protect the power of the stories they had collected. But none were like the first. None could hold *all* the stories. Only Nyame's has that power."

She paused, then smiled at me. "Open it," she said.

Didn't have to tell me twice. I reached for it and...she slapped my hand.

"Ow!" I shook away the sting. "What was—?"

She wagged a finger. "I said, open it."

"That's what I was about to do!" I complained.

The Amagqirha shook her head. "Any boy with grubby fingers can flail about. Only you can open it. You are Anansesem—act like it."

Man, I get scolded no matter what world I'm in. But I took a deep breath and focused. After a moment of searching out the story beats and the rhythm, I felt it—the familiar tingling. The electric melody built up in my fingertips, and when I couldn't hold it in any longer, I let out a whisper.

"Once, let's say a boy could fly...."

As the words zipped out of my mouth, the silver Story Box flared so bright my eyes hurt. By the time I could see again, the Amagqirha had rolled up the sleeve on her left arm and was digging around inside the chest, its lid now propped open.

"What are you doing?" I asked, rubbing my eyes.

"You will see."

She pulled something out of the chest, then grunted with approval and slammed the Story Box closed. I frowned—I hadn't gotten a chance to look inside—but she ignored me and began shaping something in her hands, whispering strange words over them.

"What are—?"

"I said, you will see." She glared at me, then returned to her mysterious activity. After several minutes, she straightened, examined whatever it was she had made, and nodded. "It will do."

She held out her hand. "Your bracelet."

"Huh?"

"Your bracelet with the charms. Hand it over."

"But—"

She narrowed her eyes and my default reaction was to do as I was told. I untied the bracelet and held it out, and she snatched it quick as lightning. The Amagqirha had a nice jab. She hunched over and murmured to herself, and I swear I saw silver symbols etched in the air before they disappeared in a cloud of smoke. Finally, she turned back to me.

"Here."

I took the bracelet and held it up, squinting in the dim light. She had strung it with a tiny silver ball, which nestled between the two adinkras.

"A bead?" What was it with Alkeans and their jewelry?

"A talisman, boy. For protection."

"From what, a loose braid?"

The Amagqirha pursed her lips. "You would be wise to take this seriously. Something is coming. Something you've seen before, and yet have never seen the like. You know of whom I speak, even if you didn't mention him to the elders."

Uncle C's cackle echoed in my ears, and I shivered. "I do."

"Then you know he brings pain. He brings terror. He brings suffering and destruction. The horror he rides in on, the old evil he's driven up from the Burning Sea, it will deliver death to us all."

The words *death to us all* echoed around the room.

"You will need all the help you can get if you are to defeat them both."

I stared down at the bead. "If? Not *when* I defeat them?"

"*If* seems more appropriate."

"And how about Anansi? Will he—?"

The Amagqirha sighed and leaned on the pedestal, and in its glow I could see just how old and tired she really was.

"Closing the tear in the sky, defeating these iron monsters— that is only the beginning." Her eyes seared into mine. "The elders have seen it. I have seen it. If you do not succeed, a terrible war will follow. This talisman will provide aid when you need it."

"Will it transform into a shield or a sword?" I slipped on the bracelet and secured it.

"No, it will help you commune with the—"

"Ouch!" I hopped up and down and shook my arm. Hot, stabbing pain shot through my wrist, and I turned it over to see Anansi's adinkra glowing orange-red. A blister had already begun to form where it had burned my skin.

"What is it?" the Amagqirha asked.

"Anansi's charm," I said, wincing. "It's—" My eyes went wide and I inhaled quickly. Before I could explain, however, a booming sound shook the mountain, sending bits of rock clattering down and the two of us stumbling. The pedestal with the Story Box began to sink into the floor, and a low rumble vibrated through the air.

"What's going on?" I shouted.

The Amagqirha's face had gone pale, and she gripped my wrist and tugged me to the door. "Something has activated the sentinels," she said grimly. "We're being attacked."

39

UNWELCOME VISITORS

THE RUMBLING CONTINUED AS WE RAN BACK DOWN THE SLOPE.
I'd been worried the Amagqirha would lag behind, but I had
to sprint to keep up as she scampered ahead, lifting her skirts
so they wouldn't drag. We tore around the curves, barely
staying upright as tremors shook the mountain.

"What's going on?" I shouted after a quake sent me stag-
gering into the wall.

The Amagqirha hauled me upright. "Isihlangu is fighting
back."

A lump of fear grew in my throat. What could have the
Ridge's defenses going full throttle? Fetterlings? Even the
bosslings wouldn't stand a chance against the giant floating
towers that guarded the foothills. They'd be smashed before
they even got close.

So what could have broken through a mountain nick-
named the Shield?

Something in me still hoped it was all just a false alarm. I mean, we'd triggered a warning boom when we snuck inside. Maybe some other group of desperate Midfolk had come for the Story Box.

Yeah, right.

We finally arrived back at the central chamber, which was in chaos. People ran left and right, searching for kieries and forebears while trying to avoid overturned tables and chairs. Guards whizzed by overhead as they raced to their posts. Children grabbed younger siblings and fled to the safety of their homes, where stone doors slammed shut and sealed themselves in bursts of silver light.

"Tristan!"

Ayanna and Thandiwe crouched behind a makeshift barricade of food-splattered tables. Gum Baby stood on top of one, screaming insults at the would-be intruders, while Chestnutt nervously recited iron-monster stats over and over. Nyame's empty Story Box rested next to them, as dull and dingy as ever. I sprinted over to them and dropped to the ground.

"Where have you been, you—?"

The Amagqirha dropped down next to us, and whatever insult Ayanna was going to fling at me dissolved into a grudging tone. "Just . . . don't scare us like that. One minute we were eating together, and the next you were gone and the mountain started shaking."

"The Amagqirha said it could be some of the rock lasers," I said.

The old lady looked at Thandiwe, who nodded, then chewed her lip. "She's right," said the Ridge warrior. "But it's not just some of them. All the sentinels activated at once. Whatever's out there is big. Real big."

As if her words signaled the next stage in the assault, the giant stone double doors to the chamber shuddered as something crashed against them. People started screaming, and Thandiwe scowled and pulled her kierie and spear free. Ayanna slipped her staff out of its holster—at some point the Ridge guards had returned her weapon/rudder to her.

And me?

Why, I had a fancy bracelet!

The expression on my face must've been a doozy, because Thandiwe chuckled and held out her club to me.

"Here," she said. "Try to be useful."

I started to take it, then thought of something. "No, I'm good."

She frowned as I pulled out the gloves John Henry had given me. When I put them on, the hammer symbol above the knuckles flared bright. I smiled at Thandiwe. "Better stick with what I know best."

She raised an eyebrow, then turned away. I let the smile fade, but the words stuck with me. I *was* good at boxing. The conviction surprised me, but I honestly believed that whatever came next, I could face it with both fists raised.

BOOM!

The main entrance doors sagged inward. Something huge moved around outside—I caught glimpses of it in the growing cracks. Large, determined, and angry. A giant three-fingered hand made of rotted wood and rusty metal appeared at the edge of the door. It tore away a chunk of stone, like a three-year-old grabbing a piece of cake, and hurled it inside.

I flinched as the boulder bounced near us with a floor-rattling crash. "What is that out there?!"

"I don't know," Thandiwe whispered, her face tight. "Let's hope the guards can—"

A fist slammed through, widening the hole, and the screech of a thousand chains scraping together stabbed our ears, forcing everyone to hunch over and grab their skulls.

"We should sneak out the way we came in!" Ayanna shouted. She pointed halfway up the mountain wall, toward the tunnel to the tram. "We're not going to make a difference in this fight. We can get a head start and be back with Nyame before these beasts even know we left. Thandiwe, you can come with us."

Thandiwe grimaced. She didn't look fond of the idea of letting her kinfolk fight without her, but she didn't argue, either. It made all the sense in the world. We could slip away and be that much closer to saving MidPass. That was the whole goal, right? Right?

And yet...

"No," I said, glancing at the Amagqirha. "We can't."

"What do you mean 'we can't'?" asked Ayanna. "Tristan, this is our chance."

Chestnutt piped up. "She's right. If we don't get out now, we might be stuck here."

I shook my head. "No. We can't just leave them when they're in trouble. They helped us, and—"

"Maybe you *should* go," Thandiwe cut in. I looked at her in surprise and she gripped her kierie and spear tight. "The Ridge can hold. It will be tough, but my people can fight them off. Your people need you."

"No!" I shook my head. "We don't abandon friends."

Ayanna groaned. "Why do you have to be a hero at the worst possible time?"

More hammering and scraping at the door interrupted the discussion. I swallowed, then turned to the Amagqirha. "You should head somewhere safe. And take Nyame's empty Story Box—just in case."

She studied me, then nodded. "I will keep it with...what I showed you. It will be safer there." She grabbed the ratty crate and trotted toward the ramp to the Atrium. After a few steps she turned. "There is strength in not fighting, Tristan. Remember that." And then she kept going.

A loud roar blasted outside the hall, and with a final punch, the doors collapsed into piles of rubble. Fetterlings swarmed in.

"Here they come!" I yelled. "Watch out for the big… whatever it is." But it still hadn't made it into the chamber.

"One thing at a time," Thandiwe said.

"Right." I ducked as a fetterling leaped over me, then I smashed it to smithereens with a right cross. "Just let me know when I need to focus on the thing with a hand the size of a car."

A group of fetterlings sprinted across the open floor toward Thandiwe and me as we protected our friends and other people crouched behind the overturned table. I balled my fists and dropped into my stance, but before I could swing again, Thandiwe shouted and smacked three clear across the room with her club. Another tried to snake around the edge of the table, but Ayanna's staff, flaring with golden light, struck out and jabbed it in the collar until it disintegrated into a tinkle of blackened fragments.

A cheer went up as the last fetterling was pinned by a Ridge guard's spear. I didn't join in. This wasn't over—not by a long shot.

"Hey!" Gum Baby shouted. "Is that it? Save some glory for Gum Baby! Y'all being greedy."

As soon as she spoke, a face—if you could call it that—lowered itself to the doorway, and I shivered at the twisted mouth of splintered wooden planks and knotted chains. It roared, and the smell of fishy water made my stomach heave. The good news was that the creature looked too huge to enter the room. How it had gotten into the mountain at all was beyond me. The bad news was that another wave of fetterlings swept through underneath it, followed by a bossling. I groaned. "You had to open your little big mouth."

Gum Baby grinned from ear to drawn-on ear. "You just stay behind Gum Baby and hush. Gum Baby'll keep you safe." She flipped in the air to land on the back of a charging fetterling, pulled its snapping manacle-hands behind its head, and used them as reins. "Wahoo! Gum Baby's on the move!"

"Be careful!" I shouted, and then I had to lurch aside as two fetterlings snapped at my wrists. By the time I had smashed the first one and launched the second into the air with my fists, Gum Baby and her mount were galloping around firing sap balls at anything that moved.

The monstrosity outside the door tried to claw a bigger opening, while inside, the bossling alternated between harassing half a dozen Ridge guards and clearing rubble from the doorway. If the two of them succeeded . . .

"Princess!" A guard coasted off of a rail to a floating stop a foot or so above the ground, his forebear humming as he balanced on it. "The Shield forces have been summoned. We only need to hold off the enemy for a few more minutes."

Thandiwe nodded, and the guard flew off to join a

squadron that was buzzing around the bossling's head, hammering blows that didn't seem to faze the monster.

"*Princess?*" I asked.

"Drop it," she said. She pulled her forebear off her wrist and switched it from a shield to its normal hover mode. She stepped on, then beckoned me to join her.

"Come," Thandiwe said.

I took a look at the board. "Nah."

"Now, Tristan. We have to hold until the Shield forces get here. If that...creature keeps digging, we don't stand a chance."

Gum Baby galloped past, still riding her fetterling and whooping and hollering.

I growled, then grabbed Thandiwe's outstretched hand and climbed aboard. "All right, but you'd better take it"—the board shot forward onto the nearest rail, and I barely had time to catch my balance—"slooooooooooow!"

We climbed high into the air, weaving in and out of stalactites hanging from the rocky ceiling, and I mumbled prayers in seven different languages as we circled the inside of Isihlangu on its glittering spiral rails. The great hall of the fortress swirled with action, and from our vantage point we could see it all. Ridgefolk fled up the circular paths that spiraled around the walls, trying to get inside their homes before fetterlings caught them. Guards rode forebears like professional skateboarders, shifting the Alkean hoverboards from rail to rail so fast Tony Hawk would've been jealous. The bossling clambered atop the stone stage in the middle of the room and screeched.

We had to do something, or we'd be overrun. I pointed at the link of chain just below the bossling's manacle-head.

"There!" I shouted. "We have to hit it there—it's a weak spot!"

Thandiwe whistled, and the Ridge guards peeled away from the iron monster and fell into formation behind her, everyone lining up on the same rail. She pointed to me. "Follow his lead. Where he strikes, we strike. Understood?"

"Yes, Princess," they all shouted, and I raised an eyebrow.

"Focus," she growled, handing me her club, "and get ready. We attack...now!"

The forebear dove, and I shouted a war cry. It sounded heroic, but honestly, it was a shriek of terror. Everyone was counting on me, though, so I gripped the kierie in one hand, held on to Thandiwe with the other, and when the bossling reared in front of us, I swung with all my might.

CLANG!

My arms shook with the impact. We whizzed by, arcing back up into the air, and the guards followed my attack with their own.

"Again!" I shouted over the whooshing air. "It's still standing."

We dove again and again, preventing the bossling from

focusing on the doorway. It screeched and swiped at us. One of its chains clipped a guard, and he fell screaming to the floor. Another swipe sent two more spiraling down, and all of a sudden it was just Thandiwe and me.

But the bossling had suffered, too. It ignored the door completely and wobbled on its coiled chains. Down on the floor, Ayanna and a stunt-riding Gum Baby were holding off a swarm of fetterlings, but more were entering. They surrounded the defenses and hemmed my friends in.

"We need to hurry," Thandiwe shouted. "Ayanna is in trouble!"

"One more attack should do it," I said, determined to end this. "It's reeling. If we can—"

But I never got to finish the sentence.

The doors buckled inward, and the wooden beams of the frame groaned like they were holding too much weight. In an explosion of dust and rock, the largest iron monster I'd ever seen bulled its way through the collapsed doorway, trampling the injured bossling in the process.

40

HULLBEASTS AND BRAND FLIES

SOME THINGS JUST SHOULDN'T EXIST.

You get me?

This creature, man... this creature was a collection of rot on four legs. Yes, four legs. Plus two huge arms that scraped the stone floor as it moved into the hall. Its extremities were soggy wooden beams intertwined with metal shackles, the iron restraints lining its limbs like veins. A piece of a thick mast served as a head, with crooked eyes made of rusted iron spars. The torso, a huge warped frame of an old ship, shook and sloshed as it walked and dribbled a wet green trail of algae behind it. It was the size of an elephant and just as intimidating.

And the smell. Holy moly.

Swamps, dead fish, sweat, dirty toilets, and straight-up-and-down funk. It washed over us and I heard more than a few people dry-heaving and vomiting, including some guards on their forebears.

"What *is* that thing?" Thandiwe gasped, holding her nose.

"I . . . I don't know, but we need to regroup," I said.

"Yes . . . yes, I think you're right."

We quickly descended, and before the forebear reached the floor, I hopped off and skidded to a stop next to Ayanna.

The monster lumbered to the middle of the room, flinging guards aside left and right. It kept one hand on its bloated chest, but the other smashed people, pillars, and furniture alike. It slammed the ground twice with one fist, then let out a roar that nearly blew us across the hall.

Gum Baby rode her fetterling up to us, flipped off of it, then pummeled the iron monster with sap. She pointed at the giant creature and said, "Y'all gonna handle that, or do Gum Baby gotta do everything?"

Ayanna ignored her and turned to me. "We still have time. We can slip out of the tram tunnel—the raft is up there."

I hesitated, then shook my head. "No, we can't leave until reinforcements come. The monsters will rip this place apart."

"No, see, I've been thinking. What if they're following us?"

I ripped my eyes away from the monster, which was batting at the Ridge warriors near its head like they were gnats, and looked at Ayanna. "What?"

"The fetterlings, the bosslings, now this thing—what if

they're following us?" She tucked a strand of hair behind her ear and grabbed my arm. "We'd be helping by leaving! Right?"

"But why would they—?"

"Because we're trying to stop them, because you're an Anansesem, because they hate us, I don't know! But it makes sense."

Thandiwe started to back up. "I think...I think we should—"

"Got it!" Chestnutt broke in. She hopped over on her hind legs and held up a single sheet of paper. "I found a list of monsters in Anansi's notes. I think I know what this is."

We all huddled behind a chipped stone table, most of its jewels shattered or missing, and listened as our bunny spy gave us the lowdown.

"Made of rotted wood and abandoned shackles," she read aloud. "Bound by rotten malevolence—"

"Eleven what?" Gum Baby asked.

"MALEVOLENCE! Evil! Bound by rotten malevolence, and carriers of disease via their...Oh no." Chestnutt looked up and gulped. "Carriers of disease via the brand flies infesting their bodies. Hullbeasts."

Ayanna panicked. "Brand flies? Did you say brand flies? Tristan, we need to get out of here. We need to go right now!"

I licked my lips. "Okay. Okay, let's—"

A deafening croak filled the hall. The monster—the hullbeast—cupped its free three-fingered hand around its wide mouth and croaked again. Something flew out into the air and hovered above everyone. A buzzing sound filled the room.

Chestnutt hopped into Ayanna's arms and shouted, "Watch out! It's a scout fly! Once it locks on to you, the whole brood—"

The scout fly shot up, then dove like a falcon straight at us. It hovered a few feet away. Two metal antennae waggled at us—no, it waggled at *me*—and started to whine.

And when I say whine, I don't mean like your little cousin when she's complaining you won't let her give you a make-over. I mean like a mosquito buzzing past your ear. But think of a mosquito the size of an eagle. And made of rusty metal.

Getting the picture?

I finally understood why the gods hadn't been able to get near the burning tear. With swarms of these things filling the sky, they'd not only have to worry about getting scorched by the fire, they'd also have to watch their backs for prehistorically large poison bugs.

Wonderful.

The whining sound filled the hall, and Ayanna tugged at my arm. "Now, Tristan! We need to leave *now*!"

We all took off running for the ramp, but then I felt a tingling in my hands, and I stopped to look behind us.

The giant iron monster opened its mouth wide—wider than a mouth should ever, ever open—and it bellowed, allowing a maelstrom of brand flies dripping with green venom to erupt from its mouth.

Not toward me, though. Toward Ayanna.

"No!" I shouted.

Horrendous screams filled the mountain. The metal bugs swarmed like bees at a picnic. Everywhere a brand fly landed, skin sizzled and welted. Victims tried to peel the flies off, but whatever type of poison those flying iron monsters carried, it was potent. After a few feeble attempts to free themselves, the Ridgefolk crumpled to the floor, paralyzed. Fetterlings snapped cuffs around their wrists and ankles and tugged them out the door. The hullbeast scooped up more by the fistful and dropped them into its swollen torso.

I turned in circles, stunned.

Thandiwe and Ayanna were surrounded up on the ramp. I watched them swing and connect, sending bug after bug tumbling to the ground. But there were dozens—no, hundreds of the insects—so many that soon I couldn't see the two girls anymore.

A brand fly zoomed at my face, but just before it landed, a glob of sap splattered on its wings and it crashed in a tailspin.

Gum Baby had flipped into the air and landed in my hood just in time. "Well? Get a move on, Gum Baby ain't got all day."

I sprinted toward the ramp. A bug whizzed past my cheek, and I ducked and put on a burst of speed. Somebody screamed behind me, and I winced but didn't stop. I cursed myself. Why hadn't I listened to Ayanna before?

A cluster of Ridgefolk tried to barricade themselves inside a storeroom near the winding ramp. They piled tables and chairs and forebears in front of the door before closing it. I thought about trying to squeeze inside with them but then saw a brand fly land, tuck its wings to its back, and wriggle through a tiny crack at the bottom.

The screams inside would follow me forever, it seemed.

I ducked my head and ran up the ramp. Gum Baby flung sap at anything that got too close. Fetterlings were on our tail, and she knocked several backward with well-aimed shots. Brand flies were sniped out of midair, each hit punctuated with an insult.

Ping

"You ain't nothing!"

Ping

"Tell 'em Gum Baby sent you!"

Ping

"Ow!"

"Well, move your big head, Bumbletongue, Gum Baby trying to save your raggedy butt."

I rubbed the back of my head and kept running. We'd just rounded the final curve, heading toward the thinning cloud of brand flies near the tram entrance, when a scream split the air.

My blood chilled. "Ayanna."

Several flies dive-bombed us as we got closer, and I swung my loaner kierie like a two-handed sword, batting them back. More peeled away from the cloud around my friends, buzzing and rattling and keeping me away. The floor began to tremble beneath my feet, and I felt my knees go weak as a fresh horde of fetterlings charged through the destroyed main entrance. Some split off and snapped up fallen Ridgefolk—no doubt hauling them back to the Maafa and Uncle C. The rest stampeded up the ramp after me and Gum Baby.

Enemies in front.

Enemies behind.

Enemies—

A three-fingered hand the size of a minivan crashed down on the ramp between us and where Thandiwe was huddled over Ayanna, swatting metal bugs left and right. I couldn't see Chestnutt anywhere. The hullbeast's ugly face peeked over the ledge, growling and smelling like a kindergarten bathroom.

Gum Baby tugged my earlobe. "Bumbletongue, Gum Baby sure hope you got a plan. 'Cause, uh . . . it ain't looking good."

Hearing the normally brash pint-size peashooter so worried made me realize just how much trouble we were in.

As if the humongous iron monster hadn't made that clear.

Fetterlings screeched and thundered up the ramp. Brand flies dipped and swooped, buzzing overhead. Thandiwe met my eyes as I dropped into a crouch with her kierie, preparing to make our last stand. I'm sure my face looked as hopeless as hers did. There were just too many of them, and not enough of us. The reinforcements had never arrived. The Ridgefolk had been either sedated, hauled away, or barricaded behind stone doors. We were on our own.

Drumbeats sounded, faint and distant, like someone was playing somewhere out on Isihlangu. Maybe it was a distress call. The hullbeast raised his arm and easily swatted aside hundreds of brand flies. Two more swings and the air cleared. Thandiwe lay on the ground, covering Ayanna, shielding her from the flies. Miraculously, though dozens and dozens of dented metal bugs lay scattered around the entrance to the trams, the princess's skin was clear. But Ayanna's . . .

"No!" I shouted.

As the fetterlings turned the final curve, I sprinted toward my injured friend. But the hullbeast was faster. Its massive arm stretched toward the prone figures, and I felt my heart drop.

I wasn't going to make it.

41

THE MAGIC AX

THE DRUMBEAT GREW LOUDER, AND THE SOUND OF FLAPPING wings floated past my ear on a faint breeze. As the hullbeast reached for my friends, as fetterlings stormed after me and brand flies circled the silver gem lights like vultures, the drums pounded harder and harder, and I stopped running.

A crow cawed and thunder clapped, and everyone in Isihlangu froze in time.

"Seems like you in a spot of trouble, sure it does."

High John stepped out of the fold of Old Familiar's wings, his footsteps sending little twisters of dust spinning down the ramp. In one hand he held an ax with a head that glowed like an angry red coal. I swear I saw a face on it winking at me.

"You came back," I half accused, half sobbed.

"Thought I wouldn't?"

I didn't answer. Instead, I pointed to where Ayanna and Thandiwe lay just past the motionless arm of the hullbeast.

"Please, you've got to help them! Ayanna's been branded, and maybe Thandiwe, too, and I can't tell if they're moving, and the hullbeast is gonna swallow them and drag them away if we don't—"

"Okay, okay," High John said. "We're gonna do this together. All right?"

I took a breath, then another, and nodded. High John grinned, clapped me on the shoulder, then backed up and turned to face the hullbeast. He eyed it, then patted the head of his ax.

"Okay, love, seems we need to go to work again." High John took a few steps back down the ramp to where the charging fetterlings were suspended in time. He motioned for me to follow. "You come help me with these fancy contraptions, let Old Familiar take care of those poison flies, and my ax will handle that giant over there, sure it will."

"Your ax will...?"

My voice trailed off as High John tossed the ax in the air AND IT STAYED THERE.

I licked my lips. *"She gifted John a magic ax,"* I recited.

"Hey now, I know that story."

"I can't believe it's true!" One of the many stories Nana used to tell us about High John was how he fell in love with the devil's daughter. In order to win her hand, the devil told him he had to clear an enormous field, plant corn, then harvest it, all in one day. The devil's daughter, in love with the man, gave High John a magic ax and plow to complete the task.

"Where's the plow?" I asked.

High John raised an eyebrow. "You want me to plant some iron monsters?"

"No, I guess that wouldn't make sense."

"I reckon it wouldn't. Now, you got any more questions, or can we mosey on about our business?"

I raised my fists and nodded. He snorted, then tilted his head at Old Familiar. The giant crow cawed once and flapped its enormous wings. The air in the great hall shimmered and rippled, like a pond when you skip stones across it, and the world came back to life.

The next few minutes were a blur.

I punched left and right, nonstop, knocking fetterlings off the ramp or smashing them into the wall. High John danced between the iron monsters, tangling them up as they lunged at him and leaving them twisted in rusty knots, juicy targets for my hooks and uppercuts. The ramp was just wide enough for High John and me to defend. Nothing got past us.

Chop chop chop

High John's ax went to work on the hullbeast. I caught a glimpse once when I spun away from an attack. It wasn't pretty. You ever see a twig get caught beneath a lawn mower? Or tree branches fed into a wood-chipper? Yeah.

Chop chop chop

Meanwhile, Old Familiar cawed and hunted brand flies. Though the bugs swarmed around him, the poison didn't seem to have any effect on the shadow bird—his black feathers just absorbed it like ink into the page. Then, with a clack of his beak, the flies were gone. I even managed to punch a few knotted-up fetterlings into the air and watched as Old Familiar snapped them up, too.

"Last one," High John called, kicking a wriggling and screeching tangle of fetterlings down the ramp toward me. I sized them up, gripped both hands together like a club, and grinned.

"Fore!" I shouted, then belted the iron monsters clear off the ramp.

"Nice!"

I grinned, but the smile fell off my face when I heard a moan of pain. High John and I sprinted up the ramp, kicking aside battered and deformed brand flies, and slid to a stop next to Thandiwe. Chestnutt lay on Ayanna's chest, listening. The tiny bunny lifted her head slowly, like it weighed twice as much as usual, and her eyes glistened.

"She's not breathing," she whispered, and my blood froze.

42

HOODOO AND CONFESSIONS

"CAN YOU HELP HER?" I ASKED. MY VOICE CRACKED AND I DIDN'T even care.

High John looked worried as he pulled the root bag from around his neck and laid it above Ayanna's heart. "This poison, it ain't something of the body."

"What?"

He pointed at the brands that marred her brown skin—dark and angry blue-purple welts. "No fever, no twitchin'—just these marks, looking like they've always been there. She's still alive, but..." He shook his head. "This is beyond my conjure, I'm thinking. I'll try, though. Just not here. I need Old Familiar for this. Let's go." He gathered Ayanna in his arms, then stepped off the edge of the ramp.

Thandiwe gasped, then gasped again when Old Familiar rose into the air with High John on his back. I immediately jumped on too, with Gum Baby in my hood.

Thandiwe took a deep breath. "You need my help," she said, more to herself than to me. "This fight is not over." She strapped her forebear to her arm, picked up Chestnutt, and joined us.

I managed a smile—leaving home was not an easy choice to make—but my eyes never left Ayanna.

Thandiwe settled behind me and asked me a question.

"What?" I hadn't heard her. My attention was on High John as he laid Ayanna down on the broadest part of the giant crow's back and secured her with rope.

"I thought you didn't like flying," Thandiwe murmured, eyeing Old Familiar cautiously.

"I don't" was all I said.

"Y'all best hang on," High John called back, and then the crow gave two powerful flaps and rose in the air.

"Tristan! Wait!"

The Amagqirha waved from the floor below. She climbed onto the stage with Nyame's Story Box in her arms. Old Familiar spiraled down, and I reached for the now irrelevant piece of junk when we got close enough.

But instead of giving it to me, she put it down and grabbed my wrist. "May your ancestors guide you. And remember—all of Alke is with you." Her eyes flashed silver, like the twists in her hair and the beads around her wrists and ankles. The Amagqirha stepped back as Old Familiar lifted into the air again, the crate in its talons, and flew out of the main entrance. I looked over my shoulder to see the diviner holding up a hand in farewell as she, the Ridgefolk, and the mountain they lived inside dwindled in the distance.

Thandiwe, sitting near the giant shadow crow's tail feathers, cradled Chestnutt, who seemed to be asleep. Gum Baby sat in Thandiwe's lap beside the little rabbit and spoke to me without looking up.

"Chestnutt's gonna be all right, right?"

Oh no. "Is she...?" I asked Thandiwe.

"Looks like she was stung, too," said the princess.

"Stupid bunny," said the doll. "Gum Baby should've been there, should've been protecting her. Bunny can't fight, she knows she can't fight. Why'd she think—?" She broke off, crossing her arms and shaking her head.

I didn't say anything as I kneeled by Ayanna's feet and held on to the rope tied around her ankles. Tears welled in my eyes. Uncle C was living up to his promise of taking everything from me.

We shot out of the mountain like a bottle rocket aimed at the stars. Outside, the sky glowed around the edges, moving from a rosy pink above Isihlangu to an angry red smear on the western horizon. The tear in the sky had spread like a crack in a windshield and was boiling the lands below with its glare. *Hurry up, then, and put us out of our misery,* I said silently to the haint.

When Old Familiar straightened out, I heard Thandiwe say behind me, "Ancestors, help us."

The mountainside below the Shield lay in ruins. Every sentinel tower was shattered. Glittering black fragments dotted the land, winking at us as we soared overhead. Deep gouges ran for yards, as if the iron monsters had taken out their wrath on the earth itself.

Thandiwe hissed in pain. I was about to go console her when High John called me from the front of the bird.

"Tristan, come here, would you?" His voice sounded calm. Like, too calm.

I stood up and took another glance around. Thandiwe, mourning her home. Gum Baby, hurting for her friend. Chestnutt and Ayanna clinging to life. Everybody fighting to hold on to something precious, at risk of losing it forever.

"What's wrong?" I asked, carefully shuffling past Ayanna and over to High John.

"Two things." He cleared his throat, then spoke in a lowered voice. "Ayanna's fading fast. Nothing I'm doing is helping, boy, it sure ain't. I'm trying, but I reckon I don't got the conjure for it."

Fading fast. His words punched me in my throat, and I couldn't speak.

High John looked out over the foothills. "She ain't gonna make it to MidPass, Tristan. Not like this. But..."

Something in his voice pulled my eyes toward his.

"But there may be someone—someones—in that shiny Alkean city yonder."

I followed his finger as he pointed to the north and west. "You mean the Golden Crescent?"

"That's the one. I know some folk who got stronger conjure than I do. Might be they can save our pilot if we can get her there in time."

I chewed my lip. "We were going to see Nyame anyway." I explained our plan to ask the sky god to repair the Story Box. Then I studied him. "You said 'two things.' What's the second?"

He crouched by Ayanna and pointed to the conjure bag he'd laid on her chest. "Like I said, this ain't doing much. It's supposed to keep her spirit close to her body, help her fight off whatever poison those metal creatures put in her soul. But she needs more—she needs your help."

"What can I do?"

He patted a spot next to Ayanna. "Sit awhile. Talk to her. You've got the spider god's gift, boy. Might be you can reach her where the conjure bag can't."

"You want me to tell her a story? What kind?"

"Just talk to her. What about don't matter much to me. Speak to her soul, distract her from the pain."

Speak to her soul. Right.

But I sat down and nodded. "I'll do my best."

He clapped my shoulder and moved up front to guide Old

Familiar. I sat there, crisscross applesauce on the spine of a giant crow, staring at the unconscious form of the girl who'd had my back from the start. No questions asked—well, lots of questions, but never about whether she should help me.

What to say?

What would...? What would...? I gritted my teeth, forcing the name of my best friend back into my head. Eddie. What would Eddie say if he were here?

Eddie would...

He'd...

A slow smile crossed my face. Eddie would introduce himself.

Alke rolled by beneath us as I gathered my words. Isihlangu's misty peaks occasionally popped into view, like EKGs by a hospital bedside. The wind pushed and pulled at Ayanna's twists. I tucked a loose one behind her ear, then cleared my throat.

"Hey. It's... it's me." I took a deep breath. I couldn't lose another friend. I just couldn't. "High John said you... you're still there, that I should talk to you, like you can hear me. Because you *can* hear me. So... I guess I'm gonna talk."

Old Familiar rose and fell with each powerful beat of its wings. The up-and-down motion reminded me of a ship fighting against the current. It should have made me feel nauseated and tense like it normally does, but my fear for Ayanna outweighed my fear of heights.

"You asked me why...back there...why I always look for a chance to be a hero. Well"—I inhaled, sucking in as much air as I could, then let it out in a rush—"the truth is, the one time I *should've* saved someone, I panicked. I...messed up and they...they died. And it haunts me. That failure haunts me every night."

Uncle C thought he was smart. The haint had left me with the one memory I hated most. The memory of Eddie's death. Well, all memories serve a purpose.... What are memories except stories we tell ourselves, right?

"We were coming home from a field trip to the museum," I went on. "In Chicago, middle of winter, so the roads were a bit icy. We were so close to making it back to the school—I think we were only a few blocks away—when we drove over a bridge and hit a patch of ice. The bus...the bus spun around one hundred eighty degrees and we slid into the other lane, right into the path of a truck."

I sensed someone moving next to me on Old Familiar, but right then I could only see snow flurries trickling through a shattered window and flashing red lights against a gray sky.

"The impact smashed the rear of the bus, where we were sitting. We always sat in the back so we could talk our nerdy talk without anyone looking at us weird. The emergency exit door was knocked off, and the floor was cracked, and exhaust was pouring in, making it hard to breathe. But I could see... I saw that the bus was hanging over the edge of the bridge....

"All the kids were screaming, and I kept hearing adults shout, 'Hold on, we're getting help, just hold on.'

"Eddie was in the back corner, trapped between two seats, struggling and failing to free himself. He asked me to save him. 'Tristan, pull me out. Tristan. Tristan.' I still hear his voice. I still see his hand reaching for me. I didn't move. I was so scared. I was scared of falling, of drowning in the water below. I didn't wanna die. I didn't wanna die, and that's all I could think about, that I didn't wanna die. And Eddie called me, and I didn't wanna die."

Tears were rolling down my face now, and I took a deep, shuddering breath. I finally looked up.

Everyone crouched nearby. Thandiwe with Gum Baby on her shoulder, and High John holding an unconscious Chestnutt.

"Some hero, right?" I said.

"Tristan, it wasn't—" he began, but I cut him off.

"Don't give me that mess. Don't even. Y'all grown folks quick to say something like that. 'Oh, it wasn't your fault.' Don't lie to me, High John. Give me that much, at least."

Silence followed the rant, and I focused on my breathing. In and out. In and out.

High John sat down and set Chestnutt in his lap. A tiny bag hung around her neck—more of his conjure medicine. He sighed, then turned to me. "Fine. I reckon I can at least be honest, sure I can. Could you have saved your friend? Maybe. But that maybe ain't gonna change anything. Can't live your life with grief whispering in your ear, pulling you this way and that. But you can't shove it in a drawer deep inside yourself, neither. Naw, you got to sit grief down and talk to it. Listen to it. Come to terms with it. Pain is the body's way of saying it's healing, so you gotta let it heal."

I shrugged. "That's what Mr. Richardson says. 'Give it time, let it work itself out naturally.' But how much time does it need?" I caught a glossy black feather that fluttered loose from Old Familiar's back. "Eddie was my best friend, and I miss him, and walking around with this hurt...well, it hurts."

Thandiwe spoke up. "The elders have a saying. *Too much is the same as not enough.*"

"What does that mean?"

Gum Baby flicked sap at me. "It means be sad, but not too sad."

"Okay, but—"

"Gum Baby ain't got time to lead you everywhere, Bumbletongue. This is one of life's great mysteries. A puzzle. Shoot, it might even be one of those hedgehog things. What are they called? Echidnas, that's right."

I stared at her. "You mean an *enigma*?"

"Why you always correcting somebody?"

"The point is," High John interrupted with a ghost of a grin, "you should grieve your friend. But remember to live your life as it is now, and not how it would have been. Never forget, but accept. Understand?"

I nodded. I thought I did.

"Hey," Thandiwe called. She pointed over the left wing, where a glimmering sliver of golden-orange land appeared. "We're here."

43
THE MMOATIA FOREST

SOMETHING WAS OFF.

The burning tear in the sky covered the Golden Crescent in an orange glow. Ghostly flames danced on the beautiful palaces beneath Old Familiar's wings, somehow throwing off real heat. Nyame's land had turned into a giant sauna, and sweat beaded on my forehead.

But it wasn't just that.

There was a . . . feeling in the air like something was lurking, watching and following us as we arrived. That familiar feeling from the Drowned Forest, and from my dreams.

They were here.

Uncle C and the Maafa.

I wasn't the only one who noticed. High John clutched his conjure bag and frowned, Thandiwe held her kierie at the ready, and Gum Baby . . . well, Gum Baby was herself.

"This ain't how Gum Baby left the place! You see? This is why Gum Baby can't have nice things. Company comes over and RUINS EVERYTHING!"

We soared over the empty city. Ivory towers, now beet red as they reflected the burning rip in the sky, stood tall and angry. The crystal-blue pools boiled and steamed, and a thick mist curled down the wide avenues and marble-lined streets.

The giant crow landed near a familiar forest with the golden fence and gate running around it. Gum Baby's eyes grew big and she shuffled closer to me.

"Say," she mumbled, "ain't this the place with those creepy whistles and where you ran away like a—?"

"High John," I said hurriedly, "how will this help Ayanna? The city is empty—so I heard."

High John slipped off Old Familiar's back. His face tightened, like he was about to do something adults found uncomfortable, like plunge a toilet, or apologize to a kid. He straightened his vest, smoothed the front of his pants, then cleared his throat.

"Can you bring Ayanna? Might be I need to have my hands free."

He frowned at the arching gate, then snorted at the crumbled gilded leaves in a pile off to the side.

Gum Baby asked him nervously, "You, uh, you know this place?"

"Yeah," he muttered. "I studied under...them, for many years. Before...Well, before."

I squatted and gently lifted Ayanna.

"Tristan?"

The whisper was so faint I almost missed it. But when Ayanna's head shifted, and I looked down to see her eyes open, crinkled with confusion, I stopped moving.

"Right here. I'm right here. We're getting help—you're gonna be on your feet yelling at me in no time. Just hold on."

"Tristan," she murmured again, and then her eyes fluttered shut.

"Ayanna?"

As soon as I stepped off Old Familiar with her in my arms, the giant crow cawed and took off, disappearing into the shadows.

My voice carried down the street as I told the others, "She woke up. She spoke, but now..."

High John's face grew worried. "Come on, we need to hurry."

The marble street echoed with our footsteps, and the mist curling around our waists was the only other thing moving as we made our way to the gate. High John raised an eyebrow at the statue with the gummy gag still over her mouth, and Gum Baby and I looked at each other. There's a time for honesty and a time to focus on the important issues possibly threatening everyone in Alke.

We crossed the threshold, and just like before, the whistling began. Thandiwe kept glancing over her shoulders as she walked, and Gum Baby hid in my hood.

"Look who's the scaredy-cat now," I said.

"Take one for the team," she whispered in my ear. "Gum Baby's too pretty to get in trouble."

High John led us to the foot of the large sycamore tree, and once again I stood in awe of its massive size. It reminded me of the Tree of Power back in MidPass, with its gnarly roots and roof-like branches. We stopped in a hollow among the roots, and High John surprised me. He got down on his knees, placed his hands on his thighs, and began to whistle.

"What is he doing?" Thandiwe whispered. "He's going to get us caught!"

The branches in the tree began to rustle, and leaves floated down around us, as though someone—or a bunch of someones—was climbing down. The mysterious whistles intensified, and High John paused, then began to whistle again.

"I think," I said, realization dawning, "that's the point. Listen. They're talking to each other. Well, signaling each other."

"Who's *they*?"

A small shadow stepped from behind the trunk, and in the fiery glow of the sky, I saw a tiny, fairylike creature. Suddenly a lot of things fell into place.

High John's mentors in conjure and rootwork.

A forest palace.

The whistling stopped, and High John said to us, "I reckon this might be a mite strange, but this is—"

"A mmoatia," I interrupted. "I mean an aboatia—one of the Mmoatia."

High John paused. "Yes. How—? No, let me guess. That nana of yours."

Thandiwe looked back and forth, confused. "What is an aboatia?"

"A forest fairy," I answered. The aboatia had a long nose and brown skin that rippled like a forest stream. Its thick braids touched the ground, and its sharp eyes followed me as I took a deep breath and gingerly stepped forward. I kneeled in front of it, still cradling Ayanna, and looked at High John. "Nana told me that Mmoatia are the keepers of healing. Illnesses and ailments are their domain—and they will teach cures to those they deem worthy."

I remembered more, but I didn't think it would be a good idea to say it out loud. Nyame had tasked Anansi with capturing one of the Mmoatia to satisfy his price for the Story Box. To catch the fairy, Anansi had used Gum Baby. (This was back when she was silent, believe it or not.) The aboatia became stuck to the little doll and—*whoosh*—Anansi took them both off to the sky god.

No wonder Gum Baby was hiding now.

High John nodded. "They've agreed to help. But . . . only Ayanna. No one else may stay. Seems they've had a recent problem with unwelcome intruders."

His eyes flashed at me and suddenly my sneakers looked incredibly fascinating. But Gum Baby rustled in my hood.

"What about Chestnutt?" she stage-whispered. "She's hurt, too!"

High John whistled with the fairy for a few minutes, then nodded. "She can stay as well. But now we must go. The others are getting agitated, and you don't want to anger the Mmoatia."

"You can say that again," Gum Baby muttered.

"What?" asked High John.

"Nothing!" I answered quickly. I laid Ayanna on a flat stretch of ground, thick with grass. Goose bumps rose on her arms in the midnight breeze, and, after a brief moment of hesitation, I took off my hoodie ("Hey!" Gum Baby cried as she tumbled out) and draped it over her.

"I'm coming back," I whispered to Ayanna. "So don't you dare go anywhere."

I wanted to ask the aboatia questions, get High John to translate. . . . Was Ayanna going to be okay? Could they help her? She was unconscious again, and it was ripping me apart inside.

First Eddie, then his memories, and now Ayanna? It all was too much.

More shadows danced beneath the tree, and the whistling

picked up again. Gum Baby danced in place nervously. A hand rested on my shoulder, and High John stood up.

"It's time, Tristan," he said. "Gotta get that box to Nyame."

"Yeah, let's go already!" hissed Gum Baby, tugging my arm.

I nodded and got to my feet. The aboatia cocked its head at the charms dangling from my wrist, visible now that my hoodie's sleeves weren't hiding them. It whistled, and High John nodded and whistled back. Then he turned to me.

"Hold out your arm," he commanded.

"Why?" I asked, even as I did so. The fairy came closer, and I tried not to stare as it hopped this way and that, peering at the charms. It whistled, and High John rubbed his chin. The fairy bowed, and he bowed in response.

"Come on, kids," he said, heading for the gate.

"What was that about?" Thandiwe asked as she and I followed. Gum Baby stood on my shoulder, one sticky hand on my head for balance.

"Turns out," High John answered, "that despite Anansi's ultimate insult, the bearers of his mark are welcome beneath the branches of the Mmoatia." He met my eyes and grinned. "Seems they have taken a shine to you, boy. You should find your way back here at some point to see why. Favors from the fairies are a powerful thing, sure they are."

I definitely planned to come back—for Ayanna and Chestnutt. Gum Baby patted my head and whispered, "Don't expect Gum Baby to go with you. Nuh-uh."

We stopped outside the gates and retrieved the Story Box from where Old Familiar had left it. High John glared at the burning tear flickering in the sky.

"Time's getting thin. The rip has nearly reached the mainland. We've got to hurry."

"Nyame's palace is this way," I said. I pointed at the trail markers Chestnutt had left during our last visit here, feeling an aching tug. At least she and Ayanna were in good hands now. "Let's go get this Story Box fixed."

44
WE'RE ALL BROKEN—STORY BOX, TOO

THERE'S A POINT WHEN I GET SO WORKED UP I CAN'T TELL MY emotions apart. Am I angry or sad or scared? Is it everything at once, or none of the above? Mr. Richardson said that when I feel that way, I should grab one emotion like a rope and pull myself back to the moment it first hit me. Retrace my footsteps. Do some mental detective work.

While we followed the silent street to Nyame's shimmering gateway, I followed my tangled and raw feelings back to their beginnings. There was anger at Eddie for leaving me. Stress over Ayanna and Chestnutt being injured. Fear of things getting even worse and my not being able to get back home. Frustration with everybody telling me *Man up*, or *It'll be fine*, or *Go punch something, because it'll make you feel better*.

By the time we arrived at the large plaza and stopped in front of the towering gateway, my hands were shaking and my heartbeat was pounding in my ears.

"You okay?" Thandiwe asked.

I wasn't sure what would come out of my mouth, so I just nodded.

High John looked around uneasily. "Something don't feel right."

"What? Gum Baby don't see anything."

"Naw, it's . . . in the air." He glanced at me. "Do you feel it, too? The rhythm, the wind—it's all wrong. That hole in the sky is turning this world inside out."

Ah yes, one more emotion I'd forgotten about.

Guilt.

High John was right. The electric rhythm, the drumbeat, the words from the land that I'd gotten used to hearing in the background—they'd all disappeared, leaving just a buzzing hum, like speakers cranked all the way up with no music playing. Like lightning about to strike.

"There's a storm coming," I said, keeping my voice low. "I can feel it. We need to hurry."

"Yeah." High John looked around one more time, then checked the sky. "Yeah, sure you right."

We ran through the gate and down the path to the sky god's palace. I felt the statues' golden eyes on me again, but this time their gaze was more appraising than threatening. The Story Box felt heavier as I lugged it past them, and when we reached the final statue, the old queen who'd saved us from the bosslings, I swear I saw her wink.

"Did she just—?" Gum Baby whispered from my shoulder, and I nodded.

"I think so."

The burning sky crackled overhead as we slammed through the giant palace door and skidded to a stop in Nyame's hall. Leopard paused in mid-paw-lick, Python raised his massive head from the stone floor, and the sky god sat moodily on the throne.

"Well," Nyame said, his eyes flashing almost as bright as the tear in the sky. "The non-hero returns. The ungrateful, the selfish, the spurner of gifts. Come to complain some more?"

His eyes moved to Gum Baby and softened, then to Thandiwe and High John, where they lingered. "And you've changed your team. Interesting. Is this a downgrade or an upgrade, young Tristan?"

High John had both hands in his pockets, but I could see the anger in his jaw when he spoke through tight lips. "Your sky god seems upset," he said. "All this gold and nobody to impress."

Nyame got off his throne and stalked down the dais stairs. "Mind your tongue, vagabond. You are here because I allow it."

"Sit back down and count your money, Pops," High John said with a sneer. "You ain't scaring nobody in here."

Leopard growled, a rumble like thunder in a forest, and

the massive beast prowled over. High John grinned, a wide, easy smile that I was starting to suspect meant the opposite of good times ahead.

"Tell your kitty to play nice before I send it outside to chase its tail." The grin disappeared and High John's shadow started to stretch and grow. "After I remove it."

Nyame's eyes began to glow, and I sighed and stepped between the two. Honestly, adults are the worst. Do-as-I-say-not-as-I-do hypocrites. Eddie and my memories were out there somewhere, and these two were having a spitting contest.

"I see you're feeling better than the last time we were here," I said, dropping the Story Box in front of the sky god. Nyame paused, scowling at the interruption, then froze.

"Is that—?" he asked, reaching out a trembling arm, and I nodded.

He traced a finger over the splintered and warped lid, then let his hand fall. The symbols etched on its sides sparkled briefly, as if they remembered their former glory, before they faded back to worn shadows.

"It's been emptied," he whispered.

"Anansi did it," I said.

The sky god looked up, his eyes brimming with the sorrows of a thousand lost happy endings.

I held up my adinkra bracelet. "It's the only thing that makes sense. We found his notes and the iron monsters he'd been researching. The Story Box—he used it to attract them, like bait. But something went wrong. There was a mishap, a fight. . . . I think he accidentally drained it of its stories."

Nyame picked up the Story Box and hugged it to his chest. "Anansi . . ." he repeated, staring blankly at a waterfall across the room.

He summoned the pedestal from under the floor and placed the Story Box gently on top. Then he leaned on the stand, suddenly seeming old and weary.

"But where are the stories now?" Thandiwe asked. "And why did the Weaver go into hiding?" She looked between me and Nyame. "When Anansi gave us the Box, you hadn't even punched the sky open yet. The iron monsters were still scattered and weak."

I winced at the reminder that most of this was my fault. "I don't know, but I plan on asking when I see him."

"So you still intend to go through with this?" Nyame asked.

"We have to. When I smashed the Bottle Tree and created this mess, something fell into this world along with Gum Baby and me—a haint. I know what he wants now. He wants the Story Box so he can get stronger."

High John thumbed his belt buckle and frowned. "You keep on saying *he*, not *it*. This supervillain of yours got a name?"

"When I saw him, he told me to call him Uncle C."

Nyame narrowed his eyes. "*Uncle*. UNCLE? You are related to the creature persecuting my people?" The suspicion in his tone made me flinch, but I stood up straight and shook my head.

"No, of course not! It's his idea of a sick, twisted joke! And he's coming for us. For me. And he's bringing the Maafa with him."

Nyame stood up straight. "Here?"

"Take a good look at the sky, Sky God," High John sneered.

The edges of Nyame's fists began to glow white-hot, and before things got any worse, I had to step in again.

"Enough! Iron monsters are coming back here, and they're just the first wave. According to the Ridge's Amagqirha, there could be a big war." I looked at Thandiwe. "She told me the elders felt it as well."

Thandiwe looked troubled. "So what do we do?"

I kept my eyes on Nyame. "We need you to restore the Story Box. Then we can lure Anansi and convince him to close the hole in the sky. That will weaken the iron monsters enough for us to be able to destroy them."

"And this Uncle C?" Nyame asked.

High John stepped up to my side. "We'll deal with him, the boy and I. Together."

I smiled sadly at him. "It will take more than just you, me, and Old Familiar. Or even John Henry and Miss Sarah and Miss Rose."

He stiffened. "I'm not going to fight with—"

"There's no other way," I interrupted softly. I turned to Nyame. "We're going to have to work together. Midfolk and Alkeans."

Nyame and High John eyed each other, and the sky god snorted. It was a very human thing, now that I think about it. Like two boxers who had just finished a match that ended in a draw, both knowing they'd fought a classic bout.

"Yeah, we'll see," High John muttered, and I rolled my eyes.

"So, can you fix the Story Box?" Thandiwe asked Nyame.

He pursed his lips, then shrugged. "I can, though I can't see what good it will do. Anansi's trickery may prove to be the end of us all."

"It be your own people," muttered Gum Baby.

Of all the sticky things that had come out of that doll's mouth, that may have been the stickiest.

Nyame sighed and planted himself in front of the dais. He grabbed the lip of the pedestal, spoke a few words under his breath, and it lifted and began to spin slowly with the Story Box on top. He muttered more incantations as he reached into thin air and pulled out things I'm not sure I can describe, though I'll try.

He filled the cracks in the wood with a father's pride and a mother's belief. He wove dying rays of sunlight and a breath of fresh air together into ribbons of ivory, which he sent over to wind around the sides of the Box, and then he pulled them tight to straighten the warped planks. The glimmer of a river was molded into place on the lid, and he added the flash of a gem to the latch. I heard laughter as he reinforced the corners with glee. Finally, he outlined the top and sides of the box with gold filigree and stepped back.

Nyame blew gently on the Story Box, and, like an artist removing shavings from a sculpture, revealed his gleaming masterpiece.

"Holy—" High John breathed.

"Sweet peaches," I said.

Gum Baby clapped.

The gold-and-ivory box was almost too pretty to look at, and the longer I stared at it, the more I was drawn to it. Deep inside me, I heard the power Nyame had called upon, and I—

High John grabbed my wrist. "Easy there."

I frowned. "What—?" I began, then stopped. I'd started walking forward without realizing it and was inches away from plucking the Story Box off the pedestal.

I swallowed and took three giant steps back. "No wonder everyone wants it."

Nyame looked proud. "I do good work."

"Yeah, yeah," Gum Baby said, crossing her arms. "Gum Baby will give you a sticker. Now where's Anansi? Gum Baby got some questions that need answering, quick, fast, and in a hurry."

Nyame eyed her for a second, then shook his head and headed for the door to the rooftop gardens. The floating pedestal with the Story Box on top trailed him, still spinning. Gum Baby made a face at the sky god's back, and we all followed.

In the gardens upstairs, Nyame settled the pedestal near the front edge of the palace roof, overlooking the marina and the bay. The sky god studied its placement for several seconds and made some small adjustments. Thandiwe looked at me and I shrugged impatiently. I wanted this to be over with. I wanted Chestnutt back with us. I wanted to check on Ayanna, to see if she had been healed.

The world may have been in trouble, but friends are friends, and I wanted them close by.

"Tristan," Nyame called. He pointed to the Story Box. "It's time. Open it."

I nodded, then wiped my palms on my shorts. This was it. The moment we'd fought, struggled, cried, and worked so hard for. Gum Baby patted my head, and Thandiwe saluted me with her fist. High John grinned and winked. I took a deep breath, then stepped in front of the pedestal.

"Find the thread," Nyame said before he stepped back.

The thread.

The common story we all share, that passes from city to city, from country to country, from world to world. The story that everyone's uncle wants to tell again and again. The story told at the watercooler. The story told around the campfire. The story told at bedtime, whether in Chicago or Alabama, the Golden Crescent or MidPass.

I closed my eyes.

Music.

Drumbeats.

Clapping.

Laughter.

Calls.

Responses.

And there, beneath it all, hanging by a silver strand of childlike anticipation, I saw it.

"Let's say there was a land where the People once lived. A land of story, of dreams, of heroes and of gods. A land born of pain and joy, for all stories contain both. Let's say this land was called . . . Alke."

The rhythm gathered beneath my skin, and my palms itched with the need to create, to shape. I grabbed the thread with both hands and opened my eyes. The Story Box burned with light so bright it seared my vision and left behind floating dots of color. It shone like a beacon, a lighthouse of hope and joy.

Thandiwe gasped.

The pedestal beneath the Story Box turned into a pillar of light, and symbols blazed to life within it. In trails of copper ink guided by an invisible hand, the symbols were applied to the magnificent chest in honor of the gods of the

Golden Crescent. Their adinkras blurred from reddish-gold to dazzling white as beneath them scenes from another time were depicted:

People danced in a circle around a glowing golden box, as a man with golden eyes watched over them.

A spider wove a web of silk that turned into words, and men and women wearing the spiderweb adinkra collected the words and marched off.

A group of people, including a spider and a being with glowing eyes, confronted a terrifying creature rising out of the sea, their hands outstretched, preventing the evil from advancing. This last image wasn't as bright as the rest, and that bothered me a bit, but then the splendor of the entire Story Box swept me away.

It was glorious.

Beautiful.

Amazing.

But...

"Where's Anansi?" Gum Baby asked. She stomped around, looking in the bushes, and splashed through the waterfalls. "Where is he?"

I could feel the energy rolling off of the Story Box in waves. Nyame could feel it, too, I knew, because the adinkra on the hems of his robes flared with golden light, and his eyes did the same. And High John could sense it—his shadow stretched across the rooftop over flowers and statues.

So where was Anansi?

Nyame turned suddenly toward the west and peered out at the ocean. He stood there, frozen, for several moments. "Something is wrong," he whispered. He turned to me. "Close the Box, quickly now!"

A loud roar sounded in the palace below. I flinched, severing my connection with the Story Box. Leopard roared again and again, and High John frowned. Suddenly he too went stiff as he looked over the ocean. Without a word, he twisted into his shadow with a gust of wind, and in the next instant he took off into the sky on Old Familiar's back. The giant shadow crow cawed as they soared above us.

"What do you see?" Nyame called.

"A burning wave, biggest I've ever seen!" High John shouted back. "It's knocking aside boats like they feathers, sure it is."

"A wave . . ." Nyame muttered. He turned to me. "Tristan—"

But I wasn't paying attention. My eyes were glued to the marina, where a tsunami carrying columns of fire was sweeping toward us. Boats and oversize yachts crashed into each other with noises that sounded like cannons and gunfire.

"What's happening?" Thandiwe shouted. Gum Baby scrambled up to her perch on my shoulder to look, and she gasped.

Before I could answer, something rose out of the sea, and out of my nightmares, too. A dilapidated vessel, bigger and more horrifying than any bone ship, split the surface, growing larger and larger. Its masts were shattered and its grimy gray sails hung limp and torn. Holes of different sizes dotted the hull, and burning seawater flooded out like lava. Figures moved on the deck.

Fetterlings.

Hundreds of them.

And with them came that familiar feeling of suffocating terror. The weight of years, decades, centuries of hate and violence—it all gathered in the air and pressed down on my shoulders. The stench of death and dying, of rot and decay, rolled over me. I knew those feelings. I knew that presence. I'd been inside that vessel. Uncle C was in that thing.

Which meant that ship was—

"The Maafa," I whispered.

45

FLIGHT OF THE MIDFOLK

"THAT'S THE MAAFA?"

Thandiwe gripped her forebear-turned-shield tight in one hand and pointed at the massive ship with the other. It vomited fire and fetterlings as it cut through the burning waves. Anything in its path was crushed beneath its hull or charred beyond recognition as it entered the bay. Gray mist and black smoke followed in its wake, while smashed wreckage floated in front of it.

Nyame whirled on me in fury. "You said my people still lived in that thing. Look at it! Tell me how *anything* could survive in that!"

"I saw them!" I protested, but a sinking feeling grew in the pit of my stomach.

How *could* anything live in that?

The sky god turned away in disgust and paced the edge of the palace roof. The leviathan of fire and iron pushed its way into the shallow harbor. The golden spire shuddered as boat after damaged boat was thrown against its base. Nyame fumed, his robes flapping in the ash-flecked wind.

"First my people. Now my land? I cannot allow it." The sky god pointed at the Story Box. "We did just what this uncle of yours wanted. The beasts will come for it, and we must not let them take it. Otherwise, this"—he gestured at the bay that slowly burned—"will only be the beginning." His eyes pierced mine. "Your world will be next."

And with that totally not-ominous statement, Nyame stepped off the roof. As he dropped out of sight, a flare of bright light exploded and streaked through the sky like a missile. It arced high—so high it appeared like a second sun, or the start of a second rip—before dropping down behind a cluster of palaces. I lost sight of it for a second, but the fifty-foot wave that raced toward the invading ship, dousing fire spouts and drowning fetterlings, let me know he had landed in the marina.

And it was because my gaze followed the path of Nyame's flight that I noticed a group of familiar faces.

Gum Baby spotted them, too. "Look!" she shouted. "It's John Henry! And Miss Sarah and Miss Rose! They made it out!"

Thandiwe grinned. "MidPass lives, Tristan. They live."

My knees went weak, but it was a good feeling, like I'd just been declared the winner of a match. John Henry waded through the bay, knocking debris out of his way with a swipe of his glowing hammer. He held a rope in his other hand, and he was pulling several rafts full of people and animals. In the air above, Miss Sarah and Miss Rose carried a large basket of additional refugees between them as they flapped to the shore. I didn't see Brer, but the rest were a sight for sore eyes.

"They rescued the Midfolk," I said. "John Henry understood my message."

Thandiwe glanced at me. "You sent a message? When?"

"Back when High John took me... It's hard to explain, but I did."

She looked skeptical, but instead of questioning me further, she pointed with the knob of her kierie. "Look—we're not the only ones who've spotted them."

A group of fetterlings were swimming across the bay toward the Midfolk. They looked like sharks as they cruised around the burning wreckage, silent and unseen.

Gum Baby pounded a fist into her other hand. "They're not going to make it."

Thandiwe placed her forebear on the ground and stepped on it, then looked at me and raised an eyebrow. "I can reach them. Can you protect the Story Box?"

"I can, but how are you going to get there in time? I thought your forebear only—"

"You think too much about the wrong things," Thandiwe said. "Do you know why we call them forebears? Because our ancestors are always there, lifting us and carrying us forward, and shielding us when we are vulnerable. Don't worry about me—worry about doing your part. You sure you can hold?"

I took stock of the scene—the flames, the fetterlings, and the Maafa, and the Midfolk fleeing them all. "I can hold," I said. "When you reach them, send Brer if you see him—a giant rabbit with scars, talks real slick. But take the rest of them to the Mmoatia forest, to Ayanna and Chestnutt. The fairies will protect them."

Thandiwe nodded, and without another word, hopped off the roof while slipping the forebear beneath her feet. She landed on a curving ivory buttress and rode it like a skate-boarder grinding a railing. The princess ended up in the plaza below with a full head of steam, and she carved down and around the wide paved street, using her kierie as a rudder. Soon she was out of sight, and I sighed.

"Girl's got skills," Gum Baby admitted. "Gum Baby taught her well."

I rolled my eyes, then shielded them as a blast of wind blew dust and ash into my face. High John stood on Old Familiar's back as the shadow crow cawed and flapped above us.

"Tristan, you've got company coming!" he shouted. "I reckon you might wanna get ready."

"What? Where?"

"Got some of them poison flies coming from the south,

and fetterlings from the north. Must've slipped by in the confusion. This old crow will take care of the bugs—can you handle them chain monsters?"

Sure enough, a dust cloud swept toward Nyame's palace, and the faint sounds of screeching and rattling carried over the roar of the chaos in the bay. I swallowed hard, then nodded. I only had to hold them off until Brer arrived. Whenever that was. "Yeah, I got this."

High John studied me and Gum Baby, then nodded. "Reckon you might need this," he said. He tossed down a sparkling, shiny piece of metal, and Gum Baby snagged it out of midair. "All them other gods giving you protection," he said. "Might as well do my part, sure I will."

I pried the charm out of Gum Baby's sticky grasp. The adinkra was two crossed swords with holes in the blades and handles, and it pulsed with dark light.

"What is this?" I asked.

High John smiled. "The akofena. The Swords of War. Symbol of courage and bravery. For when you need to defend several places at once."

Old Familiar flapped powerfully up in the air. "Take care now, you hear?" High John called. "Don't go dying—you and me got some talking to do." And with that, High John the Conqueror soared into the sky on his giant crow, hooting and hollering as he cut through smoke and flame to confront the swarm of brand flies racing toward us.

As soon as I slipped the adinkra onto my bracelet, four night-black boxing gloves shimmered into view. When I made fists, one pair of gloves floated shoulder-high on either side of me, and the second pair hovered near my waist. I now had six fists ready to pummel some iron monsters. When I relaxed my hands, the gloves disappeared.

I laughed. "Looks like we're doing some shadow boxing!" I called back to Gum Baby.

She let out a joyous whoop and cartwheeled across my shoulders.

"Bring it on!" she screamed. "Ain't nobody scared! Gum Baby got two hands eager to deal! This restaurant is open and ready to serve! Get your education for free, you thistle-heads, Gum Baby's an equal-opportunity destroyer!"

The stampede of fetterlings crashed against the base of the palace, and then the time for words was over.

A fight is a paralyzing thing.

When the time arrived for my first boxing match, I'd thought I was prepared. I mean, I'd trained forever, it seemed. Hit the bag. Ran the streets. Did whatever Dad and Granddad told me to. I was supposed to win.

But in the ring, once I was inside the ropes and everybody else was outside except the kid I had to face, all that practice disappeared. I had two heavy gloves, uncomfortable boots, and the desire to be anywhere else. Who was I kidding? I wasn't a boxer. I'd just gone along, because that's what a kid is supposed to do, right? Make his parents happy?

My opponent whupped me in all four corners of the ring.

From the first bell to the last, everything moved too fast. I couldn't keep up. My guard was too slow, my feet were too slow, my everything was just too dang slow.

But now...

Now I had purpose, which gave me all the energy I needed. I was Old Man Rawlins. I wasn't gonna lose...not today, chumps.

"Watch it!"

Gum Baby's warning came just in time—a rusty collar snapped shut inches from my neck as I jerked back.

"Get the sap out, fool!" Gum Baby flipped in midair, flinging her sticky ammunition at the fetterlings swarming over the rooftop. "Gum Baby always carrying you."

The akofena charm tingled, and my night-gloves flashed into existence. One jab, two jabs, three, and a trio of fetterlings the color of ashy scabs tumbled over the edge in pieces. I risked a glance behind me—the Story Box was still there on the pedestal—and then turned to face another group of screeching metal creatures.

We fought like that, Gum Baby and me, for what seemed like forever. Wave after wave of fetterlings swarmed over the rooftop gardens, and yet somehow we held them back. Gum Baby was a living terror. If she wasn't dancing over the heads of her opponents, she was tumbling through their chain-link bodies, depositing sticky traps that rooted them to the spot. Which left me batting cleanup.

Pop pop

My fists were everywhere.

Pop pop

Black fists in black gloves delivering black power two jabs at a time.

Pop pop

Finally, after the last group of fetterlings was repelled, we had a moment of rest. I looked out toward the water and tried to find everyone, to see how they were doing.

Old Familiar dipped and swirled, snapping brand flies out of the air like they weren't moving, the prince-turned-slave-turned-god standing atop and swinging his ax like a scythe through a field of wheat.

Nyame, like a sun flare that leaped from spot to spot, sent iron monsters flying into the bay with blasts of white-hot energy. I couldn't stare for long, or I'd be temporarily blinded. The sky god fought with the fury of exploding stars, and, as a lone god, he was targeted by most of the iron monsters.

But the refugees from Midfolk fought, too, for their very right to live, though they were far from home. John Henry, the raft line wrapped around his waist so he could use both hands, swung his hammer like he was back drilling through a mountain. Left and right, up and down, the hammer fell on fetterlings with the crash of metal on metal. No flourishes, just a steady rhythm.

Miss Sarah and Miss Rose circled and dove from above, flaying fetterlings with whiplike switches. They harried and harassed iron monsters like hawks scattering mice. As a result of everyone's efforts, the group made their way up the winding streets of the Golden Crescent unimpeded.

But, try as I might, I couldn't see Brer anywhere.

Instead, Thandiwe led the Midfolk stragglers. I don't know where she'd met up with them, or how she'd convinced them to follow her, but the warrior girl from the Ridge battered fetterlings with grim determination. She was on the ground, her forebear looped over her back, which freed her spear to pin foes to the ground while her kierie hammered them senseless.

Everywhere I looked, fetterlings and brand flies were being destroyed.

Yet, despite our progress, more and more of them were being disgorged from the Maafa. The supply seemed endless. And that wasn't all. The ship had reached the marina, and heavy troops were emerging from its fiery decks. Bosslings leaped into the waves, followed by several hullbeasts. They waded through burning waters and debris and lumbered ashore like nightmarish special forces.

"Dang," Gum Baby said from her perch on my shoulder. "Just . . . dang."

"I know what you mean." The reinforcements pushed Nyame back, even as he blasted them left and right, while still more dropped from the Maafa's decks. Suddenly my friends went from holding their ground to retreating.

And there was still no sign of Brer.

"Come on, Rabbit," I muttered. "Hurry up!"

"Tristan, look!"

A group of iron monsters broke off from the marina fight and chased after the Midfolk. Two bosslings and a hullbeast thundered up the street, and my heart plummeted. If they caught up, everyone would suffer, gods or not.

The remaining hullbeasts leaned back and belched forth a mass of brand flies. Shrieks filled the air as the charcoal cloud of metal bugs shot up into the air. High John and Old Familiar were quickly swarmed.

A shrill cry of pain dragged my attention away. I spun around, heart in my throat, as I caught a glimpse of a dark shape falling from the sky, feathers fluttering down like black snow.

Miss Rose.

She dropped out of view just outside Nyame's palace gates. "No!" I whispered.

John Henry bellowed in pain, too, and his hammer crashed to the ground like a tree falling. He backed up the curving street, his head the only thing I could see for a moment, the rest of him obscured by flowering trees and gold-covered rooftops. Miss Sarah followed close behind, the fight forgotten as a wail left her lips. More shrieks of pain and confusion rose as the rest of the Midfolk panicked.

A glint of metal winked in the corner of my eye, near the Mmoatia forest palace. Something waited in the trees, right at the spot John Henry and the others were rushing toward.

An ambush!

I had to warn them. Somehow, I had to drag the iron monsters away from Miss Rose and get the others to abandon the ambush. I needed to clear a path for High John so he could link up with the others and rescue the Midfolk.

It was time for a distraction.

Something that everyone, from fetterling to hullbeast, would focus on.

I needed the Story Box.

The restored treasure rested on the ivory column, the rose-gold symbols nearly faded away. It was closed, but I could still feel the thread of stories inside. My feet carried me over on their own, and I saw golden scenes glimmering on top of the chest.

Hold up.

One group of scenes, they showed . . .

I leaned in closer.

"Sweet peaches."

A figure standing in front of a seated group, a box strapped to his back. The same figure, his arms wide, still wearing the box, but this time it was cracked open. Symbols floating in, and symbols floating out. And finally, the figure walking away, the crowd waving, the box on his back now closed.

Anansesem didn't just tell stories, they collected them.

I walked around the Box, forcing myself to move slowly despite every urge to rush, to hurry and save my friends. And when I reached the back panel, where there were two sets of gold lines, I stopped.

They carried the stories from people to people.

"They *carried* them," I said, an idea popping into my head. "Here goes nothing." Concentrating, I reached for the rhythm of the story thread inside, and I spoke the sentence Nana started every one of her stories with.

They were the words of the Anansesem, uttered when traveling from village to village to spread the news.

"Let me give you some truth, and I hope it returns back to me."

All noise stopped.

The winds died, the waves calmed, and every iron monster—from brand fly to bossling—let out a harsh, rattling cry and charged toward Nyame's palace.

Toward me.

But I remained focused on the spectacle right in front of me.

The golden lines on the Box brightened and expanded until two straps extended from the glowing chest. I reached up and grabbed them, lifting the Story Box off the pedestal.

I slipped an arm through one, then the other, and shook my head in wonder as the Box stretched and changed and settled against my back.

It changed depending on who carried it.

I looked over my shoulder and snorted at the gold-and-black book bag I was now wearing, with golden zippers and a faint hum rippling through it. It was partially open, and the thrum of a half-finished story sent tingles up my spine and down into my fingertips. Adinkra decorated the straps—Nyame's symbol on the left, and Anansi's on the right—and I squeezed them, as nervous as a kid on his first day of school.

"What do we do?" Gum Baby asked.

I stared at her, then at the Story Box, and licked my lips. Uncle C wanted the Story Box? Then we were going to bring him the Story Box.

"Gum Baby, you're not gonna like this."

A few minutes later I walked down the stairs, the Story Box on my back, to give my first official performance as Anansesem to the most dangerous audience I could ever imagine.

I exited the palace and entered the courtyard to face a sea of fetterlings. They quivered as I approached, then parted like magic. My eyes stared straight ahead, even though I could hear them close ranks behind me, cutting off any retreat. But running away was the last thing on my mind.

I had an appointment to keep.

46
A DANGEROUS BARGAIN

IT WAS THE LONGEST WALK OF MY LIFE.

Imagine getting called to come up to the front of the class to solve a problem, but the whiteboard is a mile away. Or going up to the auditorium stage at an all-school assembly to give a speech, and if you mess up, they might drag you out of there, never to be seen again. Or your mom comes to pick you up early and catches you clowning in the back of the classroom, and now you got to walk by all of your friends as she watches you with that *Oh really?* look.

Yeah.

Matter of fact, imagine all three of those things happening at the same time.

Throw in a little terror, a little nausea, and a little *Holy moly, how am I going to survive this,* and you're halfway there.

I didn't look left or right, not even when I passed the Mmoatia grove. Not even when I passed John Henry straining against the grasp of several bosslings. Not even when I passed a quietly sobbing Miss Sarah, the limp and motionless body of Miss Rose lying in her arms. Nope, I didn't meet anyone's eyes as I placed one foot ahead of the other, following the curving street until the dented gold marina spire rose out of the bay in front of me.

And in front of it, Nyame.

Hundreds of destroyed fetterlings lay in mounds around him, like a fort made of defeated enemies, and yet several hundred more live ones circled him. As I approached, their heads snapped around like I was a magnet, and the god in the middle raised his head and glared at me.

His eyes burned like a thousand red-hot coals, and if looks could kill... What am I saying? His looks probably *could* kill. For all I knew, he was shaving off my retirement years.

"You don't know what you're doing," he snarled.

"It's this," I shot back, "or everyone gets dragged into that death ship over there. I'm doing the only thing I can."

He shook his head. "You are dooming us all." And he turned his back on me.

I clenched my fists, but the iron monsters around me began to get closer and closer. Yet they weren't attacking. It was like they were urging me on. I gave Nyame my own glare, then, with a dozen fetterlings following, moved down to the shore, where a collection of rotted planks tied together with swollen, seaweed-covered ropes awaited.

My rusty honor guard herded me to the makeshift raft.

I turned around, saying, "No way," then took a half step back when twelve fetterlings started clanking together, like metal rattlesnakes. "Fine, fine, I'm going."

I stepped onto the raft, and a wave of sadness pulled a lump into my throat. Ayanna's raft was somewhere back in the Ridge. Lost forever, probably. I shook my head and took a deep breath. *Forward*, I thought. *Have to move forward.*

I didn't have a stick or an oar to propel the raft, but the rotted thing jerked into motion by itself, floating slowly at first, then picking up speed. Debris knocked against the sides, and more than one burst of flame erupted out of the water, making me jump each time. Steam hovered over the boiling sea, and a low roar lurked in the background. The tear in the sky, directly above and stretching off into the horizon, smothered everything in a thick heat that made breathing a struggle.

The Maafa lurked just offshore, squat and ugly in the shallows like a diseased leviathan that had washed into the bay. It smelled like it looked and looked like it smelled—filthy, covered in crusty barnacles, with the rotten remains of fish caught between the splintered boards of its hull, and emitting fumes, the kind that linger in the back of your throat after you leave the gas station.

My eyes and my stomach both wanted to vomit.

The raft followed its invisible leash farther and farther

away from shore, away from safety—wherever that was. I drifted closer and closer, until the Maafa loomed over me, and still I floated on. I gagged when I smelled the greenish-black crust that lined the hull, with its odor of old vegetables and the special Alabama grease Nana always smothered on my cuts. Fetterlings, trapped against the side, wriggled weakly in the water.

I finally reached a jagged split in the hull and, as the raft drifted inside it, fetid water dripped down my neck. A familiar setting materialized out of the darkness.

Two torches.

Three steps.

A long passageway shrouded in darkness.

The raft came to a stop, and I gripped the straps of the Story Box (Story Bag? Story Backpack? I hadn't figured that out yet) and stepped onto the stairs. The soggy wooden planks of the deck squelched and sagged under my feet. My breathing echoed in my ears.

I inhaled, trying not to smell the putrid air, and then let it out.

And that's when the ship spoke.

"Thought I told you stories are powerful magic?"

I froze. The voice came from the darkness. But it wasn't Uncle C's, like in my nightmares.

"Well, my boy? Fine mess you got yourself in."

Wait a minute.

Wait. A. Minute.

I knew that voice. But the last time I'd heard it, the owner was telling me—

"Did you at least give me a good ending?"

"Brer Fox? Is that you?"

A wheezy coughing laugh echoed around me. "So it seems. I guess these old whiskers got one last job to do."

I took a step forward, then another. The darkness didn't fade away as much as part around me. The passageway grew narrower and narrower, and when I turned around I could just make out the torches near the hole I'd entered. "I'm here to speak to the Maafa."

The bulkheads groaned and the deck shifted. Boards twisted and realigned, and I threw my hands out to keep my balance, nearly falling when the planks caved in at my touch. I felt something soft and hairy. And warm. I made sure my legs were steady, then glanced over. My hand had pushed through the soggy wood, and underneath—

"Sweet peaches!"

A face.

No, dozens of faces. Some I recognized—Tarrypin, Sis Crow—and others I didn't. These were the victims, the ones the iron monsters had snatched. They'd all been stuffed into the bulkheads and decks of the Maafa.

I jumped back in horror... and their eyes followed me. They *were* alive, but just barely.

"Not pretty, is it?" Brer Fox said in a strained tone.

I pulled my eyes away from the barely breathing folk. "I came to bargain. Can you tell it that? I came to bargain!" I shouted.

"You sure you know what you're doing?"

"I do. Now can you tell it that?"

"It already knows. It—"

Brer Fox's voice cut off, and I stood in dark silence for several seconds.

"BF? BRER FOX!"

"Still here...just...translating." He sounded like he was in pain, and I squeezed the Story Box's straps. He'd gotten trapped because of me, and now he—and the others—were suffering. Just when I got worried and started to shout again, the soggy planks in the deck above my head peeled back like a banana, and Brer Fox dropped down. His limbs were tangled in chains, and a strange orange glow filled his eyes.

"What is the bargain?" he said, and I flinched.

That wasn't Brer Fox's voice. It was deeper, darker, like creaking timber and crashing waves. It was freedom denied. It was silent pain.

It was the Maafa.

"You think you have something we want?" the old evil asked through Fox. "You?"

It was weird—and scary—seeing Brer Fox's mouth move

but hearing the haunting voice of the ship. But I had to push past the fear. Everything depended on this moment. Everyone depended on *me*.

I forced myself to start talking again. "You're carrying something inside of you," I said.

"We carry a lot of things." The chains holding Brer Fox forced his legs to walk around me like a grotesque puppet. "The living. The dying. The fear that unites them both. It is what we do."

"Yeah, but you also carry a haint, and it's using you. It's using you to get to me and everybody else on Alke, so it can become more powerful than even you."

"IMPOSSIBLE!" the Maafa forced Brer Fox to snarl in my face, and I threw my arms out for balance as the ship heaved up and down in the water.

"It's true!" I yelled.

The chains holding Brer Fox grew taut, and then he was hauled up into the upper deck.

Before I could react, the planks in the bulkhead to my right split apart, and Tarrypin—his shell bundled in chains—was marched out. His eyes were glowing orange, too, and he spoke in the same ancient voice of the Maafa. "So, we have a spirit aboard. What does—?"

"It's poisoning you." I took a big risk by interrupting, but time was running out. There was no telling what was happening outside. "And it's taking the stories your monsters hunt down and hoarding them, getting stronger. Soon it will take over and make *you* a victim."

The possessed Tarrypin shook his wrinkled head. "Your story does not impress us. Even if such a stowaway existed, it could never surpass our might. We will—"

"It does, and it can, with this." I shrugged off the backpack and it transformed into the golden Story Box. I held it out.

There was a momentary pause, and then Tarrypin was yanked back into the bulkhead. A short distance down the passageway, the deck opened like a trapdoor, and a teenage girl stepped out, walking lightly despite the manacles on her ankles.

"Netta?" I whispered. "No."

But the girl I'd met back in MidPass didn't raise her blazing eyes. Instead, they stayed pinned to the Story Box.

"You carry the words of the gods," the Maafa said. "You are . . . Anansesem." For the first time, I heard a note of concern in the voice.

"Yes," I said. "And like I said, I've come to make a bargain."

I could feel the Maafa's consideration in the silence that followed. When it next spoke, the ship was almost thoughtful:

"Why shouldn't we just take the cursed sky god's treasure and rule the lands as we like?"

This I was prepared for. "Because you wouldn't rule it for

long. The haint infesting you would grow too powerful for even you to contend with, and he'd destroy you. But there's another way." I hesitated, then inhaled and let out a deep breath. "I will tell your story."

The entire ship stilled. The creaking, the rustling, the clinking chains—it all fell silent as the Maafa registered my words. Then:

"You would tell . . . our story?"

I nodded. It was a gamble, and a lot of people in Alke wouldn't like it, but it had to be done. "People don't speak of the Maafa anymore. They shush any mention of you. Children don't know your name. Soon you'll be erased from the histories of Alke entirely."

I put the box down on the floor. The images on its sides, including the one of Anansi and Nyame confronting the Maafa, were barely visible. As Netta's eyes stayed on the Story Box, I closed my eyes and concentrated on the Maafa's tale.

The Maafa is pain, John Henry had said. *It came here with the first of us. The sadness to our joy.*

Drums pounded in my ears and my fingertips tingled. I opened my eyes in time to see the Story Box glowing, and projecting images on the bulkhead. An inky black leviathan leaped forward along the planks, only to be met by a group of familiar beings: a giant man with a shining hammer, two soaring shadows with blazing wings, a man with golden eyes, and a spider clinging to a line of sparkling silk. They all clashed with the formless beast, eventually casting it back into the darkness below.

The Story Box flared white-hot in the dark before it faded to a dull glow, and a sigh seemed to settle throughout the hull of the ancient ship.

After several seconds, Netta lifted her glowing eyes to me. "You would tell this story?"

I raised my chin. "I would tell the tale of how all the gods of MidPass and Alke united to defeat a powerful foe. Yes, I would tell that story."

The open secret of the Maafa had been bothering me throughout my time here, and it had taken something High John said to make me understand. You shouldn't try to hide from your pain. You shouldn't run from it, cover it up, pretend it never happened. That's what John Henry and Nyame and all the other gods had tried to do with the Maafa. That's what I'd tried to do with Eddie. Uncle C thought he'd hurt me by taking all my good memories of my best friend, but he'd only helped me face my feelings.

As Anansesem, it was my job to carry the stories of the land to its people. *All* the stories. If we ignored the past, how would we learn from it?

I waited for the Maafa's decision.

The Story Box's light dimmed, and the passageway seemed to widen a bit. The trapdoor in the deck disappeared, and the bulkhead planks straightened. Netta, still possessed by the Maafa, raised both arms.

"We return to our rest, and you will tell our tale?"

"And," I added, "I'll even get rid of that haint for you. A two-for-one. Because I'm that kind of guy."

Netta nodded, and she stepped to the side. Two planks in the bulkhead shifted apart like they were made of rubber, and the girl disappeared into the darkness.

Something rustled in the upper deck, and Brer Fox's voice sounded above me. "I don't know how or why, or what you said, but it agreed. You have to be careful, though, my boy. Provided you hold up your end of the bargain, as soon as you rid the ship of the haint, the Maafa will return to the bottom of the sea. And if it just so happens you can't escape in time, both you and the Story Box will ride down to the deep along with it."

His voice broke off and I nodded grimly. "I understand."

"I know you do, my boy, I know you do. Forgive an old fox his worry. Take heart—you can do this." His voice began to fade away, and I stopped myself from dashing to the wall to beg him to stay and help me. A last chuckle floated in the air. "Seems like hope lives after all."

"Wait!" I shouted. "Are you—all of you—coming back?"

Silence.

Then, "I reckon some will. But I like how my story ended,

my boy. And I'm tired . . . so, so tired. Figure I might just rest for a bit."

"Fox," I called. "FOX!"

And then there was nothing but me and the empty passage-way, a nondescript door waiting at the end. Something rolled down my cheek, but I didn't bother with it. Whether it was the sea's salt water or my own, it wouldn't help with what came next. I hefted the Story Box back onto my shoulders and started walking before fear talked me out of it.

I had made a bargain with the Maafa.

Now it was time to deal with Uncle C.

47
KING COTTON

"WELL, COME ON IN, TRISTAN, DON'T BE SHY. YOU LETTING OUT all the heat."

It took a few heartbeats—several pulse-pounding heartbeats—before my eyes adjusted to the gloom. The passageway had been dim, but this room was two shadows short of midnight black.

The layout mirrored my visions. There, in the corner, the barrels stacked up to the deck. The rectangular burlap bags, their faded black letters illegible in the dark. And mounds, I mean mounds, of the white—

"Cotton," I said, astonished.

"Smart boy. Smart, smart boy. That's why I like you, wanna help you."

I didn't see the haint at first. Cotton was strewn across the floor, piled up in the corners, and bursting out of several stained, split-open bundles. But there, in the highest mound in the far corner, lay the figure of what used to be a man.

Uncle C.

Uncle *Cotton*.

From what I could see, he was stylish. He wore a pair of fine, polished patent leather dress shoes, silk dress socks, creased trousers, and had a pocket-watch chain dangling from the pocket. But that's all I could see. The top half of him lay beneath a white heap of soggy cotton. The only thing showing above his waist was the left side of his face—ashy, pale, and blistered around the lips. His eye, blue as the bay outside, blinked open, and the corner of his mouth crinkled into a smile.

"Lookie here, lookie here. Look what the cat dragged in. I'd get up, but...well, I'm a bit under the weather." He laughed, a raspy chuckle that irritated my ears like forks scraping against plates. "Well, come in, come in, don't be shy. We gots a lot to talk about, don't we?"

I studied him.

This was the architect of nearly everything bad that had happened in MidPass and Alke. The one who had stirred up the bone ships, the iron monsters, the hullbeasts, the brand flies. The evil behind the abductions of people and animals and the pillaging of their homes. Because of him, Ayanna was suffering, maybe even...

He watched me study him, but when I squeezed the straps

on my shoulders, his eyes latched on to my backpack, and a suspicious look crossed his face. "What you got there?"

For a second my heart thudded in my chest like the war drums in the Ridge. I hid it, though, and shuffled closer. Just a bit.

"I brought you what you wanted. Now give me my memories."

"I told you to bring me the Story Box, not some raggedy knapsack! Where is it?" Uncle Cotton demanded.

"Right here," I said, patting my backpack. "Where's my journal? Where are my memories?" My voice felt thick and speaking was difficult. My chest wouldn't stop heaving, and my palms were sweating.

He eyed me, then chuckled. "Straight to the point. Okay. I like that. No shucking and jiving around the issue. Well, my boy—"

"I'm...not...your...boy," I said, breathing hard after every word.

His eyebrow rose. "Okay, then, okay. No need for rudeness. I thought you were better than that. You *are* better than that, I know it. You and me, we're the same. Determined. Focused. Driven. I understand what you're going through, believe me. Having something stripped away. Ripped from you. The loneliness. The emptiness."

I squeezed my eyes shut. "Give. Me. My. Journal."

"Okay. Okay. Everything you need is right there."

I opened my eyes to see that he had shifted slightly, so his face pointed toward the corner off to my right. I spied a door, its bottom half covered in thick roots and thorny vines, and my spirits sank. "How am I supposed to get in there?"

I've never seen a half-face look more apologetic. "Tristan, Tristan. I told you, you gots to trust me. What you're missing is in that room, beyond that there tangle, and I can get you to it. I told you I could help, and I will, believe me. But I can't do nothing like this." His eye looked down at his buried torso before fixing me with a pleading gaze. "You've got to help me if you want me to do the same. I told you. Free me, and I can free everybody."

"Free you . . ." I repeated.

Uncle Cotton grimaced, a cruel twist of the face. "My own fault, really. This world is built on the power of story, boy. Seems my story is intertwined with this here floating death palace. Cotton and the Maafa."

"Greed and enslavement," I whispered.

Cotton shifted, a movement I realized was a shrug. "Nature of the beast. Funny, right? You freed me, only for me to end up tangled in something even stronger."

His pale eye flicked to the Story Box. I took a step back.

"But with that . . . Ohhh yeah, with that, I could rewrite my own story. You went from chump to champ. Imagine what *I* could become. The legends. The history! It's the only way," he said. Something rustled in the mountain of cotton, and a withered hand, with nails black and sharp, rose feebly out of the white fluff. "Give it to me. Let me help you."

I hesitated.

"Let me help you," he whispered again, and the insistent demand wormed its way into my brain.

I slipped off the backpack and held it in my right hand. "And you'll give me my memories, and the journal? Right away?"

A snarl rippled across his half-face before it faded and a smile appeared. "Sure, Tristan, sure thing, just as soon as you free me, I'll get it to you. You'll have what you want. All your stories—every single one. Heck, here's a few reminders to get you started, just so you know I'm on the level."

He took a deep breath, then blew gently on the cotton in front of him. Little strands of white, barely visible in the dark, floated toward me like a cloud. I backed up, but the threads consumed me. I froze in fear, feeling a tingling sensation that started in the center of my spine and moved upward, increasing in strength as it went, until my forehead buzzed.

Eddie's smiling face popped into my mind. Both of us, sitting at the table, going over our English project. Eddie at the corner store. Eddie holding the heavy bag for dear life as I threw hooks and crosses and jabs and straights. The memories swept over me and I felt months of stress leak out of my shoulders.

"Now then . . ." The buried haint's lone eyebrow was arched

again, and it brought me back to the present like a splash of ice-cold water to the face. Anansi's adinkra burned hot against my wrist, and I fiddled with it and the Amagqirha's bead.

"A deal's a deal, Tristan."

I nodded, swallowed, then took a step forward and dropped the backpack into his straining hand. He fumbled with it, then snagged a strap and clutched it tight. He inhaled, then exhaled, and the skin on his face seemed to ripple.

"Help me," he demanded. "Help me out of here."

This was it. Once he was free, everything would hang by a thread. I prayed I'd thought this plan through enough as I inched closer. I scooped handfuls of soggy cotton away from him, like wet sand at the beach. The waterlogged fibers weighed a ton, and they clung to my fingers as I tried to hurl piles away. Slowly, a body began to emerge from the mess.

A head with stringy gray hair slicked back tight to his skull.

Teeth bright white—so white they seemed fake, except for the single gold tooth in the back.

And he was rail thin.

He wore a matching suit jacket, and beneath it, a collared shirt starched stiff.

Uncle Cotton hugged the Story Box tight. Before my eyes his face lost its wrinkles, smoothing out to look like that of a much younger man, and the cotton . . . All the cotton in the room began to tremble. Slowly at first, but soon each dingy white ball bounced and hopped as if in an earthquake. They rolled on the floor and tumbled down from the piles in the corners, hightailing it to where Uncle Cotton lay with his eyes closed, a heavy sigh escaping his lips. They bounced down his collar, rolled into his sleeves and pant legs, even into his socks.

Soon all the cotton in the room was gone. It filled his clothes like straw in a scarecrow.

All that was left were the thorny roots digging into the bottom of the door to the next compartment.

I had to get him to remove those, too, or this plan was doomed.

"Help me up."

His voice, stronger and more confident, grabbed my attention, and I stretched out an arm. His hands felt like leathery claws as they slipped around my wrist like handcuffs. But he was light—so light it surprised me. Cotton spilled out of his jacket sleeves and pant cuffs before it was drawn back inside like a yo-yo on a string. He patted down his hair and kept the right side of his face turned away from me, though his left eye rolled toward me and winked.

"Ahhh. You don't know how good it feeeeeels, being free from that there prison. Trapped like a hog before dinnertime, I swear. And this—" He held up the Story Box by its two straps and stopped speaking as the magical treasure slowly morphed back into the shape of a chest. He giggled, and the giggle turned into a chuckle, which grew into a hearty laugh that sounded wet and loose.

"Ha-haaaaa, lookie here. Boy, I feel that power, let me tell you. I can feel it right as rain. Hoo-whee! We gonna have us a party!"

He fumbled at the lid, trying to release the catch. It held fast, and his smile slowly faded as he tried again and again to open the Story Box. He grunted, swore, dropped it to the floor and pulled with both hands. He looked up and I flinched—the right side of his face, up to and surrounding his right eye socket, was a mass of viney wood stems and shredded cotton. His eye socket blazed and he snarled.

"Why won't this thing open?"

I licked my lips. "Because only I can open it."

"Well, then do it, boy! Ain't got time for your games!"

The door behind him was still covered in roots. I took a deep breath, then shook my head. "No."

"No?" He barked the word so violently, my hands were up and my fists clenched before I realized it. His teeth were bared and his clawlike fingernails suddenly became longer and sharper, like talons. They grew and grew, twisting and turning toward me, and too late I realized they were slender branches, thin itchy switches with barbed hooks. They snaked around my wrist and up my arm, digging into my skin, and Uncle Cotton leaned in close.

"No?" he repeated.

"Not"—I squeezed the words through my teeth—"before you give me my journal. Like you said."

He looked ready to spit. Maybe worse. The branches tightened around my wrist, as proof of what they could do, and then they loosened enough so I could talk without wincing. Red marks crisscrossed my left arm.

Uncle Cotton swallowed whatever curse dangled on his tongue, and suddenly the smooth, polished smile was back. "Okay, then, okay. Sure, you're right. Gotta help. But I gotta make sure you're on the level. I need to know I can trust you, Tristan. I'm gonna have to rely on you when we get outside. We came to this world together, and if we go out there as a team and you let them know I'm here to help, to be a savior . . . shoot, ain't no stopping us. I'll be a hero. That's what they're looking for, right? A hero to come trotting along and rescue them from themselves? Well, here I am."

He preened, even as the rumbles of the Maafa smashing against the Golden Crescent shook the room. His blue eye narrowed, a calculating look entering it, and the cotton branches began to squeeze me again as he grew even more excited.

"They might give me the keys to the city. I mean, look at you—they gave you all sorts of godly charms and you just a boy with a few stories. *Anansi's chosen one*. Ha!" He scoffed.

"Wait until a *real* tale-teller, a word-spinner, a true weaver, comes along. They'll forget all about that spider and his little brood."

He froze as a thought struck him.

"They might even make me king."

His cotton-encrusted eye socket fixed on me, and terror gripped me so fiercely I couldn't breathe.

"Yeah. King Cotton. That's got a real ring to it, don't it, boy?"

A peal of thunder rumbled in the distance. Drums and shouts echoed in my ears.

My mouth moved, once, twice, three times, before something resembling a word crawled out of it. "Y-yeah."

"Aw, don't worry, King Cotton will take care of his friends. You could be my ward, my heir apparent. Play your cards right, and you could have your own little palace here. Pick any one you want—they're all empty."

He cackled and slapped his knee.

"My...memories..." I gasped out past the pulsing pain in my arm.

"Right, right. Getting ahead of myself. Well, go ahead, Tristan, get your little friend's stories and let's shut this raiding party down. You and I got some planning to do."

His right eye turned bright white as he puffed out his narrow chest, sucked in a mouthful of air, and blew a stream of cottonseed-filled air at the door. The vines creeping around the compartment shriveled and peeled away, like flowers wilting under the baking sun. Soon nothing remained but little piles of dirt scattered on the creaking wooden deck. The pain in my arm faded as the branches untwisted and retreated back into his fingernails.

Uncle Cotton beamed. "Happy?"

Memories rushed back into my mind like a floodgate had been opened. Cotton watched, then pointed to the newly opened door. Inside the cell-like compartment, a brown book lay against the wall.

Eddie's journal.

An ominous rumble rattled the deck as I crossed the few feet to pick up the little book. Its leather cover was warped and the pages were water-stained, but you know what? I didn't care. It was Eddie's, it was mine, and I had it once more.

The deck shuddered again, and Uncle Cotton looked around with a frown. "Now what's got this hunk of junk all up in arms?"

A small smile crossed my face. The Maafa was keeping its promise. I'd gotten Uncle Cotton's tendrils out of the hull, and now the ship was preparing to return to the bottom of the sea, where it belonged.

A seam appeared in the deck between two planks, and water started bubbling through. I backed away. Time was running out. I turned to head through the passageway, only to find Uncle Cotton standing in front me, the Story Box extended, a weird gleam in his blue eye.

"You ain't thinking about skipping out on me, is you? Tristan? Naw, you wouldn't do that. You a man of honor! Like me . . . I held up my end of the bargain. You got your little book. Now it's time for you to open the Story Box."

A section of the hull broke off behind him with a loud *crack*, and green seawater began to gush inside.

"Open it!" Uncle C shouted.

I flinched. "Okay, okay." I took a deep breath, then reached for the Story Box, pulling on the thread that connected tales from all over the world, and the lid opened, spilling bright golden light into the flooding room.

Uncle C started to laugh. The raspy sound grew louder and louder as the Maafa fell apart around the haint and me. "Yes! Yeessssss! Wait . . . What in the—?"

He bent his head closer to the Story Box, lifting it to his face, and then jerked back when a quick flurry of sap balls flew out and smacked him in the eyes.

"Heard you was looking for these hands," a tiny voice shouted from inside the Story Box. "Well, here they are, and Gum Baby gonna deliver them to you free of charge. Sap attack!"

The little loudmouth flipped out of the Story Box, light trailing off her like streams of glitter. Gum Baby jumped on top of the haint's head and fired sap ball after sap ball into his face, until he wore a mask of sticky dark amber.

"Return of the sap, needle-head! Don't call it a gum-back!"

Uncle C grunted as he struggled beneath the weight of the sap being absorbed by his cottony self.

"That's for Chestnutt! And that's for Ayanna! And that's for having the nerve to throw rocks at the throne, chump! You no good, mealy-mouthed, dandelion-faced thistle-head!"

"Gum Baby," I shouted, "let's go!"

"Snot-snorter!"

"Gum Baby!"

She kicked him upside the head one more time for good measure, and that last effort made the haint topple backward into the water rising around our feet. As he fell, I snatched the Story Box from his hands. After it transformed into the black-and-gold book bag, I put it on and Gum Baby scrambled on top.

"Tristan!" Uncle C wriggled in the water, his cotton getting even heavier now, and spat sap out of his mouth. "Don't you leave me like this, boy! I helped you! None of them folks out there lifted a finger for you before I did! I made you what you are, boy—don't you leave me!"

Another splintering crack echoed like a gunshot deep in the Maafa, and the ship tilted, lifting me higher while Uncle Cotton slid to the other side. Water came rushing down the passageway. There was no exiting the way we'd entered. That left the compartment behind us, where Eddie's journal had been stashed, and I darted toward it. Maybe there was a porthole I could—

"Tristan!" The lack of emotion in Uncle C's voice forced my head around before I could stop myself. His head faced in my direction, his eyes still covered in sap. The bulkhead closest to him slowly broke apart. "You know this ain't over, right? I will find you, boy. I will find you and—"

The sea stormed in, foaming and angry, carrying broken planks and limp fetterlings, and flushed the haint away in mid-threat.

The water hadn't reached the little room yet, but I could feel the ship going down. Gum Baby climbed onto my shoulder. "We need to move, Bumbletongue, and fast."

"Yeah," I said, staring at the maelstrom. "You're right."

And I entered the next room just as the upper deck fell with a groaning smash.

48
LAST STOP

"UM..." GUM BABY WHISPERED AS THE DOOR SLAMMED SHUT behind us. "This ain't what I was thinking of when I said we needed to escape."

I couldn't answer, though I happened to agree.

The inside of a school bus stretched out in front of us.

"About time you showed up, nimrod," someone said from the rear. A thin boy, wearing a Malcolm X T-shirt and sporting a DIY haircut, sat up from where he'd once been sprawled by a gaping hole in the side of the bus. "You still slower than the next payday."

"You know this guy?" Gum Baby asked.

I opened and closed my mouth several times, speechless. How? My wrist tingled, and I lifted the adinkra bracelet and stared at the silver bead. *Commune with the spirits,* the diviner had said.

I took a deep breath, then cleared my throat. "He is... was... my best friend."

Eddie still looked... like Eddie. Short and skinny. He even *felt* real—he held out his fist as I walked closer, gripping the very real green seat backs, and after a few seconds I dapped him up, staring at him when our knuckles connected.

"Is Cotton gone?" he asked.

"Yeah," I said. "Yeah, he's gone. For now."

"Try to contain your excitement, my guy." Eddie pushed his glasses up on his nose. "I heard the racket from in here. Sounded like y'all put the hurt on him. The heroes in your comics would be proud."

Gum Baby peeked over my shoulder. "Gum Baby did the hurting, ghost nerd. Respect the sap or get clapped."

I rolled my eyes, but Eddie snorted. I could see the seat through him, and it weirded me out. This wasn't a dream or a vision or even a story I'd been sucked into. My best friend was sitting right there, grinning at me. But he was dead.

"Feels weird, huh?"

"Yeah." I sat down on the seat across from him, still slightly shocked. "Yeah, I guess it does."

"Dang straight."

Mist rolled around our ankles, filled the front rows, and obscured the windows. If I didn't look around, if I kept my eyes locked on Eddie, I could imagine I was back in Chicago.

But I wasn't.

"Where are we?" I asked.

Eddie leaned back against the beat-up seat and traced a

name that had been scribbled on the vinyl in black marker. Finally he sighed and took off his glasses, cleaning them on his shirt. Funny that he even needed them anymore. "We're still inside."

"Inside?"

"Inside the Maafa." He slipped his glasses back on and bounced his fists on his knees while tapping his feet. That was Eddie. Unless he was reading, he just couldn't sit still. "Cotton, ever since he's arrived, he's been feeding your stories to this ship. Can you believe that? He was using your stories—and Nana's stories—as a way to track you. Every time you did your Anansi thing, he listened in and then sent those chain monsters after you."

I sank back into the seat, feeling sick to my stomach. Ayanna had been right. They'd been following me. I'd led the iron monsters to MidPass, to the Golden Crescent, to Isihlangu. Everyone suffered because—

"Oh, quit moping," Eddie broke in. He shook his head. "None of this is your fault. The Maafa and the monsters were already here. Cotton was the one who stirred them up, not you. Well, punching the Bottle Tree was pretty bad. And I guess that did let him loose, so, if I'm being technical, it *is* all your fault."

"Gee, thanks," I muttered, and he grinned for a second, before sighing and biting his nails.

"What?" I asked.

"What what?"

"You only bite your nails when you're nervous."

Eddie looked at his nails. "Even dead I can't stop doing that."

"So what's up?"

He didn't say anything for a few moments, then he sighed. "This is it, Tristan."

I frowned. "What do you mean?"

"I mean, this is it. After you leave, show's over. No more... no more talking."

The implications of what he was saying slowly dawned on me, and it was like someone had pulled my heart out. Again.

"But... but—"

Eddie shook his head. "I'm only here because Cotton kept me here, and you needed help. Now that you've separated him from the Maafa, I'm taking this bus to the end of the route."

I hugged his journal to my chest, and he grinned. "Cheer up, man—you're a hero! Celebrate! People are going to want you to come and tell stories. While you're at it, put my stories in a few more ears out there. Make me famous, Anansesem. I wanna be the next person to become a legend after they die. I'll be like Tupac and Socrates—Tupacrates!"

He clapped and erupted in his wheezing, nasally laugh, the one that was super contagious. Sure enough, I started chuckling too as he kept laughing. Even Gum Baby snickered in my ear.

"Gum Baby likes him. Ask him about precoffinary measures."

I rolled my eyes.

Eddie stopped laughing and sighed. He checked his watch, then pushed his glasses up again. "All right, bro, it's time to go."

"You?"

"No, you. This is your stop."

I tried to look outside the windows but couldn't see anything beyond the mist. Eddie pointed toward the front door of the bus.

"Gotta go that way. And hey, as you're leaving, check on all those folk the Maafa had stuffed in the decks and cargo hold. They're gonna need some help getting to shore."

I stood and grabbed the top of the seat, trying to figure out how to say what I wanted to say.

Eddie being Eddie, he just went ahead and said it.

"I'll miss you, too." He grinned. "Maybe I'll come back and haunt your D-twenties. Those dice are too unlucky for you."

He held out a fist again, and, with a small smile of my own, I bumped it. With Gum Baby on my shoulders, I walked backward toward the front of the bus, keeping him in sight. I fixed that image of him in my mind—the smiling, glasses-wearing knucklehead who'd always had my back no matter what. That's the Eddie I chose to remember.

"Oh hey, Tristan, I almost forgot." Eddie's call stopped me in mid-sentimental thought.

"What's up?"

He grinned, wider and more conspiratorial, and my eyes went big.

"No, don't say it . . ." I warned.

Impossibly, the grin grew even wider.

"Eddie . . ."

"Look in the next room! You're talking to the wrong one!" he shouted, and then he and his cackles were swallowed by the mist.

I sighed and faced front.

I felt Gum Baby twist around to look back. "And Gum Baby thought you were weird. No wonder y'all were friends."

"Yeah," I said, stepping out of the bus door. "No wonder."

We found ourselves in a different compartment, where the water came up to my ankles and I had to crouch to avoid bumping my head on the upper deck. The windowless space we had entered was about the size of the cafeteria at my school, but it wasn't made for tall people. Either that or no one ever stood upright in here. The bulkhead and decks were all made of rough, dark planks. Fragments of wooden crates and barrels lay in piles in different corners, along with rusted metal chains.

"Where are we?" Gum Baby asked.

"Maybe a cargo hold? Still on the Maafa, at least."

We were whispering. I don't know why, but I didn't want to draw any more attention to us than I had to. The area felt tainted . . . like at any second a hundred haints just as evil as Cotton would arise out of the wood and yank our souls to somewhere painful.

A dark lump lay on a platform sticking out of the far wall. Beside it was a door, banded in iron and bolted shut.

Gum Baby pointed at the lump.

"What's that, Gum Baby don't like it, what is it?"

Something touched my leg, and I leaped up in fright, hitting my head on the ceiling. "Ow!"

"Watch it!" Gum Baby shouted, slipping down to sit on top of the backpack. "You trying to kill Gum Baby?"

"Sorry." I held my hand over my heart. Water sloshed my ankles and I kicked off something slimy. "Looks like the ship is flooding."

"Well, get moving. Gum Baby ain't liking this place too much."

"Me neither. I think I know what kind of cargo was held here."

"Oh yeah? What?"

"People."

But instead of heading to the door, I angled toward the dark shape.

"No, fool, don't go toward the mysterious and possibly deadly trap! Head away, to the door! Oh, for the love of—"

"Eddie said we'd find something here," I muttered as the hairs along the back of my neck began to rise. "It'll only take a second."

"Well, it's starting to get mighty wet, and Gum Baby took a bath last month, so don't take forever."

I stopped a few feet away from the dark shape.

Gum Baby peeked over my shoulder. "What is it? Another ghost friend?"

"No," I said grimly, as a light switch flipped on in my head. I had an answer, but it brought more questions along with it. "You're gonna have to get back in the Box, though. I need to carry him over my shoulders."

Gum Baby looked at me in confusion. "Carry who?"

I shook my head, too angry to talk. It was time for one last confrontation.

49
TRICKING THE TRICKSTER

WHEN THE MAAFA SAID IT WAS RETURNING TO THE DEPTHS OF the Burning Sea, it meant it. A few minutes after I emerged from the door in the cargo hold and stepped onto a large floating piece of wood, I watched the giant ship sink in front of my eyes. The survivors around me—people and animals who had been trapped within its planks—cheered weakly as they clung to their own pieces of flotsam and kicked toward the shore. The giant tear in the sky bathed the beaches and coastline of the Golden Crescent in a red-orange blaze. The fires in the sea had gone out, but it looked like Nyame's city was burning brighter than ever, and the gilded domes and shining ivory towers reflected all that light back onto the bay.

Back onto the Maafa's watery grave.

And back onto me, surfing among floating debris, angry as all get-out.

The iron-monster army had disappeared along with the

Maafa. Whatever malevolent energy had been powering them was shut off, and they broke apart in screeching showers of rusty confetti. Their remains drifted down like ash onto the sand, the surface of the water, everything. Some got on me, but I couldn't muster the energy to care.

My blood was boiling.

I should have felt some relief, some happiness—the iron monsters were gone. Done for. They wouldn't be hunting Midfolk or Alkeans again.

But no—all I felt was rage.

Limp bodies littered the beach—more captives released from the hull and decks of the Maafa. They coughed and spluttered as they sat up drowsy and confused. Some I recognized. Others, Gum Baby said, had been missing for months.

"There's Old Wilkins! He went out to get some sugar and never came home."

"Mm," I grunted.

"And look! There's one of Sis Crow's nephews. That featherbrain owes Gum Baby some money."

"Mm."

"DON'T THINK GUM BABY FORGOT, BRITTLE BEAK! AIN'T NO IRON MONSTER TAKE YOUR WALLET! BETTER COME UP OFF OF WHAT YOU OWE GUM BABY!"

My heart lifted at the sight of John Henry towering over everyone as he took a head count. Thandiwe waved her kierie at me. Nyame, flanked by Leopard and Python, took stock of the damage to the marina.

A lot of folks were hurt. Miss Sarah held Miss Rose, whose right wing was bandaged to her side. The two beamed at me, though Miss Sarah's eyes flicked back to her partner with worry every so often. Even John Henry held his right shoulder where his shirt had been torn away and a leafy bandage was wrapped in place.

But...

Alkeans still stood on one side, Midfolk on the other. Even after all this, the distrust was still there. If anything, from the glares being shot across the sand, the muttering, and the buzzing tension, it looked like things had only become worse.

Because of me, yes. Because of my actions. I had to own that.

But someone had lied to me.

Someone had sent me to steal Nyame's Story Box. The assignment had sown even more distrust between Midfolk and Alkeans, dividing them at a time when, if they'd worked together, they could've stopped the Maafa before it had gotten so strong. Before Cotton's thorns had dug in so deep. And, just like the haint, this person had wanted the Story Box for its power.

But the Story Box was drained and useless, and there were only two ways to refill it. The first was by stealing tales from this world and mine, whichever ones he could get his thieving hands on. That's why he sent Gum Baby to steal Eddie's journal.

The second? An Anansesem.

All of this just so he would get all the glory and the power.

Like John Henry and High John had both told me, stories fed the gods and heroes in Alke.

I glared as that someone shouldered his way past John Henry and stood with his arms folded across his chest.

Before I approached him, I hid the bundle I was carrying behind a sand dune. I mumbled out of the side of my mouth, "Gum Baby, here's what we're gonna do. . . ." Then I brushed off my hands and walked over to the assembled crowd.

"Tristan!" John Henry boomed. "I don't know what you did, but I'm fixing to slap your back until the morning, boy. You saved us all!"

"And look who's all better," said Thandiwe. "The Mmoatia worked nonstop to help them recover." The warrior shook her head. "I'm still not exactly sure what sort of antidote they used. . . ."

Ayanna limped forward, cradling a bright-eyed Chestnutt. Ayanna slapped me upside the head, though at least this time she was weak. "I told you to be careful, flyboy, not to start a war." She smiled when she said it, though.

I gave her a gentle one-armed hug and grinned, but it didn't last long.

She noticed and elbowed me. "What's wrong?"

I didn't answer, because right then Nyame strode forward, his golden robes absorbing the light and scattering it across the beach like a million pieces of glass. He looked better than I'd ever seen him, though the marks left by the brand-fly crown hadn't completely faded.

"Well done, young Strong," Nyame said. "You—"

"Well, kiss my wrist, I bet you think you're hot stuff now!" High John interrupted loudly as he sauntered up to congratulate me. I couldn't help but notice that he still held his ax. Nyame noticed it, too, and his golden eyes narrowed. Leopard growled, and High John sniffed.

"Purr at me again, little kitty, I'll be wearing you soon."

Leopard sank into a crouch, ready to pounce, and High John's ax flared to life.

"Enough!" I shouted.

"Yes, that is quite enough," another voice piped up.

I tried not to grit my teeth as Brer Rabbit hopped forward and placed a paw on my shoulder. It was hard.

Like, really hard.

But I needed to stall.

"The boy here," Brer continued, "has done well, in spite of the many, many, *many* mistakes that we will address later. One of which," he said, twitching his whiskers at me, "was not following directions as they were given. I seem to recall instructing you to bring the Story Box straight back to MidPass. Hmm? Is that not so? I believe it is, if my memory serves me correctly, and—unlike someone I know—*mine* always serves me correctly."

The snarky chastising rubbed every single one of my nerves the wrong way. But I didn't get angry—or *angrier*.

I just waited.

Brer continued. "Had you just done what I asked, some of this unnecessary violence might have been prevented." The giant rabbit shuddered before smoothing his whiskers down and straightening his ears. "No matter. Lessons learned, I'm sure. We can't all be calm and cool under pressure, now, can we? No, don't answer—it was a rhetorical question. I'm afraid we were right—you just don't have what it takes to be the hero that unites Alke, young man. So sad. Truly. I'm crushed."

He tried to twist his mouth into a disappointed expression, but it ended up looking like a smirk.

"Now, if you'll kindly hand over that Story Box, I will start fixing this mess you caused with that temper of yours."

He held out a paw, and I resisted the urge to slap it away. Instead, I backed up.

"What are you doing? Come now, boy, this isn't the time for games."

A small dark shape flipped across the sand behind him, and I tried not to look at Gum Baby as she scrambled up John Henry's shoulder. The giant man jerked in surprise, then relaxed when he saw who it was. He opened his mouth, but Gum Baby shushed him and whispered in his ear. She showed him Nyame's bright adinkra charm, which winked under the red blaze of the hole in the sky, then pressed it against his temple.

"This is not a joking matter, Tristan," said Brer. "Hand over the Story Box!"

He lunged forward to snatch the straps of my backpack, but I skipped to the left to put some space between us. Brer tried again, and I ducked, leaving him clutching at air. Dad would've been proud of my bobbing and weaving.

"Now look, you spoiled little child," he wheezed.

I held out the backpack and taunted him. "Is this what you want?"

He glared at me. "Blast it, boy! You'd cross a hero? You are more foolish than I thought. Give me that, or so help me, I'll—"

"You'll what?" I teased.

By this time Gum Baby had leaped from John Henry—who stood awestruck by what he had just learned—to High John, and now she dropped to where Miss Sarah and Miss Rose sat. I needed her to hurry up and get to the Alkeans. They needed to see this, too.

"You'll what? Stomp your little paws again? Go ahead. The Thicket is gone, remember? Whatever magic was in those thorns burned away when the iron monsters attacked."

Brer stopped chasing me for a second to catch his breath. "Because . . . of *you*," he said, panting. "You did this! Your childish anger, your tantrums, your incessant"—he lunged forward again, but I was ready for it—"need for attention. You brat! You spoiled brat!"

Gum Baby finally reached Thandiwe and Nyame. The Ridge warrior's frown turned into a gasp when the doll touched the adinkra to the side of her head. Then the little acrobat spun through the air to land on top of Nyame's fuzzy golden-gray afro. Honestly, I was worried about the sky god the most. Sometimes the closest people fool us the longest. As Gum Baby said earlier, it be your own people.

The little doll gave me a gums-up (Arrrgh, now she had me making bad puns!) and I took a deep breath.

"You want this?" I shouted. I dangled the Story Box and pranced backward until I was on the top of the dune where I had left my bundle. "Do you? Well, come and get it!"

I took another step back and pretended to lose my balance. Brer grinned and dove forward. "Aha!" he shouted.

I pivoted and he tackled air, falling and rolling down the dune, coming to a stop right next to the creature I'd pulled from the hold of the Maafa.

"Gaaaaah!" he yelled, spitting sand out of his mouth. "I've had it with—"

I smiled when he came face-to-face with his mirror image. That's right—it was a rabbit.

A skinny, soaked, unconscious bunny with matted fur.

We'd rescued Brer from the holds of the Maafa. The real Brer Rabbit.

Which meant the rabbit we'd all been talking to, the one who'd come up with the plans, the one we'd all trusted, was none other than—

"Anansi!" Nyame shouted.

50
REVEAL

THE DISGUISED GOD YELPED AND SCRAMBLED BACKWARD. HE slipped on a piece of broken barrel and slid down the dune, landing on his fake rabbit tail in a tidal pool. He froze as the others gathered next to me, their expressions ranging from confused to disgusted to furious.

"What is the meaning of this?" Nyame demanded.

Ayanna shook her head. "How could you?"

"This whole time, you let us believe you were gone," Thandiwe spat. Her kierie was raised, and she looked seconds away from dashing down the slope to beat some honesty into the impostor below.

John Henry leaned on his hammer with his good arm. "We trusted you."

"And you played us like a new-string fiddle," High John said. "Sure you did."

"Now see here," the disguised Anansi began, getting up

and dusting the sand off his furry disguise, "whatever that devious little scamp told you all—"

Nyame stepped forward again, and the words died.

The sky god looked like the sun on earth. Everything around him paled in comparison to his shining robes, and his golden stare threatened to melt Anansi into a puddle. Even John Henry watched him warily.

And Gum Baby rode on Nyame's head like a princess in a carriage, my adinkra bracelet dangling from her hand.

"You know," I said, "the last time I was here, the sky god made me a charm. An adinkra. If I remember right, he made it out of light and air."

"I fail to see how that is at all relevant," the trickster god muttered, but he didn't move.

"Oh, it's relevant, all right. See, that charm was special. What could it do again? Oh yeah. As long as I wore it, I could see through any illusions. Pretty useful, right?"

The impostor rolled his eyes, and I shook my head and continued. "You were there when the real Brer Rabbit was taken by iron monsters. *Before* I punched the Bottle Tree, I might add. So you can't pin all this on me."

He started to protest, but I talked right over him. "You and Brer were trying to figure out how to build a Story Box when the monsters came. They were attracted by the stories you had won from Nyame, and they captured Brer."

I stopped for a minute, imagining how that scene had

gone down, with Anansi only looking out for his own butt. It made me even angrier.

"You stashed Nyame's broken Story Box in the Ridge for safekeeping," I went on. "But rather than warn everyone, and get them prepared, you hid in a bunny suit like a chump. Like a coward."

"Strange hearing that word from a boy who left his friend to die," the impostor snarled.

A week earlier, that comment would have sent me flying down the dune ready to fight. Even a day ago, maybe. But not anymore. Now those words rolled off me like drops of seawater. I smiled and shrugged, but my accusations were hard, punctuated by a jabbing finger.

"But then, when I created the tear between our worlds, you were stuck! Trapped! You needed a new plan, so you used the Warren to keep tabs on everyone. You sent us after the Story Box—the Story Box you had already drained—not to make things better, but because you still wanted its magic. You still thought you could fix it and everything else on your own."

I shook my head, disgusted by Anansi's selfishness. "You put us through all this to satisfy your greed, even though you knew it would only make things worse between Alkeans and Midfolk. You're already a god, but that wasn't enough for you. You also had to be the only storyteller. Isn't that the truth?"

Silence.

A hand dropped on my shoulder, and I ended my closing statement, balling my hands into fists. Nyame nodded at me, then turned to the sulking god below us. "Reveal," he said to him.

One word.

The power in it slammed the impostor back into the sand. "What are you—?"

"Reveal."

Suddenly I felt the urge to admit all my wrongdoings. The times I lied, the times I snuck candy home after school... That time I told Mom I was going on a run but instead I sat on a park bench and read the latest comic book releases.

And I wasn't the only one.

"Gum Baby confesses!" The little loudmouth dropped from Nyame's head and collapsed on the sand, pounding it with her fists. "Gum Baby was the one who ate the big biscuit! She knew it was John Henry's, but it was fluffy and buttery and—"

"Enough!" Nyame said, and he turned back to the impostor, who wriggled furiously on the beach. "I will not say it again."

"Clever boy." The voice coming from the shivering, twitching body sounded distorted. Like someone talking with a stuffy nose. Or with their hand over their mouth. "Clever, clever boy. Tricking the trickster. Well done."

Even with all my suspicions, and the guesses, and even the

aid of the adinkra as Gum Baby handed the bracelet back to me, I wasn't prepared for the tall, skinny, spindly-legged, deep-brown-skinned man who stepped out of the furry disguise he'd been wearing since the iron monsters first showed up. He wore pants that stopped high above the ankles and a cut-off T-shirt, and his bare toes wiggled in the sand. His eyes twinkled mischievously and he wore an infectious smile. A fickle breeze suddenly kicked up sand around us.

"So," Anansi said, "now what?"

Turns out there are some pretty steep consequences for gods who don't care for their people. Nyame had Kumi, the golden statue, march the Weaver back to the palace, where judgment would be delivered. The rest of us escorted the sick and injured to the fairy forest, where we hoped the Mmoatia would agree to help them.

On the way, I learned that MidPass was a wreck. Miss Sarah—in between worried glances at Miss Rose, who was now being carried on a stretcher—told us that the iron monsters had wrecked the Thicket, and the Drowned Forest was a stinking, swampy mess. Well, even more stinky and swampy than usual, I guess.

"Folks left everything behind, just dropped it and ran to us when they heard your message to get to the Golden Crescent. We carried some of 'em here in a basket, and it was as scary a flight as I've ever seen. But I'd do it again if it came to that." She folded her wings around me in a giant feathery hug, and I tolerated it. "Ain't no telling what it's gon' be like when we get back to MidPass. But we'll get back there—"

Miss Rose opened an eye. "Because home is still home," she finished.

Her partner shushed her, and Gum Baby and I left the two of them with the Mmoatia. Ayanna refused to stay in the sick bay, and she accompanied us, along with Thandiwe, to Nyame's palace.

"What do you think will happen to Anansi?" Ayanna asked.

Her hair was half braided, half curly afro, and I was tempted to touch it. Instead, I traced the stitching on Eddie's journal in my pocket. Its familiar weight was such a relief, I constantly patted it to make sure it was still there. "I don't know. How do you punish a god? *Hey, you, no dessert?*"

Thandiwe snorted. "Not likely. Make him work—that's what the elders would say."

We walked slowly, making sure Ayanna didn't overexert herself. I could still see some of the brands lining her skin, and the sight still made me angry. She caught me glancing at her for the hundredth time and swatted my arm.

"I'm fine, flyboy. Quit babying me."

"Who's a baby?" Gum Baby popped out of my Story Box backpack, where she'd made herself at home. She was in the middle of trying to do her hair so it matched Ayanna's. "Y'all talk too much. Hurry up! Gum Baby wants to see Nyame put his foot in Anansi's—"

"Hey, hey," I said. "Language."

"Don't shush me. Gum Baby was gonna say *web*! You always shushing somebody. Gum Baby ought to put her foot upside your big ole noggin." She scrambled up and started jumping on my head. "See? How. You. Like. This?"

"I'm gonna take you back to the Mmoatia," I warned.

She slid down to my shoulder, where she sat in a huff. "You always threatening people."

We arrived at Nyame's palace to see animated statues barring the giant doors. The leader squinted at me before stepping aside with a curt nod. I nodded back, and Ayanna raised her eyebrow.

"Careful now, your head can't get much bigger."

Gum Baby and Thandiwe snickered, and I couldn't respond, because we were in the reception hall. Nyame and Anansi faced each other, the sky god on his throne and the Weaver standing in front of the dais, hands still in his pockets. Leopard swished his tail and Python hissed as we stepped inside, but they both kept their eyes locked on Anansi.

Nyame acknowledged us. "Good. Just in time."

Uh-oh.

I narrowed my eyes suspiciously. "What does that mean?"

Ayanna sucked in a breath at my lack of godly respect, but me and the big sunny god were cool.

I hoped.

Nyame just pointed at Anansi. "I have determined a punishment befitting his disappointing behavior."

"Not covering your mouth while sneezing is disappointing," I said. "What he did seems a bit worse."

"*He* is standing right here," Anansi said with a sigh.

"And he can keep on standing while the adults talk," I shot back. He still had the same snarky attitude as when he had impersonated Brer, and it didn't irritate me any less.

Anansi just smiled, though.

"If you two are finished," Nyame said in that weary tone your parents use when you and your siblings are arguing, "perhaps we could proceed? Anansi, Weaver of both tales and tricks, the punishments for your crimes are as follows:

"One, you will immediately cease your research into the stories of other worlds and turn over any and all results to me. Two, you will travel with young Tristan and follow his instructions to the letter to fix the tear in the sky."

I grinned and Anansi groaned. That would be fun.

But Nyame didn't stop there.

"In addendum to Two, once the tear is fixed, you will accompany young Tristan into his world to assist in the completion of his story project—it having been so rudely interrupted by your efforts to steal stories from other realms—for a duration of no shorter than twenty days, as Tristan sees fit."

I choked on air in surprise. "He's staying with *me*?"

"I'm staying with *him*?" Then Anansi got a thoughtful look in his eye. "Actually, that could be—"

"I'm sorry," Nyame interrupted, and now it was his turn to get a gleam in his eye. "I was not finished. You will accompany young Tristan, but I am not fool enough to trust you any further. No, you will need... constraints."

Everyone stared in confusion as the sky god began to pull light from the ever-present sunrays beaming through the skylights and windows. He stirred in a piece of a nearby floating cloud, and then blew the glittering mixture toward Anansi. The spider god tried to duck, but the spell held him fast, and a golden whirlwind began to spin around him. Soon he was lost to view behind a funnel cloud of sunlight and magic.

"Tristan, the Story Box," Nyame commanded.

I shrugged off the treasure and handed it over. Nyame took it, dumped out a protesting Gum Baby, who'd climbed inside to take a nap, and then, before anyone could stop him, tossed the Story Box into the spinning cyclone.

"Wait!" Anansi called out. "Okay, look, I know I did a few things I shouldn't have—Ouch! That stings!—but we can work this out." His head poked from the cloud as he struggled to free himself, and Ayanna gasped. I tried not to recoil either.

His face blurred as it shifted between that of a dimpled, skinny man and that of a jeweled tarantula. Both faces pleaded with the sky god. "Seriously! Let me— Hey, my feet! Let me just make this right. I can—*Yowch!*—spin up a few— *Eeep!* It pinches—spells and have everything shipshape!"

His appeals fell on deaf ears, and Anansi turned to me as Nyame's spell pulled him back inside the funnel cloud. "Look, boy, we started off on the wrong foot. I've got eight of them! Easy to do. Look—Watch it! I can't replace those!—why don't I give you an even better scribble book?"

I crossed my arms and glared. Anansi continued to plead, even as he disappeared. Finally, after another few spins, the glittering sunlight blew away, leaving nothing behind except for—

"Is that a cell phone?" I asked.

Nyame waved at it. "The spell decided how Anansi might best serve in his, ah, new role." His golden eyes pinned me in place. "As an Anansesem carried the Story Box into the heart of evil, against my wishes..."

I started to explain, but he cut me off.

"...against my wishes—thereby saving us all—perhaps it is time for the Story Box to be carried by an Anansesem once more. Take it, Tristan, and let the stories of your world fill it. Use Anansi as you see fit. Remember, though—you are now responsible for his actions. You both will have to deal with whatever consequences result from this."

I walked over and picked up the smartphone. It had a

shiny black case, and on the back, a gold spider stretched all eight legs in the cardinal directions. I powered it on, and a spider crawled across the middle of the screen.

"This is humiliating," the mini Anansi complained. His voice came out tinny, and I grinned. "I feel cooped up!"

"Good," I said and slipped the phone into my back pocket.

"Doomed to exist in the dark, near a butt. Great."

"Better than acting like a—"

"Boys," Nyame said, pinching his brow, "go. Go away before I regret this. And, Tristan . . ." He inclined his golden-brown head. "Thank you. You have done more for Alke in a few days than many have done in years. You will always be welcome here. Just . . . next time, try not to bring any Bottle Tree friends with you, hmm?" He fixed me with an *Or else* stare and held it. "Now shoo. Safe travels."

I blushed and muttered a good-bye, then hightailed it out of there.

Gum Baby scampered up and trotted alongside me as Ayanna, Thandiwe—with Chestnutt in her arms—and I exited the palace. "Gum Baby don't envy you, Bumbletongue. Having to carry around something that small and annoying? Don't seem fun at all."

I patted her on the head. "I'm used to it by now."

We walked back to the Mmoatia forest. Ayanna was limping pretty noticeably, so, to distract her, I practiced telling her the Maafa's story. A promise was a promise, after all.

When we reached the gates, we both stopped. Gum Baby looked between us, then scrambled up next to Chestnutt in Thandiwe's arms. "Yeah...well...maybe your head isn't as big as Gum Baby thought it was. So...Gum Baby hates good-byes. Right, Chestnutt?"

The little bunny wiggled her ears. "Bye, Tristan! You have to come back so you can see my Warren Society initiation ceremony."

I gasped. "No way!"

"Yup, yup! They're gonna make me a full member as soon as MidPass is rebuilt."

I grinned. Good things happening to the best people (or bunnies, in this case) is the greatest feeling in the world.

Gum Baby gave an exaggerated sigh. "Enough with the sappy words, or Gum Baby's gonna start crying, and nobody wants that. C'mon, Ridgey, take us to go chase some fairies."

Thandiwe chuckled, then stepped forward and gave me the firmest handshake I'd ever gotten. "Farewell, Tristan. I will tell your story to the elders. And you will be admitted to Isihlangu with open arms at any time."

"Later, warrior girl," I said with a smile. "Or should I say, my princ— Ouch!" I rubbed my arm where she'd punched me, then waved as she and Chestnutt and Gum Baby took off into the leafy forest palace.

Ayanna fidgeted, and then, before I could say anything, hugged me tight. I hugged her back, and then she backed up. She looked down at the ground when she said, "You're all right."

I frowned. "That's it?"

"Yep. Well, no. Here's your hoodie. I . . . thank you."

I took the rumpled hoodie and raised an eyebrow. "That's it? That's all you want to say to me?"

She made a fist and shook it. "You need more excitement?"

"All right, all right." I tried to think of something to say, something cool to end the good-bye on, and then shrugged. Why not? "Gaaaaah."

A spluttering laugh escaped before Ayanna could stop it, and she rolled her eyes. "Bye, flyboy."

I grinned and watched as she limped off to get some rest, and then it was just me.

"That was cute."

Oh. Right.

It wasn't just me.

"Shut up, phone," I muttered and headed to the marina.

Gods. So freaking annoying.

51
GOOD-BYES AND NEW LIVES

JOHN HENRY AND HIGH JOHN WAITED FOR ME BY THE BEACH. JOHN Henry had his overalls rolled up around his knees as he stood in the water, hammering away at a bridge fashioned from the wreckage of fancy yachts. High John stood watching him, crunching noisily on an apple. The two of them together looked like uncles shooting the breeze at a family reunion. John Henry was all work, focused and determined, while High John ... well, there was no defining him.

"Make sure you fasten them planks real secure-like, hear me?" said High John. "Last thing we need is someone falling in on the way home. Oh, hi, Tristan." He put his half-eaten apple in his pocket. "Done with Mr. High-and-Mighty up there?"

I glanced back at Nyame's palace high up the curving city streets. "Yeah, I guess so."

High John muttered something and John Henry frowned.

"Now then, ain't no need for that sorta language. Not in front of the boy!"

"What are you doing?" I asked John Henry, walking up to the waterline.

"Ole Hammer Head decided to build a bridge from MidPass to Alke," High John said with a drawl. "Figures he can bring us all together real cozy-like, sure he does."

John Henry scratched his jaw and sighed. "It's gonna take some time for MidPass to get itself right again. What with Brer—the *real* Brer—being out of sorts. Old Nyame said we could hang out here in the meantime. Don't know if this bridge will do any good bringing Alkeans and Midfolk together, but I reckon it's a start."

High John grunted, then looked at me. "Well? What sort of light reprimand did our friendly spider god get? A time-out and a stern talking-to?"

I pulled out the Anansi phone and explained Nyame's punishment. John Henry whistled, and even High John looked impressed as he said, "He's trapped in there? Hmph. Well, maybe that Nyame fella's got a bit more in him than I thought. Though how's that little thing supposed to help you fix the tear? And if Anansi's in there, how's he supposed to get you up in the sky?"

I paused, my mouth frozen mid-answer. "That's . . . a good question."

John Henry chuckled as he returned to his hammering.

High John shook his head. "I knew it. Them Alkeans can't button their pants without ten sets of instructions. Of course they leave it to us to figure out the hard parts."

He whistled, and Old Familiar cawed and flapped down out of the air. The shadow crow messed with my hood, and I rubbed his beak before climbing aboard.

John Henry raised an eyebrow. "I see you got over your fear of heights."

Oh. Right.

The crow actually planned to fly.

I wobbled on my feet and swallowed several times. "Actually, I didn't, but thanks for reminding me. I'm just gonna... close my eyes."

John Henry's laugh created waves in every direction as he grabbed at his belly. He wiped a tear from his eye and waded over to hold out a giant hand. "Boy, I swear, I'm gonna miss your jokes. You be safe, now, you hear?"

I shook his hand, winced as he nearly crushed it, then grinned. "When I come back, I'll bring you some Ali posters. And Sugar Ray Leonard, too!"

"I'm looking forward to it."

He stepped back, and High John leaped aboard. Old Familiar cawed twice, and then we took off, flapping in a giant, gusty circle as we built up speed and climbed higher and higher.

As Alke receded below me, I studied it. The Golden

Crescent glistened like a jewel, and behind it the Ridge stood tall, a wall protecting a treasure. Beyond the mountains, green hills and brown deserts and blue lakes came together in a mosaic of beauty. I could hear Alke calling to me, singing the song that connected the land to its people.

"Catch you later," I whispered.

Outside the protective embrace of the bay, the Burning Sea flickered like dim coals. I didn't see any bone ships. Had they gone down with the Maafa, too?

A misty landmass rose out the sea as we flapped higher. MidPass, most of it hidden beneath fog as thick as thunderclouds. I vowed to return to it someday, if only to see it restored to the home my friends needed it to be.

"Don't fix your face too grumpy," High John called, as if he could read my mind. Shoot, he was a god—he probably could. He smiled and turned to consider MidPass, too. "You'll see it again. It'll be right as rain, sure it will."

We climbed higher still, and soon the roar of the burning rip in the sky filled my ears. It sounded like waves crashing against cliffs, like eight semi-trucks driving past at the same time, like a giant rush of wind that kept blowing and blowing.

"Hold tight now!" High John shouted.

I shielded my eyes as Old Familiar shot up through the bloodred flames. Heat pressed against every inch of my skin—a dry blast so hot that my sweat evaporated before it made it out, and yet the shadow crow made it with little effort. Helps when you have feathers made of darkness. We dodged flares and twirled between burning cinders, and still it grew hotter and hotter, until I thought this was a huge mistake, I couldn't take it anymore, we'd melt before—

"We're here!" cried High John.

We popped out like a cork, shooting high into the treetops of a familiar landscape. The cool air rushed against my face as we arced above the branches, and the forest smelled like rain on freshly dug earth. It was nighttime, and save for the stars above, the burning hole in the ground near the Bottle Tree was the only light for miles.

Old Familiar landed twenty feet away in the clearing, and I hopped off. High John took a look around, impressed. "This your home, kid?"

I grinned. "You got that right. Alabama—you in Strong country now."

High John doffed an imaginary hat and smiled right back. "Well, look whose britches decided to grow. My pardon, Mr. Strong."

"If you two are quite finished, can we get this ridiculous ordeal over with?" Anansi's tiny voice interrupted, full of impatience. "Some of us have work to do, and it doesn't involve blathering about like bumpkins."

High John eyed the phone as I pulled it out. "Bet my ax

can cut that in half." He climbed back onto Old Familiar and tossed me a casual wave. "Let me know if you need me to do that, you hear?"

"I will," I called back.

"And don't be a stranger! Them folks back home ain't nearly as fun as you. Betcha we can stir up a right amount of trouble, sure we can!" He waved again, and Old Familiar shot into the air before tucking his wings tight and diving into the hole.

And just like that, I was—

"Finally," Anansi grumbled. "Let's get this finished."

I sighed. He killed my buzz every time. But before I snapped back, a thought occurred to me. "What day is it? Brer—you—said that there was some time effect between Alke and this world."

"Yes, yes," the spider god said impatiently. "Time dilation. When the balance is disturbed—like when there's a burning hole between realms—there's no way to control the passage of time. Not that I expect you to understand that. Basically, the tear created a skipping effect, where a minute here is nearly three days there. Your High John and his feathered friend will return to find that nearly a week has passed."

I checked the phone. Sure enough, it was the same night I'd left.

"I know it's a complex topic, and I'll be sure to go over

painstaking details at a later time, after we clean up the mess you made, but right now..."

I rolled my eyes. "Fine. What do I do?"

"I don't know, I can't see the blasted thing. This is your infernal creation. Figure it out!"

I held up the phone and studied it. The screen flickered on, and Anansi sat in his human form, leaning against the edge. Several app icons flickered into view above his head, and I raised an eyebrow as I recited their names.

"Anansi Tales, Web Search—ha, 'cause you're a spider—Alke Maps, Listen Chile, Tristan-Don't-Press-This-Unless-You-Are-Really-Bored..." My finger hovered over that one for a second, until I spotted one more in the top right corner. "Oh, what's this? SpiderCam?"

I tapped the icon, and the phone's camera filled the screen. Anansi yelped in surprise as the burning hole appeared near where he sat. He got up, intrigued. He walked around the screen, studying the tear as I aimed the phone's camera lens around the clearing.

"Hold it," he commanded. "Point your projection spell right here again."

"It's a camera," I muttered.

"Point the camera spell right here, then. Yes. Hmm. I wonder..."

He walked to the tear and pulled a silver thread out of

nowhere. His hands moved in a blur, and the bottom corner of the burning gash closed.

"Whoa." I gasped. I moved the phone to see the ground with my own eyes, and sure enough, the hole had gotten smaller. "What is that stuff? That's amazing."

"Kindly keep the camera spell still," Anansi snapped, "and it's god silk, not that I expect *you* to know about such things." He went back to work, and I watched the ground, rather than the phone, as near-invisible thread pulled the hole's edges together tight with a puff of smoke. Before I could think of something slick to say in response, the tear was gone. A puckered dirt mound was the only evidence of the portal between realms.

"There, all done."

I walked around the Bottle Tree forest, amazed despite Anansi's smug tone. Say what you will about his attitude, the spider god had skills. All that trouble. All the violence, the fear, the pain. If only Anansi had . . .

A breeze rustled the trees, and the bottles on the branches clinked together. I frowned at the branch that had once held the large blue bottle. Cotton's bottle. The broken shards still lay on the ground, and the thought of him coming back to terrorize me sent a shiver down my back. I'd have to replace that bottle, and fast. Maybe Nana had some more.

The wind whistled gently, sounding pleased.

"Well, come along, boy, escort me through this rustic wonderland of yours." Despite the words, Anansi sounded peeved. "Twenty days can't end soon enough."

I thought about that as I started to walk back through the forest. This time the trees almost seemed to part before me, like they were being respectful. But that was silly. Right?

"Actually, that's not exactly accurate," I said.

Suspicion filled Anansi's voice. "And just what is that supposed to mean? You heard the sky god just like I did. He said—"

"He said," I interrupted happily, "'a duration no *shorter* than twenty days . . . *as Tristan sees fit.*'" I emphasized that last bit as we stepped onto the dirt road leading back to Granddad and Nana's house.

Anansi went silent.

Then:

"That no-good, sneaky, shiny-foreheaded, brass-eyed—"

I laughed as Anansi continued to fume all the way down the path. The edge of the sky began to lighten as morning crept up on the Strong family farm, just enough to do a bit of reading. Something Nyame said back when he'd confined the still-complaining trickster god. *Let the stories of your world fill it once more*, he'd said. Well, I knew just where to start.

I pulled out Eddie's journal. It was wrinkled and battered and just as valuable as the magic phone I held next to it.

I opened the Listen Chile app and grinned when a button labeled RECORD appeared. I pressed it and cleared my throat, then opened the first page in the journal.

"Once, the people had no stories...."

So there you have it. The tale of the tape. The story of how I went twelve rounds with an evil spirit and won. Stop the fight, ref, he don't want it with me.

I'd continue the analogy, but truthfully, I had a lot of people (and gods and creatures and one annoying doll thing) in my corner. I didn't do it alone. And if the adinkra bracelet tingling on my wrist was to be trusted, I'd need my people in my corner again real soon. But it's cool. I'm ready. I can go another twelve rounds.

'Cause at the end of the fight?

I'll still be standing.

Still punching.

Still Strong.

My name is Tristan Strong, and I've got a story to tell.

ACKNOWLEDGMENTS

It takes a village to raise a child, and a book is no different. Tristan's story would not have been told if it weren't for a bunch of people in my corner.

Thank you to all those who came before me, who paved the way for me to write and tell stories, who guided my hands, who lifted and shielded me, my own forebears. To the Nanas and the Granddads. To the nameless and missing. To the taken and stolen. To the stories that came from them and came with them.

To my mother, Doreatha Mbalia, my first critique partner and biggest fan.

To Cake Literary (Dhonielle and Sona, especially) and Disney Hyperion (Steph!), who offered me an opportunity to bring the stories of my childhood to life.

To the staff: the copy editors, the designers, the publicists, the marketing and sales teams, the assistants, and everyone else involved in bringing books to the masses, who often go unappreciated and unrecognized.

To Rick Riordan, whose books redefined the way mythology and folklore could be told.

To the many writing groups I've joined, whose encouragement pushed me through times of uncertainty and self-doubt. The Slack groups, the Discord groups, the retreat groups— you all pulled me forward.

To the chat groups whose advice I repeat to everyone who will listen, and to the chat groups whose comments I will deny ever having read.

To my friends and family, whose love and support give me energy.

To my first beta readers: my daughters.

To my wife, Mallory, whom I do not deserve.

And to my father, Ahmed Mbalia, who we called Baba, who passed several months before I started writing this book, and yet whose words still ring in my ear to this day.

Turn the page for a sneak peek at the exciting sequel
Tristan Strong Destroys the World!

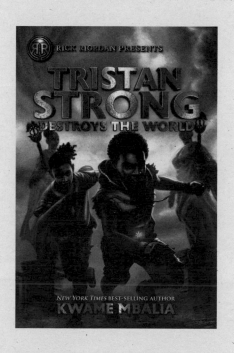

1
TRICKSTERS AND WHISPERS

NOBODY LIKES GETTING PUNCHED IN THE FACE.

Call it a hunch or an educated guess. Either way, I can confirm from firsthand experience that getting punched in the face is way down on the list of enjoyable activities. It's somewhere between eating a halfway-scraped-off piece of burnt toast and giving yourself a wedgie. Nope. Don't like it. *Especially* when it's accompanied by my grandfather's trash talk.

POP!

"C'mon, boy! Keep your head moving! Unless you wanna make your living lying down on the mat. You want me to build you a house down there? I can get you a one-room studio, utilities included."

When I opened my eyes, Granddad was standing over me with his hands on his hips. Well, his mitts on his hips. He wore gray jogging sweats and a crisp white T-shirt that he had probably ironed. His afro, neatly trimmed and nearly all gray, moved from side to side as he grumbled and shook his head. He took off one mitt and held out a massive brown hand with scars on the knuckles. When I reached up with my right glove and he pulled me to my feet, I could feel the strength that had made him a legend in the boxing circuit.

"You gotta move," Granddad said. He got into a boxer's crouch and started bobbing and weaving his head. "You're too stiff in there right now, like something's holding you back. What's wrong? You asked for this, remember? You tired?"

We were inside the old barn on my grandparents' farm. The early afternoon sun peeked through gaps in the walls, sending warm yellow rays down in stripes across the packed dirt floor. Granddad and I had been working all day—clearing out junk, sweeping the floor, stuff like that. A makeshift boxing ring now stood in the middle of the open space, and a few other adults were setting up benches.

Why, I hear you asking, did I volunteer for this?

Well, a few days ago, Granddad had gotten a call from an old buddy he knew back on the amateur boxing circuit, now a trainer himself. A practice bout for one of his new prospects had been canceled because of a storm, and he wanted to know if Granddad knew of anyone they could spar with.

Why yes, I imagined Granddad saying, *I have the perfect sparring partner. No, don't worry, he's up for the challenge.*

That, my friends, isn't volunteering. That's called being volun-told.

So I had a sparring match in an hour or so, and I was *not* looking forward to it, but Granddad had insisted I get in one good match before I left to go back home to Chicago.

Yay.

But don't get me wrong. I wasn't backing down. I wanted the challenge. Kept me distracted. Helped suppress unwanted thoughts. Mr. Richardson, my counselor, called them *intrusive thoughts*. Busy hands, calm mind.

And when you trained with Granddad, your hands stayed busy.

"No, sir, I'm not tired." I hopped up, slammed my gloves together, and started the routine again.

Granddad held up his mitts, and I let my hands go to work.

"All right, boy," my grandfather said. "One-two."

I took a deep breath and fired off the punch combination. Sharp. Quick. Had to be better. Had to get stronger. Step forward, twist the hips, snap off a punch.

Faster.

FASTER.

FAST—

"All right, boy, all right. Don't get too worked up." Granddad backed away and dropped the mitts. I stopped in mid-jab, breathing hard. "I told you, we're warming up. What's gotten into you?"

I started to answer, then closed my mouth. I didn't know how to explain my need to improve, the weight I felt on my shoulders.

Granddad watched me closely. "Take a deep breath. You sure you ain't tired? I heard you up late last night, then early this morning. You getting enough sleep?"

I bounced on my feet. "I'm okay, Granddad. I'm ready."

"I'll tell you when you're ready. Just breathe. You look tired."

I rolled my neck, trying to loosen up, looking everywhere around the barn instead of at Granddad. Pictures and posters decorated the walls, detailing fights from years past, and faded brown boxing gloves dangled from a beam running across the high two-story ceiling. But the real eye-catcher was a giant mural depicting two men, a weary boxer with one fist up as he curled a bicep, and his cornerman, towel slung over his shoulder, standing behind him with both arms flexed.

It was Alvin Strong, my dad, the night he defended his championship for the first time, and his trainer, Walter Strong—Granddad.

I once asked Granddad why he'd chosen to commemorate that night and not the time Dad had won the belt in the first place. He'd scratched his beard, then made a fist and flexed, like Dad in the mural. "Taking the belt was a feat, I'll grant you. Somethin' hard, worthy of a mural, I suppose. But it's one thing to take the belt when don't nobody see you coming. It's another to stare down an entire country while you got a target on your back, and then beat them challengers into submission. It's hard to win a belt.... It's even harder to keep it."

As I shook my arms to loosen them and then slipped my mouthpiece back in, Granddad stood beneath that mural. He might have been older, skinnier, with more wrinkles and less hair, but the same strength still radiated from him. I had that strength, too. I'd used it before, and I was going to have to use it again. Because, as much as it pained me, I *had* asked to train. I needed to get stronger.

"I'm okay, Granddad. Honest," I said, pounding my gloves together again. "I'm not tired at all."

"Mm-hmm. We'll see. Here we go. One-two. One-two. Good. Hook coming in. One-two. One-two. Tuck that chin in, boy, show these hands some respect! One-two. That's it, that's the Walter Strong special. Watch it, now. Good!"

POP! POP!

I snapped lefts and rights at the mitts as Granddad called the cadence, and for a while I did good. When the hooks came in from either direction, I ducked them, and when the straights came in, I dodged them, weaving from side to side so they went sailing by. A rhythm had me bouncing on my feet and practicing the sweet science. It felt good. I got into a groove.

POP! POP!

And then it happened.

A sound drifted past my ear. Something tiny and faint. A breath of wind brushed my cheek. A chill gripped my chest, making it hard to breathe.

Tristan . . .

Someone whispered my name. And right after that, another sound reached my ears. My heart seized up. My fists dropped as I turned toward whatever—or whoever—it was.

"Tristan!"

I recovered too late.

WHAP!

The hook came again and clipped the side of my head, sending me head over heels. It didn't hurt—it just knocked me upside down—but Granddad grew upset. He took off the mitts and tossed them out of the ring.

"Now what done got into you?! What is so fascinating that you'd take a punch from your opponent just to get a peek at it? Hmm? A piece of trash on the ground? You ain't even here—you off somewhere in your head!"

I didn't answer. Something fluttered across the floor, tumbling between the feet of the adults who were trying hard to not look at us. It was a receipt, crumpled up and harmless. I let out a shaky breath. Granddad waited, then sighed and motioned for me to come over. He unlaced the gloves and pulled them off, then undid the wraps on my hands and wrists. He worked quickly, then gathered up everything and stared at the mural on the barn wall.

"Boy," he said without looking at me. "Let's take fifteen. I need to get some water in me anyway. You look exhausted, and you're chewing on something in that head of yours and need to spit it out. Whatever it is, you can't bring that into the ring. Distractions will be the end of you before your opponent throws a single punch."

He stepped out of the ring and stuffed the equipment into a giant faded-green army duffel. He strained once, then stopped and took a deep breath. With a grunt, he lifted the bag over his shoulders and headed off. "I'll be back with the body pads," he said over his shoulder. "Then we're going to start over. I expect you to be ready to get serious."

Granddad marched out and the spectators followed him, leaving me alone in the barn, staring at the balled-up receipt. Tiny. Like a small wad of cotton. That had bad associations for me. But the piece of paper wasn't the actual distraction. I just couldn't tell Granddad that. A whisper? He would've stared at me like I'd sprouted an extra armpit on my forehead. And who could blame him?

How could I tell him that, just for a second, I'd thought I heard a faint drumbeat?

A miffed, cultured voice jerked me out of my thoughts.

"You know, boy, the least you could do is remove me from

your sweaty pocket before you start prancing about in your silly outfit and gloves. Hurry up and let me breathe. Or do you plan on moping forever?"

It came from my training shorts. I rolled my eyes and pulled out a shiny black phone with a gold spider emblem on the back, sleek and brand-new. When I raised it, the screen blinked on and a splash screen appeared—a fancy box with the word STORY written inside it. The image faded away, and in its place appeared a tiny brown man stomping back and forth, hopping over glowing app icons and kicking aside the clock. He wore flip-flops, pants that were either too short or shorts that were too long, and a T-shirt with a grinning spider on it. Anansi's sense of style was somewhere between lazy dad and retro-chic teen, and I could only shake my head.

Why was Anansi, the original trickster, the master of storytelling, the weaver of tales and webs of mischief, inside my phone?

Great question!

Because a month ago a tiny loudmouth stole my dead best friend's journal.

Because in my anger I punched a hole into a different realm where Black folktale heroes and African gods walk around like you and me.

Because I accidentally brought a diabolical haint with me, stirring up an even more ancient evil.

Because I caught Anansi trying to use all the confusion

to gain power for himself instead of helping the people, and this was his punishment.

Because I am an Anansesem, a carrier and spreader of stories, and this phone is the Story Box, the vessel in which those stories are stored, and which it is my responsibility to watch over and refill.

Because I got the hookup, that's why. Now stop asking questions.

Anyway, that was a month ago. It had been thirty days since Eddie—well, his spirit, actually, since he's my dead best friend—told me good-bye for the last time. Since then I'd read aloud every word in the journal he left me and recorded it with the Listen Chile app on the SBP (Story Box Phone—give me a break, let me be lazy).

The SBP's screen went blank, and then the lock screen appeared. Anansi glanced at the Story Box logo, then sat down and leaned his back against it. He pulled a black pixel out of the background and began to toss it against the edge of the screen like a ball.

"Look," he said gently. "I know you and I haven't seen eye to eye...."

I snorted.

"And we might've gotten off on the wrong foot—"

"You tried to get the people of Isihlangu to throw us in their dungeons," I said with a raised eyebrow.

Anansi flapped his hand and waved the words away. "Stop

living in the past. We have to look toward the future. I am due for a reprieve from this prison soon, and that can't happen if you don't pay attention to incoming fists. Who will tell old Nyame I fulfilled my obligations if you're unconscious? Who will transcribe your grandmother's fantastic key lime pie recipe for me? No, no, you must focus."

I shrugged and started rewrapping my hands. Granddad would be back any minute now, and I needed to be ready. If I could just get through this match, the rest of the week would fly by, and then I'd be on my way back to Chicago. "I'll be fine."

"It appears to me you're not acting fine."

"I'm good. Relax."

Anansi raised an eyebrow. "And the nightmares?"

Whispers drifted past my ear again. A rhythm pulsed from somewhere out in the cornfield behind the barn—a fast drumbeat that sent my heart racing. I hadn't told anyone about the bad dreams that had sent me lurching up in bed every night since returning from Alke. This is why you can't leave a trickster god on your nightstand while you sleep. I tugged on my gloves, then stood. "I'll. Be. Fine."

"You can't punch your way out of everything, boy. Sooner or later you'll find someone or something that punches harder. Trust me."

Before I could respond to *that* startling piece of wisdom, the barn door creaked open. Granddad walked in; sure enough, he wasn't alone. A crowd gathered behind him, and Nana—my grandmother—stood by his side, but my eyes were on the person standing next to him.

"By my eight ashy legs," Anansi whispered. "That boy is huge!"

"Let's go, boy—up and at 'em," Granddad said. "It's time to spar."

2
THE SPARRING MATCH

LIFE ISN'T FAIR.

That's what every adult has said when I've told them something wasn't fair. You've probably heard the same thing. *Oh, nothing's fair. You have to play the cards you're dealt.* Well, why are we even playing cards? I don't even like card games!

Anyway...

What *really* wasn't fair was my sparring partner. His name was Reggie Janson, and he stood taller than most of the adults surrounding the ring. Wider, too. I mean, even his muscles had muscles. Smooth brown skin, JAWBREAKER scrawled in graffiti print on his hoodie and trunks, and a face pulled into a scowl that made him look meaner than the neighborhood dog everyone steers clear of. His legs were tree trunks and his gloves bowling balls. In short—

"You might want to rethink this," Anansi said into my ear. I was wearing my earbuds with the hope of tuning out the prefight noise and commotion, but what I got was trickster-god color commentary over some chopped-and-screwed classic hip-hop songs. Yep, apparently Anansi had discovered streaming and was currently obsessed with Houston rap.

I ignored him. He might have been right, but still, he didn't have to come out and say it. Whatever happened to false encouragement?

I continued my warm-up until Granddad came over with a water bottle and a towel. He was chewing on a blade of grass, which he only did when he was worried. "Okay," he said, "stick to the basics. A simple sparring match, three rounds, nothing serious."

The sound of a small explosion filled the barn.

We all turned to see Reggie's trainer standing over a ruptured punching bag that had hit the floor, sand spilling out. Reggie turned, saw me watching, and shrugged, then started shadowboxing.

"Sweet peaches," Anansi and I said at the same time.

Granddad chewed the blade of grass even harder, as if he were having second thoughts, but then he shook his head. "You'll be fine," was all he said.

I nodded, then someone caught my eye. A short curly-haired woman in hospital scrubs had opened the barn doors and stepped inside. She saw somebody she recognized and waved. "Who's that?" I asked.

Granddad turned and grunted. "Hmm. Ring doctor. Travels with Reggie when he spars, just to be safe."

"Reggie travels with a doctor? Is he sick?"

"The doctor isn't for him. She's here for his opponents."

My jaw dropped, but Granddad studiously avoided my eyes and spat out the blade of grass before pulling another from his pocket. Who keeps grass in their pocket? And who sets up a boxing match like this for their grandson? I wanted to protest. Maybe it wasn't too late for me to back out and take up a less threatening sport, like staring contests. But I didn't have a chance to suggest it before Granddad turned around and started clapping. "All right, let's get started. Tony, you ready?"

Reggie's trainer flashed a thumbs-up before slapping his boxer on the shoulder.

I took out my earbuds and dropped them and the SBP onto a bench in the corner. Anansi was laying on his back with his eyes closed when I left him. *Thanks for your support*, I thought as I walked away.

Reggie and I both climbed into the ring. We had on our headgear, but I felt like I needed a football helmet as extra protection.

"All right, keep it clean, but take it serious. We ain't here to hurt nobody. It's just a tune-up, right?" Tony, Reggie's trainer, looked between us with an eyebrow raised, and we both nodded. "Good. Let's show them folks how we roll down here in Alabama." He stepped out of the ropes and put a whistle in his mouth. "Touch 'em up, then wait for my whistle."

Reggie's gloves pounded into mine as we stood face-to-face. "Why so tight, little bro? It's just a sparring match. Don't be so serious."

We backed up. I bounced on my toes, ready to do this thing.

At least I thought so.

The whistle came and my fists went up, just as a right hook came howling toward the left side of my head. I ducked, and a left uppercut streaked toward my face. Somehow, at the last minute, I managed to twist my body so my shoulder took the blow.

The impact sent me flat on my butt.

"C'mon, boy, what're you doing? Get up and get in the match!" Granddad's gruff voice and the snickers from the crowd brought a flushing heat to my face. I climbed to my feet and rotated my right shoulder. It felt like a hammer had battered it.

Don't be so serious. Right.

As if he could hear my thoughts, Reggie grinned. Jeez, even his mouthpiece said JAWBREAKER. Was there anything peaceful about him?

The rest of the round was more of the same. Me ducking. Me slipping and twisting. Me trying not to die as fists the size of my face tried to punch me into another zip code. At the end of the round, Tony the Trainer (look, it's how I remembered his name) blew his whistle and I collapsed onto the stool Granddad had waiting for me. I took a sip of water and tried to force some air into my lungs.

"You dancing or you boxing?" Granddad held up a bucket for me to spit out the water. "You know you can throw some punches, too?"

"Yes, sir," I said.

"Do you want me to call the match? Is it too much?"

"No, sir. Just—"

"Just what?"

"Just waiting for an opening."

Granddad put down the bucket and placed both hands on my shoulders. "Sometimes, boy, you gotta make your own opening. Don't wait for somebody to give you permission to do your best. You let 'em have it and leave all that other mess for the hogs. Fight for something! You got it? Grab whatever you need to grab deep down inside of yourself, whether it's pride or honor or even just the love of fighting, and you fight for it. Got me?"

"Yes, sir."

"Got me?"

"Yes, sir!"

Round two started out the same, though. As much as I

wanted to, I couldn't land a blow during Reggie's barrage. The dude had punches that threw punches. He clipped me a good one on the top of the head when I didn't duck fast enough, and it felt like a cannonball had grazed my skull.

Even so, Reggie was getting frustrated with all my defense. "You planning on fighting today?" he taunted. "Scared money don't make money."

The second round ended, and Granddad didn't say much. He rubbed my shoulders and gave me a little water, but I could tell he was disappointed.

And that wasn't even the worst part.

Just before the third round started, I heard it again.

Tristan?

A voice calling my name. Even stranger, a tingling sensation rippled down the fingers of my left hand and circled my wrist. The barn door was closed, but I swore I felt a breeze swirl around me. A humming song sounded faintly in my ears, and the dull thuds of a giant drum echoed around the barn.

"Oh no," I whispered, looking around wildly to see if anyone else had noticed. But everyone seemed focused on the match. This was something only I could hear.

Well, there was one other person ... sort of.

The SBP still lay on the bench at the edge of the ring, partially covered by a damp towel Granddad had dropped. I could just make out Anansi's worried face as he tried to peer over the edge of the screen and into the crowd. He'd felt something strange, too, and it had left him shaken.

That makes two of us, I thought as Tony the Trainer blew his whistle for the final round.

Everyone had given up on me.

Tony kept glancing at me and shaking his head as he backed up. A few of the adults who'd gathered to watch—those that still remained—were no longer paying the sparring session any attention. Even Granddad seemed disinterested. He met my eyes...then looked away.

That hurt the most.

Reggie bounced on his toes and knocked his gloves together. Every time he did, it sounded like two cinder blocks slamming together. "C'mon, man, let's get this over with. I thought the legendary Coach Strong would have some sort of prodigy for a grandson. No shade, but I guess we can't all be great."

"Yeah," I muttered. "That sorta sounds like shade to me." I wanted the match to end so I could to escape to a corner somewhere. Maybe a hole. With a bag of cheese puffs and some root beer. And—

A soft fragment of a song drifted through the talking crowd to my ears.

Tristan...

I looked up, confused. Reggie danced in front of me,

shaking out his arms and rocking his head from side to side. "Did you hear that?" I asked.

"The ringing?" Reggie's mouthpiece muffled his speech, but when he tapped his glove against the side of his head, I got the message. "Don't worry, little bro, it's only gonna get WORSE." He grunted the last word as he ripped a right hook toward my temple. It missed by inches, but he followed it up with a barrage of jabs and straights that took every ounce of Granddad's training to avoid. Bob, weave, duck, backpedal. Even with all that, a few blows landed. A right slipped through my guard and grazed my ribs. An uppercut nicked my chin when I threw my head back too slowly.

I backed up, panting. This was getting out of hand. Granddad stood on the ring apron, halfway over the ropes, shouting something at me. Why couldn't I make it out? Had I lost my hearing? Was I in a daze? Reggie stalked toward me and I was raising my fists when—

Tristan . . .

There it was again! From the crowd. I could hear a voice—a different one this time. No, several.

Tristan!

Help, please!

He's coming!

So many voices. And beneath them I heard a rhythm. *The* rhythm. The one I hadn't heard in a month. Not since a giant shadow crow had flown me through a gash of roaring fire.

Something surged inside of me. A feeling. A power. But why here? Why now? Bright light flashed and caught my eye. The SBP was ringing. Was I getting a call? Or was it Anansi? I felt the tingling on my wrist again, like when your foot falls asleep. It felt like I was trying to wake up. Or someone was trying to wake me up. They needed me. I was being summoned to—

Reggie dashed forward and bull-rushed me into the ropes. His head ground against mine, and he looked up, a sharklike grin exposing his custom mouthpiece.

"You're wasting my time," he snarled. "Do me a favor and stay down."

"What do y—"

Before I could finish, Reggie reared back, his right fist cocked behind him, ready to unleash fury. Then I understood. He wanted to end the fight now. His fist roared forward, a heat-seeking missile with a target lock on my face. If it connected it was game over, good night, thanks for playing.

I couldn't let that happen.

Fight for something, Granddad had said.

Fight for something. Fight for something!

"Alke," I whispered.

POP! POP!

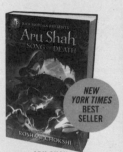

Praise for
Tristan Strong Punches a Hole in the Sky

★ "Mbalia's epic debut centers African American characters and
tradition, featuring a pantheon of legends and a plot worthy of
such tricksters as Brer Rabbit and Anansi the Weaver. Perfectly
paced, this cinematic adventure never drags, anchored by
Tristan's conversational narration and balanced by his struggle
to cope with a friend's passing. It brims with heart, humor, and
action, successfully crafting a beautifully unified secondary
world that brings the power of stories to glorious life."

—*Booklist* (starred review)

★ "Mbalia expertly weaves a meaningful portrayal of family and
community with folklore, myth, and history—including the legacy
of the slave trade—creating a fast-paced, heroic series starter."

—*Publishers Weekly* (starred review)

★ "Mbalia's African American and West African gods (with
villains tied to US chattel slavery and the Middle Passage
specifically) touch on the tensions between the cultures,
a cultural nuance oft overlooked. Readers who want more
than just a taste of Alke will be eager for future books."

—*Kirkus Reviews* (starred review)

★ "This debut novel offers a richly realized world,
a conversational, breezy style, and a satisfying
conclusion that leaves room for sequels."

—*School Library Journal* (starred review)

★ "A stellar mix of the playful and the serious, the traditional
and the original, this novel marks the emergence of a
strong new voice in myth-based children's fantasy."

—*Bulletin of the Center for Children's Books* (starred review)

KWAME MBALIA is the *New York Times* best-selling author of *Tristan Strong Punches a Hole in the Sky*, for which he received a Coretta Scott King Author Honor award. The book was also named to best-of-the-year lists compiled by *Publishers Weekly*, the Chicago Public Library, and the *New York Times*. The second book in the trilogy is *Tristan Strong Destroys the World*. Kwame lives with his wife and children in Raleigh, North Carolina, where he is currently working on the third book about Tristan. Follow him on Twitter @KSekouM.

RICK RIORDAN, dubbed "storyteller of the gods" by *Publishers Weekly*, is the author of five *New York Times* #1 best-selling middle grade series, including Percy Jackson and the Olympians, which brings Greek mythology to life for contemporary readers. Millions of fans across the globe have enjoyed his fast-paced and funny quest adventures. The goal of Rick Riordan Presents is to publish highly entertaining books by authors from underrepresented cultures and backgrounds, to allow them to tell their own stories inspired by the mythology, folklore, and culture of their heritage. Rick's Twitter handle is @RickRiordan. Visit him at www.RickRiordan.com.